Alix

&

Valerie

Ingrid Diaz

Bedazzled Ink Publishing Company * Fairfield, California

978-1-934452-04-2 paperback

First Published 2008

Front cover
Karine Brousse

Cover layout
C.A. Casey

Nuance Books
a division of
Bedazzled Ink Publishing Company
Fairfield, California
http://www.bedazzledink.com/nuance

For K, who makes each day feel special

Acknowledgements

Special thanks to Amber, Amy G., Bird, James, Cindy, Sheila and Christy for being constant sources of inspiration and amusement during the writing of this novel. Also to Lish, Cherri, Jenn, Kavin, Tricea and Coslima, for their friendship and their unwavering enthusiasm over anything I write. I'd also like to thank Lyan, Julia, Yuhwei, and Matt for making me laugh every day both in-game and out. Thank you to all of my readers. Thank you to Carrie, my editor, for all of her hard work. Special thanks to Claudia for all of her support and for having such faith in my writing. Thank you to Karine, who stands at my side through anything and everything and keeps me (somewhat) sane. And last but not least, thank you to my parents, for all of their love and encouragement no matter what I do.

Part I

Alix

Chapter 1

I told her not to choose pink. No, I *begged* her. I got down on my hands and knees and pleaded with my best friend to have mercy on my soul.

"But this dress is so nice," Jessica argued, holding it up and smiling mischievously at the torture she was putting me through. "You'll look adorable."

The lady who was helping us at the bridal shop nodded in agreement, and I resigned myself to the inevitable fate that was the dreaded dress. I grabbed it and went into the dressing room to change out of the torn black jeans and black Aerosmith tee shirt I sported that day, an ensemble that matched my gloomy mood quite perfectly. The mirror reflected a shattered heart trying desperately to hide its true state. I felt like crying, but didn't. I didn't want Jessica to see how much this was hurting me. She didn't deserve my pain being thrown in her face.

I dumped my clothes on the floor and threw the dress over my head. The material felt cool against my skin, a contrast to the cotton and denim I was so used to wearing. I had no idea what material the dress was made of, but already I hated it. I loathed what it represented: the bitter taste of hope's dying embers. And here I was . . . putting it on, like a second place winner settling for her loss.

The reflection in the mirror changed, and I was startled momentarily to see myself in a puffy pink dress. It clashed severely with the blue hue of my hair, and I felt utterly ridiculous.

I stepped out into the shop, where Jessica and the woman, whose name I think was Crystal were talking intently. They stopped when they heard me walk in and stared at me. I bit my lip, a habit I'd developed my senior year of high school unbeknownst to myself until Jessica had pointed it out. "I feel like a walking advertisement for Pepto Bismol," I muttered, glancing down at myself.

Jessica smiled and walked all around me, taking in my ridiculous attire with an amused expression. "Really, Alix, like I could pass up the opportunity to stick you in a dress?"

I narrowed my eyes at her. "You shall pay, Mrs. Collins," I told her, my tone masking the pain behind the words.

At that moment, the door to the bridal shop burst open, announcing an anxious costumer. Roxanne Perez in all of her Latina glory stopped in mid-stride and stared straight at me, her mouth hanging open in surprise. Then she started laughing hysterically, pointing at me as she did so.

I would have beaten her up, but I decided to be mature and ladylike. After all, I was in a pink dress. You can't get more ladylike than that. So, instead, I looked at Jessica for help and received a pat on the head for my efforts.

When Roxanne finally calmed down enough to speak, the first words out of her mouth were, "Alix, you look like an Easter egg!"

I didn't find this amusing, but I felt vulnerable in my pink-clad state and had no intention of encouraging any further comments on my dress. Instead, I smiled and replied, "Wait until you see your dress."

Roxanne glanced worriedly at Jessica, who smiled broadly. "What are you making me wear?"

I crossed my arms, waiting for the shoe to drop.

As if on cue, Crystal brought out Roxanne's bridesmaid dress. It was orange. It was hideous. It was the most beautiful sight I had ever laid eyes on, and Roxanne stared at it in horror for over a minute.

"I am *not* wearing *that*!"

Jessica waved away the comment. "If I got Alix to wear a pink dress, I can get you to wear an orange one." She took the dress from Crystal and handed it to a stunned Roxanne. "Into the dressing room you go." She pushed Roxanne inside and closed the door. She turned around and smiled at me. "I love weddings. They're the perfect excuse to torture my friends."

Torture. Funny she should choose that word.

Roxanne walked out of the dressing room a few minutes later, and I started laughing. Now we both looked ridiculous. "Orange is *not* my color!" she stated, holding the dress up for emphasis.

"Oh, 'cause pink is mine?" I retorted.

She looked at me impatiently. "No, you look completely ridiculous, but that's normal for you."

Jessica was enjoying this, I could tell. Her blue eyes were sparkling with held back laughter, and a smile played on her lips. It was almost enough to make me forget the hideous thing I was wearing.

Almost.

For once in my life, I had to side with Roxanne. "Jess, you know I love you, but if you don't pick a different dress for me, I shall be attending your wedding in the nude."

"Oh God, no," Roxanne muttered. "You know she'll do it."

I smiled to myself. They both knew I wouldn't.

Jessica started laughing; a hearty sound that will forever be music to my ears. "You guys really think I'd make you wear those things to my wedding?" She shook her head and motioned to Crystal who appeared with two identical dresses: one black, the other violet. Jessica smiled. "These are the real ones."

Black. I looked at Jessica at that moment, and she caught my gaze and winked. I would've worn the dreadful pink dress for her. And she knew it.

ℒ

A couple of hours later, I walked into my dorm room to find my room-mate sprawled on the floor, staring intently down at a book whose cover I could not see. I dropped my keys on my desk.

"Hey," I greeted.

"Men are evil," my roommate informed me, not looking up.

Nicole Fischer was a twenty-two year-old Women's Studies major and an avid feminist. She spoke constantly of Bell Hooks, Adrienne Rich, and a zillion other names I could never remember. At first I thought these were friends of hers, but later I learned the truth.

"So are women," I told her, collapsing on my bed with a groan. I felt emotionally drained. This wedding was wreaking havoc on my heart.

"Jessica?" she guessed, finally looking up. Her light brown eyes showed concern, and she pushed the loose strands of brown hair behind her ears.

I simply nodded. "Two days until the wedding."

"I'm sorry, babe." Nicole lifted herself up from the floor and sat down on her bed so she could see me better. "Did you get a dress?"

"It's black."

Nicole laughed. "That figures. You don't wear any other color."

"I'm in a constant state of mourning," I replied dryly. "'Black is all I see when I close my eyes, Black is in the night when the windows close, Black is all, yet nothing at all . . .'"

"Is that one yours?" Nicole asked.

"Nah. Jade's."

"Speaking of Jade, she called twice. And your sister called once." Nicole returned to the floor to continue her reading.

I reached for the phone and dialed my twin sister's phone number. Rachel picked up on the second ring. "What's up?" I asked.

"Who's this?" Rachel asked, confusion in her voice.

I rolled my eyes. "It's not a matter of who am I, it's a matter of *where* am I."

"That's better. Hi, Alix. You sounded far too normal to be yourself for a moment."

"Forgive me, Satan, if I'm not up to par. It hasn't been what you would call a good day."

"Please stop calling me Satan. It was funny when we were seven, but now it's just annoying."

"Sorry, *Lucifer*. To what do I owe the pleasure of your call?"

"Stripper," Rachel responded. "And before you reply with some smart-ass comment about incest, let me clarify. I meant the stripper for Jessica's bachelorette party."

"What about him?" I asked, annoyed at the entire concept.

"Well, did you call him? I mean, the whole thing's arranged right?"

The joys of being maid of honor. "Yeah, he's coming. Everything's set. We're meeting at Jessica's at seven tomorrow."

"Cool. See you there."

"Adios." I hung up, and dialed Jade Cooper's number. An English-accented voice picked up a few rings later. "Hey Jay. You rang?"

"It was about bloody time. Listen, do you want to go out tonight? I thought we could go clubbing. We can pick up some guys."

"Guys?"

"Or girls, whatever," Jade replied. "Pick me up around eight and we'll have some fun. We'll see about getting your mind off of Jessica getting married."

I laughed sadly. "I don't think anything could get my mind off of that." I thought about Jade's proposition for a moment, and then shrugged. I had no plans. "Okay. Be ready by eight."

♌

At seven-fifty, my vintage VW beetle putt-putt-putted its way to Jade's house. She lived with her crazy Aunt Fifi, and I do mean *crazy*, in a two-story house the size of a shoebox. I'm not sure what it was that Aunt Fifi did for a living, seeing as she should have been committed, but I've never thought to ask. It was one of those mysteries of life better left uncovered.

I pulled into Jade's driveway and honked the horn a couple of times. I turned up Aerosmith's "Angel" as I waited. This had become my theme song over the years and for the past few weeks I couldn't bring myself to listen to anything else.

A fuzzy head peered out of the window, and I waved. A second later, Jade Cooper stepped out onto the porch and joined me inside the vehicle.

The night of her graduation from high school, she had gone through with what she'd threatened to do for a year: she buzzed off her hair. When I'd first met Jade, her hair had been long and blue, it had then evolved to purple, then to red, then to orange, then to yellow, then to black, back to blue, and before I knew it, it was all gone. Two years later, it was still quite nonexistent, and I had grown accustomed to having a near-bald-headed friend. Perhaps when I'd dyed my own hair blue, it was in loving tribute to Jade's.

On this occasion she was clad in a tight black tee with the *Sliders* cast—she'd had a crush on Jerry O'Connell for as long as I'd known her—across the front, and a long black skirt, Doc Martins as usual, and her trademark fishnet stockings.

As for myself, I'd opted for the please-don't-try-to-pick-me-up look, which consisted of black Jnco jeans and a black Care Bears tee shirt with a picture of Grumpy Bear in the center. In this outfit, they'd never buy my fake ID.

"Not that bloody song again." Jade reached over, ejected my tape, and replaced it with her own. Soon Metallica filled the small confinements of the car, and I pulled out of the driveway, already used to the ritual of music exchange.

"So where are we going?" I asked, turning down the music so I wouldn't have to scream over James Hetfield.

Jade shrugged, lighting a cigarette and rolling down the window. "My friend Beth said there was this cool new club in Ft. Lauderdale. Whispers or something."

She handed me the directions, and I glanced down at them. It was near South Beach. I could find it.

"So I'm thinking of letting my hair grow out," Jade said.

I took my eyes off the road to glance at her. "Yeah? Tired of getting hit on by girls instead of guys?"

"Actually yes. My sex life is suffering." She laughed. "Actually, I'm getting bored. You can't do much with peach fuzz hair, and I miss the colors."

I nodded. "Well, I'm getting rid of the blue tomorrow."

"Going back to your original brown?" Jade inquired, flicking the cigarette outside. "I like the blue, Al, it gives color to your otherwise morbid personality."

I looked at her. "Yeah, you're one to talk." Then I shrugged. "Actually, I haven't decided on a color yet. I just didn't want to have blue hair for Jessica's wedding. She didn't say anything, but still. I was thinking of dyeing it black."

"And what color's the dress?"

"Black."

Jade started laughing. "You're going to be like a pair of green eyes against a sea of darkness. Trying to turn yourself into a cat?"

"The transformation is almost complete," I assured her. "I just decided to shave for the occasion."

Jade shook her head and turned up Metallica. "'Nothing Else Matters.' You love this song."

And I do. We sat in companionable silence the rest of the way to the club.

Chapter 2

The smell of smoke and liquor assaulted my nose and lungs upon entering the nightclub. My fake ID passed inspection with flying colors, and I wondered if my real ID would ever fare as well as my fake one when I turned twenty-one the following month.

Jade abandoned me after ten minutes to mingle on the dance floor, and I resigned myself to a table near the bar.

Whispers seemed like a nice-enough establishment and would have been graded less harshly had my mood been better. After seven years of unrequited love, one tended to grow slightly bitter at the world.

"Anything to drink?"

I looked up at the waitress standing before me. "Dr. Pepper if you have it," I replied. There was no sense in getting drunk and driving into a tree, or a lake for that matter.

"Designated driver?" the waitress guessed.

I shrugged, and she walked away, leaving me alone with my myriad of thoughts. I looked around. It was a straight club, much to my dismay, although with its location in downtown Ft. Lauderdale I couldn't attest for the straightness of the people inside. Either way, it wasn't as if I'd planned on hooking up with anyone.

Jade joined me at the table, slightly sweaty and out of breath from jumping around on the dance floor. She held up a napkin proudly and grinned. "Only been here for half an hour and already I got digits."

I grabbed the napkin and looked at it, then handed it back. "And does Katrina know you don't swing that way?"

"Actually, this is for you," Jade explained, handing it back. "She gave me her number, and I told her that you were probably more her type. And then she said she had to run."

"So she took one look at me and ran?"

"Yes. Quite literally actually." Jade shrugged. "Don't know how you do it, Al."

"It's a gift," I replied dryly.

"It's not like you're ugly or anything," Jade continued.

The waitress appeared with my Dr. Pepper on the rocks, and I was grateful for the interruption. I took a sip and tried not to sigh.

Jade regarded the waitress. "Help me out here. Would you say my friend is ugly?"

I nearly spit out the gulp of soda.

"I wouldn't say that," the waitress replied.

I looked up into light blue eyes and felt myself blush, an oddity in itself.

"So, given that you were of that orientation," Jade continued, much to my annoyance, "would you even go as far as saying that she's attractive."

"Quite," the waitress answered and winked in my direction before moving on to another table.

I shook my head, and Jade shrugged.

"So there you have it," she said, "it's not your looks." She stared at me, hazel eyes narrowing in deep concentration as she studied my face.

I frowned. "Don't look at me like that, Jade. It freaks me out."

"Hey, she didn't ask if I wanted anything to drink," Jade complained, looking around.

I placed my cup in front of her. "Here. Drink. Give your vocal cords a rest."

"You know I can't stand that crap." She made a face to illustrate her point. "It tastes like medicine."

I took back my soda and held it protectively. "Don't listen to her," I whispered to the glass. "She knows not what she says."

"I'm going to stop by the bar and then back to the dance floor," Jade announced. "Care to join me?"

I shook my head no, and Jade left in search of alcohol.

I was bored. I had anticipated that I would be so I'd brought a book, Jennifer Fulton's *Greener Than Grass*, but it was far too dark to read where I was sitting. I finished my drink and dropped some money on the table to pay for it, along with an overly friendly tip. I tended to over tip as it was, but the waitress humoring Jade went far and beyond the call of duty.

I made my way through the crowd on the dance floor until I ran into Jade. She grabbed my arms and started dancing, if you could call it that. I wouldn't. I cupped my hand around her ear and told her I was leaving, and to text me when she was done. She nodded without much protest, and I left the nightclub.

Outside, the night was warm, as most nights in South Florida tended to be. I was glad that hurricane season was ending soon, rain rendered the summer months pointless.

Whispers was located on the second floor of a two-story building in South Beach, and I walked down the stairs to the sidewalk. A tourist shop fully stocked with billions of items bearing the Florida name occupied the first floor. I made my way past the tourists crowded around the postcard displays. The Ft. Lauderdale nightlife was alive and booming all around me. People paraded back and forth in small groups, big groups, and pairs—talking, laughing, shouting.

I'd gotten lucky with a parking spot and I was grateful to find my car still there when I returned. I got in and sat there for a few minutes, trying to decide where to go. I could stay where I was. I could head to the beach. But I didn't feel like being alone. Not completely alone, and in the end, I could think of only one place to go.

I'd been to Pride Factory only once in my life, having been dragged there by Jade one night to meet her favorite gay male porn star. It wasn't the sort of place I frequented, but that's where I ended up. I'd been searching for an embarrassing gift to give Jessica at her bachelorette party and this seemed like the perfect place to find one. I walked around, wasting time by looking at their selection of pride gear before moving on to other displays.

People entered the store and people left. No one paid me much attention. I'm not sure how long I'd been there. A while, it seemed. I'd ended up in the video section, trying to find the most inappropriate gift possible. I was in the process of turning a DVD on its side to understand what exactly the people on the cover where doing, when a voice startled me.

"Thanks for the tip."

I looked up, slowly, to find somewhat familiar blue eyes gazing down at me. It was the waitress from the club. "Did you follow me here to tell me that?"

She smiled—a half-smile that might've seemed arrogant on anyone else. "I have a friend that works here. Just came to borrow something and saw you standing here, looking at . . . um . . ." Her gaze drifted over the rows of X-rated videos.

I was suddenly aware of the video in my hand. I thought of putting it back on the shelf but that would've only called attention to the fact that I was embarrassed. So I held it, proudly. "It's gift," I said and stopped myself from saying more.

Her smiled widened as if she didn't believe me. "Right."

I didn't know what to say, so I took the moment to study her. She was beautiful in a no-nonsense sort of way. Her oval face framed by long, dark blonde hair. She was wearing her uniform still, a white cotton shirt with the Whispers logo on the left breast pocket and tight black jeans. She didn't seem much older than me, maybe twenty-two or twenty-three at the most. I didn't know why she was still standing there so I said, "You're welcome for the tip."

She extended her hand suddenly. "Valerie Skye. Call me Val."

"Alix Morris," I said, shaking her hand. "Alix with an 'i.'" I restrained myself from covering my right eye as I usually did when explaining the spelling of my name. I'd been trying to get out of the habit of doing that upon arrival at college, but much to my dismay it was second nature. I barely caught myself this time.

"So, I don't mean to be nosy, but I'm a bartender, so it comes naturally to me," she began, "but did you and your girlfriend have a fight?"

Confusion must have shown on my face because she quickly added, "The girl you were with at the club."

"Oh, Jade. No." I shook my head. "She's not my girlfriend. Just a friend." She was staring at me, so I looked away. I felt like fleeing. Was she hitting on me? It was then I remembered her original question. "We didn't have a fight. I just had to get out of there."

She nodded. "I know the feeling." She was silent for a second. "Hope I'm not bothering you, coming over here like this."

"No it's okay." And it was. "I'm really just wasting time until Jade finishes having fun."

"So why aren't you out having fun?" she asked.

"Not in the mood, I guess," I said, sounding bitterer than I'd intended. "I don't find the idea of strangers picking me up at a club fun. And I bet Jade will be wasted by the end of the night, so there was no point in my drinking. So . . ."

She watched me for a long moment. "Well, this place is about to close in fifteen minutes." She paused as though arriving at a decision. "Would you like to take a walk with me?"

I opened my mouth to refuse, but then I realized I had nowhere else to go. I bit my lip, trying to decide on a course of action. I didn't know this woman. She could've been a mass murderer for all I knew. All rationality and common sense told me that this was a bad idea. To this day I still don't know why I agreed to go.

We walked outside. She led, and I followed, until we reached the sidewalk, then I fell in step beside her, wondering why we were walking when I had a perfectly good car. But she seemed content, and I said nothing. I stuck my hands in my pockets as I usually did when I didn't know what to do with them, and focused on not tripping.

Val pulled out a pack of cigarettes and waved it at me.

I shook my head no. "I find that not smoking is more rebellious these days."

She smiled and took out a cigarette for herself. "Mind if I succumb to the powers of nicotine?"

I shrugged. "Your lungs."

She lit the cigarette and took a long drag, and then put the pack and lighter away in one swift motion. "Do you go to school?" she asked after a moment.

"Baldwin U."

"I go to Miami."

I was surprised. She didn't strike me as the college type. "What are you studying?"

"Visual Arts. I'm on an art scholarship, otherwise I'd never be able to afford it."

"Yeah, I couldn't afford M.U." I relaxed a bit now that there appeared to be a general topic of conversation.

"So what are you studying?" she asked.

"Theater and Film Studies."

"Do you want to be an actress?"

I looked up at her, my eyes narrowed. "I *am* an actress. I just need to find a way to be acknowledged as such."

She laughed. "I understand completely."

I searched my mind for something to say. I couldn't stand silence. "Thanks for not calling me ugly back at the club," I found myself saying.

"Why was your friend asking?"

I shrugged. "I don't know. She's weird."

"Were you having self-esteem issues?"

I had to laugh. "Nah, she was just trying to figure out why it is that I scare people away."

Val looked down at me, and I could tell she was trying to make sense of my statement. "I can't imagine you scaring anyone away."

"Stick around, you'd be amazed."

That put a lull in the conversation, and I mentally kicked myself for bringing up the subject. This had been a bad idea to begin with. I barely knew this woman. Why was I walking down NE 13th Street with a total stranger who'd picked me up at a gay pride store? "Why did you ask me to take a walk with you?"

"You're cute," she said.

I opened my mouth to respond, but nothing came out.

She laughed and looked at me. "Actually, I wanted some company."

I wasn't sure if that meant that I wasn't cute, or that I was cute and that she also wanted some company. Either way, I decided to change the subject. "Do you live around here?"

"Yeah. About a five minute walk from the club."

"But you commute to Miami every day?"

"I only go there part time," she answered. "I work too much."

I nodded, then frowned. "Did you say you were a bartender?"

"Yeah, one of the waitresses quit today so I had to double as both." She glanced at me. "Where do you live?"

"I have a dorm at Baldwin."

"First year?"

I smiled. "Third. How old are you?"

"I'm twenty-one. You?"

"Twenty. I'll be twenty-one next month."

Val laughed. "I smelled fake ID all over you."

"Well, not for long," I countered, a little defensively.

A car started honking, and Val paused until the noise subsided. "When's your birthday?"

"October thirty-first."

She seemed surprised. "Halloween? That must suck."

I snapped my head to look at her. "It does suck. Thank you. Most people think it's the coolest thing on earth."

She shrugged. "Well, I would imagine that you'd like your birthday to be your own. It kind of takes away from its importance when you have to share it with a big holiday."

"Exactly. I usually celebrate it the weekend before, otherwise my friends would never remember."

Val just nodded.

"When's your birthday?" I asked, trying to keep the conversation going.

"June first."

I smiled. "I was expecting you to say Christmas day, or Easter."

Val laughed and shook her head. "Nah. Nothing special about my birthday."

"Sure there is. You were born then. It gives an otherwise mundane date meaning. I think that's what birthdays are all about actually."

Val caught my gaze for a few seconds. Then she looked away.

We arrived at the end of the street and before we had a chance to turn onto North Federal Highway, my cell went off. I almost missed it, drowned out by the zooming of cars back and forth.

"It's Jade," I announced, reading the text message. "I need to go pick her up."

"I'll walk you back."

We headed back in the direction we'd come. "Did you walk all the way to Pride Factory?"

"Yeah. I like walking."

"Apparently." I smiled up at her.

She smiled back.

The walk back to the car was far quieter than I would have liked, but I didn't feel as uncomfortable in the silence. When we reached the car, I was suddenly hesitant to say goodbye. "Would you like a ride home?"

She seemed torn by the offer, and I could sense a war going on in her head. "Are you going back to Whispers?"

"Yeah. Jade's meeting me outside."

"You can drop me off there, then."

I unlocked the passenger side door. "Hop in." Then I walked to the other side. When I put the key in the ignition, I prayed the car would start and was relieved to hear the engine turn. Cars were unpredictable things, very likely to embarrass you in front of people you'd just recently met. I pulled out of the parking lot and headed toward the club.

Val appeared to be searching for something in her pocket. A second later, she turned toward me and said, "Can I see your hand?"

I frowned in confusion and stole a glance at her. Hesitantly, I held my right hand out in her direction. Her hand cupped mine, holding it in place. Her palm was soft and warm against my skin, and I found myself wondering if the rest of her was as soft and warm. I mentally shook myself and looked down to see her writing something on my palm. It tickled and I almost pulled away. When she finished, she gently released my hand, and I pulled my eyes away from the road to read what she'd written. It was her name and phone number. Well, this is a first, I thought to myself, not knowing what to make of the gesture.

"You don't have to call me," Val quickly explained. "I just thought . . ."

"Thanks." I smiled, but didn't add that I would call her. I wasn't sure why. Perhaps it was because at the time I didn't think that I would, and I didn't want to lie. I stopped the car across the street from Whispers, and Val went to get out, so I searched my mind for something to say. "It was nice meeting you, Val."

She smiled. "Nice meeting you, Alix with an 'i.'"

And then she was gone. I sat back against the seat, shaking my head. My mind was a whirlpool of thoughts. What had just happened?

"Did a chick just get out of your car?" Jade asked, taking her place beside me.

I pulled out into the street without responding. I felt depressed, and I wasn't even sure why. "Yeah."

"Are you okay?"

I glanced at her and nodded. "Yeah. I'm okay. Did you have fun?"

"I met a guy."

"Really? Details please."

For the rest of the drive home, Jade told me all about the guy she'd met while smoking a "fag" outside. The first time she'd used that expression I thought she meant she'd been killing a gay guy, but after nearly five years of friendship I'd gotten used to her British jargon.

After a while I zoned her out. I didn't do it intentionally, but my mind was unable to focus on the outside world. I kept thinking about Mathew and Jessica, and how happy they were. Mathew was a great guy, and I loved him dearly. It would have been easier had I hated him, but I didn't.

Then my mind jumped to thoughts of Valerie and the phone number on my hand. Would I have the guts to call her? Did she want me to call her? I should have given her my number. Then I wouldn't have to worry about it. Did I want to see her again? Did I like her?

I pulled the car into Jade's driveway and turned to find her staring at me. "What?"

"You haven't heard a bloody thing I said, have you?"

I shook my head. "Not a damn thing."

"Well, all right, I'll call you tomorrow and repeat myself. What time's the party?"

"Seven," I responded.

Jade nodded and grinned mischievously. "Can't wait for the stripper." She winked. "Pick me up, okay?"

"Be ready by six," I said. "I have to get there early and make sure everything's good to go."

"Yep." Jade jumped out of the car, and I stayed in the driveway until she disappeared into the house.

I looked down at the number on my hand, the black ink a sharp contrast to the white of my skin; seven digits, two options, and a million possibilities. I sighed as I started toward home.

I should have given her my number.

Chapter 3

Much of Friday passed by in a blur of theater classes and acting workshops. At six, I stopped at Jade's to pick her up and headed off to Jessica's to get the party set up.

We arrived at Jessica's mansion around ten after six and set up the food in the rec room. By seven guests started to arrive. By seven-thirty I escaped to Jessica's bedroom, where I collapsed on her king sized waterbed and willed myself to sleep. My night had been restless, having tossed and turned for hours. I had a class at seven in the morning, for which I managed to drag myself out of bed. I'd been exhausted the rest of the day, weaving through my myriad of classes like a zombie on automatic pilot.

I fell asleep at some point and awoke at the sound of the door opening. I looked up to find Jessica walking toward me, holding a bottle of Dr. Pepper and two plastic cups filled with ice. She was dressed casually in blue jeans and a tight white tee shirt. By looking at her, you would never guess that she was worth billions of dollars or that she owned one of the biggest mansions in the United States. You would never guess it either by talking to her.

"Having fun?" she asked, joining me on the bed, which protested the addition of her weight by forming a series of waves across the water mattress. She sat down, Indian style.

"A blast," I responded, feeling more or less rested. "Are you?"

She considered the question. "Well, the stripper was certainly a surprise."

I grinned. "It wasn't my idea. Besides, it's supposed to be some kind of tradition."

"Of course."

"Why'd you leave the party?" I asked.

She handed me one of the cups, forcing me to sit up. "Can't have a party without my maid of honor." She poured the soda into both cups.

"Jess, you hate Dr. Pepper."

"And you hate parties. Consider it a compromise." She smiled and lifted the cup. "To my best friend."

I smiled. "To mine."

I watched her take a sip, loving the disgust that crossed her face. "I can't believe you like this stuff."

I drank the whole thing in one gulp. "It's wonderful. Did I ever tell you the story of how Dr. Pepper got its name?"

Jessica looked thoughtful for a moment, as though going through her file of memories and examining each one for the required information. "Nope. Do tell."

I cleared my throat and took on a mocking storyteller voice. "Once upon a time, there lived a young man who loved a young woman, and she loved him just as much. However, the girl's evil father, a man by the name of Dr. Pepper, refused the young man's request to marry his daughter, insisting that he would never amount to anything. The broken-hearted fellow, insistent on proving his worth to Dr. Pepper, created the formula for a deliciously refreshing soft drink that does *not* taste like medicine no matter what you people say, and named it Dr. Pepper, after the girl's father."

"Did they ever get together?" Jessica asked.

"The guy and the father? I don't think so, but you never know."

Jessica laughed and smacked my arm playfully. "You know what I meant."

I smiled, my flesh tingling where she'd touch me. "I don't know, actually."

"Well, I'm disappointed in you, Alix. You're supposed to know these things. How can I come to respect the story if I don't know the entire thing?"

I suppressed my desire to tackle her and tickle her to death for being such a pain in my ass. "I guess you're just going to have to try and move on with your life somehow," I said instead.

"I'll do my best." Jessica stared down at the cup in her hand.

"I'll drink it if you don't want it," I offered.

"No, no. I will get this. It'll be like a milestone in my life."

"'The Night Jessica Heart Drank Dr. Pepper,'" I teased. "They'll make a Broadway musical about it."

"It'll be a hit."

I smiled and watched her drink the remainder of the liquid. "You know, you're missing your party."

"They're having a bit too much fun with the stripper," Jessica said, shrugging slightly. "I didn't feel like being there."

"Know the feeling," I said. I hadn't meant to say that aloud, but it was too late to rein in the words.

Jessica stared at me for a long moment. "This is killing you, isn't it?" she asked finally, softly, perhaps even sadly.

My heart started beating faster. I didn't want to get into this now. Not ever for that matter. "Is what killing me?"

Jessica sighed, wearing an expression that let me know we were in for a serious discussion. "My getting married."

I felt like running, running right through the balcony doors, down to the pool deck, then straight down the steps to the beach. I didn't want to think about it, or talk about it, or face it. But I didn't move. I also didn't say anything.

"Can I tell you something?" she asked. "And I can't believe I'm about to tell you this."

I nodded, suddenly fearful.

She paused, and I could almost see the wheels turning in her mind. I could feel her hesitation. Was she scared? "When I found out . . . about you. The day that Lynn posted your diary, and you ran out of the school and I ran after you and you were crying and everything felt like it was falling apart. I almost told you that . . . I've been with a girl."

The plastic cup slipped from my fingers, spilling ice cubes across the comforter. "Shit," I muttered, and started scooping them up, unable to meet Jessica's gaze. I felt her hands on mine before I saw them. I dared, somehow, to look up into her eyes. She was waiting for me to say something. I couldn't even remember my own name let alone form a coherent sentence expressing my feelings. I tried to flash back to that day, out in the canal by Baldwin High, where sixteen-year-old me had sat across from eighteen-year-old Jessica, praying to a God I wasn't sure I believed in not to let her hate me. Had she told me then what she'd just told me, my reaction would have been much different; I would've felt hope. As it happened, five years later, sitting on her bed, the night before her wedding, I felt my heart shatter into a million pieces and scatter over my soul.

"Please say something," Jessica whispered.

"Who?" was all I managed to say.

Jessica hesitated, drawing in a long breath, and I could tell she hadn't wanted me to ask that question. She looked around, unable to answer for a minute. Finally, she said, "Lynn."

The world stopped. Everything around me went mute, and I was about to pass out. "Wow. If I thought my heart was broken before . . ." I shouldn't have said that. I could tell my words caused her pain, and I couldn't bear the thought of hurting her. "I'm sorry, Jess. That wasn't fair of me."

"Don't apologize, Alix. It was stupid of me to tell you this now."

She was lost, I realized. Torn between not wanting to hurt me, and not knowing how to keep from doing so. There wasn't much she could do to make everything better, short of professing her undying love for me. How could I have been so selfish? All these years, blaming her unconsciously for not feeling the same way. Pretending I understood, while secretly hoping to get what I wanted in the end. She hadn't told me five years ago because she'd known it would have given me a false sense of hope. She hadn't wanted to lead me on.

I looked right into her dark blue eyes, rimmed with tears, and did the only thing I could think of doing to put some closure between us: I kissed her. I leaned forward, over a sea of melting ice cubes, and pressed my lips to hers. It lasted all of three seconds, if that, but in that short span of time, five years of silent longing came to a screeching halt. My heart felt complete again; wounded but not broken.

When I pulled away, I waited for her reaction, worried suddenly that I'd made a huge mistake.

"I thought you promised never to do that?"

I smiled, 'cause I could tell she was teasing. "If you weren't getting married tomorrow, Ms. Jessica, a lot of my promises would be flying out the window."

Jessica laughed and grabbed my hands, pulling me in for a hug. "I love you. I hope you know that."

I hugged her tightly, letting her words coat my spirit. "I love you too." Then I pulled away and looked at her. "All right. Now you're going to have to backtrack on this. You said you *slept* with Lynn Hauffman?"

"I don't know if I'd go that far. She was my best friend at the time and we were just . . . curious."

"Ugh." I stuck out my tongue. Lynn of all people. I shouldn't have asked. Lynn had been my greatest tormentor during high school. Loathing was a mild word for what I felt for her. "How old were you?"

Jessica thought about it for a moment. "Fifteen."

I'd heard enough for now. I'd torture myself with all of this information later. Maybe I'd even bring up the subject again, someday, when all my wounds had healed. Or maybe not. Maybe it was better to leave the past buried. "So, last night of singlehood," I said, needing a change of subject.

"I know," Jessica said thoughtfully. "It seems so unreal."

I nodded. "I'm going to miss you while you're off honeymooning in Europe."

"I'll send a postcard." She laughed when she saw my raised eyebrow. "I'll send a few."

"A little better." I bit my lip, and my thoughts drifted suddenly to Val. Jessica watched me. "What's up?"

It was unnerving that she could read me so easily. I had to stop biting my lip. "I met someone last night."

That caught Jessica's attention. "Oh? Like a someone, someone?"

"Like a girl someone." I watched for her reaction. She was waiting for me to go on, so I did. "Her name is Valerie. She's a bartender at this club in Ft. Lauderdale."

"Cute?"

I sighed. "Beautiful," I admitted.

Jessica nodded. "So . . ."

"So should I call her?"

Jessica started laughing. "Well, you should if you want to." She grabbed the phone and pointed it at me. "Call her now. Invite her to the wedding. Your invitation does say 'plus guest.'"

I stared at her. "Are you crazy?"

"Some may think so. Here." She handed me the phone.

I stared down at the receiver in my hand, actually considering the idea. I'd memorized Valerie's phone number. I still don't know why. I hit the "talk" button and dialed the number. After three rings, the machine picked up and I quickly hung up. "She's not home." I was both relieved and disappointed.

Jessica shrugged. "Try again later."

I knew I wouldn't.

♌

I must have fallen asleep at some point, because the next thing I knew I was waking up to the sound of the ringing phone, and Jessica's groggy voice muttering a tired, "Hello?"

I kept my eyes closed, curious to know who was calling, but too tired to get up. So I just listened instead.

"Alix?" I heard Jessica say. "She's sleeping. Who's this?" Pause. "Valerie?"

I jolted awake at the sound of her name.

"Oh, wait, she just woke up," Jessica said, handing over the receiver. She gave me a funny look and lay back down, watching intently.

I took a deep breath and said, "Hello?"

"Hey, you called?"

I was confused. Had I left a message without realizing it? "Yes I did. How did you know?"

Valerie laughed. "Caller ID. I knew it would come in handy some day."

"But I don't live here. How did you know it was me?"

"Well, the address read Baldwin, and I only know one person from Baldwin. I put two and two together, and that's what I got."

"Most people get four," I joked.

She laughed. "Well, I never was good at math. I'm glad you called."

"You are?"

"Yeah, I didn't think you would. So . . . uh, why did you?"

I turned to Jessica. "Why did I call?" I asked. Jessica nudged me with her knee. "Well, my best friend is getting married tomorrow and she thought—I mean, I thought that maybe you'd like to come to the wedding." This was such a stupid idea. Why would she want to come to Jessica's wedding? She didn't know her. She barely knew me.

"Dammit. I have to work at two."

My heart sank. "That's all right. Another time then."

"I get off work at nine, do you think you'll be free by ten?"

I tried to think logically for a moment, but my mind failed me. "What time do you think the reception will be over?" I whispered to Jessica.

She shrugged. "Our flight is at ten."

"I should be," I told Valerie. "But I will be at my friend's house."

"Hmm." Valerie paused. "All right, how about I pick you up there?"

"Here?" I looked at Jessica, and she arched an eyebrow. "All right. Sounds good." I gave Valerie instructions on how to get to Jessica's and hung up. I sat there silently for a moment trying to digest what just happened. Finally, I looked at my best friend, the woman I loved more than breathing, and said, "I guess I have a date."

She sighed dramatically. "At last. Some competition."

I laughed, placing the receiver back on its base. I wondered if Jessica could ever have competition, and if so, if Valerie could be it. I lay down and glanced at the time. It was only eleven. Jessica had basically missed her entire party, and I was touched that she'd done so to spend time with me. "Do you think everyone went home by now?" I asked.

"I doubt it, but I'll bet you twenty dollars that someone goes home with the stripper."

I smiled at the thought. "Probably my sister. She needs to get some badly."

Jessica turned over and poked me in the ribs. "You're one to talk."

"Hey! How dare you compare my lack of a sex life to my sister's? There's a difference you see."

Jessica laughed. "Enlighten me, please."

I looked at her, quite defiantly in fact, and said, "I could get laid. I just choose not to. She wants to get laid, she just can't."

"Doesn't she have a boyfriend?"

"Yes, that's the problem. Saint Jonathan must wait for the marriage vows before he can examine anyone's no-no special place."

Jessica burst out laughing. "Oh, you're kidding? I didn't think there were people like that left in the world. Guys anyway."

"Leave it to my sister."

"Well, I think it's sweet."

It was my turn to laugh. "And you and Mathew waited how long?" I held up my hands. "Wait. Forget I asked. I really don't want to know." I turned on my side so I was facing her. "Speaking of sleeping together, can I sleep here tonight? I'm too exhausted to drive back to school."

"Yeah, just don't kick me like you usually do."

"Just for that I'll kick you twice as hard."

Jessica arched an eyebrow. "Do you want to sleep on the couch?"

"Ouch. Fine. I'll be good." I rolled out of bed to use the bathroom. I was suddenly feeling better than I had in a long time. I had a date. A date. Me. I was nervous and I was scared, but most of all, I realized, I was really excited.

Chapter 4

My eyes opened slowly and my gaze finally focused on Jessica's form silhouetted in the balcony. I glanced at the alarm clock next to me and read 5:56 before easing out of bed.

Jessica had her back to me. She was staring at the ocean in a way I'd seen her do so many times before. I wondered if this would be the last time I'd see her standing there without Mathew by her side, and my heart flooded with conflicting emotions.

I leaned against the frame of the sliding glass doors, not wanting to disturb her. Before us, the ocean roared, its surface reflecting the sky's golden colors of dawn, and I wondered what she was thinking.

"I love how you do that," she said without turning.

Her voice startled me. "Do what?"

She turned to me, and I took that as an invitation to join her on the balcony. I walked outside, feeling the salty morning breeze on my face. I leaned against the railing, waiting for her to answer my question.

"I love how you always wait for me to say something first," Jessica told me. "Like you're scared you'd be interrupting something important."

I sighed to myself. She had no idea how well I knew her. "You're up early," I said, changing the subject.

Jessica shrugged, turning her attention back to the view. "I couldn't sleep. Alix, do you think I'm too young to get married?"

I stared at her. "What?"

"You know. Should Mathew and I wait a few more years?"

I shrugged. "What's the point? You could wait ten more years and you know you'll still be with him." I touched her arm. "Look, Jess, I couldn't think of a better couple than you and Mathew. You're perfect for each other."

Jessica let out a long breath and smiled. "Yeah. It's just, I feel like I'm about to grow up, you know?"

"At least you get to grow up with the one you love."

"That's true."

"Okay, enough emotional talk," Roxanne muttered, walking out into the balcony. "That's all you two do. Blah blah blah, I love you Jessica. Blah blah blah, I love you too Alix but not in that way. Give me a break." She straightened out her bouncing brown curls and put her arms around both of us. "Girls, today is the end of an era."

The end of an era, I thought. I looked from Jessica to Roxanne to the rising sun on the horizon. It occurred to me that the end of an era marked the beginning of something new.

I put my arm around Roxanne's waist and leaned my head on her shoulder. Jessica did the same. And the three of us looked over the balcony railing to where the ocean met the sky, each of us lost in thoughts of our uncertain futures.

ℳ

I've had this recurring dream for years now, where I'm standing at the altar, and Jessica is walking toward me, wearing a beautiful wedding gown, and looking happier than she's ever looked in her entire life.

My dream came true.

Only I was wearing a bridesmaid's dress and when Jessica stopped walking, she was standing beside Mathew and not me.

But that was close enough, I think.

I looked around the church where people were gathered on both sides. The groom's side was occupied in the front by Mathew's parents and his two sisters, Nina and Sarah. Then there were other people I didn't really recognize. Jessica's side consisted of the mansion's staff. Maurice, the butler, gave Jessica away and took his place beside Rosa, the house-keeper. Jessica's grandparents had phoned in that morning to announce they couldn't make it. Jessica's parents . . . well . . . that's a whole different story. So as far as family, only Jessica's cousin, Amber, had made it. And she stood beside me as a bridesmaid.

"Dearly beloved . . ." The priest's voice rose over the silent crowd, echoing across the large expanses of the church, and I suddenly felt like I was trapped in my worst nightmare. Although, had it been my worst night-mare Jessica would've been marrying Steven Tyler instead of Mathew, so I knew this had to be real. " . . . If anyone knows of any reason why these two should not be married, speak now or forever hold your peace . . ."

That would've been my big chance to make an ass of myself, so thank-fully I stayed quiet. I really didn't know of any unselfish reason why Jessica and Mathew shouldn't be together. Still, I looked around, waiting for someone to say something. Nobody did.

Then, before I knew it, I heard Jessica say, "I do," and as those words filtered through my hazy consciousness, I realized that nothing in my life would ever be the same.

𝒮

A few hours later I was working on my fourth piece of wedding cake, looking around as the wedding reception went on around me.

The happy couple had decided to have it at the mansion, and I couldn't think of a more beautiful place for it. Especially seeing it decorated as it was. Jessica and Mathew had hired a decorator named Dominique who'd been hitting on Mathew since day one. Jessica found it amusing; Mathew not so much.

"Good cake?"

I looked up to find the groom smiling down at me. "I hate cake," I muttered, stuffing a big piece into my mouth. Well, I generally hate cake. But this one was good.

Mathew pulled up a chair and joined me at the table. "I'm hiding from Dominique."

I shook my head. "You should be hiding from his assistant. I think he's not too happy Dominique's got the hots for you, if you know what I mean."

Mathew shrugged and batted his eyes. "Why do I have to be so gorgeous?"

I choked on my mouthful of cake and managed to swallow before bursting into laughter. I smiled at him. "I don't know, Matt. I think you just got lucky. I mean, I'm having trouble containing my own lust for you."

"I guess that's why you're drowning your sorrows in cake." Mathew nodded. "I'm sorry that I have broken your heart, Alix dear."

I patted his hand. "That's all right. I'll get over you some day."

He chuckled and looked around. "I can't believe we're married."

"Yeah." I nodded, feeling melancholic all of a sudden. Mathew and I had never really talked about my feelings for Jessica. We joked around about it, but it was understood that there wasn't anything either of us could discuss that would change anything, so we kept the topic off-limits. "It was about damn time you took her off the market." I winked at him.

"Well, if you ever change your mind about that threesome . . ."

I kicked him under the table. "Jerk. What kind of girl do you think I am?"

"Well, all bisexual chicks are into that kind of thing, right?"

This time I threatened him with the remains of my cake. "Say one more thing, and this will be all over your beautiful tux."

Mathew held up his hands. "All right. I give up." He smiled. "Want to dance?"

"Yeah. Let's go make Jessica and Dominique jealous." He stood, took my hand, and led me to the dance floor. I don't remember what song was playing. It was definitely not Aerosmith. "So where's your wife?" I asked, as we joined the rest of the couples.

"I'm not sure. Maybe she ran off with someone else."

I nodded solemnly. "That's a definite possibility. You know how she is, always running off with the mailman, or the milkman, or the boogie-man."

Mathew started laughing. "The boogieman?"

"Yeah, sure. You'll like the wedding gift I gave you."

"Oh, yeah?"

"Yep. It's a leash, so you can keep your eye on her at all times. It's blue, too. Very manly color."

"I'm glad you're around to keep my masculinity intact."

I nodded. "My pleasure."

"So what did you get Jessica?"

"I got her an apron. Gotta keep those socially constructed gender roles in place."

"Definitely. Wouldn't want her getting any ideas."

The song, whatever it was, ended, so I pulled away from him, and then gave him a big hug. "Treat her well, okay? I know you will, but it's just one of those things you have to say anyway."

Mathew hugged me back. "If I ever treat her badly, I give you full permission to kick my ass."

We started walking back to the table.

Maurice appeared suddenly at my side. "I'm sorry, Miss Alix, but there is a young woman at the front door inquiring about you."

I frowned. "What young woman?" Then it hit me. "Valerie?"

"I believe that's her name, Miss."

I excused myself from Mathew and walked as fast as I could in the shoes I was wearing toward the house.

I found Valerie looking around the foyer.

"Hi," I said lamely, not knowing what else to say. She was clad in tight black jeans again, and a navy blue baby tee with the words "Save Ferris" printed in orange across her chest. Black boots completed the outfit. I suddenly realized what I was wearing and how stupid I must have looked. "You're early," I found myself adding.

"I know, I'm sorry. I'll go."

The tone of her voice made me flinch slightly, and I wondered if I'd done something wrong. "Please don't." I had the inexplicable feeling that if I let her walk out the door I'd never see her again, and for some reason I couldn't bear the thought. "The reception is almost over. Just hang around a little longer and we can leave."

Valerie looked uncertain. "I'm not exactly dressed for the occasion," she said, her tone softer this time. "I didn't realize you'd invited me to Jessica Heart's wedding."

I shrugged. Being best friends with someone famous sometimes made you forget that they were famous at all. "She's my best friend."

Valerie nodded at the dress. "Bridesmaid?"

"Maid of honor." I waited for her response, afraid that the news would frighten her off. Most people would have been thrilled, but Valerie looked ready to bolt. "I didn't know it would bother you."

Valerie was silent for a moment, and I readied myself to chase after her if she did take off.

Before she had a chance to say or do anything however, Jessica appeared at the top of the stairs. Her wedding dress was gone, replaced with a pair of faded jeans and a black Tweety tee shirt. Her long black hair hung loose as usual, and I was momentarily afraid that after seeing Jessica, Valerie would forget all about me. The irony of the thought caused me to frown.

Jessica reached the bottom of the stairs and approached Valerie with a smile. She extended her hand. "I guess you must be Valerie."

Valerie shook her hand hesitantly, glancing at me as though wondering how Jessica Heart knew her name. "Call me Val. Interesting wedding dress."

Jessica laughed. "I was going for the modern look." She turned her attention to me. "I guess you're out of here?"

"When are you guys leaving?" I asked, torn between wanting to leave with Valerie and wanting to cling to Jessica and never let go.

"As soon as I find Mathew. Have you seen him?"

I nodded and pointed outside. "I was just dancing with him, but Dominique cut in so you might wanna go out there."

"I'm sure he's enjoying it." Jessica turned back to Valerie. "Well, Val, you're welcome to anything at the reception. There might be cake left if someone over here didn't eat it all." She glanced pointedly at me, and I glared at her.

Valerie grinned slightly. "Thanks."

"I'm going to find Mathew and sneak out of here," Jessica announced. "Think anyone will notice?"

"Not a chance," I told her. "Have a great honeymoon."

Jessica winked. "I will." She gave me a hug, which felt so final in spite of the fact that I'd be seeing her again in a couple of weeks. "Have fun, girls. Nice meeting you, Val."

I watched her walk away, then turned to find Valerie gazing at me with an unreadable expression. Could she tell how I felt? Was it that obvious? I managed a smile. "Let me get out of this thing and then we can go." I headed for the stairs and motioned for her to follow me. I'd stopped by my dorm earlier that day to get a change of clothes. There was no way I was going out on a date wearing a dress. Was this a date?

"I like your hair," Valerie commented.

"I figured I'd look a little more sophisticated for the occasion." To be honest, I'd simply asked the hairdresser to get rid of the blue and make it black, but Roxanne and Jessica had insisted on her giving me a trim. The trim turned into a completely new do. Instead of black, it was now light brown with reddish highlights. Instead of shoulder-length, it was now cut short around my ears, falling forward into my eyes in a way that was becoming annoying. Jessica and Roxanne agreed that it brought out the green of my eyes, and made me look older and more mature. It only made me wonder what I'd looked like before.

"It looks nice."

"Thanks." We reached the top of the stairs where the staircase split in two. I turned to the left and headed up a new flight of stairs. Valerie followed closely, looking around in amazement. At the top, I went to the right, down a long corridor to the very last door at the end of the hallway. I threw open the double doors to Jessica's bedroom and allowed Valerie to pass through first.

"Holy . . ." Valerie's jaw fell open.

I couldn't say I blamed her. The room had nearly given me a heart attack the first time I'd walked inside. I guess after all these years one took these things for granted, so I looked around again, trying to picture it as Valerie must see it.

The area to the left had once been half of a basketball court, complete with a hoop and everything, but had been recently turned into a small gym. The wall, which had once sported paintings of an outside basketball court, had been covered with a large mirror. The hardwood floors were now carpeted in a dark blue color, as was the rest of the room.

Jessica's bed was directly in front, and the wall behind it had been painted to look like the bottom of the ocean. Jessica has a thing with the ocean. I don't think she could ever live anywhere that wasn't on the beach.

Her king-size waterbed rested on top of a wooden platform with a couple of wooden steps leading up to it. Nightstands on either side of it, along with a matching wall unit, completed the set. On either side of those, were two doors. One led to the bathroom, and the other to the walk-in closet, which was big enough to house an entire family of four comfortably.

To the right were French double doors leading out to the balcony, and a living room-type area was to the side of that. A black-leather couch faced a Phillips flat screen TV and beanbag chairs of different colors were strewn about the carpeted floor. There were a couple of wall units at either side of the TV, both housing movies and stereo equipment.

At the other side of the double doors was Jessica's desk. Her desktop computer and its many components rested on its surface. Next to that was another wall unit filled top to bottom with books. That particular wall was painted to simulate the ocean at sunset.

The wall behind me was a very dark blue, with a gorgeous, full moon glowing over the horizon, casting its reflection over the water.

"Makes your room at home feel like a shoebox, huh?" I said, after a moment.

Valerie laughed. "My entire apartment could fit inside this room about five times."

I smiled and walked over to the bed, where I'd thrown my change of clothes. I'd been in a hurry that morning, so I wasn't entirely sure what I'd selected, but I figured one couldn't go wrong with jeans. I'd chosen a different pair of black Jncos this time. The ones I'd been wearing Thursday night had a picture of a kid on a skateboard above the left back pocket. These had a mad scientist with green hair embroidered on the right back pocket. I liked these better anyway because they were baggier. For a shirt, I'd opted for a black Garbage tee shirt with Shirley Manson on the front in black and white.

I grabbed the clothes and turned to Valerie. "If I can find my way out of this dress, I'll be back in five minutes." She smiled, but I wasn't entirely sure I was kidding. I walked into Jessica's closet and shut the door.

Once upon a time, it had been filled with clothes as far as the eye could see. A couple of years ago, Jessica had decided that one person did not need so many outfits in one lifetime and gave them all away to the Salvation Army. I did manage to steal a few of her black tee shirts, though.

Catching my reflection in the mirror, I flinched. I had to get out of that dress and pronto. For a second I actually thought I looked good.

That's when dilemma number one presented itself: the zipper. "Shit," I muttered, trying to get my arms around the back and failing miserably in the process. Dilemma number two was deciding what to do about it. I bit my lip, running a list of possibilities through my mind. Granted, it was a very short list. I looked around, as though expecting Jessica's clothes to take life and help me out of the predicament.

Eventually, I gave up and walked back out.

Valerie was standing at the same spot I'd left her. She arched an eyebrow, then she grinned. "There are too many smartass comments running through my mind to pick just one."

I pointed to the back of the dress. "Can you help me?"

Valerie coughed, to keep from laughing, I imagined, then walked over to me. "Isn't it a little early in the date for me to be undressing you?"

Flirting. Definitely not one of my strong points. It occurred to me then that I was going out with this woman, whom I barely knew. What was she expecting from me? I'd never really done this before. Did she think we'd have sex that night?

Valerie reached for my dress, and I jerked back. She frowned. "I'm sorry, I was just teasing."

I made a mental note to kick myself when she wasn't looking. "My fault. You surprised me, and I've been known to be rather jumpy." We were off to a good start. I turned around so she could unzip me, which she proceeded to do quite hesitantly. I was sure that she was having second thoughts about this entire thing, and I had to admit I wasn't feeling entirely confident about the situation. But I was willing to give it a shot. "Okay, this time, I will come back out wearing something different. I hope."

I escaped into the closet and leaned my back against the door. There I was, twenty years old, and I'd never even kissed a girl. Unless you counted the two second act of desperation the night before with Jessica. So yes, I was freaking out. A lot. Especially since my safety blanket was on her way to Europe with her husband, and the girl on the other side of that door was really gorgeous and I had no idea what the hell I was doing.

Deep breaths, Morris.

I said that to myself a few times, then kicked off the dreaded shoes. Three minutes later, I was back in my normal attire. And I had to admit that the haircut did look kind of cool. I stood before the mirror, trying to imagine what Valerie saw when she looked at me. To this day I can honestly say that I have no idea.

Valerie was sitting on the last step leading up to the bed, and she rose as I walked in the room. "Feel better?" she asked.

"Yes, dresses aren't my thing. Now, if I manage to find my shoes we can be on our way." I started looking around the floor. "Where are we going, anyway?"

"I was kind of hoping you'd have some ideas."

My Airwalks peered out at me from behind the black leather couch, and I sat down on it to put them on. "Wait a second, didn't you ask me out?"

Valerie came around the couch and stared down at me. "Well, I tried to think of someplace but I don't know you well enough to know where you'd want to go, so I figured I'd let you choose."

I finished with the shoes, and my feet cried out in glee that they weren't clad in fancy footwear. I wasn't sure what to make of Valerie's inability to make a decision as to where we should go. So I put myself in her position and decided she was right. How was I supposed to know what she liked to do on a Saturday night? I had enough trouble figuring out what I wanted to do on any given day.

"The whole dinner and a movie cliché seemed a bit overdone," Valerie continued. "I thought we could be more creative than that."

I smiled and stood up. "At this rate I don't see us doing anything at all." I looked around the room for a second, gathering my thoughts. "Would you like to take a walk down the beach?"

Valerie nodded. "Lead the way."

We took a shortcut through the balcony. There were stairs leading down to the pool deck and then down to the beach. It was a private sector, but it connected with the public area about a mile down.

I took off my shoes and socks when we reached the last step. If I'd known this was what we'd be doing, I wouldn't have bothered to put them on at all. Valerie hesitated, then took off her boots and placed them beside my Airwalks.

We started off down the shoreline. I didn't get too close to the water's edge because I didn't want the bottom of my jeans to get wet, but Valerie didn't seem to care. I was sure she'd jump right in the ocean with her clothes on if I dared her. And maybe I would have had it had been daylight, but it was dark and I wasn't sure how cold the water was.

I was being quiet, which was generally unusual for me, especially when nervous. It's amazing how much babbling a person can do in the right frame of mind. Astounding how quiet the same person can become when feeling out of sorts. This was a bad day for a first impression, or second impression or whatever it was. I needed to snap out of it and quickly before I blew something I still wasn't sure was mine to blow.

"I'm usually more talkative than this," I said suddenly, my voice rising over the crashing waves, which were relatively calm that night. There wasn't much wind blowing to cause anything above a gentle roar as the water rolled in and out of the shore in a way that had become symbolic of my life.

"I have mixed feelings about this part," Valerie responded, looking down at the water flooding her feet, and the sand giving under her weight.

Until that moment I had never truly listened to the sound of her voice. I'd heard the words she'd spoken, but the actual tone of her voice had fallen on deaf ears. It was soft and strong at the same time, feminine and powerful and sweet. The kind of voice I could listen to forever without growing sick of it. "What part is that?" I inquired, mentally shaking myself from my thoughts.

Sky blue eyes focused on me for a moment. "The part where we know absolutely nothing about each other and don't know where to start."

I shrugged. "We could play truth or dare."

Valerie's eyebrows shot upward. "Seriously?"

Truthfully, I'd meant it as a joke, but I didn't see why we couldn't. "Sure."

"Okay."

"Okay." Perhaps this was a bad idea.

Valerie stopped walking, took my hand, and pulled me down on the sand so that we were sitting side by side.

I liked that she was bold enough to touch me after I'd made a fool of myself earlier. I was also grateful she wasn't as shy as I was when it came to that sort of thing. "So, who starts?"

"Well, since it was your idea, I think you should go for it."

"All right. Truth or dare?"

"Truth."

A question popped into my head, and I was happy that this didn't seem as difficult as I had expected. "What made you give me your number?"

Blue eyes narrowed slightly at the question, and she grinned at me. "That should be pretty obvious."

I shook my head. "I suck at obvious things."

"Well, I gave you my number because I wanted you to call me."

Score one for the smartass. "Touché. That's not exactly what I was going for, though."

She took a deep breath and then said, "I didn't want you disappearing out of my life without getting a chance to know you better."

"There. Now that wasn't so hard was it?"

"Truth or dare?"

Frankly, I would've preferred a third choice, but then I figured that I could always fib my way out of the truth option. So, "Truth."

"Okay . . ." Valerie leaned back on her elbows, stretching out beside me, and I did everything within my power to keep my gaze from wandering. "Why did you call me?"

It was a fair enough question, one that I nearly missed having been too busy not noticing her bellybutton ring. I wondered if she had a tattoo. "I called you for the same reason you gave me your number."

So with that it was established that we were generally interested in each other on some mysterious level. I couldn't help but think of fate, which I didn't usually believe in. Sometimes, though, fate really did seem like the perfect explanation for the more outlandish events of my life.

After a while, we dropped the game, and I lay down beside her on the sand as we continued to ask each other random questions. At some point I asked her about tattoos, and she smiled and said she had two: a small rose on her right shoulder blade and a broken heart on her left breast. I didn't ask to see them, but it made me wonder about the broken heart. Had she been hurt at some point in her life? I couldn't imagine why else anyone would choose to permanently brand her skin with such an icon. Unless there was some farfetched explanation that would never occur to me in a million years.

While she was looking up at the sky, I took the opportunity to look at her. Beautiful was all I could think of to describe her. I found myself comparing her to Jessica, though I knew it was wrong of me to do that. Still, I couldn't stop myself. Valerie didn't have Jessica's exotic looks, but there was something else that attracted me to her. And I wasn't sure what it was. Not yet, anyway.

Her skin glowed under the soft touch of moonlight spilling through the palm trees. Her blue eyes were fixed on some faraway spot, blinded by whatever thoughts danced in her mind. For one strange, irrational moment, I wished to crawl inside her mind and get lost in the maze of her dreams. Was I so desperate for love?

Her eyebrow ring shone momentarily as the metal reflected the light. She turned to me, an eyebrow arched in question. "You were staring at me."

"No I wasn't," I said, lamely, embarrassed I'd been caught.

Valerie rolled over on her side, propping her head up with her hand. She proceeded to gaze at me curiously without saying anything.

I grew slightly uncomfortable under her scrutiny. "What are you doing?"

"I'm staring at you."

"I see that. Why?"

"Why were you staring at me?" she asked, her mouth creasing into a smile.

Trapped. How did one answer that question without embarrassing oneself? "I was looking at your piercings. Did they hurt?" I congratulated myself for my wonderful bullshitting abilities as I waited for Valerie to respond.

She looked skeptical for a moment, and I wondered if she was disappointed or impressed by the skillful way I'd dodged that bullet. "They didn't really hurt, but they were sore for a while, my tongue ring especially. Plus it sucked that I couldn't do much with it for three months."

"That must have hindered your sex life," I said, and wondered if I was flirting.

Valerie grinned. "If I had one maybe."

Interesting she should say that. Why would she, I wondered? I admit I was being paranoid, but I couldn't help but question her intentions. Trusting total strangers wasn't something I was keen on doing. I had enough trouble trusting my best friends. Luckily, I could pretend not to be paranoid. "I can relate."

"Would you like to get something to eat?"

Food! I hadn't realized how hungry I was until she said something. "I would love to. I'm starving."

Valerie stood up and offered her hand to help me. "All that wedding cake is long gone, huh?"

I let her pull me up, but glared at her. "That mouth of yours is going to get you in trouble one of these days."

Valerie grinned brightly. "I hope so."

Chapter 5

Starting a relationship, in my opinion, seems like a complicated process. I mean, what marks the start of a relationship? A kiss? Does a particular type of kiss signal the start of a particular kind of relationship. Or is a kiss just a prelude of things to come? Does one sit down with the potential boyfriend/girlfriend candidate and discuss the rules? And who makes up the rules? What if one party wants a committed relationship and the other doesn't? Whose interests take priority then? Because, really, what are the odds that two random people who are physically attracted to one another turn out to both want the same exact thing at the same exact time?

These were the thoughts going through my mind at dinner, as I contemplated the meaning of what could only be construed as a date. It's amazing how important the term "date" seems when spoken of, but when you're in it, it doesn't seem like that big of a deal. Two people just hanging out. Except that with a "date" comes expectations, and these expectations had my stomach in knots.

My mind refocused on the real world, and I grew aware of Valerie watching me.

"You haven't heard a word I said, huh?" she asked.

It struck me as odd how everyone seemed to know when I wasn't listening to them. Did my eyes glow with a sign reading "vacant"? "Sorry, I was thinking."

"About?"

"Relationships," I responded honestly.

"Oh, really? Anything in particular?" She leaned forward, seemingly interested.

She was asking me to speak my mind. If she only knew what a scary proposition that was. I figured, however, that if I was going to freak her out, I might as well do it before any permanent damage was done. "I was just thinking that relationships are complicated."

"How so?"

"Well, for instance, is this an official date?"

Valerie frowned slightly. "Um . . ."

"It's like when does something become romantic as opposed to just friendly and how do you know what kind of relationship you're entering into—short-term, long-term, one night stand? And how do you know if you're supposed to be monogamous? Is monogamy even in existence these days? And if you have sex on the first date, does that speed up the relationship process or kill it altogether?"

"Anyone ever tell you that you think too much?"

I smiled. "Hey, these are valid questions."

Valerie looked around the Baldwin Lakes Mall food court. "Do you want to get out of here?"

"Sure."

We walked outside in silence, comforted by the noise of passing cars and busy shoppers parading across the parking lot. It was when we reached her car that I got the insatiable need to run. *One of these days*, I thought, pulling open the passenger side door of Valerie's Bronco II, *I'll actually dart off into the night*. This wasn't that night, so I made myself comfortable, withholding the impulse to drum my fingers on the door's armrest. Instead, I bit my lip and stole a glance at Valerie who was looking at me curiously. My heart leapt up my throat and I had to swallow it down. *Relax, dumbass*, became my mantra.

I felt her hand on mine so suddenly, that I jumped, startled. I might have let out a shriek too, I'm not sure, yet surprisingly, her hand didn't move. I looked up into a pair of twinkling blue eyes. "I'm sorry," was all I could come up with. "I'm kind of . . . I've never . . ." I half expected her to kiss me right then, if only to shut me up. Instead, she laughed, let go of my hand, and started up the car. So I sat back against the seat, feeling like a total asshole.

"I don't want to get you into bed, if that's what you're afraid of," Valerie said suddenly, her eyes glued to the road.

The statement was spoken so softly that I wondered if I'd imagined it. I repeated the statement in my mind, mulling over the meaning of each word, until I felt . . . offended. "You don't want to get me into bed?"

She glanced at me quickly, surprise written on her face. "Well, no."

"Aren't you gay?" I demanded.

"Last time I checked."

I frowned. "Well, why the hell don't you want to sleep with me then? You did say I was cute, did you not?"

"I never said you weren't."

"And you did give me your number, did you not?"

Valerie pulled the car over to the side of the road.

"What are you doing?"

"I'm pulling over so I can talk to you, 'cause it's hard to have an argument with someone while you're driving."

Argument?

She put the car in park and turned to me. "Okay. I didn't say I never wanted to sleep with you, I was just trying to put your mind at rest if that's what you were worried about."

"So you would like to sleep with me, just not tonight?"

Valerie stared at me silently for a moment. "Would you like to sleep with me?"

The question caught me by surprise. It shouldn't have, but it did, and it hit me that I was discussing having sex with a total stranger. "When?"

"Just in general."

"Well, I guess that depends."

"On?"

I sat back. "Well, on several factors. First, I'd have to get to know you better, and I doubt we'd accomplish that on a first date—"

"Are you asking me out on a second date?"

I arched an eyebrow. "Well, we never did finish establishing what this was."

"For argument's sake, let's just call it a date."

I shrugged. "Fine then. Would you like to go out with me again?"

"Sure."

"When's good for you?"

"How about tomorrow at eight?"

"Sounds good."

"Meet you at my club?"

"Okay."

Silence.

"What's the second factor?" Valerie asked.

"Hmm?"

"The second factor in your reasoning to sleep with me."

I turned so I could face her. I liked the way she was framed by the car window with zooming cars flashing in the background. It looked almost magical. "I guess, how much I like you would be factor number two."

She grinned slightly. "Is there a factor number three?"

"How good of a kisser you are."

Valerie was quiet. "Is that your way of telling me to kiss you?"

"No. I have factors for kissing too."

She smiled, throwing the truck into gear. She pulled back out into the road without saying anything.

That went relatively smoothly, I thought, feeling rather proud of myself.

"Okay, so what are the factors for kissing?" Valerie asked.

I glanced at her then shrugged. "I haven't come up with them yet, but when I do you'll be the first to know."

"I'd appreciate that."

"Any time."

"So what would you like to do now?" she asked. "Or would you like to call it a night?"

I wasn't entirely sure what I was doing, or what I wanted, but I knew for a fact that "calling it a night" wasn't it. "Let's rent a movie," I suggested. "We can take it back to Jessica's."

"Sounds like a plan."

She smiled. I smiled. We both smiled. And my heart might have even grinned a little.

But just a little.

∅

Choosing a movie that we would both enjoy was the tricky part. Maybe this would be the determining factor as to the future of our relationship. What if she wanted to watch a western? I *hate* westerns. She could've turned out to be the biggest western fanatic this side of El Paso. Then what would I do? Or maybe she was the sappy romantic type. What if she wanted to watch *Gone With the Wind*? I'd have to kill her.

Perhaps this had been a bad idea.

"What are you in the mood for?" Valerie asked, as we crossed through the doors of the video store.

"Well, I guess this would be a good time to ask what your favorite type of movies are," I commented, as we passed by the DVD selections on our way to new releases.

Valerie half turned as she answered. "Horror mostly. You?"

Marry me. Now. "Horror too." I smiled a bit sheepishly. "I also like comedies," I added, not sure why. Perhaps so she wouldn't think I was copying her. "I'll even deal with action. As long as there's a lot of blood."

She smiled. "Do you want to check out the new releases or go straight for the horror section?"

I shrugged. So we started off in new releases. Half an hour later, we walked out of the door with copies of *Blue Streak, Night of the Living Dead, House on Hunted Hill,* and *Run Lola Run.* Quite the variety, I must say. "So how many of these do you think we'll actually get through?"

"One?" Valerie guessed, starting up the car.

I nodded. "Sounds about right."

Valerie turned on the radio, and I was grateful that it saved us the trouble of making conversation. On the plus side, I was feeling more relaxed, and far less paranoid than I had been at the start of the evening.

Meanwhile, I was trying to decide whether I wanted to invite Valerie back to my dorm. I knew Nicole was gone for the weekend, so we wouldn't have to worry about that. But Jessica had the big TV, and my car was at her house. The logical thing was to go to Jessica's and watch the movies. I'd spend the night and head to school in the morning. I kept myself from nodding and instead refocused on the outside world. "What are we listening to?" I asked, noticing the music for the first time.

"Save Ferris," Valerie responded, lowering the volume so we wouldn't have to shout over the music. "Want me to switch to something else?"

I shook my head. "Nah, it's not bad. I'd just never heard them before. Are they your favorite band?"

"Yeah, they're up there. I also like Dance Hall Crashers."

"Never heard of them either."

"I guess you're not into ska."

"Can't say that I am. Although, it's more from lack of exposure than anything else."

Valerie glanced between my face and the road for several seconds before responding with, "Well, hopefully you'll decide to hang around me long enough to expose yourself."

"Do you come up with these things on the spot, or do you have this like endless storage of cheesy one-liners?"

"Both." She winked.

I smiled, turning my attention to the window.

"You're really not the flirting type, huh?"

I looked at her. "I think flirting is just a coward's way of saying what's really on their mind."

"Oh, yeah?"

"For instance, by your 'expose yourself' comment, what you were really trying to say is that you like me."

Valerie glanced at me. "Is that a fact?"

"Yes. It was either that, or you hope I hang around long enough to sleep with you."

"Can it be both?"

I laughed. "Possibly."

"So instead of flirting, you just come right out and say what you really mean to say?"

I considered the question as Jessica's mansion rolled into view. "Well, not necessarily. Sometimes, I just don't say anything at all. This saves me the embarrassment of saying something I'll regret saying two seconds later."

Valerie parked the car in Jessica's driveway, right in front of my beetle, and turned off the ignition. "You are one strange woman."

"Thank you," I responded, and jumped out of the car, carrying the bag of movies with me.

Maurice was opening the door before I even got a chance to ring the doorbell. It was uncanny. Sometimes I got the feeling that he stood at the front door, staring through the peephole just waiting for someone to show up so he could open the door for them. He bowed his head as I passed through the threshold. "Welcome, miss."

"Hiya, Maurice. My friend Valerie and I are just going to Jessica's room to watch some movies." I held up the bag for emphasis.

"Very well, miss." He nodded at Valerie, shut the door behind us, and excused himself.

Valerie watched him walk away and frowned. "You'd think he'd be a little bit more hesitant to let us in here while the owner of the house is away."

I shook my head and started toward the staircase. "Rule number one in the Heart mansion: Alix rules all."

"What's rule number two?" Valerie asked, following me up the stairs.

"There is no rule two. Rule one is all that matters." I smiled at her, then continued in silence the rest of the way to Jessica's room.

We managed to get through *House on Hunted Hill* and *Blue Streak* before exhaustion set in. It was nearly four in the morning, and we'd been on the verge of falling asleep on Jessica's couch when Valerie announced that she'd better get going.

"You can sleep over if you'd like," I offered, motioning to Jessica's king-sized bed. "You'll have plenty of room, I promise."

Valerie smiled, but shook her head and declined. "I've got to go to work in a few hours. I might as well head home."

"I'll walk you out then."

Outside, the ocean breeze planted salty kisses on my cheek as I followed Valerie across the gravel driveway to her car. I was wondering how the evening was going to end. Would she kiss me? Would I kiss her back? Would I freak out and run? Did she know this was my first time? Questions and no answers. This was the story of my life.

"I had fun tonight," Valerie announced as she reached her car.

I scrunched up my face. "Can't you think of anything better than that? I mean, that's what everyone says at the end of a date. Even if they had a horrible time, they always say the same exact thing."

"You're so difficult."

I smiled. "Much better."

She laughed and ran a hand through her hair. "So I'll see you tomorrow?"

"Yep. Whispers at eight."

There was that awkward silence that occurs when two people aren't sure what to do next and must take a moment to decide the next course of action. I was hoping she'd kiss me. I was trying to conjure up enough courage to kiss *her*. Neither choice seemed likely, and as she opened the driver's side door to get into the car, I saw my chance slipping away. Instead of taking it, I said the wittiest thing I could come up with. "Drive safely."

"Yes, mom."

I grinned, then watched her drive away. I glanced at my watch. It was nearly four-thirty and I was about to collapse. On my way back to Jessica's room, I couldn't help but think that my life had suddenly gotten interesting.

I wasn't sure if it was a good thing . . . or a bad thing.

Chapter 6

"You're home early," I stated, kicking closed the dorm room door with my foot. I yawned and took a seat at my desk, booting up my laptop as I did so.

Nicole mumbled something unintelligible from behind a book.

"What was that last word after 'bleh'?" I asked, leaning my chin on the back of the chair so I could look at her without expending any unnecessary energy.

The book lowered to reveal Nicole's face. "I said I came back last night. Where were you?"

"I spent the night at Jessica's," I answered, turning my attention to the computer.

Nicole raised an eyebrow. "I thought she was on her honeymoon?"

"Yep. She's in Paris all right. I had a date of sorts last night and we went to Jessica's to watch some movies and then I just spent the night there."

The book was shut, and Nicole was leaning forward in her bed. "Alone?" she asked carefully.

I didn't bother turning around. "Yes, alone."

"Did you kiss at least? Is he or she cute?"

"No and yes."

"No and yes what?"

I sighed quietly, signing on to America Online. "Welcome," sang the computer, followed by, "you've got mail." I clicked on the mailbox icon, then remembered I still had to clarify my answer to Nicole's question. "No we didn't kiss and yes she's very cute."

"What's her name?"

"Valerie."

"Valerie what?"

I searched my head for the answer. I knew she'd told me her last name when she'd introduced herself at Pride Factory. "It starts with an 's,' I think. S-s-skye! Valerie Skye."

"Sounds like a porn star."

I looked around my desk for something soft to throw at her, but came up with nothing. I resigned myself to the very mature response of, "It does not," then scanned down the row of e-mail, deleting junk mail as I went. Finally I came across what I'd been looking for.

From: Dreamer   *Subject: bonjour*

I smiled to myself and clicked on the letter.

Hey Al,
Well, we made it to Paris in one piece. We're about to collapse, we're so tired, but we wanted to let you know we're okay. I'll email you again in a day or two and catch you up on our exciting French adventures. We miss you. Please let me know how your date with Valerie went. I've been dying to know. Take care.
Always,
Jess

I finished reading and clicked on the "reply" icon.

Jess,
Hey, glad to hear from you. Don't mind the subject line. It was the only French thing I could come up with. Anyway, I hope Paris is treating you well, and that you're having fun on your honeymoon. No need for details in that department though. ;)

As for my date with Valerie, it went well enough. We're going out again tonight. I'll keep you posted on any juicy details, if any arise. Nothing happened last night. We went for a walk, then to dinner, then rented some movies and watched them in your room. Thrilling, huh?

Well, I'm off. Say 'ello to the Mister for me. Hope you're being a good little wife. Cook him dinner, and put his feet up. Oh, and don't forget to bring him a nice cold beer while he's watching the game. I'll shut up now before you smack me from Paris.

Love always,
Alix

I closed down AOL and glanced at the time on Nicole's alarm clock. It was only four-thirty; plenty of time left before date number two.

♌

At seven-fifty I walked through the doors of Whispers and stood off to the side trying to locate Valerie. I caught sight of her behind the bar, speaking intently with some woman whose back was turned to me. I wasn't sure what to make of the situation, so I stood where I was until I saw Valerie move on to another costumer. I took a deep breath and made my way to the bar. I didn't know why, but I was nervous.

I took the nearest available stool and waited for Valerie to notice me. It didn't take her long. A cocktail napkin was placed before me, and I glanced up into her gorgeous blue eyes.

"I was afraid you'd change your mind," Valerie said, leaning against the bar so I could hear her over the music.

"Sorry, you're stuck with me another night," I responded.

She smiled. "Would you like a drink before we go?"

"No, I'm good, thanks." Truth was, one drink and I'd be table hopping in the nude. Not good for a second impression, or third, whichever.

"Okay give me a minute and we can get out of here."

I nodded and took that moment to look around the club. It was a little less crowded than it had been the last time I'd been there, but it was lively enough. I glanced up as I noticed that the song playing was one I'd heard in Valerie's car the previous night. I felt warm breath on my ear, sending chills down my spine. I almost missed what she'd said. "Yeah I'm ready," I answered, turning to face her. *She's so beautiful*, I thought for what felt like the millionth time. I jumped off the stool and followed Valerie out of the club.

Once outside, she looked at me a bit sheepishly and said, "Do you mind if we make a slight detour at my apartment? Someone threw their drink at me and I don't feel like smelling like Sex on the Beach all night."

I started laughing as I followed her down the stairs. "Sorry that just sounded perverted."

She laughed too, then motioned down the street. "I live really close by."

"Lead the way, milady." I fell into step beside her as we made our way through the busy sidewalks of downtown Ft. Lauderdale. "So, um. Why did someone throw their drink at you?"

Valerie shrugged. "A small fight ensued and I stepped in to stop it."

"I see. Do you get fights in there often?"

"Not really. Hadn't had one in a while."

I couldn't think of anything else to say, so I fell silent, enjoying the cool breeze blowing in from the ocean. A few minutes later, Valerie turned to an apartment building, and I followed her inside. At the elevator, I paused.

"Something wrong?"

I bit my lip and looked hesitantly at the elevator. "What floor do you live on?"

"Uh, the fourth."

"Mind if I meet you there?"

She frowned. "Why?"

I wasn't sure which date was appropriate for phobia revelations, but I doubted the second was it. "I like . . stairs."

Valerie looked at me as though I'd grown three heads, then a small smile edged its way across her features. "You're scared of elevators." It wasn't a question.

I sighed to myself. "Terrified is more like it."

Valerie exited the elevator and opened the door leading to the stairs. "After you," she said, bowing slightly.

I passed through the door, feeling relieved and embarrassed all at the same time. "Thanks," I said, as we began our ascent.

"Feathers."

I glanced at her, my eyebrows narrowing in question. "What?"

"That's my phobia."

"You're scared of feathers," I said, a bit incredulously.

"Terrified is more like it," she responded with a smile.

I bit my lip to keep from laughing. "You're kidding?"

Valerie shook her head. "Nope." She smacked me lightly on the shoulder. "Don't laugh, Miss I-Like-Stairs."

I smiled. "Sorry. I should have more respect for a fellow phobic."

"Thank you." She smiled back.

When we reached the fourth floor, I followed Valerie down the hallway to her apartment. The number on the door read "413," and I memorized it for future references. Somewhere in the back of my mind I was hoping it wouldn't be the last time I ever saw that number.

Valerie's apartment was small, but cozy. Kitchen to the right, living room to the left, and a small hallway leading to, what I assumed, was the bathroom and bedroom. The hall ended with a window that overlooked an alleyway.

"I guess I could say sorry for the mess, but I'm not really sorry for it," Valerie said, shutting the door behind us.

"Good. I hate it when people are sorry for their mess. I think a mess is something to be proud of." I looked around and scrunched up my face. "Although, I gotta tell you, Val, this place is kind of a pigsty." The apartment was spotless.

Valerie laughed. "Yeah, I pride myself on that." She motioned to the couch. "Take a seat. I'll be out in a flash."

Valerie headed for what I guessed was the bedroom, and I took the moment to get a better look at the apartment. The living room featured a black couch facing a wooden wall unit, on which rested a 19" TV, a DVD player, and a stereo system. On the bottom shelf, there was a row of CDs, and I crouched down to look at the selection. I smiled when I saw that she had an Aerosmith CD. Her collection contained mostly bands I'd never heard of, although I recognized Dance Hall Crashers and Save Ferris from the conversation we'd had the night before. On the shelf above, was a row of movies. The box for *Labyrinth* was empty so I guessed she'd been watching it recently. I loved that movie.

"Do I pass inspection?"

Her voice startled me, and I jumped slightly. "You need to stop doing that," I said and turned around. My breath caught in my throat. She'd changed into a pair of tight blue jeans and a black tee. I did my best not to drool all over her carpet. Somehow, I found my voice. "Feel better?"

"Yeah, I even managed a two second shower, so I feel brand new." She grinned and stepped closer. "So, what would you like to do tonight?"

Oh, it would've been so easy to kiss her, and to hell with the "factors." Instead, I gathered up my raging hormones and spoke sanely. "I'm kind of hungry."

"Dinner it is. I can heat up some frozen dinners . . . or we can go to this great restaurant a few blocks down. Your choice."

♌

It was an Italian restaurant, and it smelled wonderful. My stomach growled in complaint, and I sent down a message telling it to shut up and be patient.

I was in the process of mentally calculating how much money I had in my wallet when Valerie said, "Dinner's on me." I must have looked surprised, because she quickly added, "You paid for the movies last night, so I thought I'd pay for dinner."

I glanced down at the prices, thinking it was kind of an unfair trade.

"You can take me to McDonald's some other time and we can even it out," Valerie suggested, reading my thoughts somehow.

I looked up. "McDonald's?"

"Well, I like McDonald's."

I laughed. "Okay. Deal." She smiled and returned to the menu, and

I was hit with the sudden realization that I'd just agreed to a third date. Third. How many until one stopped counting?

"Are you ladies ready to order?" the waiter inquired, pen and notepad in hand.

Valerie ordered first; she chose the lasagna. I still hadn't decided what I wanted so I just went ahead and ordered the lasagna too to avoid any further embarrassment.

When the waiter walked away, Valerie folded her hands on the table on and regarded me curiously. "So what would you like to do after dinner?"

"Do you always like to think ahead?" I asked.

Valerie smiled. "I like having something to look forward to."

"You're not one of those 'live for the moment' types, then, I take it?" I asked, taking a sip of Dr. Pepper.

"I didn't say that," Valerie said. She studied me silently for a moment. "What are you?"

I shrugged. "I guess I'm a seize the moment type of person, though I rarely know what I'm seizing half the time."

Valerie started laughing.

I liked making her laugh. It lit up her face. "Do you work tomorrow?"

"No I'm off on Mondays and Thursdays," she answered, then added, "I have classes."

"What are you taking?"

"Just a couple of art classes. I'm trying to save up enough money so that next semester I can attend full-time."

I nodded. "You should transfer to Baldwin. We'd be closer." I don't know why I said that. I'd always had a hard time keeping my immediate thoughts from filtering through my lips.

To my surprise, Valerie responded with, "Do they have a good art program?"

"Actually, yes," I found myself saying. "My roommate last year was an art major so I know."

Valerie seemed thoughtful. "I'll look into it."

I wasn't sure if she was serious or not. Would she really consider transferring to Baldwin just to be close to me? What would it mean if she did? I took another sip of soda in the hopes that drinking would shut my mind up.

Our food arrived shortly afterwards, and we ate more or less in silence. By then I was starting to feel pretty comfortable around her, and didn't find it necessary to fill each lull with pointless conversation. As we ate, I wondered what she was thinking. She seemed so in control and at ease in every situation, while here I was, cursed to be a bumbling idiot for all eternity.

After dinner we walked outside, unsure of where to head next. It was only ten, so we pretty much had the whole night to kill.

"See, if you'd told me what you wanted to do after dinner we wouldn't be standing out here with nothing to do," Valerie teased.

"If I knew what I wanted to do I would've told you at dinner," I responded.

Valerie took my hand; a gesture that caught me completely by surprise. I felt my heart speed up at the contact, and I begged it to slow down for fear that she might hear it above the crowds of passersby and the noise of traffic. She led me to a wooden railing which divided the sidewalk and the start of sand. She let go of my hand, and I instantly missed the warmth her touch had provided.

She sat up on the railing and motioned me to join her. When I did so, she spun around so she was facing the beach instead of the road, and I followed her example.

"Have you always lived near the ocean," she asked, breaking the silence.

Distant waves provided the background noise around us, joined on occasion by the distinct yelling of a rowdy group of people or a speeding car. "Yes," was my answer. "I've lived here all my life. What about you?"

"I was born and raised in Boston, then I moved here a couple of years ago."

"For school?" I asked.

She fell silent for a moment, then looked at me. "For a change of scenery, mostly."

I smiled. "Say 'car.'"

She looked confused. "Huh? Oh." She smiled. "I don't have an accent. You would've noticed it by now if I did."

"Yeah, that's what I figured, but sometimes I'm not as observant as I should be." I looked straight ahead, at the nothingness in the distance, trying to picture the ocean I knew was there. "Do you like Florida?"

"It's warm," Valerie responded. "Can't say I love it or hate it. Do you like it here?"

I shrugged. "It's home. Can't say I have much basis for comparison. I've never really been anywhere else, except for California to visit my cousin, Kes."

"Do you want to stay here forever?"

"Forever is a long time," I responded. Did I want to stay in Florida? All my friends and family were here. Where else would I want to go? "I don't really know. Guess I never thought about it."

Valerie smiled. "Seize the moment and don't look ahead, that's you."

I smiled back. I guess she was right. I hadn't really thought about that either. "Actually, I think I'm more of a go with the flow kind of person. Can't remember the last time I had a moment to seize."

Valerie looked thoughtful for a moment. "I doubt that's true. I bet you've seized lots of moments without realizing it."

"Oh?"

"Yep. For instance, if you were to just go with the flow, you wouldn't have called me up the other night."

I was glad it was dark, for I could feel my cheeks getting hot. "Actually, Jessica pretty much dialed the number for me."

"You didn't want to call?"

"No, I did! I just probably wouldn't have, had I not had any outside influence." I looked away, unsure of what this revelation meant to her.

I felt the warmth of her hand on mine again and looked up to catch her gaze on me. "I'm grateful to the outside influence, then," she said, grinning slightly.

What was appropriate to say? "Me too" seemed so corny. Again it was one of those "insert kiss here" kind of moments that seemed to arise between us every now and then. If I had indeed been a seize the moment kind of person, I would've kissed her. Only, I knew I wasn't.

Before I had a chance to come up with a reply, Valerie spoke up. "Do you play pool?"

I was about to tell her I was undefeated when it occurred to me that hustling her might be kind of fun. Unless she was better than me, in which case I'd feel like a fool. I guess we'd find out. "Not well," was my answer. "I've only played a couple of times." Lies, all lies!

"I'll go easy on you," she said, swinging her legs over the railing and jumping down onto the sidewalk. "There's a pool hall not far from here. We could walk, unless you'd rather take your car." This time she said car in a way that sounded like "cah."

I smiled at her New England accent attempt and jumped down from the railing. "Very cute."

She grinned. "You think I'm cute?"

More like gorgeous, I thought. I kept that to myself, however, and replied with a nonchalant, "You're okay."

We started walking.

"I guess I'll take what I can get," Valerie said. She smiled. "I thought you didn't flirt?"

I kept my face as serious as possible. "Who said I was flirting?"

She laughed. "Guess I'll just have to resign myself to the 'just okay' status."

I nodded. "Better to have someone tell you the truth now before you went the rest of your life with a high self-esteem or something."

"I appreciate your honesty."

"Any time."

We walked for about fifteen minutes before we finally reached the pool hall Valerie had been talking about. It was fairly empty, so we had no trouble getting a table, and we made our way to the one on the far right.

Valerie racked the balls, and I did my best to look clueless.

"You're holding the cue stick wrong," Valerie informed me.

And so I was. "Oops."

She smiled. "Guess I'll break then."

"Break what?"

Her eyes narrowed. My clueless routine was on dangerous ground.

So I smiled as innocently as possible and said, "Kidding."

Valerie turned to the table and got ready to break, so I moved over in order to see the shot. A second later, there was an explosion of color across the table as the white ball broke through the triangle formation and sent solids and stripes in all directions. *Not bad*, I thought, watching a couple of solids fall nicely into the pockets.

"You're stripes," Valerie told me.

"Those would be the ones with the stripes across them, right?"

"Smartass."

I smiled to myself and leaned back against the table next to ours. I held my cue stick in front of me and watched as Valerie took her shot. I loved the way her blonde hair cascaded over the side of her face as she leaned over the table.

I was too busy looking at her to notice if she made the shot or not, but the way she retreated from the table and looked at me expectantly gave me a small hint. I spent a minute trying to decide my next course of action. To miss or not to miss, that was the question. In the end, I decided to leave it up to chance.

Ten minutes later, I'd cleared the table, and Valerie was staring at me, mouth agape. "Well, it's a good thing I didn't think to play you for money," she joked.

"Well, I was going to hustle you, but then I remembered you paid for dinner and everything . . ."

"Well, thanks a lot."

We played for a little over two hours, and Valerie even beat me in one game. She kept insisting that I let her win, though in all honesty, I'd been too busy thinking of other things to remember how to shoot pool properly.

Somehow we ended up back at her apartment, on her bed . . . No, just kidding. Getting a little ahead of myself there.

We did end up in her apartment though.

"You know, I think I'm getting used to taking the stairs instead of the elevator," Valerie announced, as we walked through the door.

I laughed. "Very funny. Just for that, I'm going to get you a nice big feathery bird for your birthday."

"You don't know when my birthday is."

"June first."

Valerie seemed surprised. "You remembered?"

I took a seat on her couch and looked up at her. "Yeah. I mean, we had a nice little conversation on the importance of birthdays. Why wouldn't I remember?"

She smiled. "Would you like a drink of any kind? I don't have Dr. Pepper, sorry, but I've got Pepsi, and I could pretty much fix you any alcoholic beverage you like."

"Nah, I'm fine."

"Do you not drink? Alcohol, I mean."

"Occasionally, when I want to get really drunk. I don't have very high tolerance for alcohol and I have to drive home tonight so drinking would probably not be a good idea."

"You could always spend the night."

I looked straight at her, I'm sure my surprise was clearly showing on my face.

"Kidding," she responded, taking a seat next to me. "Well, I guess I was half-joking."

I had no idea what to say. Flirting problem, again. I wondered if they had a *Flirting for Dummies* manual.

"Would you like to watch a movie?" Valerie asked.

I snapped out of it. "Uh, yeah. Sure. What do you have?"

"*Labyrinth, Dark Crystal, The Neverending Story, Scream, Scream II, Teaching Mrs. Tingle*—"

"How about I just go up there and look?" I suggested.

"Or you could do that." She sat back, putting her feet on the coffee table and folding her hands across her chest.

I made my way to the wall unit and looked over the row of movies. There was a nice balance of fantasy and horror with a few random comedies and action flicks thrown in for variety. There weren't any I didn't feel like watching. "Tough decision. I love most of these movies."

A second later, Valerie was beside me. "How about I go down the row and you can tell me yes, no or maybe?"

I laughed. "That'll take forever. What do you feel like watching?"

"I love them all."

"Well, you're no help. How about *Labyrinth*?"

Valerie smiled. "I was hoping you'd pick that one."

I returned to the couch, while Valerie set up the movie. She turned off the lights and sat next to me. On the TV screen, the movie flickered to life. Meanwhile, I was growing increasingly aware of Valerie's warmth beside me. I wanted to touch her—somewhere, anywhere. I glanced up at her. Wasn't she nervous at all?

Valerie simply mouthed the words along with the movie. "'Give me the child. Through dangers untold and hardships unnumbered, I have fought my way here to the castle beyond the Goblin City . . .'"

I had to smile. "Seen it much?"

"Just a couple of times," she responded, with a sly grin.

I turned my attention to the film, attempting to concentrate, but not quite succeeding. Warm breath on my ear again, followed by the words, "Would you like some popcorn?" Her lips graze my skin. I jumped off the couch and landed on the floor with a loud thump.

"Sorry," Valerie said. "Man, you're jumpy. You can come back to the couch. I won't bite, I promise."

I gathered what was left of my pride and used it to lift myself up onto the couch. I didn't dare look at Valerie. I was mortified.

"Hey, look at me," Valerie said.

I took a deep breath and forced myself to meet her gaze. She appeared concerned. "I'm an idiot. I'm sorry. I don't know why I'm so jumpy."

She smiled. "It's kind of cute, actually. Anyway, it's my fault. I shouldn't have done that."

Okay so we both felt like fools, only she was better at hiding it than I was. I begged my mind to think of something to say to take the tension off the situation. "I'd love some popcorn," was what it came up with.

"Butter or no butter?"

"No butter," I replied.

"No butter? What's wrong with you?" She stood up and walked to the kitchen. "The only other person I know who doesn't like butter on their popcorn is my mother." She turned on the kitchen lights, and the living room was flooded with a faint yellow hue.

"Then maybe I should be dating her instead."

I heard Valerie laugh but couldn't quite see her. "I doubt you're her type."

"Well, damn. Unbuttered popcorn is the key to my heart."

"I'll try to remember that."

A few minutes later, the lights were off again, and Valerie was handing me a can of Pepsi and a bowl of unbuttered popcorn. "Thanks."

"Any time," she said, sitting down.

"Do you live alone?" I asked, unsure of where the question had come from.

"Nope. My girlfriend's away for the weekend."

I glanced up at her. "I hope you're joking or this bowl of popcorn is going on your head, followed by the entire can of Pepsi."

Valerie smiled, meeting my gaze. "I live alone."

I was silently relieved. "Good. I would've hated to waste the food."

We managed to get through the rest of the movie without any catastrophes. When Valerie turned on the lights, I glanced at my watch. It was nearly three and I had a class at eight. I had to get going or I'd never wake up.

"I better go," I said, rising to my feet. "Class tomorrow."

Valerie nodded. "Yeah, me too. Where are you parked?"

"Next to the club."

"Would you like me to walk you back?"

"Nah, I can find my way." I paused, smiling up at her. "Thanks though."

She shrugged slightly, and we stood there staring awkwardly at each other for a few seconds.

"Did you come up with the factors for kissing yet?" she asked suddenly.

I was both surprised and excited by the question. Seize the moment, I thought. "Yes, actually," I answered, though I hadn't really thought about it.

Valerie's eyebrows rose. "Oh?"

"Yeah, but there's really only one," I said, and our gazes met. I drowned in her eyes, losing all train of thought.

She stepped a little closer. "What is it?" she asked softly.

"You have to kiss me," I replied, the words leaving my mouth before I knew what I was saying.

And before I knew it, her lips were on mine; so soft and sweet I thought I would melt into her arms. I pulled away, overwhelmed by the rush of emotions surging through me. I wanted to throw my arms around her neck and press her close to me. I wanted her so badly I thought I would explode with longing.

Somehow, I managed to pull myself together long enough to speak. "I should give you my number," were the first words to pass through my mouth.

"Oh, right. I don't have that." Valerie excused herself for a moment as she went to find a pen and paper. I leaned against the nearest wall, trying to calm my racing heart. I'd never felt anything like this before. Maybe I was having a heart attack and didn't realize it.

A minute later, Valerie was back, pen and paper in hand. I scribbled down my number, and even my email address though I didn't see a computer anywhere in the apartment.

"Aerosmith30, huh?" Valerie said, looking down at the piece of paper.

"I don't know if you have a computer or anything. I just thought I'd give it to you anyway."

"Thanks." She opened the door for me, and I stepped out into the hall. "I'll call you," she promised.

I nodded. "Okay. Good night."

"Good night."

I smiled, and then started down the hallway, knowing she was still standing in the doorway watching me.

Chapter 7

"I am freaking out," I whined, burying my face in my hands.

Jade yawned from across the table. We were at the dining hall the following morning, eating breakfast before heading off to class. "Quit being such a wanker," she told me, without looking up from her food.

I sighed looking at her through my fingers. "I don't know what to do."

"About what?"

"About Valerie."

This time she glanced up at me. "I told you, stop being such a bloody wanker. You've spent the last few years lusting after Jessica. Give yourself a break. At least you have a chance with this one."

I knew Jade was right. I was freaking out, but it wasn't because I didn't know what to do about Valerie. It was something else. "I'm scared, Jay," I admitted.

"Of?"

"Women. Sex. Love." I shrugged. "It was easy being in love with Jessica because I knew I didn't stand a chance, so it was safe. With Valerie, though, it's something different entirely."

"Welcome to the world of real relationships," Jade told me, lifting up her glass of orange juice in a mock toast. "You didn't freak out this much when you started dating Zack."

I shook my head. "It was different. I was sixteen. Somehow, I was more together then."

"Or maybe it's the fact that Valerie is a girl . . . ?"

I looked at her sharply. "What do you mean?"

Jade pushed her tray aside and regarded me seriously. "I think you're freaked out over the fact that it's a girl you're dealing with."

I frowned, unsure of what to make of Jade's analysis. "Are you saying you don't think I'm gay?"

Jade laughed. "Oh, you're bloody queer, all right. I'm just saying you've never been with a girl before so you're scared you won't know what to do or how to act."

Bull's-eye. Score one for the Brit. "Maybe I should rent some lesbian porn or something."

"Or something," Jade responded, getting up. "C'mon, time for class."

I picked up my tray, disposed of it, and followed Jade out of the dining hall. We both had World Literature at Engelbert Hall, which was across the street from the dining commons. "Are you going out with that guy you met at the club?" I asked, taking the spotlight off of myself.

"Tonight, in fact. Wanna double?" Jade grinned. "When do you get to see Valerie again?"

"I don't know. She said she'd call me."

"Oof. Bad sign."

I frowned. "Is it?"

Jade patted me on the head. "I wouldn't worry too much about it," she said, pulling open the doors to the building and walking inside.

I caught up to her quickly. "Hold on. Why is it a bad sign?"

Jade was thoughtful for a moment. "Well, maybe it isn't. I forget men and women live by different rules. So if she said she'd call then she probably will."

I nodded, feeling momentarily relieved. "Wait, what if she doesn't call?"

Jade paused to smile before opening the door to our classroom. "Then you can quit freaking out." She smiled quickly and walked inside.

I frowned again, not particularly liking the sound of that. I sat down in my usual seat in the back, next to Jade. We were a few minutes early, so the room was still fairly empty. Our professor was writing her office hours on the board, along with her name and contact information. It was only the second week of school, so I'd only had this particular class twice, but it seemed pretty interesting. I was a little less than thrilled about the mother load of novels we had to read, but I'd have to deal with that.

Turning to Jade, I asked, "So how long should I wait for her call before abandoning all hope?"

Jade glanced at me and shook her head. "Who do I look like, Sylvia Browne? I don't know."

I propped my feet up on the seat in front of mine. I crossed my arms and sat back, waiting for the professor to commence.

Relationships were definitely complicated. Every time one of my questions was answered, a new one arose in its place. How were people supposed to get anywhere in love if nothing made any sense? Perhaps on my way to getting *Flirting for Dummies* I'd go ahead and pick up *Relationships for Dummies* as well. I figured that if the book indeed existed there would have to be a men's manual, women's manual, lesbian's manual, bisexual's manual, gay's manual, transgender's manual, transexual's manual . . . But then, if everyone was reading from a different manual, how was anything supposed to get accomplished? This probably explained the popularity of the *Men Are From Mars, Women Are From Venus* books. Of course, that didn't help me at all.

Perhaps I needed therapy.

✍

"Any calls?" I asked Nicole, dropping my keys and access card on my desk as I entered. I had to shout over the stereo. I had no idea what she was listening to now.

She lowered the volume long enough to say, "No."

I sat at my desk, booted up the computer, and hung my bookbag on the back of my chair. It was nearly five, and I had finally finished with classes for the day. After checking my email, I planned on taking a nice long shower. I had a hell of a time falling asleep, and two hours of sleep just wasn't cutting it. Maybe after the shower I'd take a nap.

The computer finished doing its thing, so I bestowed it my full attention. Once online, I headed straight for my mailbox, hoping Jessica had written me back. No such luck. In fact, I had only one message.

> *Name: DarkCrystal61@hotmail.com*   *Subject: hi . . .*

I had no idea whom the email was from, but I double-clicked on it anyway, curiosity getting the best of me.

> *Hi, Alix. I know I said I'd call you, but I was just checking my mail at the computer lab here at school before my next class and I thought I'd drop you a line to say hi. Oh, I looked into Baldwin, and you were right, they have a great art program. I just have to apply for a scholarship and maybe next semester you'll see me around campus. Unless you'll feel like I'm stalking you, in which case I'll just stay where I am. Um. I'm babbling because I'm bored. I was thinking I need a dog. Maybe Thursday after my classes I'll go buy one. Want to join me in the search for the perfect puppy? You can buy us McDonald's afterwards. ;)*
> *~Val~*

I caught myself grinning like an idiot, but I didn't particularly care. After hitting the reply button, I straightened up in my seat and began to type.

Subject: Re: hi . . .

Val,
I almost deleted your email thinking it was junk mail or porn. Lucky for you that I didn't or you'd be pet-shopping solo. Thursday I have class until 2, and then I'm free, so I'd be more than happy to accompany you in the search for Mr. Perfect Puppy. I'll have to think on the McDonald's .. that's kind of pushing it. ;) Just let me know the time and place, and I'll be there.

I told you Baldwin had a good art program. Definitely look into the scholarship. I'd love to have you around. Feel free to stalk me, no one ever does.
     Alix

I sent the email and sat back in the chair, feeling rather giddy. I turned around to find Nicole staring at me. "May I help you?"

Nicole turned off the music (if you could call it that) and regarded me curiously. "You're smiling like a loon," she observed. "Any particular reason?"

Not bothering to wipe the grin off my face I shut down the computer. "Can't a girl just be in a good mood?"

"Not when said girl is the Princess of Darkness."

"Princess of Darkness," I repeated. "I kind of like that." I rose from my chair and walked over to the closet to change into my bathrobe. "Her Gloominess is going to strip now, so please avert thy eyes lest you be blinded by her beauty."

She chuckled and returned to whatever book she'd been reading. I'd never met anyone in my life who went through books at such record speeds as my beloved roommate. Sometimes I wondered if she read them at all or if she just used them as a shield against humanity. I doubt I'll ever know the answer.

I changed quickly and headed to the girls' bathroom. Walking in nothing but a bathrobe down the hallways of the dorm was something to get used to. After three years, I barely even thought about it.

My mind kept refocusing on Valerie's email, and the idea of shopping with her for a dog made me smile all over again. Too bad it was only Monday. *Three more days to go*, I thought, and proceeded to take my much-needed shower.

♫

I'd been in the middle of a dream involving royalty and dogs, when the ringing phone brought my hazy mind to consciousness. Silently, I begged Nicole to answer the damn thing, and after a couple of rings, I heard her say, "Hello," in a soft voice. Pause. Then, "She's sleeping at the moment, and she looked pretty tired when she collapsed in her bed earlier so I don't know if I should wake her." Silence. "Okay, Val, I'll let her know you called. Bye." Click.

Val? My eyes popped open, and I sat up in bed, feeling woozy. "Was that Valerie?"

"Is that the girl you're going out with?" Nicole asked, aiming the receiver at my face.

"I guess you could call it that," I responded, grabbing the phone from her grasp before she poked me in the eye with the antenna. I yawned. "How long was I asleep?"

"Couple of hours. Are you going to call her back?" Her tone bordered on impatience, and I frowned up at her.

"Can I have a minute to wake up here?"

"Well, I have to leave for work in ten minutes, so I was hoping to get some eavesdropping time before then." She smiled innocently and made her way back to her bed. "She sounds nice. You haven't told me much about her, you know?"

"Oh, I know," I replied pointedly, playing with the receiver in my hand.

"You're stalling," Nicole informed me, as though I wasn't already aware of the fact.

Without further ado, I punched in Valerie's number. Unconsciously, I held my breath as I waited for Valerie to pick up.

Three rings later, I heard Valerie's distinct voice answer, "Yep?"

Momentarily I forgot how to speak. Shaking myself mentally, I finally found my mind buried under a pile of nervousness and senseless paranoia. Beside it was my voice. "Hi," I said, grateful to be speaking at last. "It's Alix." Remembering my own name was always a good sign.

"Oh, hey," Valerie greeted, her tone brightening. "I got your email. I wrote you back, but I figure I'd call you anyway since I told you I would."

I felt my face break into a smile. "So what inspired this sudden need to get a pet?"

"Well, I was tossing and turning in my bed, unable to sleep and feeling rather lonely when it occurred to me that I was missing something in my life. And since I figure it's a bit soon in our relationship to ask you to move in with me, I thought a dog would make a nice substitute."

My mind was reeling, her words breaking off until all I heard was "relationship" and "move in with me" cycling around and around in my head. Pulling myself together, I replied, "What kind of dog do you have in mind?"

"Hmm. Tough to say. I have a feeling that when I see it, I'll know. Like love at first sight."

I relaxed a bit, knowing we were on relatively safe ground. You couldn't go wrong talking about dogs. "Something to keep your warm on those cold South Florida nights, no doubt."

"You're mocking me now."

I laughed. "Yeah, just a little."

She laughed too, and I couldn't help but notice what a beautiful sound that was. It made me wish I was next to her so I could watch her face light up.

"I have a small confession," she said suddenly.

"What's that?" I asked, watching Nicole wave goodbye on her way out to work. I waved back and returned my attention to the phone.

"I don't want to wait until Thursday to see you again."

I was overcome with relief, though I responded with a nonchalant, "Oh?"

"Do you think we can get together tomorrow?"

I ran my Tuesday schedule through my head, then cursed silently. "I can't. I have an audition tomorrow night and classes all day." I'd totally forgotten about the audition.

"What's the audition for?" I searched her tone for a hint of disappointment, but found none. More than anything, she sounded interested.

My excitement over the audition returned, and I couldn't believe I'd almost forgotten about it. "An improv troupe. We go around doing improvisations at different places."

"Sounds like fun. Do you have a good chance of getting in?"

"Hopefully. I don't want to get my hopes up."

"Good luck, or break a leg. Whichever applies."

I smiled into the phone. "Thanks." I was disappointed, though, because I really wanted to see her. "How about Wednesday?" I suggested.

"I'm pulling a double shift at the club," she said regretfully.

I tried to keep the disappointment from my voice. "Guess we're back to Thursday."

"Guess so." This time I detected a sad note in her tone. "Hey, if we stay up all night talking on the phone, would it count as a third date?"

Laughing, I replied, "If you can keep me on the phone for more than half an hour, you'll win the record."

"Not a phone person?"

"Nope."

"I like a challenge," she replied. "So what do I get if I keep you on the phone for more than an hour?"

"The admiration and awe of all the others who failed before you," I answered, grinning to myself.

Five hours later I got off the phone with her . . . and I decided never to challenge her again.

Chapter 8

"I don't know if I can do this," I whispered to Jade, clapping more or less enthusiastically as someone who'd just auditioned finished their piece and walked off stage.

"Does that mean we can get out of here now?" Jade asked, her eyes pleading.

I smacked her on the shoulder. "You're not supposed to say that! I brought you along for moral support, after all. Your job is to keep me pumped up and optimistic."

"Rah rah, go Alix go," Jade muttered. "Now can we get out of here?"

"I hate you." I slumped down in my seat and focused straight ahead as another hopeful actor took the stage.

Jade frowned and leaned down to whisper in my ear. "I don't know how I let you talk me into coming to these things. You know how I hate theatre."

The guy on stage sucked big time, and I was grateful. "You hate theatre but you love me, and that's what matters." I clapped as the bad actor left the stage.

"Alix Morris?" someone called from the front row.

I took a deep breath and stood up. This was it. My one and only chance to join the Baldwin Players. Since it was improvisation, I was completely at their mercy. Had it been a different type of audition, I would've walked up on stage and acted out a pair of contrasting monologues, unless it was a cold reading, in which case I would've simply grabbed the script and read the lines to the best of my ability. This was a bit harder, but I just figured that my life was a huge improvisation act anyway, so if I looked at it that way I had twenty years of experience under my belt.

I took a seat on the stool and faced the darkened audience. My heart pounded as I waited for instructions on what to do next.

"Okay, Alix. You're a broken refrigerator that's been abandoned in the middle of a Laundromat. You have five minutes to find an owner. Ready . . . go."

My body sighed. This was going to be a long audition.

℘

Jade was still laughing half an hour later when we walked back to my dorm room. "That was the funniest thing I've ever seen in my life. The part where you tried to climb inside the washer!" She cracked up all over again.

I merely shook my head and opened the door to my room, allowing Jade inside. "I just hope I got picked."

"Are you kidding? You were the best one up there. It was wicked." She took a seat on my bed and broke out the pack of cigarettes. "You mind?"

I shook my head and turned on the laptop.

Jade lit up the cigarette, exhaling smoke into the air. "When do you find out if you got chosen?"

"Not sure," I replied, sitting down. "We got out of there pretty early. If I'd known I would've made a date with Valerie." I said that more to myself than to Jade, but she heard it none the less.

"I still can't believe she kept you on the phone for five hours. That's excessive for any normal person, but for you it's just mind-boggling." She paused momentarily to blow a ring of smoke. "You weren't having phone sex, were you?" She wrinkled her nose at the thought.

I narrowed my eyebrows as I glanced at her. "Yeah, that's it." I shook my head and signed on to AOL. "Oh, hey, you never told me about your date last night," I said, maintaining eye contact with the computer screen as I double-clicked on my mailbox. My email listing popped up.

> *From: Dreamer*   *Subject: Re: déjà vu*
> *From: DarkCrystal61@hotmail.com*   *Subject: Bored*

I bit my lip, trying to decide which one to click on first. Usually I left the best for last when checking my email, but in this case I wasn't sure which was which.

" . . . and then the aliens began to probe us anally which I found quite pleasurable . . ."

My head snapped in Jade's direction as my brows furrowed. "What?"

"Glad to see you were listening," she said dryly. "What were you thinking about now?"

I smiled apologetically. "I was trying to decide whether to read Jessica's email or Valerie's first."

"Oh, you're bloody kidding me." She walked to my desk and flicked me on the forehead.

"Ow!" I rubbed my forehead. "You haven't done that in ages."

"Well, you hadn't been this stupid in a while," Jade replied, leaning over my shoulder to look at the screen. "Read Jessica's first."

I looked at the computer screen. "Why?"

"Cause it's the first one there."

Not sure how I felt about her rationale, I clicked on Jessica's email first anyway.

> *Al,*
>
> *Paris is beautiful! We visited the Eiffel Tower this morning. I'm not sure what we're doing today. Mathew has our guide book. I think we're going to walk around and take pictures of things. I already bought you a bunch of souvenirs that you'll most likely frown upon and wonder why I bought them for you, but oh well!*
>
> *Mathew says hi. He wants to know if Dominique has asked about him? He really misses Dominique. Ack! Just got hit with a pillow. I better go before someone gets hurt (well, before he gets hurt anyway). I miss you!*
>   *Love,*
>   *Jessica*

"Sounds like they're having a good time," Jade said.

"Yeah," I responded. "They're one of those freak happy couples that were brought together by the pull of the moon or something."

"Are you going to reply first or read Valerie's email?" Jade inquired, voicing my thoughts.

Without really thinking, I hit "next" and Valerie's email replaced Jessica's.

> *Alix,*
> *I hope your audition went well. I had a lot of fun talking to you on the phone last night. I'm rather proud of myself for keeping you on for that long. It does wonders for my ego, which was shot after playing pool with you the other night. Well, I should go. I have a long day tomorrow. Would it be out of line if I said I missed you today?*
>   *~Val~*

I couldn't help the smile that seemed to appear whenever I read Valerie's emails . . . or heard her voice on the phone . . . or saw her. "She missed me," I said, unable to keep the awe from my voice.

Jade sighed. "You're a goner." She walked to the window and flicked her cigarette outside. "Now can you listen to my date story?"

"Oh, yeah, sorry about that," I said, turning around and bestowing my full attention on my bald-headed friend. "I'm all ears."

Jade nodded and sat on the floor next to my bed. "He took me to an art museum after dinner, where he spent about an hour staring at a painting of a yellow line crossed with a purple one. He insisted it was bloody brilliant and fantastic." She shrugged. "So I left him there."

My eyebrows rose in surprise. "How'd you get home?"

"Well, on my way out I ran into a really cute bloke who offered to drive me home, after I explained about my horrible date. He was really nice, even gave me his mobile number so I could call him sometime."

I shook my head. "I don't know how you manage to meet so many different guys just by breathing in their direction."

"Pity, isn't it, that even then I can't seem to find one worth keeping?"

I smiled. "Pity indeed. Maybe this new one will be different."

"Perhaps." Jade smiled and studied me for a second. "Y'know, I really do like this new hair style of yours. You look rather girlish but in a cool dyke sort of way."

"I'm not sure how to take that, Jay," I replied, grinning crookedly.

She laughed. "No, it looks good." She nodded toward the computer. "Are you writing back to them?"

My attention shifted back to the emails. "Yeah, I guess I should do that."

To Jessica, I wrote a quick note telling her not to buy me dumb things and to have fun and to say hi to Mathew for me. To Valerie, I simply wrote back: "I missed you too." I don't know why but it seemed too important a phrase to include among a bunch of miscellaneous meanderings and psycho babble.

Or maybe it was just the only thing I wanted to say.

Chapter 9

In my experience, love is simply pain wrapped in a pretty package of red roses and pink hearts. It becomes a series of fantasies dancing on the walls of your mind, replaying again and again at the most inopportune moments of your day when you should be focusing instead on the tediousness of reality. Then, you return to waking life and it hits you that you don't have what you want. And it hurts. Sometimes, it's just a sting. Other times, the pain is so intense that you can't even breathe. And yet, it keeps you going somehow.

I was lying in bed that Wednesday night, staring thoughtfully at a picture of Jessica. It was one I had taken of her without her realizing it. Leaning against the balcony, black hair flowing behind her in the wind, her azure eyes contemplating the distance. It was my favorite picture; the only one where the camera caught her without her defenses, without barriers. I'd never shown it to anyone, not even Jessica. Perhaps it was a bit foolish of me, but I didn't want anyone to see her as I saw her.

How do you get over loving someone? I wondered, not at all certain that it was possible. How often do you meet a person who can take your breath away with one look?

The knock on the door caught me off guard. I hesitated a second before putting the picture away, then yelled, "It's open!" When the door opened, and my visitor walked in, my mouth flew open. "What are you doing here?"

Valerie shut the door behind her and stood in the middle of the room staring at me. "Nice to see you too." She eyed me for a moment and smiled. "That's a nice look for you."

For a moment I wondered if I was lying naked in bed without realizing it. I looked down and found, to my relief, that I was indeed wearing clothing. Since I hadn't expected to leave my room for the rest of the night, I'd changed into a pair of blue and white flannel boxers and a gray tank top. My gaze returned to hers. "Thanks. What are you doing here?"

Still not answering my question, Valerie took a second to look around the room, so I took that moment to study her. Looking beautiful as usual, she was clad in faded blue jeans, a gray Miami University tee shirt, and her usual black boots. Her blue eyes ceased their exploration and returned promptly to mine. "The girl I was filling in for decided she could work after all, so I went home."

I felt suddenly bad for making her stand there, so I responded, "I'm sorry. Please take a seat anywhere." She went to the end of my bed and sat down. "I wasn't expecting you. I didn't mean to be a jerk about you showing up."

Valerie shrugged. "I should've called."

Something occurred to me and I frowned. "How did you find me? I never told you where I lived."

She looked a bit embarrassed. "I ran into your friend Jade at Whispers earlier, and she gave me directions. I really should've called, I'm sorry. I'll get out of here." She went to stand up, but I leaned forward to stop her.

"I'm glad you came," I said, meaning the words. "I meant it when I said I missed you."

This brought a smile to her face, and my heart skipped a beat. "I lied about that part, but I'm glad someone meant it."

I frowned, and she laughed. "Yeah, you better be kidding," I said, relief flowing through me. Last thing I needed was to fall for someone else who didn't feel the same way. Quickly, I pushed that last thought from my mind. "So did you have a plan for what you wanted to do, or did you just figure you'd wing it?"

"Well, I was just hoping you'd be here," Valerie admitted. "But now that you mention it, there were a couple of things I wanted to do."

"Do share, madam."

Valerie grinned. "Well, the first would probably be inappropriate at this point in time." She winked. "But, the second was for you to show me around campus, if you're willing. I understand if you're busy."

"Do I look busy?" I asked, motioning around me.

"Does that mean you'll be my tour guide?"

I smiled, meeting her eyes. "Gladly." I swung my legs over the side of the bed. "Just gotta put some clothes on first."

Valerie's eyes traveled up the length of my body, and I felt myself growing warm under her gaze. "Don't do it on my account."

Suddenly, I was at a loss for words. For a split second I wondered what she'd do if I pushed her down on the bed and started kissing her. Getting a grip, I made my way to the closet to find a pair of jeans. I debated whether or not to tell her to look away, and then noticed that she averted her eyes of her own accord. I changed quickly, and pretty soon we were walking side by side along the empty sidewalks of Baldwin University.

As we walked, I pointed out all the different buildings, and guessing that she wanted to see the art department, I led us in that direction.

"You never told me how your audition went," Valerie reminded me.

I glanced up at her, both surprised and touched that she'd remembered. "It went well, I think. Tough competition though, so I don't know if I'll get in."

"When do you find out?"

"I don't know. They're supposed to call, but I've been sitting by the phone all day and nothing. I'm not sure if that means that I didn't get in, or that they're just taking a while to decide."

Valerie nodded thoughtfully. "Got any more auditions lined up?"

"Not for a few weeks." I nodded to the building straight ahead. "That's the Art Department. Would you like to check it out?"

"I was there earlier getting information," Valerie stated. "I like what I've seen so far."

"I feel like a real estate agent," I said, laughing. "How long have you been on campus?"

Valerie stared straight ahead as she contemplated the question, then looked down at me to answer. "Several hours."

My eyebrows shot up in surprise. "All of that time and you came to visit me now?"

Valerie shrugged and looked at her feet. "Well, I didn't know whether I should bother you. It took me a while to decide."

I had to smile. The entire concept of her sitting around for hours trying to decide whether or not to visit me was endearing. "What finally convinced you?"

"I really wanted that tour of the campus," she answered, smiling.

Laughing, I looked up to catch her gaze on my face. My eyes met hers and for a brief moment I was caught in the intensity they radiated. "I'm glad I could be of assistance," I replied, looking away before my heart had a chance to beat its way out of my chest. "Is there anything else you'd like to see?"

I caught the brief smile that crossed her lips. "Oh, you mean of the school? No I think we covered everything."

"Does this mean you won't be needing my services anymore?" I teased.

She caught my gaze. "You're flirting again."

"No I'm not," I lied. "What would you like to do now?"

Valerie looked at her watch. "I should probably get going."

Keeping the disappointment from my tone, I said, "I'll walk you to your car." The walk to the visitor's parking lot was far too short for my tastes, and when we approached her Bronco II I silently searched for a reason to get her to stay longer. Coming up with nothing, I reminded myself that I'd be seeing her again the following day and chastised myself for being so clingy. "So where should I meet you tomorrow?" I asked, standing a few feet away as she unlocked the door.

Turning back to me, she considered. "Is there a good pet shop around here?"

"A few," I responded.

"Pick you up at three?" she suggested.

I nodded.

She smiled. "See you tomorrow." And then before I knew it she was driving away, and I stood there watching after her until I could no longer see the tail lights in the distance.

Chapter 10

The following morning my alarm clock didn't go off. Or else it did go off and I didn't hear it. Or else I heard it but in my sleepy state of consciousness decided that sleep was more important than classes and shut if off without further consideration. My point is, I overslept.

I was awakened instead by the ringing phone. I reached for it and without opening my eyes, said, "Hello?"

My voice was mirrored at the other end of the line. "Hey. Dinner at Mom's tonight, don't forget."

This time my eyes did open, and I ventured a look at the time. It was two. Silently I cursed myself. I'd missed two theater classes and Valerie would be there in an hour. Calculating the amount of time remaining with the amount of time it would take me to get off the phone with Rachel and take a shower, I decided I had time. I sat up and yawned, then returned my attention to my sister. "Okay. What were you saying?"

Rachel audibly sighed. "Dinner at Mom's tonight. She's been leaving messages with your roommate all week."

I walked over to my desk and looked around. A second later I spotted the message tacked to my bulletin board. *Your mom called. Dinner on Thursday at 6.* It was circled in red and underlined in blue. How the hell had I missed that? "I didn't get the message."

"Well, Mom's expecting you so you better be there. You know how sensitive she is about these things."

"But I made other plans," I whined.

"Your problem, not mine. See you at dinner. Bye."

The phone went dead in my ear, and I clicked the "end" button. Then tapped the receiver against my forehead chanting, "Think, think, think." It was too bad I couldn't lie to her. I could be an Academy Award winning actress some day and I would still not be able to pull off a lie to my mom. I dialed her number and crossed my fingers, hoping for the best. "Hi, Mom," I said, when she picked up.

"Hi, Alix. Will you pick up some milk on your way over here. I totally forgot this morning when I went shopping."

"Sure. Um, Mom. I have a bit of a dilemma."

"What's wrong?" I could hear the alarm in her tone. "Is it drugs?"

I shook my head as though to clear it. "No, nothing like that. It's just that I didn't get your messages and I made other plans today."

"You're missing my dinner?" Disappointment.

Ouch. I couldn't bear that tone. "No . . . it's just—"

"What are your plans?" she interrupted.

"I'm helping my . . . friend . . . buy a puppy." Why did I pause like that?

"That's nice of you, dear. Well, go with your friend and then come to dinner. It won't take you all day to do that." She sounded as though there was something else she wanted to add so I remained silent. "Is this friend . . . a *girl* friend?"

My heart stopped beating for a moment. This wasn't a subject we ever discussed. "Um. Not exactly. I mean, she's a girl. She's not my girlfriend. I mean I'm not dating her. I mean, I am, but it's not like—"

"Bring her to dinner."

My jaw fell open. "What?"

"Rachel's bringing Jonathan, so feel free to bring—?"

"Valerie."

"Valerie," she finished. "It was about time you started dating."

I was speechless.

"See you at six, okay, honey?"

"Okay, Mom."

"Don't forget the milk. I love you."

"Love you too. Bye." I hung up and leaned against my desk for support. That was an unexpected turn of events.

𝒮

It's amazing what cute animals will do to people. All around the pet store there was a chorus of ooo's and aww's. I looked around, watching as people turned to mush, then returned my gaze to Valerie who was holding a pug. She looked so cute standing there with the puppy in her arms that I wished I could take her home with me.

"Do you think we make a cute couple?" Valerie asked suddenly.

It took me a moment to realize she was referring to the dog. "Uh, yeah. Adorable. Is it the one?"

Valerie held the puppy in front of her and looked into its eyes. "I think I'm in love," she said, and hugged the dog to her chest, kissing it on the head.

I had to smile. "You're going to be very happy together."

Valerie grinned and headed to the counter to purchase the new addition to her household. She also had to buy dog food and play toys and a bunch of other things that pretty much cost her a small fortune. Later she revealed that she'd been saving for the special occasion, so I was flattered that she'd invited me along.

We sat in the car, Valerie playing with the puppy on her lap. "She's so cute."

I studied her silently for a moment. "What are you going to name her?"

"Alix."

I looked at her in surprise, and she smiled.

"Kidding." She looked at the dog who was now licking her hand. "I think I'll name her Loki."

"Loki?" I must have looked puzzled, because she laughed.

"From *Dogma*."

"Oh, I haven't seen that." I stared down at the dog and smiled. I'd always thought pugs were ugly, but little Loki was rather cute. I then glanced at my watch. It was a quarter past four, and I still hadn't asked Valerie to dinner. Wasn't meeting the folks a big step in a relationship? Were we in a relationship? Paranoia was becoming a constant presence in my life. "Are you hungry?" I found myself asking.

"A little," Valerie responded, her gaze fixed on the puppy.

I bit my lip, trying to come up with a casual way of asking her. "I'm having dinner at my mom's at six and she said to invite you." I held my breath as I waited for her to respond.

This time she looked up. "You want me to have dinner with you and your mom?"

I couldn't read her face and the tone of her voice revealed nothing. "My sister and her boyfriend will be there too."

She studied me silently, my heart beating faster and faster with each second that her eyes held my gaze. "I'd love to," she responded.

"Good." I felt a momentary sense of relief, followed by a new wave of paranoia. What if my mom hated her? What if Valerie hated my mom? What if a huge fight erupted?

"Are you okay? I don't have to go if you don't want me to."

Blue eyes were staring at me with concern. I smiled to put her at ease. "I want you to come." And I did. In spite of my worries.

"Do you mind if we stop at my apartment first? I need to get Loki set up."

I grinned. "I'll take the dog up the stairs with me . . . you can take the elevator with the stuff."

Valerie arched an eyebrow. "You're so generous."

"I try," I responded, reaching for the dog. "Come here Loki. You and I are going to be stair buddies. You don't like the elevator either, do you?" Loki barked in reply. I smiled, giving Valerie a satisfied look. "See?"

Valerie sighed, throwing the car in reverse. "Of all the girls in the world, I pick the one who's afraid of elevators."

"Hey at least you got a choice. I got stuck with the one who's afraid of feathers." Loki barked. "Yep, you're stuck with her too, babe," I said to the puppy, petting her. "And you have to live with her." I caught Valerie's smile, but didn't say anything. Instead I let her concentrate on driving while I played with the dog on my lap. In that moment I felt happier than I had in a long time. I glanced between Valerie and Loki for a moment, smiling to myself. I felt at home.

ℒ

When we reached Valerie's apartment building, I noticed for the first time that Loki wasn't potty trained. And if she was, she'd confused my jeans with the toilet. "Um, Valerie," I called, not wanting to get out of the car.

Valerie was already unpacking the stuff from the back. "Yeah?"

"We've got a situation here," I replied.

She appeared at my side a moment later and then started laughing. "I think you got her a little too excited."

"I have that effect on women." I smiled down at Loki, then picked her up so I could carry her out of the car.

Valerie hung a bag from one of my fingers. "There, you can carry that."

"Yeah, thanks," I replied, glaring in mock annoyance. I waited for her to grab the rest of the stuff, and together we walked into the building. "You know, you could make two trips." She looked like she was about to fall over from all the stuff she was carrying.

"No thanks. One is enough."

"Your mommy is a freak," I whispered to Loki, loud enough so Valerie could hear.

"I heard that."

"But there's nothing wrong with her hearing," I added.

Valerie and I split up when we reached the elevator and Loki and I took the stairs to the fourth floor. "One of these days," I informed the dog as we walked toward Valerie's apartment door, "that elevator is going to get stuck, and you and I are going to get to laugh at your mommy together."

"If my dog ends up being terrified of elevators, I'm coming after you,"

Valerie announced, unlocking the door and allowing us to pass through first.

"Hey, I'm the one she marked as her territory. Loki and I have bonded. What we have is special and there's nothing you can do about it."

Valerie closed the door and laughed. "We'll see about that." She walked over and took Loki, then grinned at me. "Strip."

"I guess you're not much into foreplay," I joked.

She smiled. "If we hurry I can get your jeans washed for you before we have to get to your mom's."

Take off my pants, I thought. *I can do that. She's a girl. I'm a girl.* I looked into her eyes and felt the world disappear around me. *Yeah . . . that's the problem.* I took a deep breath. "Well, if I have to take my pants off, then so do you."

She stared at me in surprise. "What?"

"Yeah," I insisted, wondering if she'd actually go for it, "if I have to parade around your apartment in my underwear, then so should you."

"They're your pants."

"It's your dog."

She narrowed her eyes, then relented. "Fine. Give me your pants though, 'cause I have to go to the basement to do it and I'm not walking down there in my underwear."

I hesitated a moment but obeyed, relieved that I'd thought to shave that day. I felt a draft on my bare legs and was extremely self-conscious under the intensity of her gaze. I handed her my jeans and tried not to blush. "You will stop looking at me like that."

Valerie smiled. "Sorry, can't help it." A couple of minutes later she walked out with my jeans, and I was left standing in the middle of her living room wearing nothing but underwear and a Nine Inch Nails tee shirt. I felt like a big dork.

Loki had ventured down the hallway so I decided to follow her. I found her in Valerie's bedroom and I stood in the doorway looking around. Like the rest of the apartment, the room was perfectly neat. There were a few posters on the walls: *Labyrinth*, Save Ferris, Dance Hall Crashers, and No Doubt. A full-sized bed rested against the wall with a night stand beside it.

I looked down and noticed that Loki had left a little present for Valerie on the carpet. I laughed to myself and then hurried back to the living room as I heard the door opening.

Valerie smiled as she entered. "You should have your pants back in an hour or so."

"Mm. Thank you. Pants off."

"I love a dominant woman," Valerie joked. She seemed to hesitate for a moment, then went ahead and took off her jeans.

I don't know why, but I blushed. I tried to keep my eyes from wandering, but I couldn't help it, which in turn made me blush more. I wished suddenly that Loki had aimed for my shirt as well, then smacked myself mentally for the thought.

"Happy now?"

You have no idea, I thought, but simply smiled. "Yep. Oh, careful where you step in your room."

She frowned. "Why?"

I pointed down the hall, and she walked there slowly as though afraid to confirm her suspicions. She stopped at the doorway to her bedroom and shook her head. "Guess we'll have to potty train her some how."

We? "Yeah or else you'll need to replace your carpet quite frequently," I replied, still wondering what she'd meant by "we."

Chapter 11

The drive to my mom's house was a relatively quiet one. I was too busy worrying about introducing Valerie to my mom and sister to come up with conversation topics, and Valerie was probably worrying about leaving Loki alone in her apartment. I almost suggested that we call the whole thing off, but I didn't. I'm not exactly sure why, but I'm pretty sure that it had something to do with the fact that in spite of my fear, I was extremely curious to see how my family would take to Valerie.

"Are you nervous?" I asked as the sign reading "Welcome to Baldwin City" rolled into view.

Valerie threw me a sideways glance and grinned. "Should I be?"

I shrugged, looking out of the passenger side window. "Truthfully I don't know what to expect. I've never brought a girl home so-to-speak."

"You've kept your other girlfriends well hidden?"

The question caught me off-guard though it didn't really surprise me. "I've never had a girlfriend," I responded quietly. I wasn't exactly embarrassed, but I was a bit worried about what Valerie would think.

"None at all?" Valerie asked, sounding surprised but not in the least bit judgmental.

"Nope."

"Boyfriend?"

"One, but it only lasted a couple of weeks."

"So you've never . . . er . . ."

I looked at her. "Had sex? No."

"Hmm."

I studied her for a long moment, hoping for further commentary. When none was forthcoming, I said, "What is 'hmm'?"

She looked at me and smiled. "Sorry, I'm just surprised."

"Why, do I look like a slut or something?" I was trying to keep the mood light because I knew we were getting close to my mom's house and this was bound to be a conversation that lasted a while. I started giving instructions as we talked.

Valerie laughed. "Yep. A big whore, that's what I thought you were."

"Sorry to disappoint."

"I'll deal with it somehow."

I'm not sure why I asked the next question. Perhaps because I was hoping zero would be her answer, though I seriously doubted it. "So what's your lucky number?"

I'm not sure if I caught her by surprise or not, but she took a few seconds before responding. She glanced at me quickly then answered, "Six."

Six. "All women?" I asked out of morbid curiosity.

Valerie nodded.

"Hmm."

She looked at me, frowning slightly. "What is 'hmm'?"

I shrugged. "Nothing. So were you in love with any of them?" I asked, not sure where I was going with this line of questioning but unable to stop myself from asking.

"Does this mean I get to question you on the way back?" Valerie asked.

"Yep. You may fire away."

She nodded. "I've never been in love."

As my street rolled into view, I focused on giving Valerie directions to the house. I wasn't sure why at the time, but her answer filled me with relief.

Valerie pulled into my mom's driveway and I noticed that my sister's car was already there. Rachel was always on time for everything. I, on the other hand, preferred to be fashionably late.

"Is there anything I should know before we go in?" Valerie asked, turning off the ignition and sitting back against the seat.

"My sister's a bitch and her boyfriend's a jerk but my mom's pretty cool when she wants to be." I smiled and touched her arm. "Don't worry about it."

We were greeted at the front door by my evil twin, whose gaze never left Valerie. It was then I remembered that Valerie didn't know I was a twin. I studied her expression, but was surprised to see no change. Usually people gaped, staring back and forth between us as though trying to make sure it wasn't their imagination. My sister was dressed in a short skirt that left little to the imagination and a black V-neck shirt. I thought she looked like a whore.

"So this is Valerie," Rachel said, more to herself than to us, and stretched out her hand. "I'm Rachel."

Valerie shook my sister's hand and we stepped inside the house. Rachel led the way to the living room, and I caught Valerie checking her out. I smacked Valerie's arm without thinking. Then the implication of what I'd just done hit me like a ton of bricks. I'd acted like a jealous girlfriend. Mentally I shook myself. If Valerie wanted to check out my sister then she was more than welcome to. At least, that's what I told myself. I never said I had to believe it.

Jonathan Green, my future brother-in-law the way things were going, stood up to greet us. He had a fake smile plastered on his face. The same smile he always used when he had to be nice to people he didn't particularly like. Needless to say, Jon and I weren't particularly best friends. "Hello Alix, who's your *friend?*"

"Valerie, meet Satan. Satan, this is Valerie."

Jonathan glared at me for a split second, then his fake smile reappeared as he stepped forward to shake hands with Valerie. "Jonathan Green, nice to meet you."

"Where's Mom?" I asked.

"She stepped out to buy milk," Rachel responded.

"I knew I'd forgotten something," I muttered. "Shit."

"Don't curse, Alix," Jonathan instructed.

"I see you have yet to take that stick out of your ass," I responded.

"Only your kind of people enjoy that sort of thing," he answered.

I was about to lunge at him because God knew he deserved a good beating, but I decided to be the better man. Plus I didn't feel like getting my ass kicked in front of Valerie. I took a deep breath. "Would you like to see my room?" I asked Valerie.

She nodded, and I led her up to the second floor. My room was just how I'd left it, if only a little neater. I hadn't felt like taking down any of the posters when I'd moved out, so the walls and ceiling were still covered with posters of heavy rock and metal bands—mostly Aerosmith of course. The walls were black in the small spaces between posters, and so were the blinds. The bed sheets were black, my desk was black, my closet was black. To make the long story short, my entire room was black.

I dropped myself on the bed the second we stepped inside. "Sorry, he just gets me so angry I had to get out of there before I punched him."

"Guess he's not a big supporter, huh?" Valerie asked, leaning against my desk.

I turned over so that I was lying on my side with my head propped on one hand. "No. He comes from a very religious, very conservative family. We put up with each other 'cause we have no other choice. He's probably going to marry my sister." I smiled apologetically. "Sorry you had to see that."

"I've seen worse," she responded with a smile.

There was a knock on the door and I quickly shouted, "Come in." It was my mom, dressed in jeans and a tee-shirt. It always amazed me the way she looked so much younger than she was.

She greeted Valerie with a smile and if that wasn't enough, she even hugged her. I tried to keep my jaw from dropping.

"It's nice that you could join us, Valerie," my mom said. She looked at me for the first time. "Stand up, let me see your hair."

I'm not sure why I had to stand up for her to see my hair, but I did so anyway and she pulled me in for a big hug. It was then that I was convinced my mother had been kidnapped by aliens and replaced by a pod. Then I remembered she'd started some woman empowerment classes and I figured that had something to do with it.

"I love the haircut," my mom informed me as she finally let me go. "Leave it to Jessica to give you a makeover."

I wasn't entirely sure how to take that comment, so I just let it go. "Thanks."

"Are you girls hiding from Jonathan?"

"Yeah, he's being his usual lovable self."

"Come back downstairs. He won't say anything with me around." My mom led the way, and we followed her back downstairs. "Did you bring the milk?" she asked, her tone revealing that she already knew the answer.

"I brought it in spirit," I responded.

Rachel and Jonathan were talking in the living room. I'm not sure what their topic of conversation was, but it most likely involved computers. They were both Computer Science majors. In other words, they were both big nerds. My sister got the logic/mathematical genes and I got the artistic ones. It was a fair deal, I thought.

"So how long have you two been together?" my mom asked Valerie, as she proceeded to work on fixing dinner. "Alix never tells me anything."

Valerie glanced at me questioningly, and I shrugged. "Well, we're not exactly together."

I felt my heart sink a little, even though I knew it was true. "We just met last week," I added as though that explained everything. I kept wondering how many dates we'd have to go on before we'd qualify as a couple. "Do you want any help, Mom?"

"No need to burn the kitchen, darling." She smiled at me sweetly, then regarded Valerie, and pointed at me with a wooden spoon. "Can't cook for her life."

"Hey I cook great spasghetti," I protested.

"Spasghetti?" Valerie asked with a smile.

"It's my own creation," I explained. "And I can bake."

My mom nodded. "That's true."

"Guess I'll cook the dinners and you can take care of dessert," Valerie said.

Had I been drinking something, that would've been my cue to choke or spit. I glanced quickly at Valerie then at my mom to catch her reaction. My mom was smiling to herself. I breathed a sigh of relief. Thankfully, my sister and her demon-spawn of a boyfriend chose that moment to join us.

"That smells great, Mrs. Morris," Jonathan said.

I rolled my eyes. I'd never seen anyone try so hard to suck up to someone for no apparent reason. Little did he know that my mom didn't particularly like him. She just pretended, like he pretended to like me whenever she was around. God forbid he show his horns around my mother.

"Thank you, Jonathan."

Halo firmly in place, Jonathan smiled at me. "So Alix, how's school?"

It was uncanny how two-faced a person could be. "Well, I haven't had much time to focus on my schoolwork, Jonathan. I've been too busy molesting little girls and sleeping with animals."

Valerie started coughing to hide her laughing. My mom gave me one of her warning looks. Rachel simply scowled at me.

Jonathan continued to smile. "So Valerie, do you go to Baldwin too?"

"Ah, no, I go to Miami."

Jonathan leaned against the kitchen counter so he could get a better look at Valerie. "Really. What are you studying?"

"Visual Arts."

"Two starving artists, how nice," Rachel commented. "You two are meant for each other."

"Rachel," my mother warned. "You and Jonathan go set the table."

I was too shocked to comment. My sister had never been nice to me but she had always been nice to my friends. "Sorry about that," I apologized to Valerie.

Valerie shrugged. "I kind of think she's right. The part about you and me being meant for each other. I have no intention of starving."

I smiled at her, and any anger I might have felt toward Jonathan or my sister completely dissipated as I stared into her eyes. "I love how you always know exactly what to say to make me feel better."

"It's a gift," Valerie responded

I almost leaned in to kiss her right then and there, but I heard my mom cough.

"You know I'm still here," she said.

☙

A few hours later, Valerie pulled the Bronco II into the nearest available spot in the parking lot near my dorm. On the ride back from my house, Valerie had bombarded me with questions ranging from what color underwear I was wearing (black, if you must know) to which was my favorite sport (basketball, but only because Jessica played it).

Valerie turned off the ignition and regarded me curiously. "I have one more question."

I turned so I could devote my entire attention to her. "I'll take Nosy Women for 500, Alex."

Valerie grinned, then turned a bit serious. "Have you ever been in love?"

I was taken aback by the question, and for a moment I couldn't even think. When my brain returned to its upright position, I bit my lip and looked anywhere but her face. "Yes I have . . ."

I heard her sigh quietly. "Are you still?"

I met her eyes at that moment and felt my entire world flip upside down. Was I still in love with Jessica? When had I not been in love with her? I couldn't even remember. If I said yes, would Valerie never want to see me again? If I said no, would I be leading her on? It was a complicated question, yet she was expecting me to answer right away. Didn't she know I never had my feelings in order? "I don't know what I feel anymore," I responded, and knew without a doubt that it was the absolute truth.

Valerie nodded thoughtfully. "I had a lot of fun today."

I frowned briefly at the abrupt change of topic, but then welcomed it. "Have you not come up with anything more clever to say by now?"

"Guess not," she responded with a smile. "I'm an artist not a writer."

"Well, I had a lot of fun too. I bet you're anxious to get home to Loki."

Valerie nodded. "I am, actually."

I nodded, taking that as my cue to get out of the car. "Thanks for coming to dinner at my mom's. I really appreciate you doing that," I said, not really wanting to part ways.

"You're welcome."

I wasn't sure whether I was supposed to kiss her goodnight or what, so I waited a couple of seconds for her to make the first move. When she didn't, I took that as a sign, and opened the car door. I wanted to ask when I'd see her again, but I was afraid I'd sound too pushy so I refrained. If I were a mind reader, my life would've been a lot simpler. "Say hi to Loki for me," I said, then followed it quickly with, "Good night." I got out and shut the car door before Valerie had much of a chance to respond, then waved as I started down the sidewalk toward my building.

Chapter 12

"Alix," Nicole said, her tone rising over the beat of the music, "if I have to hear that song one more time, I will shove the CD so far up your ass . . ."

Sighing, I turned over and shut Aerosmith's "Angel" off. "I'm confused."

"When are you not?"

"I like Valerie," I said to no one in particular. "I really like Valerie."

"But . . . ?"

I frowned, shaking my head. "That's the thing, there is no but. I mean, I keep thinking there should be but there isn't. And it's strange because it doesn't feel like anything I've ever felt before. With Jessica I was mostly just too busy hiding my feelings, monitoring every look, every word. I was so busy worrying about her getting freaked out that I didn't get a chance to really feel anything. But it's different with Valerie . . ."

"So what are you confused about?"

"I'm starting to question my feelings for Jessica," I said, knowing it was true yet completely shocked to hear the words fly out of my mouth. I sat up and faced Nicole who was staring at me expectantly. "What if I was never really in love with her? What if I just told myself that I was because I knew she was safe? Or what if, I was at one point and then I just decided to hide behind the idea of being in love with her because I didn't want to deal with my own insecurities?"

Nicole sighed, leaning back against her chair. "Alix, I could've told you this a long time ago. You need to let the Jessica thing go already. You're going to lose Valerie if you don't."

I frowned at the idea of losing Valerie. I'd only just met her but suddenly the idea of not having her in my life seemed terrifying. "I'm gonna go see her," I decided, rising to my feet.

Nicole arched an eyebrow. "Don't you have class in twenty minutes?"

"Some things are just more important," I responded, grabbing my keys from the desk. "Thanks for listening, Nicole."

"Like I had a choice."

I grinned and left the room. I wasn't entirely sure what I was going to say when I got to her apartment, but I'd think of something.

⌀

Half an hour later I was standing in front of her apartment door wondering what the hell I was doing there. I half expected her to open the door and find me standing there looking clueless. Then the possibility of her not even being home struck me and I almost hoped that was the case.

Still clueless yet brave, I knocked. When nothing happened, I knocked again.

She wasn't home.

I stood there staring at the number on her door as though willing it to change into an apartment in which Valerie was home. That didn't work very well. I'd seen in movies how there always seemed to be a spare key hidden above the doorframe, so out of sheer curiosity I reached up to check. I found dust but no key.

Not exactly sure what to do next, I ended up sitting down against the door. I decided that I'd wait for a short while and if Valerie didn't show up then I'd take it as a sign and leave. But somewhere between me waiting and Valerie showing up, I somehow fell asleep. All I know is that one minute I was sitting there staring at the wall in front of me and the next, I was waking up in a strange room.

"Long night?" Valerie asked.

I blinked until my eyes focused on my surroundings. I was lying on Valerie's bed and she was sitting next to me watching TV on mute with the closed captioning on. I couldn't decide if I was more exhausted or more embarrassed. "How did I get in here?"

"I dragged you across the carpet."

For a moment I thought she was serious until I caught the smirk on her face. I sat up, running a hand through my hair.

"Actually I carried you," she said.

I looked at her in surprise.

"Good thing I work out," she joked.

"Why didn't you wake me up?" I asked, still not fully awake. I kept thinking I was dreaming because the situation seemed so unreal.

"Hey, I tried, but have you ever tried waking you up? It's no easy task. Carrying you in here was the easy way out."

I laughed. "I didn't mean to fall asleep on your doorstep."

She shrugged dismissively. "Don't worry about it. It happens all the time. Girls fall asleep at my doorstep almost every day."

"Yeah I'm sure this is true in the fantasyland in your head," I teased.

"Ouch." Valerie feigned pain to her heart, then turned off the TV and regarded me curiously. "So now that you're conscious more or less, what can I do for you?"

I tried to remember if I'd actually come up with anything remotely intelligent before I'd zonked out from boredom, but nothing came to mind. So I decided to wing it. "Well, remember when you asked me last night if I was in love still and I said I didn't know how I felt?" She nodded, so I continued. "Well, I came to tell you that I know for sure that I'm not . . . in love still." It seemed like such a silly reason to drive all the way over there and then choose to wait outside for her to come home, but it was important to me.

"So what are you?" Valerie asked carefully.

I had no idea. "Thirsty," was what I answered and she smiled, offering me her hand.

"Well, you've come to the right place."

I let her help me up and then followed her out of the room. Loki met me in the hallway, and I picked her up. "Miss me?" I asked the dog, who in turn licked my cheek. I headed toward the kitchen. "You know, you could've opened the door for me," I informed the puppy. "Where are your manners?" I glanced up to find Valerie looking at me curiously. She stepped forward and offered me a can of Dr. Pepper in exchange for the dog. It was a fair deal, so I traded. "Sweet ambrosia." I sighed, taking a sip of soda.

"Pardon?"

"Food of the gods," I replied. "If I were a goddess, Dr. Pepper would be my ambrosia."

"And you'd be the goddess of what exactly?" Valerie put Loki back on the floor and leaned against the kitchen counter watching me with interest.

I thought quickly. "Well, I'd be the goddess of Dr. Pepper. My name would be Pepperite. Like Aphrodite, with a kick."

Valerie smiled. She paused for a moment, then asked, "So what made you realize you weren't in love any more?"

Full circle and back to square one. I sighed quietly, then met her gaze. "It just sort of . . . dawned on me." I bit my lip and looked down at the can in my hand. "Actually, my feelings for you sort of help put some things in perspective." I kind of mumbled that last part, but Valerie heard it anyway.

Sounding surprised, she asked, "What are your feelings for me?"

I wasn't used to talking about my feelings to other people. It was easier for me to hide everything because it's what I'd always had to do. So her question threw me off. It didn't surprise me; on the contrary, I'd been expecting it. But I had no idea how to answer it. So in the end, I offered her the truth, "I don't know." Knowing that wasn't enough, I added, "But I've never not known how I felt exactly. I mean, I'm never sure about most things, but I thought I at least knew how I felt about . . ." I stopped to look at her, not sure if I should say her name.

"Jessica?" Valerie guessed.

It was my turn to sound surprised. "How'd you know?"

She shrugged. "Call it a hunch."

I took a deep breath, not sure of what my point was or if I even had one. "I guess, even though I am generally unsure about everything I thought my feelings for Jessica were the one thing I knew for sure. And then you came along and all of a sudden I've started to question my old feelings . . . and I'd never done that before." I stopped, not quite certain that I'd made any sense whatsoever but hoping for the best. I'm not exactly sure what I thought Valerie would say . . . but what she did was unexpected.

It happened so suddenly that I don't even remember how it started, but suddenly her lips were on mine and she was kissing me so gently I never wanted to pull away. I felt her arms tighten around my waist and her body press slowly against mine. My body responded in ways I'd never imagined were possible and I wanted nothing more than to remain in her arms forever.

I'm not sure how long we stood there, but eventually Valerie pulled away. Around me the world spun. I have no idea how I managed to stay on my feet.

"I . . . umm . . . wow . . ." Those were Valerie's first words.

"Umm . . . yeah . . ." Were mine.

We stood there looking awkwardly at one another. And then we moved to the couch.

Chapter 13

The first thing my eyes focused on the following morning was a tack on the wall. I remember because I stared it at it for a very long time, wondering why I had never seen it before. The second thing I noticed was that my bed seemed a lot softer than usual. The third thing I noticed was that I wasn't alone, at which point my mind rose to full consciousness and I blinked a few times to make sure I wasn't dreaming.

I wasn't.

I replayed the events of the previous night over in my mind and my face broke into a slow smile. Biting my lip, I rolled over to face a still-sleeping Valerie. Loose strands of blonde hair fell haphazardly across her face and I struggled to keep from clearing them away. Instead, I pressed my cheek to the pillow and proceeded to study her quietly.

It's so easy to look at another person while they're sleeping. While their eyes are closed and their minds unaware that you are studying every feature of their face, attempting to memorize it so when you avoid their eyes later on in the day you can at least remember what they look like. I was sure that if I were told to close my eyes, I could've drawn Valerie's face to picture-perfect precision. It was a shame, however, that I couldn't see her eyes.

While Jessica's were dark blue, a blue that was almost black in coloring, Valerie's were lighter, with little specs of turquoise in the mix. They were a nice contrast to her light skin, which wasn't pale exactly, but not dark either.

Her eyes suddenly blinked open and I knew I'd been caught staring. Valerie didn't seem to mind, and she smiled as her eyes met mine. "Morning," she whispered.

I grinned back. "Morning."

"Guess it wasn't that difficult to get you into bed," she teased.

I arched an eyebrow and pulled the covers off both our fully-clad bodies. "Literally no . . . metaphorically speaking, however, you're going to have to try a lot harder than that."

Valerie smiled and leaned forward to kiss me briefly. "Details details."
She offered me her hand. "Can I interest you in some breakfast?"

I let her drag me off the bed. "Only if you make it."

"Deal. I don't want my apartment blowing up today." She laughed at
the glare I sent her way and led the way to the kitchen. Once at her
destination, she leaned against the counter. "What would you like?"

"What, don't I get a menu or something?" I joked, going to the couch
in the living room. Loki appeared a second later and jumped onto my lap.
"Make that two menus."

Valerie opened the refrigerator. "I've got eggs, bagels, English muffins,
and bacon."

My eyebrows shot up in surprise. "Wow, you're really into breakfast
huh?"

"It's the most important meal of the day," she responded.

"That's what they tell me," I replied. I usually found midnight snacks
to be the most important meals of the day. But what did I know? I stood
up, grabbing Loki as I went, and joined Valerie in the kitchen. "Tell you
what, you take care of the frying and I'll deal with the no-brain
appliances."

Valerie stared at me curiously. "What are we making?"

"Everything!" I answered, putting Loki on the ground. "I'm starving."

∅

A couple of hours later I stumbled through my dorm room to find a
bunch of messages on my desk. The one night I'm not there and everybody
decides to call me. Figures.

"Long night?" Nicole asked from her trademark spot on the bed. She
was watching TV for a change. She lowered the volume. "I wasn't sure
whether to be worried or elated. Guess I'll go with the latter."

I rolled my eyes. "Nothing happened, Nicole." I paused for a moment,
then allowed myself a grin. "Well, nothing *much*."

"Ah-huh. If nothing happened then how come you're wandering in
here at one in the afternoon?"

A slight knock on the door was followed by, "You just got in now?"
Jade stepped inside the room. "From nun to hooker. That was a fast
transition."

I frowned. "What are you doing here?"

"I was calling you all night," Jade answered, lighting up a cigarette. "So
I thought I'd show up today and see how things were going. By the looks
of it you were pretty busy last night, eh?" She nudged me and winked, then
crossed the room to sit on my bed. "Please tell all."

"Was it as good as you'd imagined, or were you disappointed?" Nicole wondered, leaning forward in her bed.

I felt as though there was a giant spotlight focused directly on me. Shaking my head, I closed the door and took a seat at my desk. "*Nothing* happened," I repeated.

"Nothing at all?" Jade pressed.

I bit my lip. "Well . . ."

"Spill it, woman!" Nicole insisted.

I decided I needed to get myself a set of new friends. The kind that minded their own business and didn't press me for personal information. Ha, right! Resigned to the inevitable, I finally answered. "Well, we kissed for a while."

"And . . . ?" Jade.

I frowned. "And then we watched TV for a while."

"And . . . ?" Nicole.

I sighed. "Well, then it got kind of late and Valerie suggested I sleep over. So I said sure."

Jade walked to the window to flick her cigarette. "That's it?" she asked, turning to face me.

"Well, yeah." I smiled. "I wasn't going to have sex with her."

"Why bloody not?"

I shrugged. "Well, for starters, I just met her. I'm not ready to rush into anything. And besides . . ." I trailed off, biting my lip.

"And besides . . . ?"

Sighing, I walked over to my bed and lay down. "What if I don't know what to do? You know . . . in bed."

Jade shook her head and flicked the cigarette out the window. "Maybe we'll just go ahead and get you that lesbian porn."

Nicole rose to her feet. "I see that no more juicy information will come out of this conversation, so if you girls will excuse me, I'm going to the student center to grab lunch." She grabbed her purse and keys and headed out the door.

Jade watched the door slam closed and laughed. "Wow that lesbian porn thing really gets her outta here."

"I'd say."

Jade sat down at the edge of my bed and regarded me curiously, waiting for me to say something.

I sighed. "It's not the mechanics of it. I know what to do." I tried to pinpoint the exact source of my worries but couldn't. "I think it's more of an emotional fear."

"Are you worried your heart will overload?" Jade grinned.

Shrugging, I sighed. "Maybe." I let my head fall back on the pillow.

"What if I'm no good? What if I'm so bad that all her feelings for me instantly evaporate at my utter incompetence in the art of lovemaking?"

Jade cracked up. "You're a nut! That's ridiculous."

"I don't think so. I mean, what if I'm like *really* bad?" I sighed. "I wish there was a way to test my abilities."

"I'm not sleeping with you if that's what you're thinking."

I nudged Jade in the leg with my foot. "Very funny. I was thinking more along the lines of those *Seventeen Magazine* quizzes."

Jade laughed. "Oh, right. 'Lesbian Sex: Do you have what it takes?' I can just see it now."

She was right. It did sound pretty ridiculous and not at all helpful, but I still wondered if there was some way, outside of the traditional mode of information, for finding out. "Hmm. What about a psychic?"

"You wanna sleep with a psychic?"

"No! I mean . . . go to a psychic. To ask them."

Jade raised both eyebrows and stared at me. "I truly hope you're not serious about any of this." She frowned. "Oh gods, you are."

"Well, no." Not entirely, anyway. "Guess I'll just have to find out when the time comes."

Jade was quiet for a moment. "Do you think you'll sleep with her?"

My gaze snapped up to her. I was silent, then I looked away and sighed. "I hope so. I've never wanted anyone so badly in my life."

"Jessica?"

I met her gaze and held it, shaking my head. "Not even Jessica."

⌘

I spent the rest of the day at the student center trying to catch up on some reading for my World Literature course. I'd been so busy balancing my heart between Jessica and Valerie that I'd totally forgotten about my schoolwork. I'd already missed a couple of days of classes in the name of love. Well . . . maybe not love. Obsession and infatuation was more like it. But those were the roots of love, no?

I managed to get through half of Fae Myenne Ng's *Bone* before my brain stopped accepting intellectual stimuli. On the way back to my room I gave myself a mental pat on the back for having been productive. I was at least ahead in one of my classes. *One down, four to go*, I thought.

My room was empty when I stepped inside, but there was a new message waiting on the answering machine. Pushing the door closed with my foot, I managed to press "play" simultaneously. I'm not sure why I did that . . . maybe just to see if I could. Anyway . . .

"You have one new message." There was a short beep, and then

Roxanne's voice filled the room. "Hey Al, just wondering what you were up to since I hadn't heard from you since the wedding. You didn't run off and join a convent or something crazy like that, did ya? Well, anyway. Call me. Maybe we can chill."

Hanging out with Roxanne hadn't been on my list of things to do that evening but I acknowledged the fact that I had no plans with Valerie and thus had nothing else to do. Besides, I wanted Roxanne's take on the matters of my heart. So without further delay, I grabbed the phone from its base and dialed Roxanne's number.

"Peek-a-mon," came the response on the other line a couple of rings later.

I smiled into the receiver. "Hi Alisha."

"Peek-a-" Alisha was cut off mid-babble only to be replaced a second later by Roxanne's "Hello?"

"Just got your message."

"Oh, hi, Alix. Hold on." I heard the distinct sounds of a phone getting dropped on a counter, soon to be followed by Roxanne's voice in the distance. "Alisha, c'mon, baby, let's watch some TV . . ."

I waited patiently for Roxanne to return, busying myself by staring at the poster of Steven Tyler on my ceiling. It was the only poster I'd bothered to remove from my room. It was my favorite and it would continue to reside above my bed until my dying day.

"Still there?" Roxanne breathed a couple of minutes later.

"Yeah. How's Alisha?" The entire concept of one of my best friends having a four-year-old child was mind-boggling. I thought with time it would become less shocking, but it only got worse. It served an up-lifting reminder that we were getting old. Jessica was married, Roxanne had a kid . . . Guess both of those were out of the question for me. I'd have to get creative if I wanted to compete. Like go through menopause at twenty-five or something.

"She's good. You know, Pokémon this, Pokémon that. The usual. What's up with you? You sort of dropped off the face of the earth since the big day."

Shrugging, I responded, "School keeps me busy enough." I was trying to think of a good way to introduce the Valerie subject.

"So I heard you went on a date . . . ?"

Or she could just introduce it herself. That worked too. "I've been on a few since then," I admitted, grinning slightly to myself.

"Same chick?"

"Yep."

Motherhood had not impaired her nosy nature. "Well, what are you waiting for, tell me everything."

And so for the next twenty minutes or so I caught Roxanne up on all of the details. It would've taken less but Roxanne had to keep interrupting me to attend to Alisha. When I was through bearing my soul, Roxanne paused to absorb the entire story. I waited silently for her to comment.

"So are you guys an official item?" Roxanne asked after a minute of silent contemplation.

Frowning, I said, "Uh, I'm not sure."

"How can you not know?"

"How *can* you know? I must have missed that course in high school. Is there some kind of announcement ritual that I'm not aware of?"

Roxanne laughed. "I don't know. I just figured you would've talked about it by now. But I forget you're not one of those talk-about-your-emotions kind of person."

Now what was that supposed to mean? "I do too talk about my emotions. I'm doing it right now in fact. It's all I've been doing for the past seven years, or were you not paying attention?"

"Oh, you talk about them to your friends, but not to the person your feelings are targeted on. Besides, you didn't whine about Jessica for seven years, because you kept your feelings hidden for three. And even after Jessica and the rest of the world found out, you still refused to talk about it unless it was forced out of you."

This wasn't at all how I'd expected this conversation to go. Why was she lecturing me? "What's your point, Rox?" I asked, a bit more harshly than I should've.

"Hey, calm down, woman. I'm just saying that a lot of your problems would be solved if you'd just open your mouth once in a while and say what's on your mind. I mean, there was a time when one couldn't shut you up for anything, but ever since the Jessica thing you've turned into this shell."

My frown returned. I'd turned into a shell? "What?"

"Never mind. Look, all I'm saying is that if you're confused, and I know you are 'cause I *know* you . . . then you should just talk to Valerie and clear things up."

She made it sound so simple. But I was willing to give it a shot. I didn't want to be a "shell" anymore, whatever that meant.

"So when do I get to meet her?" Roxanne continued.

"Well, she's probably at work tonight. I don't know when I'm going to see her again." I felt suddenly depressed at that realization. I should know when I'd get to see her again. Right? "I'd invite you to go to the club, but finding a babysitter at this hour . . ."

"Actually I had Zack on-call just in case you wanted to hang out."

I smiled. "Such a good uncle he's turned out to be."

"Yeah, I don't know what I'd do without him. So do you want me to pick you up? Where are we going?"

"Well, if you want to meet Valerie, then we're going to South Beach."

"Great. I'll pick you up once I get everything settled over here."

"Sounds good. See you then." I said good bye and hung up the phone, wondering why I had just offered to introduce Valerie to Roxanne. I didn't even know where Valerie was. What if she wasn't at work? Would I go as far as showing up at her doorstep again?

Sighing, I leaned back against the wall. Only one way to find out.

☒

An hour and a half later Roxanne and I arrived at Whispers. It was about twice as crowded as I'd ever seen it so finding an available table took a while. As we walked through the mobs of people I kept my eyes peeled for any sign of Valerie but didn't catch sight of her.

"So which one's yours?" Roxanne asked, surveying the crowd.

"I don't see her," I answered, unsure of whether I was disappointed or relieved. "I wasn't sure if she worked tonight or not." In fact I had no idea when she worked. Although I thought I remembered her saying she was off Tuesdays and Thursdays. So did that mean she worked all other days?

Roxanne shook her head then continued looking around, tapping her fingers on the tabletop to the beat of the music. "I like this place. It's got atmosphere."

Atmosphere? I looked around again, trying to observe the so-called atmosphere Roxanne was referring to. All I saw were sweaty people jumping up and down and drinking and laughing while red, green and blue lights flashed above their heads. The Whispers logo was a pretty blue color and I liked that, but as far as atmosphere was concerned I couldn't very well attest to its existence. A *pleasant* one anyway. Loud people, loud techno music . . . not my scene at all. But I was a girl on a mission. Sacrifices had to be made for the greater good.

Bestowing my undivided attention on Roxanne, I was about to open my mouth to suggest we try Valerie's apartment when I suddenly took notice of the song that had just started. It was one of those bands that Valerie liked. I turned in my seat to glance around one more time. Chances were I'd missed her in the crowd.

Then I saw her.

And the music stopped, the lights stopped, the time stopped, my breath caught in my throat and I'm sure my heart stopped beating as well. It was as if the world had stopped spinning and all that existed was Valerie and whomever it was she was kissing.

I blinked a few times, willing it to be an illusion, a trick of the lights. Perhaps it was just someone who looked like Valerie.

The music returned at full blast, startling me. And I heard a distant voice calling my name. It took me a second to register what was happening. I felt a hand on my arm, and I turned slowly to face a concerned Roxanne.

"Are you okay?"

I shook my head and went back to staring at Valerie. They'd stopped kissing. Valerie was laughing at something the woman had said.

I had to get out of there. Otherwise I'd start crying and I didn't want to cry. "Let's go," I told Roxanne and walked out without waiting for her to catch up.

Valerie never saw me.

Chapter 14

It had taken me forever to fall asleep that night and I probably would have slept through my entire Sunday had the phone not awakened me around one. I grabbed the receiver from its base, not bothering to open my eyes, and murmured a groggy, "Hello?"

From the other end of the line, I heard a breath and knew who it was instantly. By the time she said, "Hey," I'd already hung up the phone.

When it rang again a few seconds later, I turned off the ringer and slammed the receiver down on the base, making a noise which caused Nicole to lift her head from her latest novel.

"Everything all right?" she asked.

"No," I answered harshly, turning over in my bed so that my back was to Nicole. I didn't want to talk about it.

"Suit yourself," muttered Nicole.

I lay there for a while, staring at the wall and pouting to myself. I'm not sure what I was feeling exactly. It was a mixture of things, jealousy and anger to name just a couple. In the midst of my introspection, I remembered what Roxanne had said about me not talking about my feelings and turning into a shell. I bit my lip, then turned over so I was facing my roommate. She looked up as I did so. "I caught Valerie with another girl last night."

The book was put away in a matter of seconds, and her full attention was bestowed on me. "Tell me everything," she said.

And so I recapped the events of the previous night as best I could.

"Wow," Nicole muttered when I was through, "I didn't see that one coming. How long were they kissing for?"

I shrugged, shaking my head. "I don't know. It all happened so fast . . ." I shrugged again. "I just got out of there as fast as I could."

Nicole nodded. "Wow. I really don't know what to tell you, Al. That really sucks."

Yeah, it really sucks, I remember thinking. It sucked a lot. I grabbed my bathrobe and headed off to the bathroom to take a shower. There was no point in going back to sleep, I'd never manage it.

ℒ

Later, after a few hours of non-productivity, I sat in front of my computer and booted it up. I hadn't checked my email in days and I wanted to see if I had mail from Jessica.

My box was full, as expected, but most of it was junk mail. I deleted everything except four emails. Three of them were from Jessica. The fourth one was from Valerie. I stared at it for a long time, debating whether or not to open it. She was probably confused as to why I was ignoring her . . . but I was too hurt to care.

Still unsure about reading it, I decided to read Jessica's emails first. I opened the first one.

> *Alix,*
> *All right so I decided to stop buying stupid things, and decided to get you tee shirts instead. Now, before you start whining that you will never wear a shirt that says Paris or Rome on it, let me just say that you won't be disappointed at all. Intrigued yet? Well, you'll see what I mean when I get back. Anyway, I hope that everything is going well over there with you and your new woman. How is she?*
>
> *Mathew and I leave for Athens tonight. So I have to get going. See you Saturday!*
> *Always,*
> *Jess*

I didn't reply, and instead hit next to read the following message.

> *Alix,*
> *Hey I haven't heard from you. I hope everything's okay. Well, Mathew and I are now in Greece. It is beautiful here. For the Holidays we should plan a trip back here so I can show it to you. I think you'll love it in spite of your stubborn nature. What do you think? If you and Valerie are still together then she can come too. We'll double! It'll be fun. Anyway, we're off to do some more sightseeing and buy more tee shirts. Haha! Write me back, it's weird not hearing from you right away.*
> *Love you,*
> *Jess*

Next.

Alix,
Okay, where are you?? I'm probably worrying for absolutely
no reason but write me back and put me out of my misery. You
know how paranoid I am about these things. I miss you.
  Love,
  Jess

I sat back in my chair, smiling slightly. Jessica really was a paranoid being.

Sitting up, I hit reply to the last message.

Jessica,
I'm sorry I hadn't responded to you sooner. I just hadn't
checked my email the past few days. Everything's fine. You
can resume breathing now. I'm sure that Greece is beautiful
and I'll think about your offer to go for the holidays. But
I'd prefer going somewhere more interesting. Like Australia.
They have kangaroos. You can't beat seeing a real live
kangaroo, Jess. And Koala bears. I mean, really. Greece just
has rocks.

Say hi to Mathew for me. I can't wait to see you guys
when you get back on Saturday. I'm very excited about these
mysterious tee-shirts of yours. Do they get up and dance or
something? Well, anyway . . . Have fun.
  Forever,
  Alix

Once that email was sent, I stared at my inbox and let the cursor hover over Valerie's email. To read it or not to read it, that was the question. I slid the mouse down the mouse pad, dragging the cursor over the delete button, and double-clicked.

Not to read it was the answer.

✄

The following afternoon, I was sitting at the student center with Jade, working on a junior bacon cheeseburger from Wendy's and a Biggie Dr. Pepper. Jade had turned vegan on me and so her lunch consisted of unidentifiable goop and a bottle of water. We were both equally disgusted with the other's meal choices and had no other choice but to agree to disagree.

"So anyway," Jade was saying, "Did you and Valerie ever establish that you were in a monogamous relationship?"

I glanced up from my burger. "Well, not really. No. Why?"

Jade shook her head. "Are you even together?"

I frowned. "Well, I don't know . . ."

She rolled her eyes and took a sip of water. "You can't be mad at her for kissing someone else if you guys aren't even together. If you want to be in a relationship with her then you should tell her so."

Why did Jade have to make sense all the time. It was unnerving.

"Look, did it hurt you a lot to see your woman with that other chick?" Jade asked.

I nodded.

She shrugged as though the answer was totally obvious. "Well, there you go. It was sign."

"A sign?"

"Yeah a sign that you should get your butt over there and tell the girl that you want to be with her. Otherwise you're gonna lose her to that other chick and you'll be back on square one. Lusting over a now married woman. How pathetic is that?"

Very pathetic, I acknowledged, though not aloud. I sighed. "I just don't know if I want to be with her anymore. I mean, I thought we had something going, and although we never officially signed any monogamous relationship papers, I thought we were . . . something." I put my burger down. I'd suddenly lost my appetite. "If she was kissing someone else then obviously she wants to be with other people. I can't just swing over there on a vine and dub myself queen of her jungle."

Jade shrugged. "All's I'm saying is that you should at least talk to her. Just because she was kissing somebody else doesn't mean she doesn't have feelings for you."

"If she has feelings for me she shouldn't be kissing other people," I argued.

"Ideally, no. But this is the real world."

"Well, the real world sucks."

"I kind of liked the London cast," Jade joked. She caught the look I sent her and became serious again. "Look, Alix, I know where you're coming from but you have to remember that Valerie is probably not the sexual hermit that you are."

First a shell, then a hermit. Did my friends discuss these things with each other when I wasn't around? "I'm not a hermit. But I'm not a sexual vending machine either. A person can't stick their tongue down my throat and expect me to put out. I don't work that way." I was angry and I didn't want to be. "And anyway, that has nothing to do with it."

"Talk to her," Jade advised me.

I didn't respond. Instead I grabbed my tray, got up, and walked away. I wanted to get my hermit-self back into its shell before I turned into queen crab.

ℒ

Hours later I found myself standing before door number 413. Jade had been right of course, but it took me a while to come to terms with what she'd said. In the end, there was only the bottom line: I didn't want to lose Valerie.

And so there I was. Except that as I'd gone to knock I'd been hit with a horrible thought, which had caused my arm to lower back to my side and my feet to take a step backward.

What if she was with someone?

Seeing her kiss someone else had hurt enough without me having to interrupt her in the middle of something more . . . elaborate.

I bit my lip, torn between actions. I decided to think logically. It was Monday night, she was probably at work. And if she was at work then she wasn't at home. And if she wasn't home, then I had nothing to worry about.

"Isn't it beautiful?"

I turned to find Valerie studying her door in mock-appreciation. Then she smiled at me and continued, "When I first saw it I thought, 'That's the door I want to live behind.'"

She was carrying a few grocery bags and as a reflex I grabbed a couple of bags so she could her keys. "I wasn't sure if you were home."

"So you were using your X-ray vision to determine whether or not I was in?" she asked, unlocking the door and kicking it open.

Under different circumstances I would have laughed. Or I would have come up with something witty to come back at her with. As it happened, I barely managed a smile as I walked inside the apartment and closed the door. "You don't work on Mondays?" I put the bags on her kitchen table and stepped back, giving her room.

She was putting groceries away as she answered. "I work in the mornings."

"I didn't realize people went to nightclubs during the day."

"Well, Whispers is a restaurant-slash-night club. The bar is open during the day, however, and that's where I come in."

"Oh," was my reply.

Her back was to me as she said, "I didn't think I'd be seeing you again."

Her comment caught me by surprise and I was suddenly at a loss. She chose that moment to turn around and I could see the pain in her eyes. I remained silent.

"Any reason why you've been avoiding me?" she continued. "If you didn't like my cooking, I'm sorry. I'll take some classes."

I felt like crying. I wanted nothing more than to forget I'd seen anything and just throw my arms around her and kiss her . . . but I couldn't. "I saw you," I found myself saying. "At Whispers on Saturday night, with that other woman . . ." I studied her face for a reaction. Expecting to see guilt or shame . . . something to let me know she felt bad about it. I wanted her to say she was sorry and that she'd never do it again. That it had been a moment of weakness or something corny like that. I would've accepted that excuse because I wanted to. However, she did none of the above.

Valerie started laughing. Then she took a seat at the table and shook her head, her laughter shifting into an angry sigh. "You saw that? Of course. She called you didn't she?"

Needless to say she'd lost me. My eyebrows furrowed as I stared at her. "Did who call me?"

"Robin. She probably plotted the whole thing." The last part was said more to herself than to me.

I blinked. "Who the hell is Robin?"

Her eyes snapped up. "You mean she didn't call you?"

"Valerie, I have no idea what you're talking about. I went to Whispers to introduce you to my friend, and then I saw you . . . and—"

"So she had nothing to do with it?" she asked incredulously.

"What? No. Who's Robin?" Somehow this conversation had turned weird. And it wasn't supposed to be weird. At least, I didn't think it was. I made a note to watch more romance movies instead of action and horror ones. I'd obviously missed something.

Valerie stood up suddenly, grabbed my hand, and pulled me to the living room where she sat me down on the couch. "Okay, it's not what you think."

Well, this line I knew. "It never is," I muttered under my breath.

"Robin Graham is my ex," Valerie explained, obviously ignoring my comment. "That's who you saw me with on Saturday. And I wasn't kissing her—"

"Could've fooled me—"

"Look, the woman is insane. She came to Whispers on Saturday and pulled me aside, claiming she had something important to talk to me about. Out of the blue she starts kissing me and I pushed her away—"

I frowned. I didn't see her push her away, although I *had* looked away to talk to Roxanne. Then I remembered the second bit of information. "But I saw you laughing with her."

"She said she knew I still had feelings for her. I was laughing *at* her not with her." Valerie sat down next to me. "Look, Alix, I know it must have looked bad but I swear it's not how it looked—at all!"

Psycho stalker ex girlfriends. This is where we started running for our lives. I had no idea what to believe. "This is awfully bizarre."

Valerie sighed and nodded. "I know. But why would I lie?"

Why indeed. "Well, I still don't know you very well. You could be a player for all I know."

"Want me to take a lie detector test?"

Not a bad idea, extreme, but not a bad idea at all. I sighed to myself and searched her eyes, finding all the truth I needed right there. "I didn't really come here to demand an explanation from you . . ."

She seemed surprised and a bit confused.

I ran a hand through my hair and begged my mind to form the correct sentences in expressing what I'd come to say. "I'm sorry that I hung up on you when you called and then turned off the ringer and refused to respond to your messages or your emails. I was angry, but then I realized I had no right to be because we've never really discussed our relationship, or lack thereof. So what I came to tell you was that . . . I would very much like . . . the right." I looked into her eyes, waiting for her to say something.

She was quiet for a moment, then ventured a small smile. "Do you have rules for relationships too?"

I laughed. "I've never really been in one so I guess I'll have to play it by ear."

She grinned. "Well, then I bestow on you the right to be angry at me for kissing other women, although you won't have to exercise it often."

My heart filled with relief and it was all I could do not to jump up and start dancing with joy. "That's good," I replied, instead. "You don't want to see me angry."

"No, I don't."

I brushed my lips against hers. And that was the end of that conversation.

Chapter 15

I spent most of Tuesday and Wednesday floating a few inches off the ground, unable to wipe an ever-present grin from my face. I didn't get to see Valerie either of those days, unfortunately, because of school and her work, but we made plans for Thursday night.

We met on the sidewalk across from Whispers, then walked the rest of the way to the beach where Valerie proceeded to spread out a blanket so we could sit on the sand. I stood off to the side of her while she did so, looking around the fairly empty beach. There were a few people with the same idea camped in various spots across the sand, but for the most part we were alone.

"Come here often?" I asked, taking a seat on the blanket and leaning back on my elbows. It was a nice night for sitting out on the beach. Clear skies, nice breeze, wonderful company.

Joining me, Valerie smiled. "Yeah, this is where I bring all my girlfriends."

"Yeah? Well, let me know when your next hot date is so I can kill her," I responded, grinning. Valerie sent a surprised look my way and I simply shrugged. "What? You think I can't play the jealous girlfriend role? I'll have you know, I won Best Actress in high school for my role as a jealous girlfriend."

Valerie laughed. "I don't doubt it for a second." She reached into one of the pockets of her cargo pants and pulled out a can of Dr. Pepper. "I picked this up for you a little while ago."

I couldn't help my smile. I took the can gratefully and leaned forward to kiss her cheek. "Thanks. I think I'll keep you, if only because you supply me with my favorite soda all the time."

"It's all part of my plan," Valerie said, nodding and rubbing her hands together in an attempt to look evil and mischievous.

I took a sip and watched her carefully. "What plan is this?"

"Well, I can't very well tell you that," Valerie responded, frowning slightly. "Disclosing the plan is *not* part of the plan."

"Is my pouring Dr. Pepper over your head part of your plan?" I asked innocently.

Valerie laughed aloud and lay back on the blanket, staring up at the sky. She didn't say anything, and for a few minutes, neither did I.

As she contemplated the heavens, I stared down at the sweating can in my hands, wondering if I should bring up what I'd been wanting to bring up. There was so much about her I didn't know, and I wanted to know everything. But what if she didn't want to tell me everything? What if I scared her off?

"Tell me about Jessica," she said softly.

Her request caught me completely by surprise and I turned to look down at her face. She was staring up at me curiously. I took a deep breath. "What do you want to know?"

She shrugged, seemingly uncomfortable. "I want to know how worried I should be about her."

"Worried?" I smiled. "Well, seeing as she's married and straight, I don't think you have very much to worry about."

"And if she wasn't?" Valerie asked, catching my gaze and holding it as though searching my eyes for the truth.

If she wasn't? I frowned, unsure of what she was asking or what she wanted to know. Could I picture myself having a relationship with Jessica? Not one in the fantasyland that was my mind, but a real one? No. Not if I was honest with myself, as I hadn't been the past seven years. She was my fantasy. One that seemed to be ever-presently fading with each second that Valerie's eyes bore into mine. "If she wasn't . . . then she should be the one worried about you."

This brought a smile to Valerie's face.

Relieved that I'd said the right thing, I contemplated how to phrase my own request. In the end, I decided to follow her example. "So, tell me about Robin Graham." Just saying her name left a bad taste in my mouth. I quickly took another sip of Dr. Pepper to wash it away. I looked down and caught Valerie playing with her tongue ring. Every few seconds the metal ball would probe through her lips only to disappear again. She was silent for so long I was afraid she had either not heard me or wasn't going to answer. I was about to repeat myself when she finally spoke.

"What would you like to know?" she asked, glancing up at me.

"Everything."

Valerie nodded and seemed to sigh. "Well, we were together for about a year. She was a bartender at Whispers for a while and got me the job there. Then she and Dean, the owner, had a fight and Robin got fired. That was about three months ago. Robin was really pissed and wanted to leave Florida. She asked me to go with her but I had school and I liked my job at the club. So I told her no and that pissed her off even more. She always had this really bad temper. Anyway, she moved her stuff out of my apartment and disappeared. She resurfaced a couple of weeks ago, begging Dean to rehire her."

"So you lived together?" This new revelation caused the dull ache in my heart to worsen. I hated feeling jealous.

Valerie nodded in response. "Yeah, for about five months." She sat up on her elbows. "I wasn't in love with her or anything. Just lonely."

I nodded and forced a smile. "You don't have to explain." She didn't. But it made me feel better that she cared enough to do it anyway.

She took a deep breath and looked into my eyes. "Since we're on the topic of personal questions, can I ask something else?"

"Sure." There really weren't that many personal things about me. "You can ask me anything."

"What happened to your dad?" she asked gently.

My breath caught in my throat, and I looked away. "He died when I was twelve," I answered softly. "Cancer."

Valerie nodded and took my hand. "I'm sorry."

"It's okay." I bit my lip. "What about your parents?"

The tongue ring again. This time she answered quickly, as though she'd been expecting the question. "My dad is still in Boston. I'm not sure where my mom is." She shrugged and looked down at the blanket. "She left when I was two." Then without warning she leaned up to kiss me briefly on the lips. She pulled away and smiled. "It's okay. About my mom, I mean."

I nodded mutely, feeling shocked and sad at the same time. Perhaps we needed to stop with the painful memories line of questioning. Still, there was one more thing I wanted to ask her about. "What does your tattoo signify? The one with the broken hearts. I mean, why did you choose that one?"

Valerie smiled. "I got it when I was fourteen. It was a reminder to never fall in love."

My eyebrows shot upward. "Why?"

She shrugged. "When my mom left my dad, I saw what it did to him. He was heartbroken. Still is. I didn't want to end up like that."

"Seems to have worked so far," I said, feeling depressed all of a sudden, even more so than I already was.

Valerie shook her head and sat up so she was eye level with me. "It had been working." She leaned forward until her lips were inches from mine. "Until now."

And then she kissed me, taking my breath away. I lay back on the blanket with her on top of me, our lips never breaking contact. Her tongue parted my lips as her hands traveled down the side of my body. My mind was reeling. My heart was racing. I almost forgot we were in the middle of the beach.

Valerie pulled away hesitantly and smiled down at me. "Maybe this isn't the best place."

I grinned. "No, probably not."

⌀

So we left the beach in search of a better place. This ended up being Valerie's apartment, her room to be more precise.

We were kissing on her bed. We'd kissed before, but this time it was different. This time there was the promise of something more. I'm not sure how it happened; how we made up our minds. Or maybe our bodies made the decision for us. Or maybe it was our hearts. Or all three of them together. But suddenly, it seemed out of my control.

"Does this mean I passed all the sex rules?" Valerie whispered, staring intently into my eyes.

I smiled. "What sex rules?"

Valerie laughed and rolled off the bed. I watched her walk to her stereo, raising my eyebrows in silent question.

"What are you doing?" I asked.

A few seconds later, The Cranberries' "Dreams" filtered through the speakers. "Inspirational music," Valerie announced, heading back toward the bed.

"The Cranberries?"

She shrugged and smiled. "Actually it's the *Boys on the Side* soundtrack. It's on shuffle." She kicked off her shoes as she joined me back on the bed.

That's when I noticed she was trembling slightly. I frowned and stared up at her. "Are you cold?" I couldn't imagine how she possibly could be. I felt like I was burning.

Valerie shook her head and lay down beside me. "No. Just nervous."

I was taken by surprise. "You've done this before."

"Not with you."

I stared at her for a long while. I'm not sure what I was thinking about. Perhaps I was trying to figure out why such a beautiful woman would be interested in me in the first place, let alone be nervous about sleeping with me. Or maybe I was just swallowed whole by the intensity of her eyes. "Would it make you feel better if I told you I was nervous too?"

Valerie smiled. "A little."

"Okay. Well, I'm terrified."

She laughed quickly and then kissed me, making me forget all about being nervous. Her lips traced their way down my neck as her hands made their way down the length of my body. Everything blurred. I couldn't even hear the music anymore, even though I knew it was playing.

Articles of clothing started flying across the room, and before long I was staring at a very naked Valerie. Just looking at her took my breath away. I lost track of where she was touching me and with what. I just closed my eyes and surrendered myself to the feel of her lips and hands and tongue caressing every inch of my body.

I don't remember every detail but I do remember screaming her name some time later. And some time after that she screamed mine. And at some point before dawn, we managed to fall asleep in each other's arms, both of us trembling . . . but no longer afraid.

Chapter 16

I'd always imagined the morning after to be something memorable and magical; a point in time designed to reflect back on an important milestone in one's life.

But it wasn't.

By the time my mind seeped into consciousness, it was far from being morning. In fact, the alarm clock beside Valerie's bed read 5:46 pm and I blinked a few times to make sure I was reading it correctly. I'd never slept so late in my life. But at least I had good reason. This thought caused me to grin and I shifted my gaze from the alarm clock down to Valerie's slumbering form. Sunlight from the nearby window cast a soft glow on her golden hair. I thought I'd never seen anything so beautiful.

I lay there quietly for a long time, watching her sleep. At 6:23 she opened her eyes slowly and stared right into mine. This time I didn't care if she'd caught me staring. A lot of things didn't seem so important anymore and it struck me as amazing that we'd only known each other a couple of weeks.

Valerie was the first to speak. "Good morning."

"Hardly," I responded, nodding to her alarm clock.

She half turned and saw the time. "Oh, man." She turned back to me, looking sad. "I have to work at seven,"

I shrugged slightly. "I know."

She leaned forward to kiss me and in one swift move lifted herself on top of me, slipping her thigh between my legs. I gasped and pulled away in surprise.

"Are you trying to make yourself late?" I whispered.

She smiled and shrugged. "That's your job."

I arched an eyebrow at the challenge and in a swift move of my own had her on her back. "Don't say I didn't warn you."

Needless to say she was late to work. Three hours late, in fact. And I whistled proudly to myself as I drove back to school.

Instead of driving directly to Baldwin U, I made a detour and ended up at Jade's. I didn't want to be alone for some reason. Perhaps because I was too happy and too excited and needed to share some of my joy before I exploded.

At the front door, I hesitated. If Jade wasn't home then Aunt Fifi would undoubtedly sweep me aboard her sinking ship of madness and I might never get to shore. On the other hand, if I turned around and went home I'd have to sit in my empty dorm room staring up at Steven Tyler wishing Valerie didn't have to work so I could go back to her apartment. After weighing the pros and cons of each possibility, I decided to knock.

Aunt Fifi opened the door a few seconds later and I instantly regretted my decision. I hadn't seen the woman for a month or so, since Jade usually preferred to leave her house at all possible moments, but she hadn't changed much. On this particular day, she was clad in a grass skirt and a coconut bra, holding what appeared to be a piña colada in one hand.

I smiled and then bit my lip to keep from laughing. "Uh, is Jade home?" I ventured to ask, though this question very rarely received an answer. A helpful one anyway.

"Alix! What are you doing in Hawaii?"

Her learning my name had been a big step toward progress. Initially, Aunt Fifi had welcomed her visitors by screaming bloody murder and shutting the door in their face.

"I came to see Jade," I responded.

Aunt Fifi shook her head and stepped aside to welcome me in. "She's still in Florida. I'm on vacation with my monkeys." She shut the door and pointed to the living room.

It looked the same as always. A brown couch facing a thirteen-inch TV set, with an old wooden coffee table resting in between. I nodded as though I was really seeing Hawaii and Aunt Fifi's imaginary monkeys. "They look like they're enjoying themselves."

"Yes, but they're bad boys."

"Most monkeys are."

Aunt Fifi nodded as though I'd said a very deep and philosophical thing. "Would you like some suntan lotion? I wouldn't want you getting burned out here." She handed me a bottle of SPF 20.

I spread some on my arms to humor her and handed the bottle back. "Thanks. Do you mind if I go back to my hotel room? I have a headache."

She patted me on the head and spanked me on the butt. "You go right ahead, sweetums. I'm just gonna go on ahead and get the monkeys back to their tents." She said the next part in a near whisper. "If you see the chickens, please don't tell them about the skinny dipping. They're *very* sensitive about that."

"Your secret's safe with me," I assured her and managed to escape up the stairs as fast as I could. Safely on the second floor, I sighed with relief, then headed to Jade's room. I was even more relieved to hear loud music coming from her room. I knocked loudly so she could hear it over Nine Inch Nails.

I heard the volume lower and Jade shout, "I haven't seen your bloody chickens!" Then the volume went right back up.

I shook my head, smiling, and opened the door. When Jade saw it was me she turned off the stereo and moved away from the telescope. The girl had been obsessed with aliens for as long as I'd known her. She spent hours staring through the lens of her telescope in the hopes of catching some sign of extraterrestrial life.

I closed the door behind me and looked around the room. It had been a while since I'd been there. As usual, *X-Files* posters covered most of the walls along with miscellaneous posters of aliens here and there. Behind me, her favorite poster of Jerry O'Connell covered the door. Her bed was more like a mattress thrown over large piece of wood which balanced itself on the four cement blocks at each corner. Next to that was the window and the telescope hanging partly outside. And to my left was the desk, which was a cluttered mess of books and notebooks. She had a laptop computer, too, and a printer, but the computer was hidden under the piles of crap on her desk and the printer rested atop a black egg crate on the floor.

"Well, this is a surprise," Jade said, grinning at me as she sat down on the bed. "What are you doing here?"

I walked to the desk, put the stuff that was on her chair on top of the stuff on her desk, and sat down, swiveling the chair around to face Jade. I sat back and simply grinned.

Jade stared at me with a clueless expression for a few seconds, then her jaw dropped. "You didn't . . ."

My grin turned into a full-smile and I blushed.

She started laughing. "You little whore! I thought it was 'too soon' and all that other nonsense?"

I shrugged and said, "Well, I decided that twenty years was more than enough time."

Jade leaned forward. "So? Was it good?"

Why did people always ask this question? It was like a reflex or something. "Well, not that I have much basis for comparison, but I have no complaints."

"Leave it to you to give me such a vague response," Jade said, rolling her eyes. "You're an actress, you should be more expressive."

"Want me to act it out for you?"

Jade sighed and leaned back against the pillows. She crossed her arms against her chest and studied me quietly. "So what's your crisis now?"

"I don't have a crisis," I answered.

"You always have a crisis."

Thinking hard, I attempted to locate any crisis sources laying about in my mind but I couldn't come up with anything. I shrugged. "I don't have any." I smiled. "I'm really, truly happy."

Jade made a face. "This is so depressing. Pretty soon you're going to be wearing pastel colors instead of black; giving Valentines' Day gifts on V-Day instead of setting the card shops on fire—"

"I never did that."

"No," Jade allowed, "but you thought about it." She sighed in an exaggerated manner. "*C'est la vie*. So, how are you going to tell Jessica that her seven-year reign over your heart has come to a brutal end?"

I bit my lip nervously. Hadn't really thought about that. Then again, it wasn't like Jessica hadn't been begging me to get over her for years. "She'll be happy for me," I responded quite confidently. "She wanted me to move on all along."

Jade shook her head. "For a lesbian you sure don't know women very well."

⚕

In the world according to Jade Cooper, Jessica was going to be jealous. She was going to be jealous while pretending she was happy. She was going to feign her love and acceptance of Valerie, meanwhile attempting to find the most insignificant of reasons to dislike her. Then she was going to try to convince me that Valerie was not good enough for me and eventually break us up.

On my way to Jessica's mansion the following day, I mulled over everything that Jade had told me the previous night. And although I had reminded her several times that it had been Jessica who had practically forced me to go out with Valerie, Jade insisted that she was right. But I didn't think she was. Jessica wasn't like that.

It was almost six in the afternoon and to be honest I hadn't been up for very long. My sleepover at Valerie's had screwed up my entire sleeping schedule. I'd stayed at Jade's until nearly three in the morning listening to her talk about lunar eclipses or something of the sort. By looking at her you'd never think that my best friend was such a nerd, but she was.

At the circular driveway, I parked my yellow bug and jumped out. I looked up at the sky momentarily, stalling in spite of my excitement because I was feeling kind of nervous about seeing Jessica. It was a cloudy day for a change, making the air humid and hot. To make matters worse, there was no wind blowing in any direction. It was one of those days where it was best to stay inside until the Sunshine State went back to living up to its name.

Slowly, I made my way across the gravel driveway to the front doors, the rocks beneath my feet crunching loudly under the assault of my weight. As expected, Maurice was already standing at the doorway. "Hey Mau. Long time no see."

He nodded his reply, closing the door behind me. "Mrs. Collins is in her quarters."

Mrs. Collins. How strange to hear him call her that. I headed across the large foyer to the master staircase and ascended two steps at a time. I reached Jessica's room a short while later and found both doors wide open. A few open suitcases lay on the waterbed, slightly sinking into the mattress, but Jessica was nowhere in sight. Out of habit and perhaps even instinct, I headed to the balcony and found her in her usual spot against the railing. As she turned, I gasped. "What did you do to your hair?"

Jessica's gorgeous black mane was gone; cut short, spiking up on the sides. She looked beautiful but I was in shock. "You don't like it?" she asked, observing my expression.

I stepped forward to get a better look and shook my head, smiling. "No, I love it. You look great. I've just never seen you with short hair before."

Jessica smiled and closed the distance between us. "I've missed you," she stated, pulling me close for a hug.

She always smelled like vanilla. I'd never figured out if it was some kind of body spray or her shampoo or both things mixed together, but she always smelled fantastic. I swallowed and forced myself to pull away from her embrace. "Where's Mathew?"

She motioned for me to sit down on one of the lounge chairs. "He went to visit the in-laws." She smiled at the term as though getting used to the idea of calling them that, which I figured she was. "And to give Nina and Sarah their gifts from abroad."

"And you didn't go with him?" I asked.

Jessica shrugged, then sat down in the chair next to mine. "I wanted to wait for you." She smiled. "Besides, I'm going to dinner over there later tonight so I figure they could live without me for a couple of hours."

I nodded, suddenly feeling strange. Later, I began to recognize that strange feeling as indifference. Jealousy is an odd thing. Even if you manage to control it, to push it to the back of your mind, it still finds a way to hurt you on some level. Like a sharp pain that fades quickly but still impacts you at that moment. I was so used to its ever-present hold over my heart that not feeling it was an odd sensation. It threw me for a loop.

"You okay?" Jessica asked, seemingly concerned.

Smiling, I started to nod again, then decided it was more convincing if I actually spoke. "So, where are these magnificent gifts you've been collecting for me all over Europe?"

Jessica was on her feet at once, moving swiftly into the room. A minute or so later, she was back, holding a really big, and really *full* bag. "Go nuts."

I took the bag, put it down on the lounge chair, and sat up straighter to make room. I looked inside and laughed out loud. "You weren't kidding when you said you were gonna start getting me shirts." There had to be about twenty or so tee shirts neatly folded into squares. I pulled out the first one and unfolded it, expecting to see a picture of the Eiffel Tower or one of those " . . . and all I got was this lousy tee shirt" tee shirts, but my jaw dropped when I saw the picture. It was Aerosmith. "Where did you get this?" I asked, glancing at Jessica in surprise.

She was grinning. "We found this one store, purely by accident, and it was mostly rock and roll memorabilia. We went a little overboard."

I was already pulling out the rest. There were about ten different Aerosmith shirts that I'd never seen before in my life, an oddity considering my obsession. And about ten more that varied from Nine Inch Nails to Garbage to Marilyn Manson. I was in tee shirt heaven. When I was done unfolding and refolding my treasures, I leaned over the mess to hug Jessica. "Thank you so much. I thought for sure you were bringing me back snow globes or something."

Jessica laughed as she hugged me back. "Nah, I would never torture you that badly."

As I started putting the shirts back in the bag, I was aware that Jessica was studying me quietly. I looked at her expectantly.

"You never told me how things were going with Valerie."

I was unsure as to how to proceed. Revealing everything in one sentence didn't seem like the way to go, so in the end I went with the subtle approach. "They're going really well, actually," I responded, resuming my task.

Jessica leaned back in the chair. "Really well as in . . ."

Hesitantly, I answered, "Really, well, as in we're a couple now."

I could tell Jessica was surprised though she tried hard not to show it. "Wow, I really missed a lot while I was gone, huh? So how long has it been?"

This conversation was inevitable, so I sat back, ready to bare all. "Only a few days. Since Monday."

Jessica nodded thoughtfully, absorbing the information. I searched her face for any sign of Jade's paranoid-delusional predictions but found no traces of jealousy upon her lovely features. Finally, she asked, "Are you happy?"

The question made me smile. "Yes. I really . . . like her." Granted, I'd done a lot more than *like* her on Thursday night . . . and then again Friday evening . . .

Jessica caught the blush that crept up my face and she arched a curious eyebrow. "Is there something I should know?" She was watching me carefully and I knew there was no way out of the situation unless I managed to lie, which I could never do. Not to Jessica.

I decided to go with the subtle, I'm-too-shy-to-say-the-words approach. "We . . . um . . . you know . . ." I chewed on my lower lip and watched for her reaction.

What sat before me was a very stunned Jessica. "You slept with her?" she asked incredulously. "Already?"

Nodding, I said, "Yep."

Once again, Jessica retreated into internal calculation mode. She was silent for about thirty seconds and then responded with, "Was it good?"

I suspected that I'd be answering that question a lot in the near future. Not that I was going to advertise the loss of my innocence, but news seemed to spread like wildfire in our small circle of friends. "Define good . . ."

Jessica stared at me for a moment then said, "Did you . . . ?"

"Did I what?" I knew what she was asking but that didn't keep me from teasing her. Besides, it wasn't every day I got to see Jessica Heart blush.

Her dark blue eyes narrowed. "You know very well what."

Grinning, I said, "I don't think I have to answer that question, Mrs. Collins."

She sighed dramatically and shrugged. "Fine. Be a brat. What are you doing tomorrow?"

"Nothing in particular."

"Come to dinner with Mathew and me," Jessica suggested. "Bring Valerie if she can make it. I'd love to get to know her better."

"I'll run it by her when I see her tonight." Valerie had offered to cook for me that night and I was pretty excited about it. No one had ever gone through all the trouble of cooking for me before. Besides my mom, of course, but that didn't really count. "I should probably get going and let you get to Mathew's. You know how in-laws can be."

Jessica smiled. "Not really. But I guess I'm about to find out."

Chapter 17

The smell of chicken and garlic reached my senses before I even stepped foot inside Valerie's apartment. I had no idea what she was cooking but it smelled delicious.

Valerie opened the door and stood before me wearing an apron which read "Kneel Before the Cook" and a matching chef's hat.

Giggling, I planted a kiss on her cheek. "You're cute," I informed her and entered the apartment.

"Thank you," she answered, shutting the door after me. She turned to address me but by then I was already in the kitchen attempting to identify the meal in progress. I had no luck.

"What are you making?" I asked, leaning over the stove to take a peek at the contents in one of the pots. "I see noodles. I see green stuff. What is this?"

Valerie was beside me a moment later. "The green stuff is spinach. And *we*," she paused to hand me a wooden spoon and place the chef's hat on my head, "are making Chicken Penne."

I pushed the hat up a little to keep the rim from covering my eyes. "We?" I looked at the spoon in my hand. "Do I look like Emil to you?"

She looked confused. "Who?"

"You know, that guy on the Food Network. He likes to kick things up a notch by adding alcohol to everything and saying 'bam' a lot." I demonstrated with a hand gesture.

"You mean Emeril." She smiled. "I didn't take you for the Food Network watching type."

Shrugging, I responded, "Well, I love food. I just prefer not to cook it myself. Watching other people make it, however, is quite exciting." I pointed to the wooden spoon in my right hand with my left. "What do you want me to do with this, Fat Lady Number One?"

Valerie went to answer then paused, frowning. "Are you calling me fat?"

I held up the handle of the spoon next to her and looked back and forth between them as though trying to compare. "Yes. Obese. Now, hurry up and give me instructions, I'm starving."

Valerie stuck a piece of chicken in my mouth. "Work on that." Then she motioned to the pot of noodles. "Stir."

I saluted while chewing. "Mm, good chicken." Then I proceeded to stir. I fell quiet as I did so, suddenly remembering a couple of things that had been bothering me. Well . . . not bothering me exactly, but definitely nagging at me. Well, one was nagging at me, the other I was just curious about. I had no idea how to bring it up, so I just focused on the stirring.

"You know, you're allowed to talk and stir at the same time," Valerie informed me.

I half turned to look at her. She was sitting at the kitchen table, reading a magazine. I furrowed my eyebrows. "Ahem. What are you doing?"

"Reading the latest lesbian rumors from Hollywood," she responded, not bothering to look up from the issue of *Curve*.

"And this helps to expedite dinner *how* exactly?"

She glanced up this time and said, "I'm waiting for the noodles."

Turning back to the task at hand, I told her, "They look pretty done to me." I pulled one out by balancing it on the wooden spoon and dropped it on the table next to Valerie. "Try it."

She put the magazine down and made a grab for the noodle. Chewing, she nodded. "Almost."

I resumed my stirring. At the very least, this was good exercise for my arm. Who needed a Bow Flex machine when you had simmering noodles? "I really don't see why I need to keep stirring these things. I'm sure they'd manage along fine without my help."

"Hey, what you're doing right there is an integral part of my recipe. Don't sell yourself short."

"Are you calling me short?" I turned around, pointing the wooden spoon menacingly in her direction and narrowing my eyes in a feral look.

"Yep."

"Hmph," I responded and turned my back to her once more. At least the noodles appreciated me. Of course they'd probably get mad at me for eating them after we'd built such a strong bond . . . Or maybe they wouldn't mind at all, seeing as they were pasta noodles and therefore incapable of such emotion. Behind me, I heard the rustling of magazine pages. "What time do you get off work tomorrow?" I asked without turning.

"Five."

"Would you like to go to dinner with Jessica and Mathew?" I wasn't entirely sure how Valerie would take to being around Jessica, but I figured it didn't hurt to ask. "She invited you," I added, not sure if that made any difference one way or the other.

"Are you going to be there?"

I smiled to myself. "Yes I am."

"Then sure," she answered, suddenly standing at my side. She stole back the chef's hat and the wooden spoon. "Thank you for your help, madam."

I bowed and took a seat at the table, happy that my job had been completed without any major catastrophes. I wasn't a klutz—not exactly—but kitchens and I didn't really mix, unless of course *spasghetti* was involved. Then I was the Iron Chef. I grabbed the magazine from the spot Valerie had left it and busied myself by reading up on queer culture.

A few minutes later, a plate was placed before me and I looked up to see Valerie smiling down at me. "Your dinner, madam," she announced. She put down silverware on a napkin and motioned to the fridge. "Grab a Pepsi if you want."

"This looks great," I said, reaching over to open the fridge door. I leaned over and grabbed a couple of cans of Pepsi without getting up (laziness knows no bounds). I placed the second can in front of Valerie's place setting and waited for her to sit down.

She joined me at the table a moment later. The apron and chef hat were gone and I saw that she was wearing a black and blue soccer jersey with the number twenty-three printed across the back below the name "Skye." Light blue jeans I'd never seen on her before and her usual boots completed the outfit. I was pretty sure she was one of those people who could make even the most hideous of outfits look sexy.

"You know, you have yet to take me to McDonald's," she reminded me, with a grin.

I nodded, grabbing the fork. "We'll make that our next date." Which one was it now? Six or seven . . . I'd finally lost count.

"Aren't we having dinner with Jessica tomorrow."

I nodded. "All right, then the next one after that." I took the first bite and decided at that moment that I was going to marry this girl. I restrained myself from making those moaning noises from *What About Bob?* though it was exactly what I felt like doing. "I must say, you are one skilled woman."

Valerie grinned. "Thank you kindly. Do I pass?"

"You more than pass. Your cooking patch is in the mail." We fell silent for a while as we both enjoyed our meals in companionable silence. Eventually, I dared to break the silence. "Can I ask you something?"

Valerie looked up from her plate and stared at me expectantly. "Sure."

I chewed on my lip wondering why I didn't just let it go. "Well, I'm probably going to sound like a really big jerk for asking this, but it's sort of been bothering me."

If I didn't have her full attention before, I clearly had it now. "Go ahead."

"Well, you said your mom left you when you were two," I started, feeling really stupid for bringing this up but knowing it was a bit too late for backtracking, "yet you told me your mom was the only person you knew who liked popcorn without butter."

Valerie stared blankly at me for a moment. "This is what's been bothering you?"

I'm sure I blushed.

She smiled. "Remind me never to lie to you, since you're obviously a stickler for details."

I arched a brow. "Did you lie to me?"

"No! I just didn't tell you the entire story." She shrugged. "The topic of my mother isn't one of my favorites so I tend to be vague on the subject."

I nodded, curious to know the rest of the story, yet afraid to push her any further. I didn't want to force her to tell me something she didn't want to talk about. Especially since it was obvious the matter caused her pain.

She was quiet for a few seconds then looked up at me. "She left when I was two. Then she came back when I was eight, begging my dad to take her back. Apparently things didn't go well for her wherever it was she'd run off to and she was desperate. I knew she was just using him but he didn't care 'cause he was too blinded by love or whatever." She shrugged again. "Well, anyway, she stayed around until I was about thirteen, then she ran off again. Last time I heard from her she was in Miami. But that was a long time ago . . ."

"Is that why you moved down here?" I asked carefully.

Valerie looked away. "No . . . not exactly. I mean, it had been my plan to find her when I turned eighteen. I vowed to move down here and track her down wherever she was and give her a piece of my mind." She paused and I was afraid she was going to cry. "I was really angry." She glanced at me. "But then I got the scholarship with Miami and the job at the club and somewhere along the line I stopped caring. Or at least, I stopped trying to justify my screwed up existence with her absence. I mean, what would I even say to her if I found her? 'You suck. I hate you'? What would that accomplish in the grand scheme of things? So I let it go."

I had the urge to get up and hug her but I was afraid to move. I know how much it hurt me to lose my father. I couldn't imagine how I would feel if he'd up and abandoned me instead. "Thanks for telling me," I said lamely, not knowing what else to say.

Her eyes softened as she smiled at me. "I'd tell you anything."

I smiled back, feeling flattered. She didn't strike me as the type to go around sharing personal anecdotes with people.

"Is there anything else you'd like me to clear up?" she asked, taking a sip of her Pepsi.

Well, there was one more thing and as insignificant as it was, I couldn't help but wonder. "I was just curious as to why you were working that Thursday we met."

Valerie laughed out loud. "Do you lie in bed thinking about all of these random things?"

Well, yeah. Didn't she? "Random things just pop into my head." . . . As I'm lying in bed thinking about them.

"Well, one of the waitresses quit that day and Dean called me in to help. That's why I was doubling as both waitress and bartender, but I think you asked about that on our walk that night."

I felt quite foolish, yes I did, but at least my curiosity was satisfied. For now. "So I guess it was fate that we met." Since when did I start believing in fate, I wondered.

She studied me silently and half-smiled. "Perhaps."

Starting to nod, I suddenly said, "Wait, I have one more question."

"Can I buy a vowel?"

I shook my head. "Wrong game show."

"Damn. Okay, shoot."

"Do you have any brothers or sisters?"

"Nope," she answered quickly. "Are you done now?"

I nodded and finished off the remainder of my dinner. "That was the best meal I've had in a really long time. Although, I'm rather fond of my junior bacon cheeseburgers."

"Thanks. I think." She snapped her fingers. "I keep forgetting to ask if you ever heard back about your audition?"

I shook my head sadly. "No. Guess I didn't get it." Then I shrugged. "That's all right though, 'cause there's a play coming up I want to audition for and being in the Baldwin Players would've taken away most of my free time."

"Well, we wouldn't want that."

"Indeed not." I sat back and patted my stomach thoughtfully. "So what's for dessert?"

Valerie arched an eyebrow and smiled suggestively. "What would you like?"

I knew where she was going with that look, but I wasn't about to give her the satisfaction that easily. Not yet anyway. "I'd like some ice cream."

She blinked a few times, clearly caught off-guard. "I don't think I have any."

I stood up and reached for her hand. "Well, then we'd better get some."

℀

Somehow, dinner with Mathew and Jessica had turned into a high school reunion. I'd called Jessica Sunday morning to tell her that Valerie could make it and she informed me that she'd gotten us reservations for seven at *Pepe Le Pew's*. Well, no that doesn't sound right. But it was something French and expensive and had something to do with a Pepe that was hopefully not of the skunk variety. After much complaint on my part, however, plans changed and we agreed to meet at Chili's. No way was I dressing up for dinner. She'd gotten me in a dress only two weeks prior and my dress-up quota had been met for the month. Besides, Jessica hated fancy restaurants. Had the honeymoon in Europe warped her fragile little mind?

By the time Valerie and I showed up it was 7:42 and I was surprised to find that the guest list had been extended. They'd pushed together a couple of tables to make room. Jessica and Mathew were seated next to each other. To the left of Mathew were Jade and some guy I didn't know. Across from them were Sarah (Mathew's thirteen-year-old sister) and Roxanne.

Taking a seat across from Mathew and next to Sarah, I said, "Sorry we're late we were . . . um . . ." My mind went blank and I looked at Valerie who was in the process of sitting next to me.

"Stuck in traffic," she supplied in a way that made it obvious that it was *not* in fact where we'd been.

I caught the blush that crept across my face in the mirror behind Mathew and Jessica and decided that I had to stop doing that. I'd been blushing too much lately. The madness had to stop. I cleared my throat. Then I proceeded to introduce Valerie to everyone and vice versa. When I came to the guy sitting next to Jade, I paused.

"Oh. This is Jeremy." Then she mouthed the words "the bloke."

For a moment I thought she'd said "the blow" and I furrowed my eyebrows in silent question. Then comprehension dawned on me and I nodded. "Nice to meet you, Jeremy," I said politely. "So did you guys order already?"

"What do we look like, barbarians?" Mathew asked. "We have some manners."

"They were making us wait until eight," Roxanne added from her spot beside Sarah.

"Well, then I'm glad we managed to get away from traffic just in time." I said this from behind the shielding comfort of the menu. I was scanning the rows of equally tempting food when I felt warm breath tickle my ear.

"Wanna share an order of Chicken Fajitas?" Valerie whispered.

I nodded. She could've asked me if I wanted to jump off a bridge after dinner and I would've still nodded in agreement. Obsession and infatuation at its worst . . . or best depending on how you looked at things.

Jessica spoke for the first time. "So, Valerie, Alix tells me you're an artist. What kind of art do you do?"

Good question. I'd never seen any of Valerie's work.

"Mostly charcoal portraits," Valerie replied. She glanced at me. "Nude portraits."

Five pairs of eyes focused in my direction and I hid my face behind the menu again. Even if I said I'd never posed for her they would never believe me. I kicked Valerie's foot under the table. If her plan was to embarrass me, she was doing a good job.

Thankfully, the waiter chose that moment to make an appearance and I made a mental note to leave him an extra big tip just for showing up at the right time. Once our orders had been placed, random conversation broke out at the adjoining table.

Sarah was trying to summarize to Roxanne the finer plot points of *Gossip Girl*. Across from them, Jade and Jeremy were discussing Britney Spears. I decided right then to maintain my attention focused far away from their conversations. Across from me, Jessica appeared to be silently studying Valerie while Mathew seemed focused on Sarah's conversation with Roxanne.

I was feeling very awkward. Here I was with my closest friends and I couldn't think of one thing to say to any of them. Valerie being there was making me feel self-conscious. Not to mean that I didn't want her there. I just wasn't sure how to bridge the gap between her and my friends. Searching my mind for something that would spark some type of general topic of discussion, I finally came up with, "So are we doing anything after dinner?"

"Did you have something in mind?" Jessica asked.

"Uh. No, I just thought we could all hang out later."

To my surprise, Valerie spoke up. "Maybe we can go bowling?"

Jessica grinned. "Yeah," she said, nodding, "we haven't done that in a while."

Mathew smiled. "It's a plan." He turned to the others and asked if they were up for a night of bowling. Nobody objected.

I let out a deep breath, thankful that my question had killed a few minutes of silence.

"Do you like M.U.?" Mathew asked Valerie.

Valerie nodded. "It's a beautiful campus but I'm thinking of transferring next semester."

"Where to?" Jessica asked, leaning forward.

"I told Valerie that Baldwin had a great art program," I interjected.

"Everyone I've spoken to there seems very nice," Valerie added. "I just have to look into any potential scholarships so that I can attend full-time instead of part time."

"Leave it to me and you won't have to worry about that," Jessica said, taking a sip of her drink.

Valerie seemed disturbed by the comment, and I glanced sharply in Jessica's direction. I knew what she meant by it, but it was so out of character that I frowned. It was true that with one phone call Jessica could have Valerie set up at Baldwin with all expenses paid and no financial worries whatsoever . . . but the way she'd said it almost sounded as if she were flaunting her power. First the expensive French restaurant, now this. What was going on with her? I glanced at Jade and she was staring at our side of the table. She caught my gaze and gave me a look that I took to mean "I told you so."

But I refused to believe it. Jessica high on mind-altering drugs or kidnapped by aliens and replaced by a pod or her being possessed by some evil spirit, *that* I would believe. That Jessica Heart was jealous of Valerie . . . well that was ridiculous.

∾

"You're kind of quiet," I noted, speaking over the constant sounds of rolling balls and scattering pins. "We can leave if you want to."

We'd all met at the bowling alley and broken up into teams. Jessica, Mathew, Valerie, and myself comprised team one. Jade, Jeremy, Roxanne, and Sarah made up team two. Thus far, team one was in the lead with . . . well I never did look at what the score was, but we had more of the red X's than the other team did and that's really all that mattered.

Valerie smiled at me and shook her head. "No, I don't want to leave. I like your friends."

Relieved, I smiled back.

Sarah walked to us at that moment. Well, she headed toward Valerie, actually, but I was sitting next to her so I decided to include myself. The thirteen-year-old plopped herself beside my girlfriend and said, "Do you know karate?"

I'd always liked Sarah. Nina, Mathew's older sister was cool too but I'd never gotten much of a chance to get to know her. Sarah reminded me a lot of Mathew. They both had dark brown hair and green eyes, though Mathew's bordered more on hazel, where Sarah's were lighter.

"Yes I do," Valerie replied in a gentle voice which she reserved for me and I guessed women under eighteen as well. Though hopefully not for the same reasons.

Sarah's face lit up at the confirmation. "Do you beat guys up?"

I hadn't been aware that Valerie knew martial arts. It made me wonder what else I didn't know about her. I turned away from their conversation for a moment to see who was up. Jade stepped up to the lane, sat down, placed the bowling ball on the wooden floor before her and let it roll. Somewhere along its merry way, it fell into one of the gutters and Jade stood up and started clapping happily. She was such an odd child.

I turned my attention back to Sarah and Valerie just in time to hear Sarah ask, "Do you and Alix have sex?"

"Val, you're up," Jade called, walking past us.

Well, she certainly dodged that bullet, I thought as Valerie excused herself as quickly as possible and headed off to retrieve her ball from among the others. I settled back to watch her, but was interrupted by a tap on my arm. *Uh, oh.*

Sarah was looking up at me expectantly. "So?"

So . . . right. "So, how's school?"

"It's good," she answered. "Do you not want to answer my question? You don't have to tell me if you don't want to. But if you're doing it then you should at least be mature enough to admit it."

Was she calling me immature? I arched an eyebrow in her direction. "I am *too*, mature enough to admit it," I countered, feeling extremely immature for finding the need to justify my maturity to a thirteen-year-old.

"So you admit it?"

Had I just been tricked? "Uh. . ."

Valerie returned at that moment and said, "Your turn, Sarah."

Sarah smiled at me before getting up. "You're a dork, Alix."

"Thanks," I replied and watched her walk away for a second. Then I devoted my full-attention to Valerie. "How'd you do?"

"Another strike," Mathew answered for her, giving Valerie a high five.

I jumped up to hug her. I didn't really care about the strike but it seemed like a good excuse for physical contact. I grinned, stepping away from her. "At least I can beat you at pool."

She nodded and sat down. "And that's probably the only thing you'll ever beat me at," she replied teasingly.

Reclaiming my seat beside her, I said, "Don't be too sure. I'm also *very* good at air hockey."

"Oh, yeah? I'll have to see that one of these days," Valerie said, looking rather smug. "Are you good at basketball?"

I thought about it for a second. "I believe I managed to get the ball through the hoop once . . . but I'm not sure." Then I poked her in the ribs. "You never told me you knew Karate."

"You never asked," she said simply. "I know Tae Kwon Do, too. And I'm pretty good at fencing."

"Fencing? Is that where people wear those tight clothes with the ugly masks and jump back and forth trying to poke each other with wobbling swords?"

Valerie smirked. "Something like that." She looked around for a moment, then grinned. "Looks like your friend Jade is getting along well with her date."

I followed her line of sight and cocked my head to the side. Jade and Jeremy were making out quite fervently. They needed to get a room and pronto. "Well, at least she's having fun."

"I'd say." Then she nudged me with her foot and motioned with her head, letting me know that it was my turn to bowl.

Bowling, unfortunately, does not fall into the glorious list of activities that I do well. And frankly, the shoes don't help make the experience any more enjoyable. However, I must admit that the moment just before the bowling ball hits those pins is one of the most exciting things I've ever experienced. How pathetic am *I*?

There must be a method involved in throwing the ball just so, in order to achieve that perfect strike. But I wasn't going to find it and I had to accept that fact. So I made my way toward the edge of the lane, threw my arm back and swung it forward, letting the ball do its thing.

Its "thing" turned out to be rolling off to the far right side and hitting all of one pin before falling out of sight. Sadly, that was an improvement to the assortment of gutter balls I'd been throwing all evening. I grabbed another ball, ignoring the mock-clapping of my fellow companions and went back to repeat the process. This time, the ball decided to visit the left hand side, meanwhile missing all the pins in its allotted path.

I sat back down beside Valerie and received a pat on the head for my great performance. "Your evil mockery shall stop."

"Or what?" Valerie challenged.

"Or I'll call Sarah back over here and tell her to ask you embarrassing questions." That was probably the lamest threat in the history of threats, but it was the only thing I could come up with.

Valerie's eyebrow arched in response, then she proceeded to pat my head again.

ɞ

Some time later, I decided to challenge my girlfriend to a game of Monopoly. I wasn't sure what the game was supposed to accomplish, but it seemed like a fair enough competition. Besides, there were interesting odds at stake. The winner got to have a wish granted by the loser. I wanted to win, but to be quite honest, I didn't particularly mind the idea of losing either.

We were sitting across from each other on Valerie's bed with the game spread out between us. A sleeping Loki rested beside me and every now and then I reached out to stroke her fur.

It was now close to one in the morning and I kept glancing at the clock, willing time to stop turning. I had class in the morning and I couldn't miss it, but I couldn't bring myself to leave Valerie's company either.

As though reading my mind, Valerie said, "We can finish the game another day. I know you have school tomorrow."

"I'm not sure I trust you with the game," I replied, though it wasn't true. I knew she wouldn't cheat.

Soft blonde hair fell against her face as she laughed. "We can add everything up and see who has the most money."

To this I agreed. Mostly because I really did have to get going or I'd never get up in time for class. I wasn't sure I'd make it as it was.

We spent the next few minutes adding up all the money and the values of all the properties along with the houses and hotels on each monopoly. I didn't have much hope of winning since Valerie had pretty much shattered my dreams by acquiring Boardwalk and Park Place early on in the game, but it didn't hurt to check. As it happened, once everything had been methodically calculated and verified by both parties, it turned out that I did lose after all.

"Okay," I said, doing my best to appear like a mature woman capable of admitting defeat with minimal amounts of pouting. "What's your wish?"

Valerie was in the middle of putting the Monopoly money away and she looked up at me in confusion. "Huh? Oh . . ." She returned to the task of clearing the board without responding. I figured she was trying to come up with something to wish for, so I didn't press the question and instead started helping her put away the game pieces. Once the game had been neatly put away in its box, Valerie took a deep breath and said, "I would like you to pose for me."

I blinked.

"You don't have to do it," she followed quickly. "If it makes you uncomfortable. I mean, just 'cause I won in a board game doesn't mean you owe me anything. You don't have to do it," she said again, lowering her head in embarrassment.

"Are you blushing?" I asked in wonder, trying not to laugh, but unable to keep from grinning. I leaned forward to brush the hair from her face so that I could see her better. "Your wish is my command," I whispered softly.

She raised her head. "What?"

"Yep. I just have one condition."

"What's that?"

I grinned. "If you're gonna draw me in the nude, then *you're* gonna draw me in the nude."

Valerie arched an eyebrow, not understanding my meaning. Then she got it. She opened her mouth to reply but then shut it again and frowned at me. "What if I let you wear a scarf?"

"Then you can wear a scarf," I replied, laughing.

"Damn." She started crawling toward me, forcing me to lie back. "You're not going to make things easy for me, are you?" she said, straddling me.

I put my hands behind my head as I lay back on the pillow and smiled up at her. "Never."

"What if I tickle you?"

I stared at her. "You wouldn't."

She would.

Chapter 18

Somehow, I managed to get up for class Monday morning and even met Jade for our bi-weekly pre-World Literature breakfast. I was quite impressed with myself actually, seeing as I'd only gotten about three hours of sleep.

"You look like bloody hell," Jade informed me as she cut her bagel in half and took a big bite. Her hazel eyes darted around the student center as she chewed, then her gaze landed back on my face.

Instead of responding, I stared down at my own bagel and contemplated eating it. I wasn't sure I had enough energy to pick it up, let alone cut it and smear cream cheese on it. Perhaps it was a better idea just to sit there. Although, I was hungry. "Jade, would you cut my bagel and put cream cheese on it?"

"You're joking, right?"

Yawning, I mumbled, "I'm too tired to do it myself."

Jade shook her head and grabbed my bagel. "Well, maybe if you hadn't spent all night doing the humpty dumpty with a certain someone, you wouldn't be quite so tired."

"We were playing Monopoly," I replied, a bit defensively.

Jade smirked and placed the now cream cheese covered bagel back on my tray. "Is that what they're calling it these days?"

"Hey, if I recall correctly it wasn't me getting all frisky at the bowling alley." I grabbed one half of the bagel and took a bite.

She grinned. "He's pretty cute, huh?"

"Um. Sure." I took a sip of orange juice. "What the hell was up with his sideburns? I kept wanting to call him Elvis all night."

Jade leaned over the table to flick me on the forehead.

"Ouch!" I cried, rubbing my now stinging flesh. "Jeez, Jade, can't you come up with a more painless method of expressing your disapproval? A dirty look will convey the same message."

"Yes, but it's not as fulfilling," Jade replied. "I think the sideburns are cute."

I rolled my eyes. "Hey, before I forget, do you want to go to the mall with me after classes today?"

"What for?"

"I wanted to get Valerie something," I said. Then I paused. "Do you think that's too corny?"

Jade nodded.

"Hmm. Well, we could just go see what they have. Maybe buy a CD or something."

"Sure, whatever. Beats going home to deal with my aunt. Remember Hawaii?"

"Far too clearly."

She nodded, then proceeded. "Well, now she thinks she's in a nudist colony in the south of France."

"Eww! Jade! Not while I'm eating."

"Hey, I'm the one that has to live there," she countered, shuddering. "I really need to move out."

"Why don't you?"

Jade shrugged, not looking at me. "I don't want to leave her alone there. I mean, she needs someone to take care of her and I don't want her getting put in an asylum or something. I know she's nuts, but she deserves better than that."

"You should really get her some help, though, Jade. It's only going to get worse otherwise."

She nodded, but said nothing.

Sensing we were getting into dangerous territory, I decided to change the subject. "So, what did you and Mr. 70's do after steaming up the bowling alley?"

"We played Monopoly," she said with a wink.

Laughing, I said, "And you called *me* a whore."

She wrinkled her nose. "It was the sideburns. I couldn't resist." She shrugged. "But he has the tiniest dick I've ever seen."

I choked on the piece of bagel I'd just stuck in my mouth. I made a grab for the orange juice.

"You all right?" Jade asked after a second.

"Fine," I croaked, still coughing. When I managed to get the coughs under control, I asked, "So are you going out with him again?"

She nodded and said, "Of course. I mean, he's a nice guy. Plus, he seemed really at home with my lopsided boobs."

This time, I choked on the orange juice.

❧

"Check it out, Al," Jade called. "Jessica's on the cover of *People* again."

We'd been at the mall for over an hour, and most of it had been spent at the bookstore waiting for Jade to decide what books to buy.

Jade held the front of the magazine so I could see.

I put the comic book back in its bag and quickly grabbed the *People Magazine* from Jade. The picture of Jessica was from the wedding. It was of Jessica and Mathew walking out of the church after the ceremony. "Yeah," I said, flipping to the part about Jessica. "I remember them being at the wedding. Jessica let them take a few pictures."

"Is there an article?" Jade asked, walking behind me so she could look over my shoulder.

I nodded, finding the spot. "Four pages worth. Are there any more magazines with her on there? I keep forgetting to check for these things."

"And as Jessica Heart's number one fan you must have everything, right?" Jade joked, looking through the different entertainment magazines for any more articles.

"Why yes! I buy all of the Heart Corporation products and I even got her autograph once."

"*Entertainment Weekly*'s got her too," Jade said, handing the magazine over.

I flipped through that issue and then shrieked when I saw that I'd made it into one of the pictures. Granted, I was way in the background, but it was still me. "With luck, a talent scout will spot my picture and go out to find me. This could be my big break. Someday, when they do me on *Before They Were Stars*, this picture will be among all the other embarrassing ones they manage to dig up of me."

Jade shook her head. "I still don't see why you don't use Jessica to land yourself on TV. She could set you up in two seconds."

"First of all, I do not *use* my friends. Secondly, Alix Morris is no cheater. And C, when Jay Leno interviews me one day and asks me how I got my first big break I would rather say that a talent scout spotted me on the background of a picture on *Entertainment Weekly*, than tell him that my very rich best friend made a few phone calls and hooked me up."

"Suit yourself," Jade responded, handing me a few more magazines with Jessica in them. "But when you turn eighty and realize that the high-light of your career was waitressing at a dinner theater, don't come crying to me."

"I appreciate your faith in me."

"No problem." Jade nodded to the other side of the bookstore. "Let's go look at the sci-fi section."

She started in that direction and I followed closely behind, carrying the stack of magazines. I was still trying to come up with something to buy Valerie. She seemed to like silver, so maybe I'd check out the jewelry store after we finished with Jade's reading materials. Valerie worked mornings on Mondays, so I was thinking I'd pick up some McDonald's and surprise her at her apartment. I nodded to myself, thinking that was a good idea. I was getting the hang of this relationship thing.

A hand touched my arm, and I jumped, dropping all the magazines in the process. Then I looked up into a pair of apologetic brown eyes.

"Sorry," Zack Woods said, kneeling down to pick up the items.

"Zack, you scared me," I said.

My ex-boyfriend smiled. "I noticed." He handed me back the magazines and stood up. "I always seem to run into you at bookstores."

"That may well be because you live at bookstores," I replied. I hadn't really talked to Zack in a long time. We'd been in a two week relationship in tenth grade that ended abruptly when the news of my feelings for Jessica were made public. Needless to say, he hadn't taken it well. "I heard you've been playing babysitter to your niece."

Zack nodded. "Yeah. I love Alisha. I really wish Alex was around to see her grow up."

I bit my lip and looked down for a moment. For most of us, the subject of Alexander Woods had been filed into the "Memories Too Painful to Talk About" folder. He'd been Zack's older brother, Roxanne's boyfriend, Alisha's father, and a very good friend. He died in a car accident a couple of years ago.

Zack ran a hand through his light brown hair, pushing it away from his eyes. It was a gesture he made whenever he was thinking of something to say.

Thankfully, Jade came to the rescue. "Hey, Zack," she greeted. "Do you know where the World of Darkness books are? They switched this bloody place all around."

"Hmm. World of Darkness?" Zack asked. "Role-Playing books, right?" He turned and pointed behind him. "I think they moved them over there, but I'm not sure."

Jade patted his shoulder as she darted off in that direction. "Thanks."

Zack cleared his throat and turned back to me. "I really like your haircut. I saw you with it at Jessica's wedding, but I didn't get a chance to comment on it."

"Thanks," I said. "It wasn't really my idea, but I guess it's all right."

"So I heard you were seeing someone."

"Ah, yeah I am."

He nodded. "That's cool." He paused uncomfortably for a moment. "Well, I should be going. It was nice seeing you again, Alix."

"Nice seeing you too, Zack." I watched him walk away, then went in search of Jade. I found her on the floor, staring at a row of books. "Find what you were looking for?" I asked, sitting down beside her.

"Yeah I did," Jade told me without looking away from her precious books. "How's Zack doing?"

"Fine, I figure."

Jade glanced at me and smiled. "I still find it funny that after he dumped you for having the hots for Jessica, he ended up hooking up with her cousin."

I shrugged. "They're still together so I guess they did a lot more than hook up."

"Yeah what is it with those Heart women?" Jade asked, shaking her head. "They're gorgeous and yet they go for those nerdy type of guys."

"Unlike a certain fuzz-headed girl I know who has *much* better taste in men."

Jade faced me. "Yes, but I'm not gorgeous."

"Jade, you're beautiful."

Jade held up her hand to stop me. "Let me break it down for you. Jessica and Roxanne are the gorgeous should-be models. I am the eccentric foreign exchange student from England. You are the untapped resource."

"Excuse me?"

"Yeah, like if this were a teeny-bopper flick, you would be the chick who they make-over at the end and all the guys oooh and aaah at the incredible difference that a little make up and a dress can make. See, because underneath all those layers of baggy jeans and black Aerosmith tee shirts there is this supermodel just dying to come out."

I had no idea what she was talking about. "Where are you going with this?"

Jade shrugged and turned back to the books she'd been looking at. "I'm not going anywhere with it. I'm just breaking it down for you. I was trying to explain why I can't be beautiful."

"How does my being an 'untapped resource' make you not beautiful?"

"It doesn't. My being an eccentric foreign exchange student from England makes me not beautiful."

I stared at her. "You are such a freak."

∅

It took me about two hours to find the perfect gift for Valerie. I hadn't found anything at the mall that called to me. I mean, I didn't want to buy her something stupid just for the sake of buying her something. I wanted it to be special. Jade told me I was turning into a sentimental fool, but I didn't care.

After the mall, I drove around Baldwin in no particular direction, dragging a complaining Jade along for the ride. Eventually, I parked in front of a store whose sign advertised movie memorabilia.

Jade headed off in search of alien stuff and I went up to the guy behind the counter and asked him if he had anything pertaining to the movie *Labyrinth*. He said he didn't have much except a poster, which turned out to be the same one Valerie already had in her room, and a ring. It was this ring that ended up being the perfect gift. It was silver, with an "L" engraved against the carving of a maze. The words "Nothing is as it seems . . ." were engraved on the inside of the band. Those words should have given me a clue as to what was to come, but of course they meant nothing outside the context of the movie. Now when I look back on it, I see it as a sign.

As planned, I stopped by McDonald's and gotten us both dinner. I wasn't entirely sure what Valerie usually had at Mickey D's but I could give an educated guess. Then I headed off to her apartment, hoping that she was in.

When her apartment door opened, however, it wasn't Valerie standing in the doorway. It was a woman in her late twenties-early-thirties and she looked none-too-thrilled to be standing there. "Can I help you?" she asked impatiently.

For a moment I wondered if I'd knocked on the wrong apartment, but I could clearly see the 413 marked on the door. "Is Valerie in?" I asked, feeling stupid all of a sudden, and confused. And a mixture of a few other emotions that bordered on jealousy and nervousness and fear.

The woman rolled her eyes. "She's kind of busy at the moment."

Valerie stepped out of the bedroom at that moment, wearing a bathrobe and nothing more from what I could tell. When she saw me standing there she froze. "Alix."

I tightened my grip around the McDonald's bag so that I wouldn't drop it and somehow found my voice. "Uh. I was just delivering some food." I handed the bag to the woman who now just looked confused. "I didn't mean to interrupt anything."

I slowly backed away from the doorway and then started running down the hall. I don't know why I was running. Perhaps because I wanted to get away from the pain as quickly as possible and somehow I figured I could achieve it quicker by transporting my body to a different location. I didn't stop running until I reached the sidewalk outside the apartment building and felt Valerie's hand on my arm. I whirled around to face her, though I didn't want to.

"Please wait," Valerie said. She wasn't even out of breath. "It's not what you think."

I, on the other hand, was out of breath so it took me a moment to respond. "I'm having a lot of trouble believing that. You're naked under that, aren't you?"

Valerie looked down at the robe she was wearing. "Yes. But—"

"And you're the artist, so don't give me an excuse that you were posing for a portrait."

"It's not—"

"And that wasn't Robin, so you can't tell me that she just showed up out of the blue to pick up some hair pin she left when—"

"Alix!" Valerie yelled. "Listen to me."

I took a deep breath, trying desperately not to cry. Not yet. Not in front of her, in the middle of a sidewalk in downtown Ft. Lauderdale. "I'm listening."

She paused, looking around. She ran a hand through her hair and chewed on her lower lip. Then she looked around again. "Fuck it all to hell," she muttered, more to herself than to me. Then she met my gaze. "I'm not . . . I'm not Valerie Skye."

Chapter 19

I was ready for anything. I was ready for her to claim that the woman had been her long lost sister. Or a cousin. I was probably overreacting anyway. Just because she was . . . naked . . . and there was a strange woman in her apartment didn't necessarily mean that Valerie was cheating on me. There were a million and one explanations. And I was ready for any of them, really. Except that one.

"I mean, my name *is* Valerie Skye," she continued, looking very flustered. She paused for a long time. "Look, Alix, there's nothing going on with me and that woman up there. She's just a friend."

That's really all she had to say to begin with. "Then what did you mean when you said that you weren't Valerie Skye?"

She visibly swallowed. "I can't . . . I can't tell you. I shouldn't have . . . Look, I'm just not who you think I am . . ."

This had to be a dream. I looked around expecting Jessica to appear out of the blue and claim to be my father, or Jade to appear hovering in the air like a genie, something, *anything* to let me know that this was in fact a dream and that what I thought was happening wasn't really happening at all. When nothing of the sort happened, I turned back to Valerie. "You're really confusing me."

She took a step toward me, but I backed away. "Alix . . . I swear there's nothing going on between her and me."

"What did you mean when you said you weren't Valerie Skye?" I asked again.

I'd never seen her look so pained as she did at that moment. Like the world was falling all around her and she couldn't do a thing to stop it. She took a step away from me. "I'm not who you think I am," was her answer, once again.

This wasn't supposed to be happening. We weren't supposed to be standing outside her apartment building having this conversation. We were supposed to be inside, eating McDonald's. And then I was supposed to give her the *Labyrinth* ring and then we'd talk and watch TV and spend the night together. This . . . whatever this was . . . wasn't part of the plan. Where was the rewind button so I could start everything over?

"I guess I can't ask you to pretend I didn't say anything, huh?" Valerie asked sadly.

"If you're not who I think you are," I started, ignoring her question, "then who are you?"

She stared at me, shaking her head. "I can't tell you."

"Why not?" I demanded.

"Because I can't," she said, sternly this time.

I frowned at her tone. All I wanted was for her to make everything okay again. Why wasn't she? "Call me when you can," I said, my voice breaking from emotion. Then I walked away from her, hoping she would stop me. Hoping she would run after me. Hoping . . .

But she didn't stop me. And she didn't run after me. She just stood there and watched me walk away.

Part II

Valerie

Prologue

This is the story of my life. My very fucked up, made-for-TV, be-glad-it-wasn't-you life. Sit back for a while and grab a shot of hard liquor to aid you through this tale. Better yet, make it a double. Or not. Whatever . . .

Let's start at the very beginning . . .

Once upon a time (twenty-four years ago, to be exact), in a mansion by the sea, there lived a couple. Man and woman, by the way. And they had been trying for ages to conceive a child, much to their unfortunate failure. They couldn't adopt, you see, because such an action would disgrace the family name. And nothing else seemed to work.

So the one day came when the couple met another couple. A teenage couple. A very poor and desperate teenage couple who had just become pregnant and had no idea what to do. So our first couple, being that they were so kind and generous, offered the second couple a whopping twenty million dollars cash in exchange for the baby once it was born. It was a very hush-hush, top secret operation that managed to occur undetected by the media by the grace of God, or perhaps . . . lots and lots of money.

Nine months later, a baby girl was born. Twenty million dollars were passed to the second couple. A newborn baby was passed to the first, and voila, there is a new heiress to the fortune.

So, the second couple took the twenty million dollars and went on to lose the entire thing on some stupid gambling bet. Twenty million dollars, can you believe it?

You're probably wondering what any of that has to do with me. Well, I'm getting to that. You see, the teenage couple had two more children. A girl and a boy. Guess which one I am?

My name is Valerie Michaels. I have a younger brother named Aaron and an older sister named Jessica, only she doesn't know that I exist. Or, at least not in that context. It was never my intention to get involved in her life. Far from it, in fact, but I was put into a situation where I had no other choice.

You see, Aaron started stealing from the wrong people (I'm not sure there're right people to steal from, but if there are, these people weren't it). He managed to embezzle seven hundred and fifty thousand dollars before getting caught. I managed to get them to spare his life by promising to double the amount. Lucky for me, and most importantly him, their leader owed me a favor. So she granted me the chance.

I came up with a plan. It was a very good plan and would have worked wonders if I hadn't ended up falling in love . . .

Chapter 1

The way I look at things, we're bound by decisions. Good choices built upon bad choices built upon good choices. Except that in my case, unfortunately, I had bad choices stacked atop an endless line of more bad choices that were in the process of collapsing all around me. How very ironic my life had turned out to be.

She walked away from me and I couldn't do a thing to stop her. So I watched her, from the middle of the sidewalk through the lenses of Hell, until she was gone, swallowed whole by the cloak of darkness and distance, leaving me all alone to battle demons she didn't even know I had.

I tightened the white robe around my naked body and sighed loud enough for nobody but myself to hear. There was no way to fix the tangled web my life had become. So I turned on my heel, my back to the street, my face to the building and walked forward, wishing nothing more than to go back. Back in time . . . to somehow keep everything from going wrong . . .

The door was wide open when I reached my apartment, and I slammed it shut upon stepping inside, taking out my anger and frustration upon the object as though it was to blame.

The smell of fries and burgers assaulted my nostrils and my eyes narrowed. My suspicions were confirmed a moment later as I crossed the short distance between the door and the kitchen.

"Did you thank your girlfriend for bringing us food?" Chris asked through a mouthful of fries.

Somehow I managed to find my last remaining ounce of self-control. I wanted nothing more than to rip the hamburger from her hands and throw it across the room. "What are you still doing here?" I asked instead, keeping my voice even and controlled. Never let them show you hurt . . . And I was hurting. I was hurting so much I was amazed that I could still walk let alone speak.

Christina Walker put the burger down, fixing her dark brown eyes on mine with a look of utter annoyance. Her brown curls bounced as she shook her head at me. "Don't start with your pissy attitude, Val. You know very well what I'm still doing here." With her chin, she motioned to the seat across the table from her. "Sit."

I complied, if only because I needed to sit down. Rubbing my temples with both hands, I looked down at the light blue surface of my kitchen table, then closed my eyes, wishing for silence and getting nothing but the irritating sounds of Chris chewing and swallowing as background music.

"You look like shit," Chris commented, between bites.

I said nothing.

"So what'd you tell her?" Chris asked.

Silence.

Chris studied me, her eyes burning into me. "*What* did you *tell* her?"

"Nothing," I snapped, my patience bordering on non-existent. Then I sighed, looking away. "I started to . . ."

Chris was on her feet in a second. "Have you lost your mind?" she howled, and I closed my eyes wishing somehow to shut out sound along with sight. "If that bitch—"

She didn't get a chance to finish the sentence. I had her pinned by the throat against the kitchen wall so fast she didn't know what hit her. I glared into her eyes, daring her with my gaze to attempt breaking free. "Don't *ever* call her that," I hissed, suddenly feeling the crash of a massive headache split my head in two. I let her crumble to the ground in a heap of desperate breaths, as I stumbled toward the cabinets in search of aspirin.

By the time I found it, Chris was on her feet again, attempting to pull herself together. "Do that again and I won't wait for the goddamn money."

Her threat echoed through my brain as an angry voice in my head asked what I'd been thinking. I couldn't let my anger take control. Not with Chris. There was too much at stake . . .

"You weren't supposed to fall for her, Val. You getting all emotional for that girl was not part of the plan."

"Screw the plan," I muttered, wishing I could mean the words, knowing I couldn't. I downed two Advil.

My comment drew a long laugh from Chris. "Right," she responded, lowering herself down onto the chair. "No woman is worth that much. Your brother's life is on the line here."

Her words stung me, and I did everything in my power to avoid her gaze. I swallowed hard, wishing I was somehow strong enough to cry. Human enough, even.

"Have I told you that you look good as a blonde?" Chris said, following the comment with a sip of Passoa. "Makes you look almost angelic." She had a good laugh at that.

I caught my reflection on the microwave door; distorted and unclear. How perfect. I noticed the blonde hair that framed my face. Angelic. Is that what Alix thought of me? Is that how she saw me? Is that how she wanted me to be? What would she think . . . if she knew the truth?

"I still say you should've left it dark though," Chris continued, smirking. "She seems to go for the black-haired, blue-eyed type, no?"

My gazed darted to Chris's face, and I wondered what was stopping me from putting my fist through it. Too many things, unfortunately.

Chris let out a long, over dramatic sigh as she stood. "You're talking to what's-her-face tomorrow." It wasn't a question. "She can get Alix to forgive you like last time." At the door, she paused. "And quit fucking up. You're running out of chances and excuses . . . and *time*." The door slamming shut announced her departure.

"Satan has left the building," I muttered on my way out of the kitchen. Loki made her appearance down the hallway and met me half-way. "You were hiding, huh? Smart girl." I picked the puppy up and carried her back to the bedroom, kicking the door closed with my foot. I put her down on the bed and walked to the closet so I could change into something a little less comfortable. Black and red flannel boxers and a white tee shirt replaced the robe. I padded across the black carpet to the bed in three long strides and buried my face under a pillow. Somewhere within my head my brain screamed to be let out. I believed it was actually attempting to pound its way through my skull.

After all of the oxygen had escaped the tiny space between my nose and the mattress, I decided to roll over. Loki was staring at me curiously, her little head cocked to the side as though attempting to comprehend my sadness. "This is so messed up, girl," I told the dog, believing that she understood me somehow.

In response, she jumped onto my stomach and lay down there, staring up at me expectantly.

I scratched under her ears and sighed. "How will I get out of this one?"

Loki seemed to shrug.

I closed my eyes, wishing for rest I knew would never come. It would be more peace than I could ever deserve. The only time I managed to sleep at all these days was when Alix was beside me. How long until that happened again? Never if she was lucky. But of course, it wasn't as easy as me just letting her go. I would've done it in a heartbeat if at all possible. But she was part of the plan.

No woman is worth that much. Chris's voice echoed through my head. No woman.

Chapter 2

Tuesday afternoon I waited at Whispers for my scheduled lunch date, something I was not looking forward to. I suspected that she would bring only the confirmation that I had indeed fucked everything up in a completely irreversible way. What would I do then? Fall to my knees and beg for forgiveness I didn't deserve. How much longer until I could stop hurting her?

I shifted uncomfortably in the booth I'd selected. I hated waiting. It was a nerve-wracking and upsetting waste of time. I glanced at my watch. She was twenty minutes late. Tapping my fingers impatiently on the tabletop, I stared at the bottle of Corona in front of me. It was open. Why wasn't I drinking it? Probably for the same reason I seemed to have quit smoking.

My head fell against the wall behind me, and my gaze traveled around the club. There were a few people dancing and a few people at the bar. It was a large crowd size for such an early time. La Rissa's "I Do Both Jay and Jane" sifted through the speakers and I rolled my eyes at the music selection, thankful that it was my day off.

"Sorry I'm late. I know what a sod you are about punctuality and the lot."

I looked at Jade as she slipped into the seat across from me. I'd known her for a year almost. I'd found her outside once, getting hassled by some idiot guy whose ass I proceeded to kick. We sort of became friends after that. Not best friends or anything, but friends. I'd confided in her about my brother and she'd agreed to help. I'm not entirely sure why she would go through all the trouble of helping me get money from Jessica. I never did ask her why she helped me. We shared that same sort of privacy issue that I think helped to make our friendship work, and I didn't want to break that silent agreement between us.

Nevertheless, whatever her reasons, I appreciated them. She told me the only person besides Jessica and maybe Mathew who had access to any of the safes at the Heart mansion was Alix. And if there was any document I needed to find, then Alix would probably know where to find it. The problem was, I couldn't tell Alix the truth. It was risky enough getting Jade involved. I couldn't risk putting Alix's life in danger. I cleared my throat before responding. "Did you talk to her?"

The fuzz covered head shook side to side. "What the hell did you do to her? She won't even talk to me. I sat in her room all day today and she ignored everything I said; spent the entire time writing."

My eyebrows rose in question. "Writing what?"

"Hell's if I know," Jade responded, motioning for the waitress. Then she paused and stared straight at me, her hazel eyes narrowing suspiciously. "You didn't tell her did you?"

"No." As Julie approached to take Jade's order, I let my head rest back against the wall. Holding it up was requiring an unbelievable amount of effort that I was unable to expend at that particular moment. "I started to tell her," I said, once Julie had walked away.

She stared at me in disbelief for a second, then shook her head again. "Why didn't you?"

I sucked in a deep breath and shook my head. "I couldn't risk it."

"I told you from the beginning that she would understand."

Silence.

Jade sat back and studied me for a long moment. "You're totally crazy about her, aren't you?" My silence was all the encouragement she needed. "It's not too late, you know? You could tell her."

Didn't I wish it were that simple. "You don't understand . . ."

"You're right, I don't," she said, her voice taking on a sharp edge as she looked at me. "You promised me that no one would get hurt."

I met her gaze. "No one has gotten hurt."

"I believe there's a heartbroken twenty-year-old who would kindly disagree." She paused to grab the proffered blue Curaçao from Julie. She drank some before placing the glass on the table and returning to the conversation. "Look, I just think you'd get better mileage out of this entire thing if you just went up to Jessica and told her the truth."

I almost laughed at the absurdity of her suggestion. "Yeah, right."

"You don't know Jessica very well. She'd give you the money."

"It's more complicated than that."

Jade whipped out a pack of cigarettes and pointed the box in my direction.

I shook my head.

Jade rolled her eyes as she lit one up. "She's been trying to get me to quit since high school." She blew a ring of smoke. "So, what are you going to do about Alix? The typical arrangement of flowers and box of chocolates will get you absolutely nowhere with that one, I'm afraid. Just a warning."

"What's your suggestion then?"

Jade fell silent as she contemplated my question. Meanwhile, I back-tracked to her comment about my telling Jessica the truth. Which truth? There were so many to choose from, so many choices . . . and all of them were marked for disaster. Between death, chaos, and broken hearts . . . how could I decide? How could I *not*?

"I'd wait a while," Jade finally answered, nodding thoughtfully. "Give her a couple of weeks to sort everything out. If you show up now she'll just slam the door in your face."

"I don't have two weeks."

"You asked for my suggestion, and I gave it to you. Take it or leave it, that's up to you. But for the love of Metallica, quit fucking with her heart. I'm begging you, from the very bottom of my being, give the girl a break."

My gaze lowered. "I never meant to hurt her in the first place. You told me she wouldn't fall for me."

"I didn't think she would. I figured she'd give you a date, *max*. She's been gaga for Jessica since forever, who would've thought *you* would be the one to break the spell." She took a long sip from her drink. "Whatever you did, I commend you. I bow to you. I'm just depressed as hell that you aren't the real thing."

Her words caused me to frown. I wasn't the real thing? I'd never been more real than when I was with Alix. I'd had to adlib a few details about my past, granted, but I'd meant everything I'd said to her. Being with her, I almost forgot who I was and what I was supposed to be doing. What was that she had said once? Something about fate. Yes. Evil, twisted fate. Indeed. "I never meant to hurt her," I said again, as though the words served to absolve me of all responsibility in the matter.

"Yeah, well it's very nice that you seem to have fallen for her and all but what are you going to do when this is all over? Tell her the truth? Tell her more lies? You'll lose her eventually either way if you go through with it and don't tell her. Why did you sleep with her if you didn't want to hurt her, anyway? I still don't understand your reasoning there. I was so pissed at you for that. Do you have any idea how much it took for her to do that?"

That marked the end of that conversation. I rose to my feet and glared down at Jade. "Two weeks," I said and walked away, wondering if the shattering of my heart was audible over the music.

ॐ

Chris was already in my apartment by the time I got back and all I could do as I closed the door behind me was wonder what on Earth I'd done in my past lives to deserve this kind of torment.

She put out the cigarette she'd been holding and sat back leisurely on my couch, staring up at me expectantly as I entered. On this occasion, she'd opted for the silky look, and was clad accordingly in a black button-down silk shirt and maroon silk skirt. Dangling jewelry hung from various limbs on her body and I suspected she'd either come from or was headed to some important meeting.

"How sweet of you to dress up for me," I commented dryly, throwing my keys down on the table beside the door.

"Actually, I was just visiting your brother."

My eyes snapped to her, as she knew they would. If my gaze could kill, she would've been dead a while ago.

"I'm afraid he's losing faith in you," Chris continued, rising to her feet. Her arrangement of necklaces and bracelets clanked against each other. "Can't say I blame him. Even if you are Super Girl, seven hundred and fifty thousand dollars is a lot of money."

"I will get you the money."

"Your persistence is admirable, Val," she responded, walking over to me. "Frankly, if he were my brother I would've just let me kill him." She shrugged. "But I do want my money back."

I fought the urge to get away from her. "You'll get it."

She studied me for a long while, her brown eyes burning into mine, trying to find any ounce of untruth. Convinced there was none, she nodded and returned to the couch. "I trust I will. Now. What did your little contact on the inside have to say?"

"She said Alix needed a couple of weeks."

Chris snorted. "That's ridiculous. This is taking too long. Put a gun to her head, get the money, hand it over and your brother goes free. I'm tired of watching you parade around with that little *bitch*—" she emphasized the word for my benefit, "—like you're a couple of high school lovebirds. If you're just wasting my time, Valerie, let me know now."

"I'm not wasting your time," I said slowly. "Let me do it my way and you'll get your money. But I need more *time*."

Chris shook her head and stood once again. "You're not the one calling the shots around here. It's *your* brother's life on the line here, or have you forgotten that little detail?"

I closed my eyes. "I'll get you more," I found myself saying, feeling desperate. "I'll double it if you just let me do it my way."

She drew in a long breath. I could almost hear the cash register in her head processing the information. "How do you plan to pull this off?"

"Trust me," I said. "A million and a half, in exchange for more time."

A short pause, then, "How much time?"

"I'm not sure."

Chris nodded. "Tell you what. I'll give you a month. If you still need more time after that, it goes up to three million." She started toward the door. "See you in a month," she announced, before slamming the door shut behind her.

Chapter 3

I spent the next two weeks—when I wasn't working, that is—trying to come up with some way of getting Alix to talk to me. I couldn't just disappear from her life and then show up at her doorstep saying, "Hi honey, I'm home," and expect her to welcome me into her open arms. She'd most likely smack the living daylights out of me and *then* slam the door in my face.

So I considered all of my options, again, for the millionth time, and kept arriving at the same conclusion: Alix couldn't know. Jessica couldn't know. I couldn't involve any more people in this mess . . . I just couldn't risk it.

Two weeks came and went and I still hadn't figured out what to do. So, on a Tuesday, two weeks later, I'd decided to spend the day drawing. I skipped my classes at the university and stayed in my apartment all day long.

Still in my pajamas, I set up my easel in the living room and stared at the blank canvas for a long time, trying to find inspiration. Once I thought of Alix, it didn't take long for my hand to start moving over the white surface, tracing lines and molding them into shapes. Time eluded me as I sketched the outlines of her face . . . her body. Night fell and I hadn't moved from the spot I'd claimed that morning. I was wishing that the drawing would come to life, somehow, and put me out of my misery. My heart was breaking and I couldn't piece it back together, no matter which way I turned, which road I chose.

Then, there was a knock at the door.

At first, I decided to ignore it. It was probably one of the neighbors asking for a cup of sugar or something like that. Then I stopped to wonder when a neighbor had *ever* stopped by my apartment. There were only two people who ever came by. And only one of them ever knocked. My gaze darted from the drawing to the door, wondering if I was being too hopeful. I decided there was only one way to find out. Piece of charcoal in hand, I walked to the door and opened it slowly. The first thing I noticed was her eyes, green and sparkling as always. The second thing I noticed was the feather in her hand, and I swallowed, taking a step backward.

Alix walked into the apartment and closed the door behind her, looking around as though expecting someone to pop out of a corner or something. Then her eyes met mine and she aimed the dreaded feather in my direction.

"I'm here to announce that I'm mad at you," she said. "And I'm ready to throw this at you if you don't tell me what's going on with you."

She was so beautiful. I doubt that she knew it, but she was. I loved the way her short hair fell forward, strands covering her eyes at times. My gaze drifted over her, as it always did. Baggy clothing concealing the beautiful body beneath. She was dressed in black as usual. Black Airwalks, black jeans and a black Aerosmith tee shirt I'd never seen on her before. Too cute. It was then I remembered that she'd said something about being mad at me. "I think you're being a bit harsh with the feather. Perhaps you'd like to continue this conversation in the elevator?"

She took a step forward and waved the feather around menacingly. "Not funny," she replied. It was then that she noticed the easel and the canvas and seemed momentarily distracted. "What's that?"

Trying not to blush, I said something really clever and intelligent. Something along the lines of, "Umm . . ."

Feather and anger forgotten, she walked to my drawing and stood before it, studying it intently. "Is that me?" she asked softly, not taking her eyes away from it.

I took a second to decide which answer would get me in less trouble. I cocked my head to the side and scratched the back of my head as I looked at the drawing. It was pretty obvious that it was her, so I couldn't very well deny it, even if I'd wanted to. So, "Yeah," I said, coming up behind her, wishing I was brave enough to touch her. Perhaps I would've been, had she not been holding that evil feather. As it happened, though, I was too frightened of what she'd do with it if I dared cross the line. I cleared my throat as I always did when I was nervous and asked, "Do you like it?"

She turned around to face me, her body so close to mine I could feel the heat she radiated. She was kind enough to put the feather down on the coffee table before answering. "I love it," she said, her gaze not quite meeting mine. "Guess you didn't need me to pose for you after all."

I ventured a grin as I stared down at her beautiful face. "No, but it would've been a lot more fun to draw." I saw the sadness in her eyes, and my heart shattered all over again. I couldn't bear to look at her any longer. What could I say to her that would make everything all right? Jade was right, I was going to lose her either way if I didn't tell her the truth. But would I lose her anyway? How much could I say before I said too much? "What made you come over?" I asked her softly.

She took a step away from me and then sighed, biting her lip in a way I'd seen her do a million times before. "I've been thinking a lot about us. Actually, that's all I've been doing." She pushed her hair back with her hands and let out a long breath. "I was writing this story and when I started it, I meant for it to be about Jessica, you know? And then, somehow, it ended up being about you. And somewhere along the line, I realized that I don't know how to let you go." She smacked her forehead. "Oh God, now I'm quoting Sarah McLachlan." She smacked my shoulder. "Do you *see* what you've done to me?"

I rubbed my shoulder, though she hadn't really hurt me. I couldn't help the small grin that crossed my lips.

"Anyway," she continued, "I thought I'd come by and give you one more chance. Besides, I wanted to exercise my right to be mad at you." She crossed her arms and looked at me expectantly. "So feel free to grovel any time starting now."

Grovel? She stumped me, truly. I stared at her, dumbfounded, and blinked a few times. I finally came to the realization that too much was resting on my shoulders to blow it all away simply because I was too blind and stupid not to trust the one person who was starting to mean more than the air to me.

Her eyes pleaded sadly, and I could feel my resolve breaking. I looked all around the living room for a moment, my eyes narrowing. My apartment was probably bugged for all I knew. I was probably being paranoid, but I couldn't take the chance. Not when Alix's life was at stake. Besides, I hadn't yet decided how much to tell her. "Let's go for a walk."

"Where to?" she asked, looking confused.

"Just to get some air," I replied.

"Okay." She nodded in my direction. "You're going dressed like that?"

I half-smiled, a bit sheepishly, as I recalled that I was dressed in less than suitable attire for any activity that wasn't sleeping. "Let me get changed."

She nodded and took a seat on the couch. "You might wanna try a shower, too. But that's just a suggestion."

I would've grinned but I was suddenly too overcome with nervousness to do anything but secretly panic. Was I really going to tell her? I wondered as I headed toward the bathroom. I decided to take the shower after all, if only to prolong the situation while I came up with what exactly I was going to say. Cause quite frankly, I hadn't the slightest idea.

Chapter 4

You know how in movies every scene seems to have appropriate background music that works to depict how the characters are feeling without them having to say anything? Well, picture this. We were walking side by side, down the practically deserted beach. Meanwhile, the theme song to *The Twilight Zone* kept echoing in my brain over and over again. All around me, the crashing of the waves seemed to say, "Tell her." The wind, too. I thought I was going insane.

The night was humid with the promise of rain. A look at the dark sky confirmed that indeed a storm was approaching. Perhaps walking down the beach hadn't been the most intelligent of ideas, but it had seemed like an appropriate locale for revelations. The waves were getting restless and the wind was starting to blow colder, but it hadn't yet begun to rain, so we kept on walking. If it started to pour, we could easily make it to shelter.

I made a point of staring down at the sand, pretending to concentrate on the crunching noises my boots were making as they made their marks, leaving behind the traces of my existence. Beside me, Alix walked with her hands in her pockets. I wished that I hadn't allowed things get so serious between us. I'd lost track of everything. I'd jeopardized everything and I wasn't entirely sure that I could make things right again.

Yet, the fact remained that I needed Alix's help and I was running out of time to do anything but tell her the truth. Regardless of the consequences.

Surprisingly, it was Alix who spoke first. "Would it make it easier on you if I told you a secret too?" she asked, not looking at me. She sounded like she usually did, cheerful, but I could detect something else in her tone that I couldn't quite identify.

My eyebrows shot upward. "I guess it depends on the secret," I responded, wondering what anyone like her could possibly have to hide.

"Well, I'll measure the shock factor of whatever it is you need to tell me, and then I'll reveal myself accordingly."

I doubted she could possibly say anything that would measure up to my dirty dish of secrets. "So, I've got to go first regardless?"

She glanced at me, and I caught the sparkle in her eyes as she said, "You did tell me that you liked having something to look forward to."

I smiled briefly. "Indeed I did." My gaze wandered off to the ocean for a moment as I decided what to say. Did I tell her about Jessica first? How much about that did she know? Probably nothing. Or did I start with my brother? Which way would make me seem like less of an asshole?

Neither.

Sighing, I turned my attention to Alix. "Let's sit down," I suggested and proceeded to plop down on the sand. It was rather moist but I didn't particularly care one way or the other. Alix was a bit more hesitant, but then dropped down beside me anyway.

"If I get struck by lightning," she began, "I'm going to do inhumane things to you with that feather. Just a warning."

Glancing at the sky, I saw no signs of lightning. Not yet anyway. "What do you think I'm going to tell you?"

She shrugged and played absently with a handful of sand. "We can go back to your apartment and play pictionary until I guess. Or even charades, I'm good at that." She caught my gaze. "I'm not sure, Valerie. But I'd wish you'd hurry up and tell me 'cause the suspense is kind of killing me here. You can trust me, you know? I am the queen of keeping secrets."

"Oh?"

Alix nodded, paused as though recalling something, and shook her head. "Yeah." The next thing she said almost to herself, but I heard her anyway. "I think Jessica's alone are enough to land me that title."

It made me wonder how many of Jessica's secrets she actually knew. All of them? If so, perhaps it wouldn't be so difficult to explain everything. But would Jessica really tell her? I doubted she even knew herself.

"Jessica has secrets?" I wondered, hoping to sound casual.

She snorted at that. "Yeah. Probably one for every dollar in her bank account."

"And you know them all?"

Instantly, her gaze darted to mine. "What does this have to do with anything?"

If she only knew. I paused, wondering how blunt I should be, then deciding to just go for it. Like a band-aid. The faster the better. "Do you know about her parents?"

Alix frowned, staring at me. "What do you mean? That they died?"

I studied her for a moment, searching her eyes for a sign that she knew more than she was letting on. I doubted that she knew. If she knew, that meant that Jessica knew and her parents wouldn't have told her before they died. Would they? I decided to press forward. "No not exactly. Do you know anything else?"

"Why are you asking me about Jessica's parents?"

"Which ones?" I asked, under my breath. I didn't intend for her to hear me but she had somehow.

There was silence. Then, "What are you talking about?"

"Huh?"

She was watching me intently now. "What did you mean 'which ones'?"

Shit. How did I explain this?

"Are you a reporter?"

A reporter? I would've laughed had she not sounded so serious. "No. Not even close."

Alix was biting her lip again. She was watching me with a look that bordered on confusion and something else. Fear perhaps? I didn't want her to be afraid of me. "Valerie, I'm two seconds from kicking you in the face and running for my life, so you better start talking *now*."

I ran a hand through my hair, swallowing hard. "Okay. Uh, once upon a time, in a mansion by the sea—"

"What?"

Perhaps that wasn't the best approach in these circumstances. I decided to just explain the easy part first. Maybe we'd actually get somewhere that way. "Remember when you asked me if I had any siblings and I said no?"

"Right . . ."

"Well, I lied." I looked at her to see her reaction, she appeared to be waiting for more, so I continued. "I have a younger brother named Aaron. He's eighteen, and sort of a computer geek. Anyway, he was involved with these people—"

"What kind of people?"

I hesitated. "Drug people." Before she had a chance to react, I continued. "He was in charge of keeping all their information on the computer. Client information and money and so on. Well, he started stealing from them. Little bits at a time, so it wouldn't be noticeable, except that it was. He'd stolen seven hundred and fifty thousand dollars by the time he got caught." I shook my head, feeling stupid for my brother. "Their leader, which you briefly met the other night, owed me a favor, which is why Aaron had gotten the job with her in the first place, and why she hadn't immediately killed him. She contacted me, told me what he'd done, and I rushed over to see if I could talk him into telling me where the money was. If he gave them the money back, they'd let him go. He'd have to leave the state but at least he'd be alive. Well, he wouldn't tell me. I suspect it's long gone by now. Well, needless to say, Chris was furious when I came back and said he wouldn't tell me. She was ready to kill him right there in front of me, but I asked her to give me a chance to get her the money. She said no. I told her I'd double it and she relented." I looked at her then.

Alix was staring down at the sand. "So you were using me to get to Jessica so you could get the money for your brother?"

She made it sound so . . . simple. I didn't know what to say.

"I'll get you the money from Jessica," Alix announced, though her voice was distant and cold. She wouldn't even look at me. "You could've just asked from the beginning. You didn't have to go through all the trouble of pretending you were interested in me."

I parted my lips to respond but nothing came out. How could she think that? Then I sighed. How could she not. "Alix," I started, attempting to get her to meet my gaze. She wouldn't. I kept thinking that letting her go was for the best. She was better off without me. I should just get the money, get my brother, and forget all about this and her . . . but one look into her eyes and I knew it was easier thought than done. "I wasn't pretending."

She shook her head, looking anywhere but at me. "Sorry if I have a hard time believing that." She looked up at the sky then back down at the sand. "It's gonna rain. We should get out of here."

Mutely, I nodded. I got up, then reached out to help her, but she was already on her feet and walking away from me. "Alix," I called.

She didn't turn.

Running a hand through my hair in frustration I looked around as though expecting the palm trees or the waves to have the answers I needed. Sighing, I started to run after her. I caught up soon after and fell in step beside her. She still wouldn't look at me. And then it started to drizzle. "If I told you there was more, what would you say?"

"That I don't think I can stomach anymore revelations for one evening," she said, looking down, her hands in her pockets again. "You know, whatever it was that I expected you to tell me . . . I never thought it would involve you using me for money. The thought never entered my mind." She shrugged. "Guess I've been pretty naïve. I should've expected it. You were too good to be true."

"I wasn't using you for you to ask Jessica for money," I told her, not sure why. This admittance wouldn't do me any good. It would only make me look like even more of a jerk but as long as I was being honest. "I wanted you to help me find a document I wanted to steal from her so I could blackmail her."

She stopped dead in her tracks and only then did she look at me. "What?"

Oh boy.

"What kind of document?" she demanded.

I'd never seen her angry before and I decided right then and there that as beautiful as she looked with her eyes flashing in rage I never wanted to see her mad again. "Her birth certificate," I confessed and felt myself sink further into the grave I was digging.

She blinked then her anger dissipated into confusion. "Why would you blackmail her with her birth certificate?"

How did I even begin to explain this? Then I paused as I notice her face change from confusion into something that resembled recognition.

"You *know*?" she yelled. "How do you know?"

My turn to be confused. "Know what?" Then I realized and I winced in surprise. "Wait, *you* know?"

Alix looked distraught. "How did you find out? Nobody knows except Jessica, Mathew and me." She stared right into my eyes and asked, "Valerie, how do you know that?"

Sighing, I said, "I overheard my parents talking about it numerous times."

"Then how did your parents find out?"

I closed my eyes for a moment, willing myself to find the strength or perhaps the courage to say it. I looked right into her eyes and replied, "Because they're her parents too."

It's amazing the effect that five little words can have when put in the right order and used in the right context. For the next few seconds I watched as Alix processed the information I had just provided her. My heart stopped beating, I was sure of it, and I wasn't entirely certain that I was breathing either.

"I think," Alix stammered, looking incredibly pale all of a sudden, "I think I need to lie down."

I caught her before she had a chance to hit the ground and I thanked whatever gods had blessed me with fast reflexes because the girl had fainted fast. "Well, damn. That's a first."

By the time she came to, which was only a few seconds later, it was already pouring. She blinked through the rain, appearing confused.

"Hey," I said, "we have to get out of here."

She nodded slowly and I helped her to her feet. When I was certain she'd remain in an upright position, I grabbed her hand and led her in the direction of my apartment. It wasn't far and I knew a shortcut. We'd just get really soaked along the way. She didn't say anything and neither did I. Instead, I focused on avoiding most major puddles, though it didn't seem to matter because the rain was coming down hard and my tee shirt and jeans were sticking to me like glue.

Personally, I didn't mind, but Alix appeared uncomfortable and I guessed she didn't like getting wet. We passed by people under umbrellas and people under the protection of outstretched newspapers hurrying to find shelter. Cars swished by, cutting through the layers of water accumulated on the pavement.

We reached my building a few minutes later and I opened the door, letting Alix pass through first. A gust of cold air hit my body as I stepped inside and I saw Alix shiver. I didn't even bother glancing at the elevator as I headed for the stairs. The swooshing of our shoes as they met the carpet almost amused me. We sounded like a couple of ducks walking down the hall.

At my door, I paused. If my apartment was indeed bugged, then Alix and I couldn't discuss anything pertaining to any of the topics we'd touched on that night. But what was the likelihood of that? Could I risk it? Did I have a choice? I rubbed my forehead for a moment, trying to think logically. Chris knew I never had visitors. If she'd bugged anything it would've been my phone.

"Why are you pausing?" Alix asked, watching me curiously.

Glancing at her, I shrugged. "Just thinking of something," I replied and proceeded to unlock the door. I flipped on the light, did a quick survey of the room, determining that no one had been there while I'd been gone and most importantly, that there was no one currently inside. Only then, did I allow Alix through. "I'll get us some towels." From the linen closet in the hallway, I grabbed a couple of towels and made my way back to the living room. Alix was staring curiously at my phone. "Something wrong?" I asked, handing her one of the towels.

She looked at me. "Do you have another phone besides this one?"

"The one in my room." I was confused. "Why?"

She appeared thoughtful for a moment, then she caught my gaze. "You don't have caller ID."

"No, I don't." I started to ask why, when I remembered why she was asking.

She pinched the bridge of her nose, closing her eyes, as though attempting to halt the assault of an impending headache. When she opened her eyes she laughed slightly. "That shouldn't really surprise me." She studied me quietly. Then asked softly, "Did I hear you correctly, before I passed out?"

I nodded.

"You're Jessica's sister?" The words sounded awkward, and I couldn't decide if it was because she wasn't used to saying them or because I wasn't used to hearing them. Perhaps both.

Instead of responding to her question, I said, "We should get you into some dry clothes."

For a moment, I thought she was going to refuse. In fact, I thought she was going to throw the towel at me and storm out. She looked torn and awkward and hurt and I felt so helpless I wanted to scream.

"Okay," she said, to my surprise.

In my bedroom I found a change of clothes for the both of us. I gave her a pair of black sweat pants and a green tee shirt. As for myself, I opted for black cotton boxers and a light blue tee shirt with the Whispers logo on the back. While we changed, I politely turned my back to give her privacy. I found it depressing that I felt it necessary to do so, since I'd pretty much memorized every curve of her body, but as much as I hated to admit it, everything had now changed between us.

The room was momentarily lit by lightning, followed almost immediately after by a clap of thunder that made the lights flicker and my skin crawl. Feathers and thunderstorms. Anything else I could handle. When I turned around, Alix was dressed and seated on my bed, petting a blissful Loki. Unsure of what to do, I did nothing. Just stood there watching her silently.

Green eyes rose to meet my gaze. "Are you going to tell her?"

Jessica. Was it always about Jessica with her? My sudden anger unsteadied me, and I turned to stare out the window, attempting to find some mode of control. I had no right to be jealous.

"No," I said. "I was going to get the proof, blackmail her with it, get the money and then return the birth certificate to her." I paused to look at the ground before continuing. I wasn't sure what it was about the floor that provided me with comfort. "I just wanted to help my brother out of the mess. I never had any intention of hurting anyone."

"So, have you been spying on me?" she asked.

Her question made me turn around to face her. "What?"

"How did you know I called you that night at Jessica's?"

"My phone rang and you're the only one who has my number." Well, *that* number. I had two.

"Then why didn't you pick it up if you knew it was me?" she pressed.

"Because I was having second thoughts about the whole thing," I admitted. She seemed both surprised and confused by my answer, so I decided to continue. "I had expected you to be different. I knew you were friends with Jessica and I just assumed that you'd be another rich snob. I didn't think you'd be so . . ." Unable to pick an appropriate adjective, I intended to let it just hang in the air. Of course, I should've known better.

"So what?" Alix asked.

A stream of words floated through my mind, but none served to accurately describe her. "I don't know," I stammered. "So *you*."

Alix was silent for a moment, then said, "So you went ahead with it anyway, 'cause of your brother?"

I nodded.

Another bolt of lightning crashed nearby and I jumped.

"I'd get away from the window if I were you."

I started walking toward her, expecting her to stop me and tell me to sit on the floor or in the corner or something. Instead, she moved to the side to make room for me and I crawled across the bed to lean back on the wall the bed rested against. Her back was to me for a moment and then she turned around to face me.

She stared at me quietly for a long time, studying me. I was thankful for the silence. All of the talking was making my head ache and my heart pound. I felt so drained, both physically and emotionally. "I have so many questions I don't know where to begin," she said finally.

"Well, what do you most want to know?" I asked.

She shrugged. "I don't know. I don't think any of this has really hit me yet. I mean, I heard everything you said and I understand it . . . but it hasn't *hit* me. I'm sort of numb inside."

Instead of answering, I reached over to open the drawer of my nightstand. I dug around with my hand until I found my copy of Ayn Rand's *Anthem* and pulled it out. All the while, Alix watched me curiously. I flipped through the novel until I found what I was searching for. "Here," I said, grabbing the photograph that stuck out between the pages. I glanced at it for a moment, then handed it to Alix.

She stared down at the picture, then looked up at me. "Oh . . . wow."

It was a picture of me and of Aaron, taken a few years back. I'd been eighteen, he'd been fifteen. There was nothing special about the picture, really. Just the two of us standing in front of a car, looking annoyed at getting our picture taken. The only reason I kept it was because it was the last picture we'd taken together and for some reason I liked it.

"Your hair," Alix said, staring at the picture. "I mean I knew you weren't a natural blonde . . ." And she blushed. She looked up. "But why?" Then she looked down at the picture and nodded. "'Cause then you'd look too much like Jessica." She continued without waiting for me to answer. "Is this your brother? Aaron?"

"Yeah."

She stared at the picture for a moment longer. "We'll get him back," she assured me gently. "But I won't help you blackmail or steal from Jessica."

"I know."

She handed the picture back. "Is there anything else I should know before I call Oprah?"

Well, there was the small Jade factor, but did I really want to go there? No. I decided it was best if Jade told her herself. "Not really. Are you okay?"

"Not really." She smiled weakly. "I wasn't ready for this."

Would she pull back if I reached for her? Fearful of rejection, I didn't attempt to move in her direction. "I'm sorry," I said, like two words would do any kind of good. "I never—"

"You don't have to explain," she said. She didn't sound angry, just tired. "I understand."

Leaning my head against the wall, I focused on the sound of raindrops pelting my window. It sounded like a ton of little rocks getting shot at the crystal. Loki padded across the mattress and came to rest between Alix and me. She yawned and closed her eyes, resting her head on her paws. "So, what's your secret?" I asked, letting myself fall into her eyes.

Alix looked around thoughtfully, then returned her gaze to my own. "I'm really a man."

My lips twisted into a smile. "Is that so?"

"That is so."

She had no idea how badly I wanted to kiss her at that moment. If she was indeed a man, she was the sexiest one I'd ever seen.

"I should get going," she said suddenly.

A quick glance at the window let me know that the storm was nowhere near being over. "You can't drive in that," I said, turning back to her.

She was on her feet already, searching her wet clothes for the car keys. Finding them, she rolled the clothes into a ball and started toward the door. "Why not? I've driven in worse."

"You don't have to go," I insisted, jumping off the bed to follow her out of the room.

"I really think I do," she answered, turning briefly in the hallway to give me a meaningful look. "I'll get you back your clothes," she added as she reached the door.

Short of jumping on her and tying her down—as tempting as that would've been under different circumstances—there wasn't much chance of my stopping her from leaving, so I let out a deep sigh, resigning myself to the inevitable. "Will you call me when you get home?" The request sounded pathetic to my own ears, I shuddered to think how it sounded to hers.

She paused, standing with half her body out the door and the other half still inside my apartment. "Why do you want me to call you?"

"So that I know you made it okay," I replied, feeling incredibly foolish.

I couldn't read her expression, but if I had to guess I'd have to say she appeared surprised.

"Why?" she asked.

"Because you're my girlfriend," I responded and then proceeded to roll my eyes and wish I were alone so I could have the honor of kicking myself. What was this, middle school?

Her expression turned dark. She slipped from my view and shut the door without responding.

I stared stupidly at the door for a long while. Well, I'd gotten my wish.

I was alone.

Chapter 5

Loneliness will drive the sanest person over the brink of madness. Take loneliness and combine it with desperation and you might as well mix Potassium and water together; the result is the same.

The next morning, I found my pathetic self on the grounds of Baldwin University, feeling like a stalker on the loose and not particularly caring. I stood against a tree, my back glued to the trunk as I struggled to maintain a casual stance. My gaze was fixed upon Turner Hall and the window I'd calculated to be Alix's. I wondered if she was inside. I wondered if she'd seen me. I wondered what I could possibly say to this woman once I was standing in front of her. *I'm sorry. I'm sorry. I'm sorry. If I could do it all over again* . . . Such bullshit. There was nothing I could say.

I scanned the area around Alix's dormitory building. Fragments of conversations floated by me. What I wouldn't give for simplicity.

I fixed my gaze on the entrance door of Turner, half-hoping and half-fearing that the next person to exit would be her. But it never was. From my jeans pocket I withdrew a pack of cigarettes and a lighter. I looked down at both objects as if they were the embodiment of something important. Without a second glance I threw them aside. The lighter hit the concrete and bounced away, ending up at some college kid's feet. He cast a confused glance in my direction, then continued on his way. I have no idea where the cigarettes landed.

Sighing inaudibly, I leaned my head back against the tree trunk and returned to the task of staring up at Alix's building. The red-brick structure stared back at me, patient and mocking, as though somehow knowing that it possessed within its walls the very thing I was searching for.

The front door opened and my heart sped up. Once again, it was a false alarm. Out of impatience, I did something I hadn't planned on doing. "Excuse me!" I called, half-jogging to meet up with the blonde. Catching up to her, I put on my sweetest smile and said, "Do you know Alix Morris?"

She looked me up and down for a moment as though attempting to assess any potential damage her answer could evoke. "Yeah . . ." she responded after a moment, dragging it out as though unsure of her answer. "She lives across from me," she added.

"Do you know if she's home?"

Blonde curls bounced side to side as the girl shook her head. "She's got a directing workshop right now."

"You wouldn't happen to know where that is . . . ?"

The blonde proceeded to give me directions and I thanked her a few times before heading off in the direction she'd instructed. I figured a directing workshop would house a lot of students and so sneaking into the auditorium shouldn't present much of a problem. Truthfully, I just wanted to see her. To sit in the back and scope her out among the crowd and just stare at her for however long her class lasted. This plan however, was short-lived.

Finding the building didn't prove difficult. I knew my way around Baldwin University pretty well and so I had a fairly good idea where Atkins Theater was located. Once I spotted the large building with its prominent columns announcing its superiority over the less intimidating structures on campus, I proceeded to cross through the doors in search of Auditorium B. This, too, was not difficult. What I wasn't expecting, however, was what lay at the other end of the double doors of the room.

I opened the door quietly, as to not disturb the professor, and set foot inside the room. As expected it was large and full of students whose attention was fixed solely on the figure standing atop the gray-carpeted stage. Nobody looked my way as I entered. In fact, they were all so transfixed with whatever was going on onstage that my gaze darted in that direction. That's when my breath caught in my throat.

"Okay, Melanie," Alix was saying, her body half-turned to the audience. In one hand she carried a script, and with her free hand she was pointing at something on the paper. A short girl with purple-dyed hair and gothic-looking clothes looked at her intently as if Alix contained the answers to the world's best-kept secrets. "Why don't you try to block this scene?" At this point, she turned to the audience, and I ducked down to find the nearest seat. I was thankful for the sunglasses. "I need a couple of volunteers."

Hands shot up in the air and I did my best to hide behind the people in the row in front of me.

Alix picked two random people from the audience, a girl and a boy, who quickly made their way up onto the stage. Once there, they were handed each a script and told to read over the parts they were going to portray.

"Okay," Alix said, standing off to the side so that the three other people had center stage. "Melanie, I want you to block this scene to the best of your ability, taking into consideration that this stage is a lot smaller than the one you would be performing on."

The girl started telling the two volunteers where to stand on stage and on what lines to cross from one side of the room to the other. From time to time, Alix interrupted to make suggestions, but for the most part she stood to the side quietly, paying intent attention to the actions unfolding a few feet before her. I'd never seen her this focused on anything before and it took my breath away. She appeared so much older. I was so used to her shyness and awkwardness; this was a side of her I had never imagined.

I'm not entirely sure how long it all lasted. It could've been an hour or fifteen minutes, but before I knew it, everyone around me was packing up their notebooks and Alix was wishing them all a good week.

My plan of escape was a simple one, simply merge in with the exiting crowd and make myself scarce. For some reason this proved more difficult than I had otherwise expected and five minutes later I found myself still sitting in the same spot.

Alix still hadn't noticed me, or if she had she was doing an excellent job of pretending she hadn't. Instead of leaving, I managed to move up toward the stage while her back was turned to the audience so that I could hide to the side of her. I felt like such a fool.

On the stage, Alix was having a conversation with that girl Melanie and I figured that since I was already stalking, eavesdropping was only the next logical step.

"I was really hoping you could help me out with this monologue I have to do for my audition tomorrow," Melanie was saying in such a way that made it clear to me that practicing the monologue was not at all what this girl was after.

"What are you auditioning for?" came Alix's response, and I could tell by her tone that whatever force of strength had kept her lively just minutes before while she was teaching, was gone now.

"It's for *Little Women*. I'm auditioning for Jo in Miami tomorrow and I'm really nervous about it. I could really use your help."

Say no. Say no. Say no.

Sensing Alix's hesitation, Melanie continued. "I'll buy you dinner as a thank you."

My eyes narrowed in reaction to this latest development.

"You don't have to do that," Alix said, and I could tell she was about to give in. Apparently I wasn't doing a very good job of implanting my thoughts into her brain. "When are you free tonight?"

It was all I could do not to jump out of my hiding spot. Somehow I managed to stay still. *I don't own her. She can go out with this girl if she wants to.* I told myself these things, but they weren't sinking in. Mostly because I didn't want them to.

"Oh, whenever!" Melanie sounded a little too content for my personal comfort, and a growl escaped my lips. "Whenever you're free, since you're doing me the favor."

"I have a class in about twenty minutes," Alix responded, sounding thoughtful. "How about afterwards, around six? Meet in my room?"

My ears perked up at the mention of the word "room." Did this girl know where Alix's room was? Had she been there before?

"Perfect," Melanie was saying. "See you then."

I didn't have enough time to be annoyed because it occurred to me at that moment that Alix was about to leave the auditorium and if she chose to exit through the doors next to me, I was going to have a lot of explaining to do. So before I had much of a chance to rethink my plan, I flew out the doors to the open air outside. I jogged to the nearest building and hid out of sight.

A few moments later I watched Alix walk out of the doors I'd just passed through and I breathed a sigh of relief that I'd thought to get out of there instead of leaving it up to chance.

I leaned against the nearest wall and banged the back of my head against it a few times. What the hell was I doing? I stood there for a few minutes and then walked back outside. The intelligent thing to do was to go home and take a long, hot shower and get away from Alix for the rest of the day. Obviously, sanity was a fleeting entity whenever she was around.

Of course, if I just went home I'd inevitably spend the rest of the night thinking about how I really needed to talk to her. This had, of course, nothing at all to do with the fact that I knew she'd be spending the rest of the afternoon with that she-demon, Melanie.

Not even a little bit.

⚐

Needless to say, I didn't go home. I spent the next couple of hours walking around campus and buying crappy coffee from the student center. I found it amusing when random students would stop me to ask for directions. In the mood that I was in, the only rational thing to do was point them in the wrong direction. Which I did.

At around six o'clock, I planted myself on the lawn across from Alix's building, leaning against the same tree I'd befriended earlier in the day. I sat there, nursing a cup of coffee and feeling extremely creepy. I hoped the coffee at least made me look semi-normal, though I doubted it. I should have brought my textbooks with me. Of course, I hadn't entirely planned out this particular adventure. In fact, I hadn't planned to visit Baldwin University at all. I was going to do what any normal, sane, twenty-one year old girl would do after a night like the one I'd had: wander around the apartment, moping.

So how I got from A to B is beyond me, but there I was, sitting on the lawn across from my girlfriend's (ex-girlfriend's?) dormitory building, sipping lukewarm coffee and waiting patiently for who knew what.

The "what" in question crossed in front of me promptly at six o'clock. I watched as her purple head with its black-clad body firmly attached made its way up to the entrance. The door opened on cue and she stepped inside, while a tall guy wearing a baseball cap walked out.

Sighing to myself, I took a sip from my caffeinated companion. Frankly, I hadn't yet decided what I was going to say to Alix once I knocked on the door. I was quite aware that following her around campus and planting myself in front of her building for hours at a time was probably not the best way of going about getting to talk to her. But it's not like I'd been scoring any points with her recently.

Forty-five minutes later, I disengaged myself from the tree and threw away the empty coffee cup in the nearest trashcan. Then I stood by the entrance to Turner Hall and waited for someone to either enter or leave the building so that I could sneak in. It took about five minutes of standing there like a loon, but finally a guy opened the door for me and I walked inside. Alix's room was on the third floor and I passed by several open doors, which reeked of stale smoke and incense. Loud, unidentifiable music drifted down the corridor, muffling the sound of random conversations.

Despite the fact that I took my sweet time getting there, I soon found myself standing before room 335. I stared at the door for a few minutes, as though captivated by the decorations adorning the wooden surface. Half the door was occupied by a large bulletin board, which housed a dry-erase board. Someone had written the message: *Alix, Jade called @ noon* in red ink. I could feel my bravado weakening with each passing second, so I forced myself to knock on the door before it disappeared all together. The first knock was soft and received no acknowledgement. So I knocked harder the second time, putting as much will power and determination as I could muster into each stroke of my knuckles.

As the door opened, I held my breath.

Confused green eyes stared up at me from the crack in the door. "What are you doing here?" If she was angry with me she didn't sound it.

It was my turn to say something so ingenious that she would have no choice but to kick the other girl out of the room and invite me in. "Is this a bad time?" I asked, giving myself more time to think of why exactly I was there. I was also giving her an opportunity to turn me away . . . but I had to give her that option. She deserved that much. *She deserves a lot more than that, you jerk*, my conscience promptly supplied. My brain nodded in silent admission.

Alix glanced warily behind her shoulder. "I was kind of in the middle of something," she said, turning her attention back to me. I could tell by her tone that whatever it was she'd been in the middle of doing didn't fill her with joy.

Feeling a burst of confidence, I said, "Well, I kind of wanted to talk to you about something." Not knowing if that was enough to convince her, I quickly added, "It's important."

She hesitated a second longer, then opened the door and walked away. I took the gesture as an invitation to step inside. I closed the door behind me and stood awkwardly for a moment before taking note of Melanie sitting Indian style on Alix's bed. She did not look at all happy that I'd shown up. Quietly, I studied the dorm room, not because I didn't remember what it looked like, but because I had no idea what to say.

Alix's side of the bedroom remained wallpapered in posters in much the same manner that her room at home had been. I particularly loved the solo shot of Steven Tyler hanging vicariously over her bed. I wondered if that was whom she prayed to instead of God . . . Or maybe she just found comfort in not having to stare up at a blank ceiling all the time. Who knew? She was certainly still a mystery to me.

Her desk, which rested directly to the right as I walked through the door, was kept neat. There wasn't much on it, except for a gray Toshiba laptop and accompanying printer. A copy of *Stone Butch Blues* rested over the computer. *Interesting choice in literature. I would've never taken her for a Fienberg fan.* Next to the desk was her bed, neatly made for a change, and covered in black sheets. Her roommate's bed served to form an "L" against the adjoining wall. Next to that bed was her roommate's desk, which was currently stacked with books. There were a couple of dressers standing side by side against the other wall, and a Persian rug on the floor.

Once my inspection ended, I returned my gaze to Alix who was standing with her hands in her pocket in the center of the room. Melanie was still sitting on the bed, looking suddenly confused and out-of-place. Ignoring her presence completely, I said, "You didn't call me last night."

Alix glanced at Melanie, then sharply at me as though wondering why I was starting this while her guest was in the room. "I never said that I would."

I pulled the desk chair out from under the table and took a seat. I couldn't believe my own nerve. Had I been Alix I would've taken a bat to my head eons ago. I nodded in Melanie's direction. "Would you mind giving us some privacy?" *That's right. Be all the bitch that you can be. That's the way to her heart.*

Melanie turned her head toward Alix, as if hoping that Alix would come to her defense by kicking me out of the room. When Alix didn't say anything, she rolled her eyes and picked up her books. "Later, Alix."

Awkward silence lingered between us even after the door slammed shut. There was so much I wanted to say but no words with which to say them, so I said nothing.

Alix sighed, crossing the room to sit down on the bed. "I can't decide whether I'm more annoyed that you showed up here like this or more grateful." She ran a hand through her hair, letting it fall back around her eyes. I couldn't help but stare at her.

"I suppose both would be equally valid," I said, tearing my gaze away. Her beautiful eyes always managed to wreak havoc on my senses. I sat back on the chair, wishing I'd rehearsed some kind of speech before barging in here. "I'm not entirely sure why I'm here," I found myself admitting.

"I thought you said it was important?"

I forced myself to look at her, attempting to read her mind. "It is." Shrugging slightly, I added, "I just haven't figured out what *it* is yet." Feeling frustrated, I rose to my feet with no particular destination in mind. I just couldn't sit. I avoided her gaze at all costs as I paced around the room. Her eyes followed me for a moment, then she lay back on the bed and stared up at the picture of Steven Tyler. I wondered what she was telling him.

Feeling foolish, I sat back on the chair and stared down at the rug. After a few minutes I cast a glance in her direction, surprised to find her staring at me. She quickly looked away. "What?" I ventured to ask.

Green eyes darted back to meet mine. "Nothing," she responded, and the lead singer of Aerosmith reclaimed her attention once again.

Why did women have to be so complicated? "What are you thinking?" I asked, and subconsciously cringed, half-expecting her to repeat her earlier response.

She seemed to hesitate, her gaze still glued to the ceiling. "Did you figure out why you're here?"

I know why I'm here . . . I just don't know how to make you understand . . .

"I talked to Jessica."

Already? Hiding my surprise, I said, "Oh?"

"She wants to talk to you personally." She paused, then added, "I didn't tell her anything. Just that you were in trouble and needed her help."

Shit. "Thanks."

"So, if that's what you wanted to talk about . . ."

"It's not," I added quickly. *Not even close.* "I'm not entirely sure that what I want to talk about is really . . . something we can talk about."

Alix stared at me expectantly.

So, I searched my mind for the right words; for a way to explain everything that I wanted to say. In the end, I just went with the truth. "I couldn't let things end with last night . . ."

She regarded me, her face impassive. "Isn't that why you told me? So you could end things?"

"Not with you." Never with you . . .

She sat up, running a hand through her hair again. "What with me, then?"

I stared at the Metallica logo on her tee shirt. "I don't know. I just didn't want to lie to you anymore."

She fell silent, her gaze dropping down to study the intricate patterns on the solid black comforter. I sat back in the chair, wondering if I'd ever get myself out of this mess.

My eyes wandered to where she was sitting, taking the opportunity to study her now that she wasn't looking. I took note of the black Joe Boxers that had replaced the baggy jeans I was so used to seeing on her. I tried not to frown at the thought of Alix dressing so casually for Melanie and a pang of something I vaguely recognized as jealousy shot through my heart. "What are you thinking now?" I asked softly.

She lifted her head slowly to look at me, and it was then I noticed the tears trailing down her cheek. I'd never felt so helpless. "What do you want from me, Valerie?"

My brows furrowed in surprise. "What do you mean?"

"You don't want things to end with last night. How do you want them to end then?"

My mouth opened to respond, then shut again.

"What do you want me to do?" she continued, her voice rising with desperation. "Tell you I forgive you so that you can feel better? Pretend that nothing happened? I can't do that," she said, softly. "I can't forgive you for this . . ."

Every nerve in my body felt numb. The pain so intense I felt my body shut down. "I didn't expect you to forgive me," I whispered, but I had. Some deep part of me had hoped that she'd do just that. That she'd understand why I'd done what I'd done and be able to look past all the lies and the deceit. But no one was that forgiving. I knew that now.

The numbness turned to anger. Without a word, I rose to my feet and walked out of the room, hearing the door slam shut behind me. In a daze,

I walked past decorated doors, down the blue-carpeted floors, down the stairs, through the front doors to the world outside.

Fuck it all, I thought, as I jumped into my car and drove off into the night. The broken-heart tattoo gleamed proudly on my breast, reminding me of my promise. *Never fall in love. Never fall in love . . .*

Chapter 6

"I want to see him."

Chris's eyes darted up from the paperback novel in her hands. If she was surprised to see me, she hid it well. With a flick of the hand, the book landed on the wooden surface of the coffee table in front of her, making a sound that reminded me of my first grade teacher's ruler hitting my desk. I did my best not to flinch at the memory.

Chris rose from the black leather couch in the living room of her expansive estate. "How'd you get through security?" Her question bordered on rhetorical. She walked across the white carpet on her way to the mini bar and poured herself a drink.

"You should get better security," I responded. "Any idiot could get in here."

Chris smiled and sipped from her glass, her eyes fixed on me. "You're hardly an idiot," she said finally. "Although your behavior recently has been a tad questionable." She returned to her spot on the couch.

"Let me see Aaron."

Dark brown eyes narrowed for an instance then relaxed. "Sit."

I hesitated briefly, but complied.

Chris studied me for a long moment, taking occasional sips from the amber liquid. "You look like shit, Val. Wanna talk about it?"

My brow rose. "You're not my friend."

"I'm not your enemy either."

"Aren't you?"

Her mouth creased into a smile. "No. An enemy would not have allowed you such liberty in this matter."

I acknowledged the truth of her words. "Why then?"

She shrugged. "You saved my life. It's not something one's bound to forget." She leaned forward, placing the now empty glass on the coffee table. "It's really a shame that this had to happen, Valerie. You and I were close once."

"Too close."

Chris glanced at me, a smile playing at her lips. "Is that how you look at it now?"

"I'm starting to see things differently."

She studied me again then shrugged away whatever thought she'd had. "They were fun times."

Fun. I wasn't entirely sure I'd grasped the concept of fun in my lifetime. "I guess."

"So what sparked this sudden need to see Aaron? Need to be reminded of why it is you're putting yourself through this?"

"Maybe."

Chris seemed to hesitate. She sighed. "He's in the basement." She nodded to a door in the far right side of the room. "Make it quick."

I nodded my appreciation and headed off to the door. I opened it and was immediately bathed in darkness. I almost regretted this decision. There was an incline of steps leading down to a corridor dressed in fluorescent lighting.

"Aaron?"

"Val?"

I hurried in the direction of his voice and found him a moment later, sitting on a mattress on the floor, his back against the wall. He jumped to his feet as he saw me. "Did you get the money?"

"No," I responded simply, glancing around my brother's confinement. Flickering blue light on the ceiling, mattress on the floor, toilet, and a tray of half-eaten food. He might as well have been in jail. "Nice place."

Aaron snorted, sitting back down. He no longer seemed excited to see me. "What's with the hair?"

"Plan A."

He nodded, running a hand through his own hair. It bordered on black but not quite. "What plan are we on now?"

"No plan."

His face paled slightly. "Are you giving up?"

I just shrugged. Truth of the matter was, I had no idea where to go from here. "There have been some complications."

"Fall in love?"

I glanced at him sharply. "What?"

"Chris said something about you falling in love with some girl. Great timing."

His sudden sarcasm grated at my nerves. "I'm not in love with anyone," I responded and I felt a sinking feeling in my heart as the words left my mouth.

"So what are the complications then? Can't you just show up at what's-her-face's door and demand that she give you the money? She doesn't deserve it any more than we do. We might as well prosper from her good fortune."

"I don't want her to know," I answered sternly.

"Well, fuck that!" he yelled suddenly, his voice echoing down the desolate corridor. "It's my life on the line here. Who cares if she knows or doesn't know? I'm sick of protecting her feelings. It's about time the little princess got a shot of reality."

Sighing, I took a seat against the opposite wall. I understood my brother's frustration and empathized with his anger, for it mirrored my own at one point in time. "Calm down, you got yourself into this. If it weren't for me, you'd be fingerless and dickless at the bottom of the Atlantic."

"What do you want me to do, kiss your feet in endless appreciation?"

"Just giving *you* a shot of reality."

He let out a long breath. "Why are you here?"

"Just checking up on you."

"And what do you think?"

"Could be worse."

Blue eyes focused on my own for a long moment. "When are you gonna get me out of here?"

When . . . not "how" . . . The "how" was up to me. I sighed. "I don't know." Then I added, "But I will. I promise."

He nodded, closing his eyes. "I know you will. There's nothing you can't do."

My heart ached. I stood, unable to bear this scene any longer. "Be good."

He didn't respond so I started walking down the corridor. I was almost at the stairs when I heard, "Val?"

"Yeah?" I called back, not turning around.

"Be careful."

I fought back the tears the sentiment caused and climbed the stairs.

♄

My decision to meet with Jessica sprung from a moment of complete boldness and determination that seemed to pass as the Heart Mansion rolled into view. The exaggerated pace at which my heart was beating washed away my last remaining traces of courage.

I parked the car on the circular driveway and sat back, staring straight ahead. There was no use in stalling, I told myself. She knew I was there. I unbuckled my seatbelt, withdrew the keys from the ignition, threw the door open, and jumped down into a pool of noisy rocks.

I stared up at the mansion. It always reminded me of the castles in

Disney movies. The one in *Beauty and the Beast* maybe. I wasn't sure how many floors it had. Windows—hundreds of them—peered at me like judgmental eyes; watching and waiting. I forced my unwilling legs toward the door. The gravel ended as a couple of concrete steps began and I quickly ascended and stopped and stared up at the imposing doors.

Before I had a chance to ring the bell, the door on the right began to open. The butler appeared in the doorway and gave me a curt bow before stepping to the side. He motioned me in. The entire butler concept seemed a bit surreal to me but I played along, feeling extremely out of place.

I had often entertained fantasies—mostly in my younger years—of switching places with Jessica Heart. *If I'd been born first, all of this would be mine*, I thought, looking around the foyer.

A bright chandelier hung over my head, illuminating the entrance in a way that seemed smug to me. A long and expensive-looking rug welcomed my feet, then ended a few steps away to reveal black marble tiles.

The butler—Maurice was it?—closed the door and stretched his arm in a pointing motion. "Ms. Je—Mrs. Collins is in the study," he informed me, obviously embarrassed by his slip of the tongue. I hid my smile as I followed him.

The only place I'd visited in the mansion was Jessica's bedroom and to get there I had to take the red-carpeted staircase a couple of yards from where I currently walked. We were veering away from it, to the right, down a corridor I hadn't noticed existed. It was darker there and the wood-paneled walls disturbed me. They were decorated with paintings that reminded me of the ones I'd seen in my art books from school.

Maurice stopped in front of a set of double-doors, identical to the ones I'd passed along the way. He knocked and waited for permission to enter. Then he stepped forward and announced my arrival.

I somehow kept myself from rolling my eyes as I entered the room. He shut the door quickly, leaving me alone with my sister.

She was sitting behind a large oak desk which was scattered with papers. The room was lit by a couple of lamps that stood at each side of the large window behind her. I could see my Bronco from where I was standing and I wondered if she'd watched me as I'd arrived.

Jessica stood to greet me and I swallowed as I stepped forward. She was breathtakingly beautiful, no doubt about it. Her now short hair lay atop her head in a fashionably messy style, partly spiked in the back and held at each side by a couple of miniature butterfly clips. She was dressed casually, as I'd come to realize was her style, in a pair of faded light blue jeans that hugged her curves quite perfectly. A small white shirt with an oceanic print in the center completed her look. Her face was unnervingly expressionless as she took me in.

I wasn't sure what kind of impression I was making; or had ever made. I hadn't been entirely sure what kind of attire was appropriate for this kind of meeting (*Vogue* didn't have any fashion tips for meeting with your long lost sister who didn't know she was your sister). So I'd opted for my usual Levi 501's and a black tank top that reached just above my belly-button, allowing a clear view of the ring therein. My blonde hair was loose as usual, framing my face and cascading down my back.

We stared at each other. I had the oddest feeling that I was staring into a mirror. A strange look passed across Jessica's face but she masked it before I had a chance to interpret its meaning.

"Take a seat," she instructed neutrally, reclaiming her chair.

As I settled into the soft cushions of the proffered chair, I felt a strange sense of sadness wash over me and I struggled to suppress it with little success. What would it have been like to grow up with her as a sister? How much different from me was she? How alike? My heart ached and I begged my mind not to go there.

"Would you like anything to drink?"

"No, thank you," I said, though I could've used a shot of something. I kept my gaze far away from the intensity of my sister's. I wanted so badly to hate her. Hating her made everything easier. I'd expected her to be different. I'd expected her to be snobby. I'd expected her to be a bitch. I'd expected her to be someone deserving of my actions. But she wasn't. And all I could do was wonder what she thought of me.

"Alix told me you needed my help." Her blue eyes fought to meet mine and I lost the battle. Her face remained as impassive as I imagined mine to be.

Inwardly, I cringed at the mention of the word "help." Help was something I'd never asked for, regardless of necessity. I felt my pride deflating. Here I was, groveling at the feet of a sister who didn't know she was my blood. Resigned to begging for the sake of a brother who cared for little beyond his own needs. And where did I fit into all of this? "I do," I finally replied, my voice empty, as if I'd said those same words so many times that they were void of emotional meaning.

"What do you need?" she asked.

I locked our gazes together. "A million and a half."

She sat back, and I attempted to read her mind. She continued to hold my gaze. "Why should I help you?"

Her tone wasn't threatening and I suspected that she was testing me. "Because if you don't, my brother will die. You have no reason to help me, but I'm out of options and he's almost out of time."

Her features darkened for an instant and I wondered if she knew the specifics of how she came to be at the other side of that desk. Twenty million for my sister, one point five for my brother. And me? How much was I worth?

Jessica took a deep breath. "I'll give it to you. On one condition."

My eyebrow arched in silent question, my heart speeding up in excitement, my mind racing to figure out what she could possibly ask of me.

"You stay away from Alix." I felt the sting of each word upon my heart.

"Is that how you operate? My brother for your best friend? That's blackmail."

"Not blackmail." She shook her head slightly. "It's my right to be concerned for Alix's well-being, after everything you've done to her." She shrugged. "I don't think it's an unfair request, considering what I'm giving you."

Bribery. That's what it was. I began to reconsider all the nice thoughts I'd had about Jessica Heart. "I won't agree to that."

Jessica contemplated this for a long time. "You'd really give up your brother's life for the off-chance that Alix may someday forgive you?"

"I will not let my future or Alix's be determined by your bank account."

"Just your brother's life?"

Our brother! I was dying to scream. I felt so cornered and frightened and helpless. If that was her request, I couldn't turn it down. But I couldn't agree to something like that for money. Alix deserved better than that. If I was going to stay away from her then it had to be for a reason. "I'll stay away from her but not because you told me to. I have no intention of causing her anymore pain."

"How awfully noble of you," she said.

I bit my tongue to keep from lashing out at her. Of course she hated me. I'd betrayed and used and lied to her best friend and now I was politely asking for money.

Money to save a brother she didn't even know she had.

The mixed emotions surging through my soul were overwhelming. This was too much. I blinked back tears I couldn't share. I wouldn't break down. Not here, after all of this.

"I'll transfer the money to whatever account you want. It's yours, no questions asked. Just get the hell out of Alix's life and never come back."

Chapter 7

Chris had been cynical about my call. Yes I had the money. Yes I could have it transferred within a few days. Yes. Yes. Yes. Just let Aaron go . . .

Of course she refused until the money was in her account. She didn't ask how I'd gotten the money. But blackmail would've been my answer, had she inquired. Either way, I kept feeling restless.

I decided that getting out of Florida was probably for the best. I'd go pick up my brother and then I'd get the hell out of the Sunshine State. Maybe I would head up to New York City or L.A. Somewhere interesting but far away. I had enough money in the bank. College could wait.

Jessica set about transferring the money to some bank account Chris had set up for special business transactions. I didn't ask. I certainly didn't want to know.

Chris promised that Aaron would be free by Friday. By Saturday morning, I planned to be gone. I'd decide where to end up on the way.

But it was only Thursday and that meant that I had hours of waiting until I could breathe again. And there was still something I had to do before I left. Something that couldn't wait another minute.

I drove up to the University that afternoon. I just wanted—no, I *needed*—to set everything straight before I disappeared from her life forever. I ignored the pain that surged through me whenever I tried to picture the rest of my life without her. How emotional pain could manifest itself into physical pain so easily was beyond me. But somehow it was happening.

I didn't notice the red Camaro in the spot next to mine, and even if I had, I wouldn't have known to whom it belonged.

I found Alix's door slightly ajar and I was about to knock when a voice stopped me cold.

Jessica.

I felt my heart speed up as something that resembled fear welled up in my being. I had to get away from there. I had to leave. But I felt compelled to listen, if only for a moment.

"So you gave it to her," Alix was saying. "Just like that?"

"Isn't that what you wanted?" Jessica inquired gently.

"No. I mean, yes! Yes, of course." Alix sounded unsure, and I could almost hear her pacing around the room.

"I haven't transferred the money yet," Jessica began. "You've still got time to change your mind."

"No!" Alix replied quickly. "She needs it."

Jessica paused for a beat. "Do you really believe the story about her brother?"

"Don't you?"

From the crack in the door I could see Jessica shrug. She was seated patiently on Alix's bed. Alix was standing nervously in the center of the room, hands delved deep into the pockets of her black jeans.

Finally, Jessica responded, "Quite frankly, I don't see how you can believe anything she says."

Alix sat down. "I have to believe her."

"Why?"

"Because. Because if I don't I'll fall apart."

Jessica was silent for a moment. "It's going to be okay."

"How can it be?"

"She can't hurt you anymore."

Alix rested her head on Jessica's shoulder. "Then why am I still hurting?" She sighed. "I'm never going to see her again, am I?"

"Explain to me how that's a bad thing."

Alix didn't answer.

Jessica pulled away to stare at her. "Alix, she used you! She lied to you. She betrayed you. For crying out loud, she even slept with you!" Jessica's anger soared with each syllable, her voice rising. I couldn't see her face but I could almost picture her dark blue eyes glazing over in anger. "I shouldn't give her the money. Who knows what she'll use it for. Drugs, maybe. She's probably a professional con artist."

"She's not like that."

"How do you know what she's like?" Jessica demanded. Alix said nothing so Jessica continued. "What I don't understand is why you even care if she ever walks through that door."

At the mention of the door, I drew away from it, fearful that I'd be spotted.

"Because . . ." Alix started, and I could hear the frustration in her voice.

"Because why?"

"Because I'm in love with her!" Alix snapped.

And as those words reached my ears, a gasp escaped my lips and I sank back against the wall, feeling the impact of each word as it all slowly sank in. *She's in love with me?*

"You're in *love* with her?" I could hear the mattress adjust to the missing weight of Jessica's body. "How can you *possibly* be in love with her after all she did to you?"

"You don't understand."

"What could I possibly not understand? She knew you were my best friend, probably read about it in *People* magazine or something. Stalked you down, seduced you to get to me and then got you all emotional over her so that you'd convince me to give her the money. It's a genius plan and you fell for it hook, line and sinker!"

"It wasn't like that! You don't understand."

"Then make me understand!"

Alix was quiet.

"I should just call the police and have her thrown in jail. Why did I let you talk me into giving her the money . . . ?"

"Please don't . . ."

"Why? Just give me *one* good reason why I shouldn't."

"Because she's your sister . . ."

Chapter 8

Oh shit! I thought, my heart suddenly beating out of control as Alix's revelation reached my ears. I swallowed as I waited for Jessica's reaction.

"What are you talking about?" Jessica asked.

There was silence, and I leaned forward so as to not miss what was being said. *Please don't decide to storm out of the room*, I secretly pleaded.

"Alix . . ." Jessica insisted, her tone bordering on impatience. "What are you talking about?"

"Hmm? What did I say?"

"Did you just say that Valerie's my sister?"

Alix laughed nervously. "Is that what you heard? Boy, Jess, you should really get your ears checked. What I said was that I really miss my sister. Don't know why. Momentary lapse in sanity, I guess. You know how it is. Are you hungry? I'm hungry. Let's get some food."

"Alix . . ."

"Hmm?"

"I am two seconds from losing my tempter."

"I just meant . . . she's your . . . sister . . . in that way . . . that two women are . . . when they're not really. You know?"

"*What?*"

"I was speaking metaphorically. You know, sisterhood. Without the traveling pants."

"You do realize you're making no sense whatsoever, right?"

"No? Funny, that. So . . . lunch?"

There was a brief pause, and then, "I can't. I'm meeting Mathew. In fact, I should probably get going."

I glanced frantically around, trying to find some way to hide. I should've made a run for it right then, but Alix's next words kept me glued to my spot.

"Are you going to give her the money?" Alix asked softly.

There was silence for a long moment, then Jessica whispered, "Do you really love her?"

"Yes."

A sigh. "Then I will."

My eyes burned with unshed tears and I felt my heart aching with emotions I couldn't decipher. I had to get out of there.

I heard Alix say, "Jess . . . ?"

But I don't know what she said after that, because I ran as quietly yet as quickly as I could toward the end of the hallway, where I hid inside the stairwell. After a minute, I peeked around the corner to see Jessica's retreating back heading toward the opposite side. She disappeared down the stairs a moment later and I leaned back against the wall, and let out a breath I didn't realize I'd been holding.

I stood there for a while, enduring odd looks from people heading up and down the stairs. Then, when I could no longer justify my standing there, I took a deep breath and abandoned my hiding spot. At Alix's door, I paused. Then knocked more confidently than I felt. I no longer had a plan of action. From here on end it was all improvisation.

"It's open!"

I turned the handle and opened the door fully. Alix was sitting at her desk, her hands on the computer keyboard. She didn't glance up at me right away and I stood there awkwardly for a few seconds before her emerald eyes finally drifted up from the monitor.

She blinked a few times as though she couldn't believe she was really seeing me. "Hi," she said softly.

I shut the door behind me before turning my full attention back to her beautiful face. "Hi," I replied, lamely. "You're probably wondering why I'm here . . ."

"I wasn't sure I'd ever see you again," she admitted.

I leaned back against the door. Her eyes had this amazing way of disarming me. It was unnerving yet enchanting all at the same time. "Did you want to see me again?"

"I'm not sure."

Well, at least she didn't say no, I thought dryly. "I just came to say goodbye," I said, thinking it a good opening.

Her eyes reflected surprise. "Where are you going?"

"New York," I said without conviction. "Perhaps California. I'm not sure yet."

She nodded mutely. Then said, "Okay."

"Thanks for everything," I added.

"You're welcome."

I nodded. "Well, goodbye." I reached for the handle, waiting for her to stop me. But she didn't. I opened the door. Then I shook my head, slammed the door closed, and turned back to Alix. "Look, I can't do this."

"Do what?"

"Walk out of your life like that," I explained. "I can't do that." I ran a hand through my hair in frustration. "I need you to know a few things first."

Alix leaned back in her chair, crossing her arms against her chest and staring up at me with a look I couldn't quite interpret. "I think I know everything I need to know."

"No. You don't." I glanced quickly around the room, trying to buy time. "Look, I know that I lied to you. There's no excuse for that and I can't expect you to forgive me. But if I walk out of that door right now, I'm going look back on this moment when I'm eighty—provided I live that long—and wish on every star out there that I could go back in time and do this all over again. So I'm going to save myself the heartache and just say what I need to say. And if you still want me to walk out the door and never return, then I will."

"Valerie—"

I held up my hand to stop her. "Just listen." I took a deep breath then proceeded. "When I first saw you that night at the club, I nearly dropped the tray of drinks I was carrying. Alix, you were so beautiful and so not what I was expecting that I have no idea how I even managed to make my way to your table without stumbling all over myself. And I was so torn between wanting to ask you out just because I wanted to and wanting to run because I knew if I went through with my plan it would be you I'd be hurting. But I *had* to go through with it for my brother's sake." I searched her eyes for some kind of reaction but she was just waiting for me to continue. "When you asked me if you could give me a ride home that night, I knew it was my chance to walk away from all of it. I could've refused and never seen you again. I could've figured out some other way to get the money from Jessica that didn't involve using anybody, but at the same time I couldn't bear the thought of never seeing you again." It was so hard to explain everything without mentioning Jade's involvement. But I wasn't going to drop that bombshell on her. No way.

"Valerie, what are you trying to say?" Alix asked softly.

"I'm trying to say that—" I'm totally in love with you. "I really did like you . . ." Why couldn't I just say it?

"Oh," she said, her eyes flashing with disappointment. She cleared her throat. "Look, I want you to know that I understand everything. And that there's no hard feelings." She nodded, more to herself than to me. "I do have one request, though."

My gaze flew to hers. "Anything."

"I want you to tell Jessica the truth."

Jessica. Of course. "I can't do that."

Alix rose to her feet. "Why not?" she demanded. "She *deserves* an explanation, Valerie! And if you don't give it to her, I will."

"Alix—"

"You owe her that much . . ."

I sighed. She was right. I did owe Jessica an explanation. I owed her a lot more than an explanation. Resigned, I nodded. "Okay."

She seemed surprised I'd relented. "You'll tell her?"

No. No. No. Every fiber of my being was screaming against it, yet my mouth spoke the words. "I'll tell her."

Alix searched my eyes. "Do you promise?"

"Would you trust my promise?"

"Yes."

I almost smiled. "I promise." I took a deep breath. "Alix, I—"

"Why is it so bloody hot—" Jade saw me and stopped. She threw me a questioning glance but I ignored it.

"I was just leaving," I announced. I glanced quickly at Alix, then excused myself, nodding politely at Jade as I exited the room.

℘

Making a promise and keeping one are two totally separate entities, and I knew that the longer I prolonged telling Jessica, the closer I'd get to chickening out. I kept running the conversation with Alix over and over in my mind as I drove to Jessica's.

"Would you trust my promise?"

"Yes."

One simple word and I was mush.

Three hours later, I found myself on Jessica's property. If I'd been nervous the last time, it was nothing compared to the marathon my heart was running at that moment.

Always on cue, the door opened as I ascended the steps to the entrance and Maurice informed me that Jessica was out by the pool. I was surprised he didn't take me there himself like he had last time. Instead, he simply pointed in the direction I was supposed to go and I headed off that way, willing my heart to slow down. *I can't believe I'm doing this. I shouldn't be doing this. Why am I doing this?*

Alix.

Oh, right.

I took a deep breath as I reached the pool deck. The pool came complete with a Jacuzzi and what appeared to be a small waterfall off to the side. It reminded me of one of those pools in an expensive beach resort.

A burst of female laughter caused my head to turn, and I found its source a second later. Jessica was splashing water toward Mathew who was holding up a blue floatation device as a shield.

I stood there awkwardly for a few seconds, trying to decide on a course of action. Finally I decided that coming back some other time was probably a good idea. As I started to turn away, however, I was spotted.

"What are you doing here?" Jessica called from the edge of the pool.

Walking a few steps so I wouldn't have to yell too loudly, I responded with, "I need to talk to you. It's important."

"And that's my cue," Mathew said, leaning over to kiss his wife before exiting the swimming pool. He grabbed a towel from one of the lounge chairs and disappeared inside the house.

Jessica proceeded to pull herself up from the water, a puddle forming at her feet. She grabbed a towel and motioned for me to sit down. "I transferred the money, if that's why you're here."

I sat and stared up at her as she dried herself. "I'm not here about the money."

A dark brow shut up in silent question, and she paused in her actions. "Well?"

I shifted in my seat. "It's about my parents . . ."

Jessica snorted and took a seat in the lounge chair next to mine. She hung the towel around her shoulders and grabbed the bottle of water resting on the floor between us. As she uncapped it she said, "Do they need money too? No-no . . . let me guess, they were kidnapped by the mafia?" She laughed at her own sarcasm and took a long swig of water.

I waited until she swallowed, doing my best to ignore her attempts to mock me, and then said the only thing I could think of that might catch her attention. "Thomas and Leigh Michaels."

Jessica's expression changed from impassive, to confused, to something else I didn't understand.

When she didn't say anything, I continued. "I'm their daughter."

Jessica blinked a few times, as if trying to comprehend the meaning behind my words. "You're trying to tell me that you're Thomas and Leigh Michaels' daughter?" she asked, and I could tell she was trying to remain calm.

"My name is Valerie Michaels Skye," I began, "I know—"

"Stop," she said, holding up her hands. "What do you want from me?"

I opened my mouth to respond but nothing came out.

"Do you want more money, is that it?" Jessica asked. "How much to keep you quiet?"

I narrowed my eyes in confusion. "Quiet? I—"

Jessica was laughing nervously as she paced. "It was only a matter of time before this got out. Shit." She turned back to me, her unreadable mask firmly in place. "How did you find out about it? Must have taken a lot of research. *Man*, you're a sneaky bastard."

Something was totally wrong with this picture and I couldn't even begin to fathom what the hell she was talking about. *Did she lose her mind?* "Research?"

She rolled her eyes. "How much do you know? The whole thing?"

"Well . . . yeah . . . but I—"

"Okay, let's cut some kind of deal," Jessica said. "Name it and it's yours."

I blinked a few times and it started to dawn on me that she wasn't believing me on the whole daughter issue. "It's not," I began, stumbling to form the right words. "I don't want anything from you. I just thought you should know that . . . well, that I'm your si—"

"No!" she said, loudly, emphatically. "Don't even think of finishing that sentence." She continued to pace, and I could tell she was starting to panic.

God, this was such a bad idea. How did I expect her to react? I rose to my feet though I wasn't entirely sure that I could be any more useful that way. "Jessica, you have to listen to me—"

Her eyes bore into mine. "I don't have to do anything."

Sighing, I reached into my pocket and withdrew the only thing I could think of that would serve as evidence: my birth certificate. I placed it on the lounge chair I'd been sitting on. "I can't force you to believe me, but I can prove it to you. Keep that. You can have it checked out if you don't think it's real." I stared into her eyes sadly. "I don't want anything more from you, Jessica. Thanks for all of your help, regardless." I turned around and walked away. Not looking back.

Chapter 9

"I have no idea how you did it," Chris said, laughing, sitting back in her office chair. She was dressed in a silk kimono which did little to conceal the fact that she had nothing else underneath. I doubted that was coincidental. She held up her hand to stop me in case I was about to speak. "And I don't want to know," she added, rising to her feet.

My patience was wearing thin. I'd arrived at my apartment to find a message from Chris. The money had been transferred. Mission accomplished. Relief and regret hung over me like a cloud during the entire drive to Chris's mansion. I could barely stand to stay in my own skin. And now I was being forced to stand there listening to Chris babble on.

"When will Aaron be released?" I asked, impatience winning out.

Chris lit a cigarette and offered me one. I refused and she shrugged. "You sure have gotten boring." She placed the lighter back on the desk and stared at me inquisitively. "You don't seem particularly happy."

"Just let me take Aaron home," I said, and hoped I didn't sound as whiny to her as I did to my own ears. "You've got the money."

"Touch-y," Chris drawled, flicking the cigarette on the ashtray. She leaned against her desk. "What are you going to do about your hair?"

"Chris . . ." I began, impatiently.

She laughed. "It's so much fun to toy with you, Valerie," she admitted and returned to her seat behind the black desk. To my surprise, she turned serious. "You know, they wanted me to kill him anyway."

My heart leapt up my throat at the thought.

Chris winked. "Don't worry though. He'll live." She stared into my eyes. "We're even now, understand? No more favors."

"Don't worry," I assured her, "you'll never see me around here again."

Chris glanced me up and down for a moment, not bothering to disguise her appraisal. "I wouldn't mind seeing you around here all the time. Your brother, however, must leave Florida. I can't protect him once he's off my property and quite frankly, I don't care enough to try."

I nodded.

"He knows all of this, of course," Chris continued. She paused. "I suppose it would be out of the question to ask you to come and work for me again?"

In spite of my awful mood, I nearly laughed. Instead, I gave her a look which I hoped conveyed exactly what I thought of that proposition.

"Okay, I'll take that as a no." Chris put out her cigarette and stood. "He's free to go. You know where he is." She started to walk away, then stopped and turned back to me. "Take care, Val."

I watched her walk away, until I no longer had an excuse to stand there. Then I headed down to the dreaded basement.

"Aaron?" I called. I found him at his usual spot on the mattress, looking like he was in desperate need of a shower and a decent meal. "Are you all packed?"

He stared up at me in surprise. "You mean . . . ?"

"I got the money. You're free."

He was on his feet at once, hugging me so tightly I couldn't even breath. "Aar—" I coughed.

Letting up on me, he laughed through his tears. "Oh God, Val. Thank you so much. I thought for sure I was gonna die in this place."

"Hey, I thought you said I could do anything," I complained.

"And I was right."

I rolled my eyes. "Come on. Let's get you home and into the shower. You smell like crap."

♌

"So," I started, eying my brother curiously as he proceeded to consume his third serving of Chinese food. "Hungry much?"

He grunted a response.

I sat back on the chair, watching him for a minute. I couldn't believe he was sitting at my kitchen table, shoveling away at pork fried rice like nothing had happened. No apologies. Nothing. "What are you going to do now?"

Aaron wiped his mouth with a napkin and shrugged, his gaze never rising from the plate of food. "I'm leaving for Brazil tomorrow afternoon."

Somehow I managed to hide my surprise. "Brazil? Why Brazil?"

"Just feel like getting in on some tourist action, seeing as I've got to leave the state anyway," he answered, and I could tell he was hiding something.

"The *state*, Aaron, *not* the *continent*," I reminded him, though I didn't think I needed to. "Why Brazil?" I asked again.

He finally put down his fork and gazed up at me, his blue eyes troubled. "Look, Val," he began, and I could sense that I wasn't going to like what he was about to say, "I have some business I have to take care of down there. I don't want to involve you any further into my affairs. So let's just leave it at that." He resumed his meal without further commentary.

"Aaron . . ." I warned.

"Don't worry, sis. You won't ever have to worry about me again."

"Yeah that's what I'm afraid of," I mumbled under my breath. "Will you promise to stay out of trouble . . . and keep in touch . . . and not do anything crazy . . . ?"

Aaron laughed. "I promise."

Did I believe him? Not even a little bit.

"So," he said, raising the bottle of beer to his lips, "what's been going on with you?"

"What's been going on with me?" I asked incredulously. "Aaron, how can you ask that when you know perfectly well I've been doing nothing but trying to get your stupid ass out of the mess you got yourself into."

"Geez, chill out, sis."

I was this close to strangling him. "Do you have any idea what I have gone through the past few weeks?" I nearly yelled. "Worrying about what they were doing to you, about what they *would* do to you if I didn't get the money in time. I've barely slept in ages, Aaron, and all because you had the *brilliant* idea of stealing a hell of a lot of money which seems to have disappeared off the face of the planet! And now you want to scamper off to South America to do God-knows-what, which will probably get you either killed or thrown in jail. And the part that *infuriates* me, is the fact that none of this seems to have affected you at all!"

Aaron gazed at me curiously for a moment as if trying to analyze my outburst. He took a swig of his beer, calmly, as if nothing I had said had penetrated the lump on his neck he liked to call a head. "PMS?" he guessed.

"Ugh!!" I yelled, frustrated beyond words. "I'm going to bed before I kill you myself." I stomped to my room and slammed the door shut. Loki lifted her head from her spot on the bed. "Sorry," I apologized to the dog. "He just gets me so mad, you know?" She blinked in understanding, and I walked to the closet to get changed. One boot flew in one the direction, banging noisily against the wall. I glanced quickly at Loki. "Hey, don't look at me like that." The other boot followed suit. "Okay. Okay. I admit this has more to do with Alix that it does with his moronic attitude."

I replaced my blue jeans with a pair of black pajama pants and headed toward the bed. Joining the puppy, who, truth be told, looked quite bored with my attempt at a conversation, I settled on top of the comforter and stared thoughtfully at the wall. "I can't believe this is over," I muttered to no one in particular. "And now Jessica knows. That's if she chooses to believe me. I wouldn't be surprised if the FBI blew down my door and had me arrested for harassing the Queen."

Almost on cue, I heard the distant sound of a knock. I frowned, glancing at the time. It was nearly one in the morning. "Who the hell . . . ?" I wondered out loud, rolling out of bed.

I got the door to my room open in time to hear Aaron say, "Damn, you're hot! Tell me you're here for me."

Rolling my eyes, I was about to step out into the hall, when I heard Alix's voice respond with, "Ah, sorry. Is Valerie home?"

Alix. I glanced questioningly at Loki and she looked back at me as if to let me know she had nothing to do with it.

"She's sleeping," Aaron answered. "Can I be of service in any way?"

I'm going to kill him. Totally kill him. I stepped out of the room, trying desperately to calm my heart. *What is she doing here?* I kept wondering. When my eyes focused on her, I very nearly tripped right over my tongue. Instead of her baggy attire, she was clad in a velvet green evening gown that clung quite tightly to her every curve. *Oh, my gentle Jesus . . .* I swallowed hard.

Unsurprisingly, it was Aaron who broke the silence. "Wow, talk about sexual tension," he said. "I'm out of here. Don't wait up." He chuckled and exited the apartment, closing the door behind him.

Alix reached down and took off her high heels, then threw them aside. "I nearly killed myself on the stairs," she joked.

Clearing my throat, I attempted to speak, but failed.

"Jessica had a . . . *thing* . . . at her mansion tonight," she said. "And I had to go. Well, I didn't *have* to go. It's not like my life depended on it or anything. I probably would've chosen to die, had that been the case. But she convinced me and then I was thrown into this . . . *thing* . . . and well . . ." She shifted uncomfortably. "Please stop looking at me like that . . ."

"I'm sorry," I said, finding my voice somehow. "You look great," I added, thinking that was a horrible understatement. *My God she's gorgeous.* "So . . . umm . . . ?" *That's right, Val, stick to monosyllables.* "Do you want to sit down?"

She nodded as she moved toward the couch. "My feet are killing me." She glanced at the door then back at me. "Why is it that every time I come here, someone different answers the door?"

Her tone was teasing, and I was surprised. "I'm sorry about him," I apologized, taking a seat on the table in front of the couch. "He was dropped on his head as a baby."

Recognition flashed in her eyes. "Was that your brother?"

"In the flesh," I responded, not really wanting to get into the subject.

She seemed to sense this. "I'm glad he's okay." She looked down for a moment before continuing. "I came to thank you."

My brows furrowed in confusion. "For what?"

"For telling Jessica the truth," she answered. "I know I said I believed your promise, but truth be told, I half expected you to skip town."

This admission sent a pang of sadness through my heart. *She doesn't trust you.* Then the more logical part of my brain responded. *Can you blame her?* "I keep my promises. Especially to you."

"Are you really leaving?"

I stared into her face, feeling my heart break in two all over again. "I'm not sure I have reason to stay," I responded, hoping she would give me a reason.

"Well, I just thought since you told Jessica and everything . . . that you'd . . . stay and try to work things out with her."

Her words tore through me like a knife through my heart. *Jessica.* "Look, I promised you that I would tell her. So I told her. You were right, if nothing else, she was owed an explanation. But I have no intention of spending any more time in her company."

"But you can't just drop a bombshell like that on her lap and disappear from her life," Alix argued.

I stood, feeling frustrated. "What is it you want from me?"

"I don't know," Alix said, equally frustrated. "Jessica hasn't had family in so long . . . she doesn't say anything, but I know it hurts her. And then you come along with so many answers and . . . she needs you, Valerie . . ."

Tears stung my eyes, and I fought them back. "You're asking too much, Alix."

"Why? She's your sister . . . you should—"

"The answer is no," I responded firmly.

"But why?"

"Because I'm in love with you!" I blurted out. "And you're still in love with her. And I couldn't bear to be constantly reminded of that fact."

She stared up at me, stunned.

Good job, Val. That was a hell of a performance. Way to be dramatic. I mentally sighed. But damn if it isn't the truth. "Alix—"

"No. It's okay," she said, standing. "You don't have to say another word." She made a grab for her shoes and walked to the door. At the doorway, she turned around. "Thanks for telling her," she said again. Then walked out.

I stared at the closed door, wondering what the hell had just happened. Resigned, I walked back into my bedroom and carefully shut the door.

Loki once again stared at me. "I really hope you're straight," I told the puppy. "'Cause women are just . . . insane."

Loki agreed.

♌

The next morning I stepped into the kitchen to find Aaron at the table, sipping a cup of coffee and scanning the Miami Herald. I walked over to pour myself a cup as well. "When did you get in? I didn't hear you."

"Late," he responded. "Or early, depending on your point of view." He winked at me and focused his attention back on the paper.

It's simply mind boggling. "You do realize that you were headed toward being fish food not twenty-four hours ago?"

He lowered the paper. "Which is why I've decided to live life to its fullest." He rose to put his empty coffee mug in the sink and turned to kiss my cheek, before reclaiming his seat. "Speaking of which, where's that hot little number you had in here last night? Still sleeping?"

I sat down across from him. "I wouldn't know."

Confusion branded his features as he gazed at me. "You mean she's gone already? Damn, sis, I didn't think you kicked them out of your bed that fast."

Patience was not something I'd awakened with that morning. However, I willed myself to breathe in and out and keep away from any homicidal thoughts. "I didn't kick her out. She was never *in* my bed."

"Straight?" he asked hopefully.

"Hardly."

He frowned. "Then what's the problem? Did you see those legs? Wow . . ." He grabbed at his chest. "Be still my heart."

Thankful that there were no sharp utensils within easy reach, I said, "I don't want to talk about it." Then to make my point, I changed the subject. "What time's your flight?"

"Anxious to get rid of me already?" he teased.

"Curious, as to when it is that I have to drive you to MIA."

"Never, actually. I've scheduled a ride with a limo service. You don't have to worry about a thing."

"You know, every time you tell me not to worry about something, the hairs on the back of my neck stand on end."

Aaron laughed soundly.

I nodded to the paper. "Are you done with that?"

He slid it across the table. "Since when do you care about Florida news?"

"Since right now," I told him, staring down at the newspaper with mild interest. At least it gave me something to do besides having to partake in conversation with my brother. I really wasn't in the mood. And yet my mouth couldn't keep quiet. "You didn't answer my question."

"Which one?"

"What time is your flight?" I repeated.

"It's in three hours," he replied, almost regretfully.

"So soon?" Yes he was a pain in the ass, but that didn't mean I wanted him gone already.

Aaron sat back in the chair, his arms across his chest. He was wearing a suit I'd never seen before. I didn't even want to think where he'd gotten the money to buy that. "Was that the girl you are *not* in love with?"

I frowned at his change of subject. This was how it always had been with us. We kept switching back and forth between subjects the other didn't want to discuss. It was like verbal ping pong. I had no idea how to answer his question. So I didn't.

He chuckled. "You should've seen your face last night. Your tongue hit the floor. Not that I blame you."

On second thought, it was probably a good thing he was leaving so soon. I wasn't sure he would live very long otherwise.

Aaron suddenly turned serious, as if it finally occurred to him that I was not the least bit amused by his teasing. "Hey, Val, I'm sorry. I'll stop." He paused for a moment. "You should tell me what the problem is, maybe I can help."

"You can't help."

"Well, then at least I can listen," he replied earnestly. "I know I can be a total asshole at times, but you can always count on me to lend a friendly ear."

Had I not been so depressed, I would've smiled. Then I sighed. "I lied to her. She hates me. The end."

"I see," he said. "Well, it's none of my business, but if she hates you so much, why did she show up at your apartment at one in the morning wearing *that*?"

I stared down at a random picture in the newspaper for a moment. I don't remember what picture it was, nor what the heading of the article read. I didn't look up when I said, "She just wanted to thank me for keeping a promise. She'd stopped by on her way home from some . . . 'thing.'"

"But, Valerie—"

"Look, she's Jessica Heart's best friend," I stated flatly. "I used her to get the money. She's not happy about it. Now drop it."

Aaron stared at me for a long moment, then he said, "So it's my fault."

I looked at him sadly. "It's not your fault. It's mine. I'm a total idiot."

"Ouch," he said. "You must be really upset. That's the first time I've seen your self-esteem waver." He was silent for a second. "Do you love her, Val?"

"Yes," I replied softly, too tired to deny it.

"Does she know?"

"She knows."

He seemed thoughtful. "Does she love you?"

I paused, remembering what Alix had told Jessica the day before. "She's never told me."

Aaron stood, then walked over to me and wrapped his arms around my shoulders, resting his cheek against my head. "I'm really sorry, sis. It may not seem like it, but I am."

I rose, too, so I could give him a proper hug. "Please stay out of trouble, Aaron," I said, holding him tightly. "I really have no interest in flying to Brazil."

He laughed softly. "I will do my best." He kissed my cheek and let go. "I should get going."

"Already?" I glanced at the time. It was almost noon.

"Yeah, I have some things to take care of before my flight," he announced, moving toward the door. He paused before leaving. "I love you, you know?"

"I know. I love you too."

He smiled brightly and winked. Then he was gone. And the emptiness that swept through me at that moment nearly knocked me off my feet.

Fighting back tears, I headed back into my room to get changed for work. It hit me at that moment that I'd finally gotten my life back.

And I didn't have the slightest idea what to do with it.

$\mathcal{S}$

"Two Gin and Tonics!"

"Rum runner!"

"Martini, sweet!"

Orders flew at me from all directions and I moved behind the bar to get them done as quickly as possible. I poured gin into two highball glasses filled with ice, then filled the contents with tonic water. "Two Gin and Tonics?" I yelled, over the music and the crowd. A pair of hands shot out from the masses of sweaty bodies and gave me the money in exchange for the drinks.

I moved on to the next order.

Time flew by as it always did on nights that were busy. I'd been at work since two in the afternoon and Whispers had gotten progressively busier.

I'd totally lost track of time, and though my shift was supposed to end at eleven, I was willing to stay there until closing. Anything to keep my mind off of my chaotic existence.

Eventually, the crowd at the bar dispersed slightly and things calmed down a bit, allowing people to sit on the stools and enjoy their drinks without getting pummeled by the masses.

"Hey beautiful."

I cringed internally at the sound of her voice, then turned around to gaze into the familiar brown eyes of Robin Graham. "Hey," I said, wishing someone would order a drink so I wouldn't have to stand there and hold a conversation with this woman.

"Rough night?" she inquired, leaning back against the bar so she could face me.

I shrugged noncommittally. Ever since her little kissing spree I'd made sure to keep a safe distance from her.

She pursed her lips and smiled. "I thought maybe you wanted to step out for a cup of coffee or something after your shift is over." She glanced at the neon blue clock on the wall. "Which will be in about fifteen minutes."

"No thanks," I said, hoping she'd get the hint. Though she never did.

A short guy with glasses approached the bar. "Can I have a Snowball please?"

Thankful for something to do, I moved about getting the ingredients. Gin . . . Anisette . . . light cream . . . shake with ice . . . strain into a cocktail glass. Voila. I placed the drink in front of him and grabbed the money from his hands. "Have a good night," I told him. Much to my dismay, Robin was still there. "Shouldn't you be tending bar or something?" Robin worked in a different section of the club. I tended the main bar, she took care of one of the smaller ones.

"I got off at ten-thirty," she said. "Want to get something to eat instead?" She smiled suggestively.

I rolled my eyes.

"Why do you hate me so much, Valerie?" she asked, seriously.

"Why?" I asked incredulously. "You left me! No explanation. No note. No 'Sorry to throw away the past year but I'm sick of Florida.'"

"You knew I was leaving. I asked you to come with me."

"And you knew I wasn't going to leave!"

She held up her hands. "Look, let's not discuss this here."

"I'm not discussing this anywhere, Robin," I said, hoping it would sink in this time. "It's over. It was over the moment you walked out the door." I glanced at the clock. Five more minutes. Suddenly I wanted nothing more than to get back to my apartment.

"Fine," she said gruffly. "Have a nice life." She stormed off and I breathed a sigh of relief. My replacement arrived a minute later and I headed home.

Back in my apartment I stared at the contents in my refrigerator. Finding nothing there, I turned to my freezer. I settled for a weird frozen lasagna concoction that I hoped wouldn't kill me. I was halfway through the meal when I heard a knock at the door.

"Who is it?" I called.

There was a pause, then, "It's Jessica."

I blinked a few times as I recovered from the shock, then threw the door open. Jessica was standing in my doorway, holding my birth certificate in one hand. She wasn't quite looking at me.

"Come in," I said.

She entered and looked around for a moment. I felt a bit embarrassed about the size of my apartment. It was small by normal standards. It must have looked like a cardboard box to her. Jessica stared down at the paper in her hand. "You were telling the truth," she said.

I closed the door and leaned my back against it. "I know."

She handed the certificate back to me. "I came to return it. You might need it . . . sometime."

"Thanks," I said, feeling incredibly awkward. "How'd you know where I lived?"

"Alix told me," she said. "I hope you don't mind my showing up like this. I came by earlier but you weren't here."

"I don't mind," I said, meaning it. "Would you like to sit down? Would you like a drink?"

"No thanks," she said.

An awkward silence settled between us. I had no idea what to say and I doubted she did either. I took a moment to study her. She looked like she hadn't slept much, but she looked beautiful as always. She was wearing a pair of blue jeans and a blue tank top. Her gaze wandered briefly over my apartment.

"I'm not entirely sure what to say," she admitted.

"Look, I just want you to know that I don't expect anything from you," I assured her, feeling like I had to for some reason. The last thing I wanted was for her to think any less of me than she already did. I don't know why, but that mattered to me. "I just thought that you deserved to know the truth."

"Plus Alix made you promise," she said.

I smiled sadly. "Yeah, that too."

She nodded. "Yeah, she told me she pretty much had to force you . . ."

So she knows I went to see Alix. I wondered what else Alix had told her.

"This is kind of . . . overwhelming," she said. "How long have you known?"

I shrugged. "A really long time, actually. It's been a subject of discussion around my house for a long time."

"Does anyone else know?"

I thought about it. "My brother, Alix . . . That's about it. It's never been anyone's intention to make it public knowledge."

"Why not?"

I shifted uncomfortably. "Because, Jessica, you're their daughter. They gave you up 'cause they knew you'd have a better life with the Hearts than with them. Mom was only seventeen."

"I'm sure the twenty million dollars didn't hinder the decision any," she said, more than a little bitterly.

This I couldn't argue with. "Look, I'm not going to defend them. It's not my place to do so."

She nodded, looking a bit flustered. "Listen, I actually came to talk to you about Alix."

I stared at her expectantly, not sure where she was going with this. Was she going to yell at me for seeing her after I'd promised I wouldn't?

"I wanted to let you know that I don't want to intervene in your relationship," she said. "And I'm sorry that I used the money as collateral for doing so. Whether or not you see her shouldn't be up to me. And I know you know that, but I wanted you to know that I . . . I'm sorry . . . for attempting to blackmail you like that. It wasn't . . . right."

To say I was surprised was putting it mildly. "You had a right to be concerned. I know I would've been had the roles been reversed."

She nodded.

"You came all the way over here to tell me that?" I asked softly.

"And to give you that back." She motioned to the paper in my hand. "Anyway, I better be going."

I opened the door so she could pass through.

"Thanks for telling me," she said sincerely, yet sadly at the same time.

I simply nodded and watched her walk away. I turned back to my empty apartment and wondered how it was possible to have so many important people in my life . . . and yet be totally alone . . .

Chapter 10

Saturday morning found me sitting on my couch, wearing pajamas and a frown, staring thoughtfully at the portrait of Alix I had drawn. The light from the window cast a soft shadow across the canvas.

Folding my arms, I slouched down further on the soft cushions, my legs resting comfortably on the coffee table. "What do you think I should do with it?" I asked the slumbering dog beside me. Loki softly snored in reply. I nodded as if she'd suggested something wise. "I wouldn't mind hanging it over my bed . . . but I think that's hardly appropriate given the circumstances."

Shaking my head, I started flipping through the channels on TV. I stopped briefly at the Home Shopping Network, just to verify that indeed I did not want what they were selling, then resumed my surfing. As I was about to give up and watch *Labyrinth* for the millionth time, I found an interesting documentary on the Travel Channel. *This will do.* I dropped the remote beside me on the couch and settled in.

I managed to concentrate on the thing about Egypt for about five minutes before my gaze casually drifted back to the canvas on the easel. "Maybe I should just give it to her?"

Glancing at Loki, I quirked a brow. "What do you think?" Getting no response from the dog, I stared at the portrait. "Well, that's settled."

A commercial for American Airlines caught my attention and I was reminded of the flight I had not yet booked.

Grabbing for the phone, I silently sighed. *Let's do this.*

✄

"Quitting?" Dean Jacobs said the word as if he'd never heard it before in his life. His dark brows narrowed and his forehead wrinkled in the process. Brown eyes bore into mine. I wasn't sure if he was going to explode in rage or start laughing hysterically.

I braced myself for either. "I'm leaving town."

"For good?"

A shrug was all I allowed. Truthfully, I didn't have an exact plan of action. All I knew is that I had to get out. Get away from long lost sisters and would-be girlfriends and mistakes and regrets and . . . pain. Maybe if I changed my address, if I changed myself, I could start everything over again, without the emotional baggage. Somewhere in the back of my mind I knew this was impossible, but I was determined to at least spare Alix the hurt of ever having to see me again.

You mean, spare you the hurt of ever seeing her again.

I pushed the thought away and focused instead on my conversation with Dean.

"Valerie, you're the best bartender I've got," he said, running a frustrated hand through his graying black hair. "Hell, you're the best bartender anyone's got."

Twenty-one years on earth and my greatest accomplishment was mixing liquor. I was flattered.

He sighed loudly, if a bit dramatically, and sat back on his chair. He started clicking the pen in his hand and I had to remind myself several times that though a karate chop to his head would rid me of the misery, it would also land me in jail.

"So where are you going?" he inquired.

"New York," I replied, as if I had it all figured out.

"Got something special there?"

"Not exactly." *More like I'm leaving something special here.* "Just need a change of scenery is all."

He scratched the back of his neck with the pen and nodded thought-fully. "Running away from the world, eh?"

The world. "Something like that," I answered, shifting slightly in my seat.

He nodded again and clicked away at the pen. An eternity seemed to pass before he placed the pen down on the desk and stretched out his hand. "It was a pleasure working with you, Valerie. If you ever change your mind about never coming back, know that you'll always have a place here."

I shook his hand and rose as well. "Would you like me to work the next two weeks until you find somebody else?"

"When were you hoping on leaving?"

"As soon as possible," I replied, honestly.

"Then, no. I've got someone who can cover your shift." He said this almost regretfully, and I instantly thought of Robin.

"Thanks for everything, Dean," I said. Then I walked out of the office and through the familiar corridors of the club. I had wanted to not look around, to pretend that it didn't hurt me, even a little, to be leaving everything behind. But in the end, I ended up heading over to the bar—to *my* bar—for one last drink.

I ordered my usual Corona and sat in a booth in a corner, away from everything.

"This seat taken?"

I hesitated.

"I heard you were leaving," Robin said, taking the seat across from me without waiting for permission.

"Good news travels fast," I commented dryly.

"Yeah, well, Dean called me in after you left. Looks like I'm taking over your shift." When I didn't answer, she continued. "Pretty ironic, don't you think?"

I managed a shrug. When Robin had left, I'd taken over her shift. Seemed like the tables had turned once again.

She was silent for all of three seconds. "So why are you leaving?"

Silence was my response.

Robin smiled, nodding knowingly. "Relationship issues, huh?"

Was it written on my damn forehead? I glanced at her without commenting but I'm sure the look on my face was all the confirmation she needed.

"So are you keeping the apartment here?"

"For now."

"What are you doing with all your stuff?"

I caught her gaze. "What is it you want, Robin?"

She paused, then took a deep breath. "Look, I just wanted to apologize for . . . you know, for kissing you that night."

"Oh, so you admit that it was all you?"

Robin nodded. "I admit, I got carried away. I thought about you a lot while I was gone. You were the reason I came back, actually." Her gaze was fixed on a spot on the table.

I stared at the label on the bottle before me.

"I didn't want you to leave without at least hearing my apology," she continued. "I had way too much to drink that night. I was way out of line. I'm sorry."

I nodded.

"So, where are you going?"

I hesitated a moment, then realized I had nothing to lose by telling her. "New York. Aaron has that apartment there he never uses."

"Ah, yes, I remember it well." Her voice was filled with mirth as she winked at me.

I almost smiled, but it proved too much effort. I drank the last of my beer and rose. "Take care of yourself, Robin."

And I left Whispers without looking back.

ℒ

At my apartment, I sat in bed with a yellow legal pad on my lap. An empty page stared up at me, and I didn't doubt its fate would match that of his companions. I glanced wearily at the pile of crumpled paper on the bed beside me.

"A poet, I am not," I informed Loki. "Can you write this for me?" When the puppy made no effort to grab the pen from me, I glanced back down at the page. "I shouldn't even leave her a note. What could I possibly tell her that she would want to hear?"

Still, I felt I had to do this. It didn't even have to be long. A sentence would do. *Short and sweet. Just tell her how you feel.* I snorted. *That'd take a novel.*

Pen to paper, I began to scribble . . .

> *Alix,*
> *Should I become famous someday, you can sell this on eBay . . .*

Right. Another crumpled sheet joined the others.
I tried again.

> *Alix,*
> *This is a gift from the heart*

Um, no.

> *Alix,*
> *I'm leaving for New York and I'm never coming back*

Not at all dramatic . . .

> *Dear Alix,*
> *I thought you might like to have this. I thought it would be selfish of me to keep it, seeing as I've already got the memory of you to keep me warm at night*

Ha! She'll burn it . . . I tapped the pen against my forehead. *Think Alix. She hates corny. Whatever you write . . . it's gotta be . . .*

I hesitated a moment, then scribbled something fast. I folded the paper in half before I had a chance to change my mind. *Here goes nothing.*

Chapter 11

It didn't take me very long to pack all my stuff, seeing as I planned on leaving most of it behind. Aaron's apartment was fully furnished and all I really needed to take with me were the bare necessities of life (CD's, movies, etc).

I struck a deal with my landlord. His daughter needed a car for college and since I didn't know what to do with mine, I agreed to give it to him in exchange for a couple months' rent. I figured that would be enough time for me to decide whether I wanted to keep the apartment in Florida or get rid of it. He also agreed to mail me the few boxes I had to leave behind. As an added bonus, his daughter also offered to drive me to the airport in her brand new car.

Seemed fair enough to me.

And then the fateful day was upon me and I sat in my car a few hours before my flight, trying to convince myself to drive.

Finally, I turned the ignition. Then I sat back without moving the car.

"Drop off the picture and leave," I said to myself. "No knocking. Definitely no knocking." Nodding, I pulled out of the apartment's parking lot and headed toward Baldwin.

"Okay," I said out loud. "I can't just leave it against her door. What if someone steals it?" I paused. "So I'll knock and then I'll run. But if she sees me running, that would be embarrassing." I paused again. "So maybe I'll just leave it against the door."

By the time I parked the car, I still hadn't decided what I was going to do exactly. After hesitating for a few moments, I grabbed the portrait and headed toward Alix's Hall.

This wasn't so difficult when I'd pictured it in my head. I waited by the door about ten minutes until someone was kind enough to leave the building so that I could step inside. *Please be home, but don't come out.* As I neared her door, I noticed it was open. I stopped in my tracks, suddenly at a crossroads.

If she's there, I'll feel stupid. If she's there with company, I'll feel even stupider. If I just leave, I'll regret it. Glad I didn't choose to major in decision-making.

A minute passed. Maybe two.

Finally, I threw one foot forward and headed toward the open door. I knew Alix wasn't inside before I even reached the doorway. The room, however, wasn't void of human life.

"Uh, hi," I said, standing awkwardly at the threshold.

A head popped up from behind an open book and light brown eyes focused in my direction. "Can I help you?"

I was glad I'd thought to cover the canvas. "I just wanted to drop this off for Alix."

She nodded toward Alix's side of the room. "Leave it wherever." Her gaze followed me as I crossed the room to place the picture on Alix's bed. "Have we met before?"

I turned to her. "Uh, no, I don't think so. I'm Valerie."

An eyebrow shot upward. "*You're* Valerie," she said incredulously. "Not at all how I pictured you." She stretched out her hand. "I'm Nicole. Alix's roommate."

"Nice to meet you," I replied politely, shaking her hand. "I should get going."

"Are you sure you don't want to wait for her? She should be back any second. Her class ended about fifteen minutes ago."

I felt my heart skip a beat. "No, thanks. I really must get going."

She nodded as if she'd been expecting that answer. "I'll make sure she gets your gift."

I thanked her and headed out of the dorm room as quickly as possible. Back in my car, I breathed a sigh of relief. I sat there for a few minutes, trying to get a hold of my emotions.

I don't know how long I sat there, staring off into space. The time on my watch read 1:20 and my flight was at four o'clock. I had to get going if I was going to make it in time.

Pulling out of the parking lot, I glanced wearily at the reflection in the rearview mirror. I could see part of Alix's building as it grew smaller and smaller and then disappeared altogether.

I wondered if that's how love worked. If distance could make it disappear all together. I glanced at the reflection once more . . . and then sped up.

Part III

Alix & Valerie

Chapter 1
Alix

Head-banging is a surefire way to get a headache. I learned this lesson well on my way home from my Voice III class, as I got a bit carried away listening to Aerosmith's "Dude (Looks Like A Lady)." Hey, it's not my fault the lyrics are so compelling.

"Any messages?" I asked my roommate, upon entering my lovely boudoir. I was trying desperately not to think about anything meaningful. So far, I'd succeeded admirably. That is, until I noticed the object on my bed. "What's that?"

"Valerie dropped it off," Nicole answered casually, though I could tell by her tone that she was dying to know what it was.

At the sound of Valerie's name, I whirled around to face my roommate. "Valerie? When was this?"

"She left about ten minutes ago," Nicole responded, the book she'd been reading now lay open on her chest. I had her full attention. "I told her to wait for you, but she bolted."

"Huh." I turned back to my bed, or more specifically the item thereon, and tried to keep a frown off my face. I doubt I succeeded. *She bolted. Of course. What'd you expect the way you walked out of her apartment the last time.* I bit my lip.

"Are you going to see what it is?" Nicole asked, with a hint of impatience.

"Huh? Oh. Right." I walked over and grabbed a hold of the black sheet covering the object and pulled it off. For a moment, I was speechless.

Nicole was looking over my shoulder a second later. "Oh, wow. Did you pose for that?"

I knew I was blushing furiously. I was about to answer her, when I noticed the yellow piece of paper tacked to the corner of the canvas. I pulled it out and unfolded it.

Alix,
I meant what I said the other night. I hope, if nothing else,
you at least believe that.
Love, Valerie

"What did she say the other night?" Nicole asked.

It was then I realized she was reading over my shoulder. I folded the note and stared at the drawing of me for a moment. There were various emotions surging through my heart at that moment, none of which I could possibly understand fully. So instead of trying to analyze the tempest in my brain, I headed for the door.

"I'll be back," I said and slammed the door behind me, leaving a very curious Nicole behind.

ℋ

"Alix."

"Huh?"

"You're making me dizzy."

I stopped mid-pace and smiled apologetically at Jessica. Then went ahead and took a seat on one of the bean bag chairs she had randomly strewn about the place. If you must know, I chose the black one. "So, what do you think?"

"About?"

"The ozone layer," I replied dryly.

Jessica quirked a brow in my direction. She was sitting on the floor, leaning against the back of her couch. I don't know why she didn't just sit on it. "I suppose I like it."

I sent her what I hoped was a dirty look. "Focus," I instructed. "Valerie. Alix. Confusion. Help."

Jessica shifted uncomfortably. "I really don't think I'm the one you should be talking to about this."

Still sitting, I used my legs and feet to drag myself closer to her. This proved to be harder than I originally intended, but it's amazing what one won't do just to keep from having to get up. Finally, I was sitting in front of her. "Just tell me . . . what do you think I should do?"

She was silent for a long while. Finally, she met my gaze. "I think you should follow your heart."

I blinked, stood up, and resumed my pacing. "Follow my heart? My heart is stationary, Jessica. It goes nowhere. How am I supposed to follow it?" I ran both hands through my hair in an attempt to rein in my frustration. When that didn't help, I stopped. "Okay. I'll just do this the rational way." I walked to Jessica's desk and grabbed a piece of paper and a pen.

"What are you doing?"

A moment later, I was back in the bean bag chair. "I'm going to make a list of pros and cons." I said this very matter-of-factly, then shrugged. "I saw it on *Friends*. You know when Ross . . . nevermind." I drew a line down the middle of the page and labeled each side accordingly.

Jessica watched me for about five seconds. "Alix. Is this really necessary?"

"Well, you're not helping any," I replied pointedly. "If you would give me some concrete advice then maybe I wouldn't have to resort to this kind of behavior."

She grabbed the paper and the pen away from me and put it out of my reach. "Alix, listen to me. You're going to take a deep breath and then you're going to get back down from Cloud Aerosmith."

I took a deep breath, but was a bit more hesitant to give up my lovely apartment on Cloud A. It had a beautiful view. And Cloud 9 was within drifting distance. "All right. I'm calm. I'm grounded. Lay it on me."

"Close your eyes," she instructed, grabbing a hold of my hands.

I frowned slightly, then complied. "Is this some kind of guided meditation? 'Cause I tend to have trouble reaching that happy place—"

"Alix . . ."

"Sorry. Okay." I kept my eyes closed.

"Now. Do you want to be with Valerie? Yes or no."

I was about to protest but she interrupted me.

"Yes or no, Al. C'mon."

I sighed. "Yes."

She let go of my hands, and I opened my eyes. "Well, there you go," she said, as if everything was incredibly obvious.

I bit my lip thoughtfully. And I guessed it was.

&

I believe, and I'm adamant about this, that dresses and high heels cloud the mind. Because I was definitely *not* thinking clearly when I'd shown up at her apartment wearing the atrocious attire Jessica had stuck me in. Had I been thinking clearly, I would've gone home to change, and then visited her. Then perhaps I wouldn't have walked out of her apartment the moment she put the words "love" and "you" in the same sentence and directed them toward me.

This is what I was thinking while I stared at the number 413 on Valerie's door. Daydreaming is the most sincere form of procrastination.

I pushed a strand of hair out of my eyes and knocked on the door. Several times. I kicked it once. I even did the hokey pokey and still nothing.

It didn't immediately occur to me that she might not be home.

Not feeling patient enough to sit around and wait for her, I went straight for plan B.

On my walk to Whispers I went over what I'd decided. I could give us another shot. But we needed ground rules. Lots of ground rules. Perhaps maybe some underground rules to go with the ground rules.

I walked into the club feeling confident. And a bit excited because I'd finally come to a decision I could live with. We'd just take it slow. Very slow. So slow in fact, that it would give off the illusion that we were going backwards instead of forwards.

I'd expected to find Valerie at the bar, but she wasn't there. The club was relatively empty, and scanning the crowd proved simple, but fruitless.

"Can I get you something?"

I turned to the bartender. "Nothing to drink thanks," I said. Before she had a chance to move away, I added, "But, uh, can you tell me when Valerie is working next?"

The woman studied me for a moment, her eyes narrowing. She looked vaguely familiar though I couldn't really place her. "Valerie quit a few days ago."

I'm sure I did a double-take. "What?"

She nodded. "Sorry to say."

I placed my hands firmly on the bar top, trying desperately to hang on to my fleeting self-control. "Why did she quit? Did she get a better job somewhere else?"

"She was leaving for New York."

I blinked a few times as if by clearing my vision I could somehow clear my hearing as well. Or at least, change what I'd just heard into something that . . . Suddenly, her words hit home. "*What?*" This I nearly yelled.

Brown eyes regarded me curiously. "Are you a friend of Val's?"

Biting back a sarcastic remark, I said, "Something like that. Do you know when she was planning to leave?"

"Not a clue. Last I talked to her was a few days ago, but I'd bet on anything she's gone by now."

I looked around, feeling desperate. *No crying. No crying.* "Do you know where in New York she was going?"

I could tell by the way she looked at me that she had an answer but it didn't appear like she was going to give it to me.

"Please," I said, noting the touch of desperation in my voice. I tried not to cringe at this. "It's really important."

The woman stared at me for a second longer, then grabbed a napkin and pen from under the bar and wrote something down. "Her brother's apartment in New York. That's where she told me she was going to stay." She hesitated, then handed it over.

"Thank you," I said. Had there not been a counter between us, I would've hugged the woman. "I really appreciate this."

She nodded. "No problem."

As I left the club, it didn't even occur to me to wonder how this woman knew the address by heart.

♉

"I need to go to New York," I announced, throwing open the door to Jessica's room without bothering to knock.

"Alix!" Jessica and Mathew chorused.

"Whoops." I did an immediate U-turn and headed out into the hall. *This is not shaping up to be a good day.* I tried not to shudder.

A couple of minutes later, the door opened and Jessica was standing there, dressed and a little annoyed.

"Sorry," I said, crossing into the room. "You should really put a sock on the door or something. Where's Mathew?"

"Shower."

I decided that I should start talking before Jessica killed me. "I need to go to New York."

"Like . . . for your birthday?"

"No, I mean, I need to go to New York *now*. Valerie's gone."

That got her attention. "What?"

"Gone," I repeated. "As in, no longer here. As in, now entirely elsewhere."

Jessica shook her head. "And you want to do what? Follow her to New York? Stand in the middle of Times Square shouting her name? Pass out flyers with her picture on them?"

I smiled at the thought, then dug in my pocket and came up with the napkin. "I know where she's staying. Detective work pays off."

Jessica crossed the room to sit at the edge of the waterbed. "Alix, this is crazy."

Mathew walked out of the bathroom at that moment, dressed elegantly in a navy blue bathrobe. "Hey, Al. Excellent timing."

"You know I do my best," I said, giving him my most charming smile.

He smiled. "What's going on?"

"She wants to follow Valerie to New York," Jessica told him.

Suddenly, I felt like I was eleven years old and asking my parents for permission to go on a school trip.

"What about school?" Mathew asked.

I frowned at both of them. They'd make wonderful parents some day, I was just glad they weren't mine. "Okay, let me put it another way. I'm *going* to New York."

Mathew and Jessica exchanged a look.

Then Jessica said, "We're coming with you."

"That's really not necessary," I argued. "I'm perfectly capable of taking care of myself."

They exchanged another look, and I started to get annoyed.

Impatiently, I folded my arms. "Are you going to help me or am I going to have to prostitute myself on the streets of Ft. Lauderdale in exchange for a plane ticket?"

℘

The next day I sat impatiently in the terminal waiting for Jessica who had dropped me off and said she'd "be right back." Half an hour later, she was still not back and I was getting annoyed. But then, there she was, running in my direction. What I wasn't counting on was the bald-headed girl running behind her.

Rising to my feet, I frowned as they reached me. I looked at Jade. "What are you doing here?" I noticed then that she was dragging along a suitcase.

"I'm going with you," Jade said, somewhat gleefully, and waved a boarding pass in the air. She motioned to Jessica with her head. "She made the arrangements."

Jessica nodded. "Oh, and—" She took out her wallet. "Credit cards. You should only need one but just in case."

She handed over like five of them. I arched an eyebrow as I sorted through them. "Bloomingdale's?"

"You never know."

Why were my friends insane? I stuck the credit cards in my wallet. "Is that it, Mom?"

"Do you have cash on you?"

I nodded. "Stop worrying."

She hugged me tightly. "Call the second you get there. And be careful."

It was a good thing I hadn't decided to go away to college. I wasn't entirely sure she'd be able to handle it. "I'll be in touch," I assured her.

Eventually, Jade and I managed to make our way down to the gate, where passengers were already boarding.

Half an hour later, we were safely in the air. Or at least, I hoped it was safely.

"So what are you going to do once you track Valerie down?"

"I have no idea," I said. "But I'm sure I can wing it."

"Are you sure you want to do this?"

I glanced at her. "Well, it's a little late now."

"It's never too late."

I frowned. "Do you think this is a bad idea?"

She shrugged. "What I think doesn't matter. Love, romance, the whole bit is a load of bollocks, if you ask me. So I wouldn't go by what I think." She smiled crookedly. "But truthfully, this whole thing, you flying off to New York to find her, it's corny as hell but I think it's kind of cool. And not just because I get to tag along. Love kind of suits you. Weirdly enough."

"Thanks," I said, and suddenly felt uneasy. Ever since I'd found out about Valerie leaving the only thing I could think about was running after her. But what if she didn't want me to run after her? What if she had someone else there?

Jade touched my arm gently. "Are you okay?"

"I have no idea," I responded. "But I guess we'll find out."

Chapter 2
still Alix

The plane managed to land without crashing, and for that I was thankful. We grabbed a cab from Newark Airport to New York and instructed the driver to deposit us at a nice hotel. He drove around for a while, trying to decide on which hotel would be best suited for our needs. I thought it was sweet of him to take the time to do that.

He finally settled on the Hilton. Or the Hyatt. It was one of those "H" names. Maybe it was the Holiday Inn. I was way too preoccupied to notice.

Our suite consisted of adjoining rooms and as I stood there pacing around my section, Jade entered. "So, what's the plan? Or are we just winging it?"

I fell back on the bed and stared up at the ceiling for a few moments before answering. "I guess I just show up."

Jade sat down on the bed beside me. "Don't you think she's going to find this just a wee bit obsessive?"

"So what's your suggestion? That I parade aimlessly around Manhattan in the off-chance that I'll bump into her somewhere, and then say, 'Gee, fancy meeting you here'?"

Jade grinned. "You're right. Now matter what you do, it's going to seem obsessive." She patted my knee.

"Thanks."

"Any time."

"So what are you going to do tonight?"

Jade appeared surprised. She stood, then walked to the window, spreading her arms toward the view outside. "Alix, look around. This is New York! What am I *not* going to do tonight."

I grinned at Jade's enthusiasm. I wished I could share in the excitement, but I'd barely even noticed the view. "I'm going to shower . . . and then . . . I'm going to find Valerie."

Jade stared at me, shaking her head. "My friend, you've got more balls than the entire NBA."

I chose to take that as a compliment.

ॐ

The cab dropped me off across the street from the address the woman at Whispers had given me. It hadn't occurred to me to wonder if it was the right address. That is, until I heard the taxi screech away. I found myself standing alone in the middle of the sidewalk, staring up at an unfamiliar building, wondering how the hell I'd gotten there.

I stood there for a long moment, trying to rehearse the speech I'd been rewriting over and over in my mind.

Across the street, a figure caught my eye. I frowned suddenly, wondering why I felt compelled to stare at her. It looked like Valerie . . . but it couldn't be . . . Valerie didn't have dark hair . . .

The figure turned into the building.

Oh . . . God . . .

I sprinted across the street, not caring if I got run over on the way there. Fortunately, or perhaps unfortunately depending on how things turned out, I made it safely to the other side. Once inside the building, I looked around until I caught a flash of black hair disappear around the corner. I dashed in that direction, rounded the corner, and found myself face to face with Valerie.

For what seemed like ages, neither of us said anything. She was looking at me as though she couldn't believe she was really seeing me. And I was looking at her like . . . Well, I'm not sure how I was looking at her, but I'm sure she could tell you. Finally, I broke the silence. "I bet you're wondering what I'm doing here . . ."

Valerie's face was unreadable as always. "Actually I was wondering if you'd noticed that you're in an elevator."

I blinked a few times, then saw the doors to the elevator swoosh closed and felt the box-object-of-death begin its ascent. I swallowed, leaning back against the wall and holding on for dear life. *Please don't let me die. Please don't let me die.*

Bing!

I shut my eyes and screamed, "Oh shit, we're going to die!"

The doors swooshed open.

"My floor," Valerie announced.

I peered out through one eye, then the other. "Oh." With as much dignity as I could muster, I stepped out into the hall.

Silently, I followed Valerie down the dimly lit corridor, focusing intently on the dark blue carpet at my feet.

Once inside the apartment, we stared awkwardly at one another.

"Okay, *now* I'm wondering why you're here," Valerie said.

I took a deep breath. "And what an excellent question that is. It's a funny story, really. I went to see you and you weren't home. So I went to Whispers and I was informed of your departure. And I thought, 'Hey, I've always wanted to see New York in the fall.' So, here I am."

"And you just happened to be walking by this building?"

"Uh . . ." I ran a hand through my hair nervously. "Well, someone might have clued me in as to where you were staying . . ."

Valerie sighed. "Alix, why are you here?"

"I wanted to thank you for the picture."

"That's what you flew all the way here to tell me?"

"No," I admitted, suddenly wishing she'd offered me a drink. "I didn't want things to end how they did."

"So how did you want them to end?"

I stared at her, trying to put my thoughts into words somehow. "Well, . . . you know . . . without the . . . um . . . I didn't want them to end. Not really. Not with this kind of finality."

Her expression remained impassive but I could swear she looked surprised for a second. "What are you trying to say?"

Instead of answering, I said, "When did you dye your hair?"

She didn't seem surprised by the change in conversation. "Yesterday, the second I got here. I never felt quite right as a blonde."

She didn't ask if I liked it, so I didn't say anything. But I liked it a lot. *And here I'd thought she couldn't get any hotter*. I cleared my throat. I knew I had to answer her question but now my actions were starting to seem crazy. Obsessive, even. What *was* I doing there?

"Would you like to get something to eat?" Valerie suggested, much to my surprise.

I was sure I'd forgotten to pack my appetite when I'd left Florida but I could use the time to think of what to say. "Sure." I glanced nervously at the door. "But could we maybe take the stairs this time?"

She nodded and turned toward the door, but I could've sworn I saw a ghost of a smile pass across her lips.

∅

We ended up at a pizzeria in Greenwich Village. I sat down at a table and looked around. There were about seven tables lined up against the wall. Then some walking space between the table and the counter where one ordered. That was about it. I mostly sat there and concentrated on breathing.

Outside, a couple of men holding hands passed by. I raised an eyebrow. *Guess we're not in Kansas anymore.*

Valerie joined me at the table soon after and placed a large pepperoni pizza between us. I entertained ridiculous thoughts. I imagined that this steaming pile of melted cheese was the only thing keeping us apart. Like the Great Wall of China, only edible. And that if we managed to eat it all, everything would be fine.

Too bad I wasn't hungry.

I grabbed the smallest slice. Then, lazily picked off the pepperoni.

Valerie sat there silently for as long as she could. Then asked the inevitable, "I thought you said you liked pepperoni pizza?"

I looked up at her, and said quite seriously, "I love it." Then picked off the last remaining piece.

We ate silently. Well, she ate silently. I just sat there staring down at the slice of pizza and wishing it would get up and dance so I'd have something to distract me from the situation at hand. But, it too, sat silently. And I knew that if one of us didn't say something soon, I'd go insane.

"You never answered my question," Valerie said softly.

"I know," I said, daring to look up at her. It amazed me how different she looked with dark hair. It made her eyes look bluer; more intense. I looked away. "I'm not exactly sure why I'm here."

Valerie didn't respond, but I noticed she'd stopped eating.

"I couldn't just let you run off like that," I continued. "A girl needs closure."

"Closure?" Valerie repeated, her eyebrows raised.

"Yes." I nodded. "A hundred years from now—" I paused to rethink this. "I'll be a hundred and twenty and quite possibly dead. Scratch that." I shrugged. "I just don't want to look back on this and wonder what-if. I figured that regardless of what happens from here on end, at least I'll *know.*"

"And what do you want to happen?" Valerie asked softly.

Uhh . . . "I'm not sure. What do you want to happen?"

"I don't know."

Glad we got that settled.

"Not hungry?" Valerie asked, glancing at my plate.

"I can't eat when I'm nervous," I admitted.

She didn't respond to that. Instead, she stood. "Ready?"

I nodded and followed her outside. I had no idea where we were exactly, but I assumed that Valerie did. At least, I hoped she did.

"How long are you staying?" Valerie asked.

"As long as it takes," I responded.

This answer caused her to look at me briefly, then she turned her attention back to the view ahead.

"Where are we going?" I asked.

"Nowhere in particular," she said. "I just like to walk."

I almost smiled, remembering the night we'd met. I suddenly felt nostalgic.

Since neither of us were talking, I focused instead on the scenery around me. I have one word to describe it all: stores. Granted, that's not an adjective. But trust me, it applies here. If I'd liked shopping—which I didn't—I would've been in heaven. As it happened though, I merely found it interesting. We passed by countless shops selling everything from leather whips to incense and candles. I lost count of how many Starbucks I saw. Although, we could've been going around the same exact block for all I knew. I hated feeling like a tourist.

"What's your full name?" I found myself asking.

"What?" She seemed taken aback.

I shrugged, keeping my gaze on the ground. "Well, I figured that if we're starting over, then we may as well redo the introductions."

Valerie stopped walking. "Start over?"

I turned to face her and somehow managed to meet her gaze. "Would you like to?"

Her eyes studied mine intently. "What are you saying?"

"You. Me. Us. Start over." I grinned awkwardly. "I thought I was pretty clear."

Valerie didn't respond. I had no idea what she was thinking.

"Look, I'm not saying it's going to be easy . . . but I'm willing to give it a shot."

"Give what a shot?" Valerie asked uncertainly.

"*Us.*" I was getting impatient. "I want to give us a second chance. You know, minus all the lying and deceiving and stuff."

"Why would you want to do this?"

I locked our gazes. "Because losing you is not an option."

Instead of responding, she started walking. I sighed, then followed after her. She wasn't speaking and I had no idea what else to say, so I just walked beside her, wishing for telepathic abilities just so I'd know what she was thinking.

I have no idea how long we walked, but eventually we found ourselves back in Valerie's apartment. By this time, I was beginning to panic.

"Alix, you shouldn't be here," were her first words to me.

I swallowed back my fear. It would've been so much easier to just walk out the door and return to the hotel room. I could've been back in Florida the next morning, working on ways to write Valerie out of my life forever.

Anything would've been easier than standing there, facing the possibility of rejection. But stand there I did.

"Shouldn't be where?" I asked. "In New York, or in your apartment?"

Valerie looked at me sadly. We were both standing in the middle of the living room. She was leaning against the side of the couch. I was staring down at the white carpet, awkwardly contemplating the absence of color. "You shouldn't have followed me out here."

"It's too late for that. I'm here."

"Alix, you deserve so much better than me. You deserve to be with someone . . . normal."

"Normal?" I asked, frowning. "Valerie, name *one* thing that's normal about me?"

"That's not the point."

"So what's the point?"

Valerie clenched her jaw. "I'm not good for you."

I shook my head, walked to her, and grabbed her hand. I led her around the couch and sat her down. "Just listen to me for a moment. Before you came along, I had spent the past seven years of my life lusting after my straight best friend. *That* wasn't good for me. I spent all of that time being totally bitter and angry at the world. I didn't look at other people. I didn't go out with other people. I didn't even think about other people. *None of that* was good for me.

"But then you came along, and all of a sudden I'm fainting in thunderstorms and jumping on airplanes and riding on elevators. Do you think I would've done any of those things if I didn't think you were worth it?"

She opened her mouth to respond, but nothing came out.

"Exactly," I agreed, hoping I'd made my point. "So what do you say?"

Valerie stared up at me for a long moment, her face betraying nothing. Finally, she rose to her feet and stretched out her hand. "Valerie Anne Michaels, nice to meet you."

I grinned brightly, my body flooding with relief. "Alix T. Morris."

"What's the 'T' stand for?"

I snorted. "It stands for 'There's no way in Hell you're ever going to know.'"

Valerie smiled. "So what happens now?"

"This is where you ask me out on a date." Wow. New York sure brought out the feistiness in me. I kind of liked it.

"Are you free tomorrow?"

"No, sorry. I'm booked solid. Interviews, photo shoots, you know how it is."

Valerie smiled. "How about we meet here . . . around two?"

"It's a date." I smiled, then headed for the door. "See you then."

I left, then, all the while thinking that maybe that night and everything before that night had been nothing but a dream. That I'd wake up, days before the wedding, and think only of the laborious tasks still ahead. And then at some point, sometime between the pink dresses and the stripper, I'd remember that I'd had a silly dream involving Jessica's long lost sister. And I'd tell Jessica all about it and she would laugh as she straightened out the large pink bow at the back of my dress. We would both giggle at how ridiculous the dream was. And then I'd stand in front of the mirror and think how ridiculous I looked. And it wouldn't occur to me to realize how ridiculous life is sometimes and how seriously we take it.

Because in spite of everything that had transpired in the past few hours, in the past few days, in the past few weeks . . . there was only one thought running around in my mind as I headed out of Valerie's apartment.

I'd have to start counting the dates all over again.

Chapter 3
Valerie

I couldn't sleep. I kept listening to the DJ on the radio announce song after song, in that resigned, monotone voice reserved for the graveyard shift. I kept glancing at the clock, daring time to pass. The patterns on the ceiling began to form constellations only I could see. I wondered if this was insomnia.

"Why did I agree to start over with her?" I asked the air. "It's never going to work."

Loki lifted her head and I frowned as I listened intently for a moment. There it was again. Definitely a knock. "Who the hell . . . ?" I rolled out of bed and grumpily made my way across the apartment, muttering incoherent things under my breath. Loki followed behind me, suddenly excited by the prospect of a guest.

At the door, I hesitated. "Who is it?"

"It's the bloody Tooth Fairy, open up."

I rolled my eyes and opened the door. "Do you have any idea what time it is?"

Jade entered the apartment and shrugged. "Three? It's not like you were sleeping any."

I shut the door and leaned against it. "How do you know I wasn't sleeping?"

"Just a hunch," she responded, looking around. "Nice pad."

"It's my brother's," I answered.

"Doesn't seem like he was all that tight for money."

The comment stung for a variety of reasons, none of which I wanted to particularly think about at that moment. So, I decided to change the subject. Or at least, get to the point. "So what can I do for you, Jade?"

"I wanted to make sure we're even."

"We're even."

Jade nodded, taking a seat on the couch. I hesitated only a moment before sitting across from her on the loveseat.

"She's really intent on making things work out with you two," Jade told me. "We just want to make sure that she's not going to get hurt again."

"We?" I wasn't entirely sure where this was going but it was starting to sound like something I wouldn't like.

"Jessica and I."

"So she sent you here to supervise?" I asked, my jaw tightening.

Jade shook her head. "Look, I want nothing more than to see you and Alix work out."

"And Jessica? What does she want?"

Jade looked confused for a moment. "She wants to see Alix happy."

I stood, unable to sit still any longer. "Happy without me."

"You and I both know that's not true," Jade argued, but I could hear the uncertainty in her voice.

Taking a deep breath, I sat back down. "Be honest with me, Jade. Jessica doesn't want Alix to end up with me, does she?"

Jade looked away for a moment, then met my gaze. "She doesn't think you can give her everything she deserves."

That statement hurt more than I could ever express, but I'd be damned if I'd let Jade know it.

"But she would never do anything to keep the two of you apart," Jade added. "She trusts Alix's judgment." When I didn't say anything, she continued. "Look, regardless of what Jessica might think, I have never seen Alix happier than when the two of you were together."

"So why are you here?"

"Because I need to know that I can trust you not to hurt her again," Jade answered. "For my own peace of mind. I feel bad enough about my hand in all of this."

"I won't lie to her again," I said.

Jade looked relieved. "Good." She smiled. "I'll let you get back to not sleeping." She stood and headed for the door.

"Jade," I called. "Are you going to tell her that you were involved?"

Jade shook her head. "I'm too much of a coward." She went to open the door, then paused. "But if you have to tell her, then tell her. No more lies between you guys okay? I'll deal with the consequences."

I nodded and watched her leave. Then I headed back to my room, feeling a rush of emotions.

"I can give her all she deserves and more," I promised to no one but myself. "And more."

∅

At precisely 2:03 pm there was a knock at my door. "You sure are punctual," I said, as I let Alix into the apartment. She was clad in her usual black, though the jeans and the shirt were tighter than usual. No complaints here.

She shrugged, as she turned around to face me as I closed the door. "Actually, I've been standing outside since one-fifty-five, but I thought I'd be fashionably late."

"Of course," I said, trying not to stare at her.

"What?" she asked, self-consciously. Then she must have noticed where my gaze was directed. "I had a disagreement with the dryer. I told it to keep my clothes nice and baggy, and it decided to shrink-wrap me. But we compromised."

I cleared my throat. "How'd you compromise?"

"Well, it kept them black."

"Isn't that the washer's job?"

She was thoughtful for a moment, then narrowed her eyes, which seemed greener than usual. "Yes. You're right. That sneaky bastard."

I grinned.

She smiled. Then she whirled around and started walking toward the TV in the living room. "Oh my God! I love this video."

I followed behind her to see what all the commotion was about. Aerosmith. Duh. I struggled to figure out what she saw in the group but for the life of me . . .

"Isn't he hot?"

"He? Steven Tyler?" I took a seat beside her on the couch. I laughed. "You're kidding right?"

She frowned as she turned to me. "No. Why? Don't you think he's gorgeous?"

I arched a brow and turned back to the TV. She had to be joking. "Uh . . . no? But his daughter's pretty hot."

"Nope. He's hotter."

I frowned. "You *are* a lesbian, right?"

She smiled, her gaze glued to the screen. "Sort of."

"Sort of?" I must have missed this particular subject while we were playing truth or dare on our first date. "What do you mean by sort of?"

"I've gotta get this CD today," she said. Then she realized I asked her a question. "Oh. Well, I'm mostly a lesbian."

"So you're bi?"

"Sort of." The song finally ended, and I had her attention back. She grinned. "You're cute when you're all confused." She tapped my forehead. "You have like a vein that bulges out right here."

"I do not!" I argued, swatting her hand away. "Now answer my question."

She cocked her head. "Why is it important?"

Um . . . "I guess it's not," I said, though I was still curious as hell.

She stood, grabbing my hand. "Come on. Take me somewhere interesting. It's my first time in the Big Apple."

I let her pull me to my feet. "Hungry?"

"Always."

"How do you feel about peanut butter?"

✑

"I'm torn," Alix announced, as she stared up at the menu posted behind the counter of the restaurant.

The girl behind the register was subtly checking her out, and I found myself taking Alix's hand in a possessive gesture. Fortunately for her, the chick took the hint and disappeared into the kitchen while we decided on our order.

Alix glanced down at our interlocked hands.

So I pretended it was no big deal and focused on the menu. "I think I'll have the Spicy Peanut Butter."

Alix glanced up and squinted at the ingredients. "Grilled chicken with peanut butter? You're a freak."

"Yes, you're one to talk."

The girl reappeared and gazed at us expectantly.

"Ready?" I asked Alix.

She nodded. "Fluffernutter," she responded confidently. "And milk." She started to reach into her pocket to get out some money but I stopped her.

"I've got it," I said.

"Yeah?" She turned back to look at the menu. "Too bad they don't sell lobster here."

"Lobster and peanut butter? And you said I was weird."

She grinned and walked over to look at the items they had for sale.

I turned to the girl and instantly offered her my most charming smile. "I'll take a Spicy Peanut Butter, a Fluffernutter, and two whole milks."

"Crunchy or smooth?"

What kind of peanut butter did Alix like? If I turned to ask her it would look like our relationship wasn't serious enough to call for peanut butter preference knowledge. Then Miss Thang over here might start getting ideas. On the other hand, if I picked the wrong type of peanut butter, Alix would be unhappy with her meal. Not an option. Oh well, it was time for Plan B. "Actually, can I have two Fluffernutters instead? One with crunchy the other with smooth." There. That should solve the problem.

The girl shook her head but rang up the order. I paid the bill and picked a table in the corner. We were the only people there.

Alix joined me a moment later. "This is a really cute place," she said, glancing around. "You seem to know New York City pretty well. How long did you live here?"

Q&A time. Here we go. "A little less than two years."

She nodded, clearly wanting to know more, but afraid to push the subject.

I sat up. "Tell you what. I promise to answer all of your questions, if you promise to answer all of mine."

She nodded. "Deal."

"Shoot," I said, sitting back. Hopefully she'd start with the easy ones first. What's your favorite car? That sort of thing.

Alix was thoughtful for a second. "Okay. Why did you sleep with me if you knew you were lying to me?"

"Two whole milks." The girl placed the two cups in front of us. She winked at Alix and gave me a disapproving look before returning to the kitchen.

Wonderful. "Are you sure you want to discuss this here?" I asked, when I was sure the girl was out of earshot.

She took a drink from her milk. "Sure."

How did I even begin to explain this? "I shouldn't have allowed it to happen. I talked myself into doing something I knew was wrong and I'm sorry." Oh, good one. Tell the girl that you regret sleeping with her. Nice move.

The hurt on Alix's face was crystal clear.

"Sorry. That came out totally wrong." I was trying to think back to what I'd been thinking. Truth was, I hadn't been thinking. "I don't know why I did it. I just know that I'd never wanted anyone as much as I'd wanted you. It wasn't about sex. I just wanted to express how I felt about you. No words meant no lies."

She nodded.

"I really have no way of justifying it," I admitted. "It was wrong on so many levels but I couldn't have stopped myself if I'd wanted to. Unless you had wanted me to. Then I would've stopped, of course." *Shit, now I'm babbling.* "I just meant—"

"It's okay," Alix interrupted. "I know what you meant."

"Okay."

She smiled, instantly making me feel better. "Your turn."

Did that mean I answered correctly? This relationship thing was a lot more complicated than I'd imagined it would be. They made it look so easy on TV. "What kind of peanut butter do you prefer? Crunchy or smooth?"

Before Alix had a chance to respond, our delightful hostess appeared beside us, carrying two plates. "Two Fluffernutters," she announced. She turned to me. "Crunchy or smooth?"

So much for Plan B. Time for Plan C: Deductive reasoning. She liked to wear black all the time. And she thought Steven Tyler was hot. So, what did that tell me about her preference in peanut butter? Not a damn thing. "Smooth," I guessed.

The girl put one plate in front of me and the other in front of Alix. "If I can get you anything else, let me know." Then she walked away.

I turned to Alix, waiting to see if I'd guessed correctly. She was picking up the sandwich. She was biting it. Guess I was right after all. "So you like crunchy better?" I asked casually.

She shrugged. "It's all the same to me," she responded. "This is really good. Try the chips."

All that work and she didn't even care one way or another. I popped a chip in my mouth. Served me right.

♌

"You know she was totally checking you out back there?" I asked casually, because subtlety is my middle name. To express my complete neutrality on the subject, I kept my gaze focused on the sidewalk.

"Hmm?" Alix asked, seemingly distracted by whatever thoughts danced in her head. "Oh, you mean Susan?"

My eyebrows lifted. "Pardon?"

"Girl back at the peanut butter place?"

She knew her name? I must have missed something. "Yeah," I respond carefully.

"Yep, I know."

Deep, calming breaths. "You're friends?"

Alix laughed. "Hardly."

I see. "So how do you know her name?"

Alix dug her hand into her pocket and withdrew a small piece of paper. "She gave me her number while you were in the bathroom." She shrugged and put it back in her pocket.

I wondered if she really planned on keeping that. Worse yet, if she planned on actually dialing the number.

"Where are we headed?"

I looked around for a moment. "Christopher Street? Unless there's something in particular you want to see?"

"Nope. Lead the way."

We walked in silence for a few minutes. I wasn't particularly content about this whole Susan issue. Did Alix want to get back together at all? Did she just want us to be friends and see other people? I wasn't particularly sure I could handle that particular arrangement. I was having enough trouble keeping myself from turning around and telling off that . . .

"So, my turn to ask a question."

I glanced down at Alix. "No it's not. Our food arrived before you had a chance to answer."

"Then you asked again, and I answered."

Fine. If she wanted to play it that way. "But then you asked where we were going and I answered. So technically, it's my turn."

She narrowed her eyes at me. "Cheater."

I smiled proudly. "So, let's see." What did I want to know? Lots of things. "What are the rules?"

"To the question game?"

"No, to our current relationship."

"Oh." She looked away before answering. "Well, I figured you and I should figure that out together. I mean, it is 'our' relationship."

Fair enough. "All right." Might as well get to the heart of matters. "Are we seeing other people?"

Green eyes met mine. "Do you want to?"

Hell no! "Do you?"

She shrugged, placing her hands in her pockets. "Not particularly."

I hoped she hadn't heard the huge sigh of relief that escaped my lips. "Me neither," I said, trying not to sound as happy as I felt.

Instead of saying anything, Alix handed me the scrap of paper with the phone number on it.

My eyebrows narrowed in question.

"Well, I don't want it," she said, by way of explanation.

I smiled, crumpled the paper in my hand, and threw it away in the nearest trashcan. Better luck next time, Susan.

$\varnothing$

"H-O-R."

"Who you callin' a whore?" Alix asked.

"You," I responded simply, dribbling the ball away from her. "Why didn't you tell me you were this bad?"

Alix crossed her arms. "Valerie," she said, her voice controlled. "I told you on the way to your apartment that I sucked at basketball. Then I told you all the way here. And I told you the first time I lost. Then the second. And even the third. I think you just like the fact that you're winning."

I hid a grin. I did like winning. But I much preferred watching the cute look of concentration that passed across Alix's features right before she made a shot. Granted, she hadn't gotten the ball in the basket once since we'd arrived at the basketball court, but I was still enjoying myself. "Let's see if you can make it from here," I said, mockingly. I stood as close to the basket as I could without being directly under it, and made the shot. I caught the ball as it fell from the net and passed it to Alix.

Resigned, she walked over and stood at the same spot I'd been standing. "I really hate this game. Why is it called HORSE anyway? Can't we spell something cooler?" She bounced the ball a couple of times and stared up at the basket. Then came the concentration look that never seemed to work. Then the shot.

Missed by a mile.

"Ooh, it *almost* touched the rim that time," I teased, running to catch the ball before it interrupted someone else's game.

"Why don't we go play pool?" she suggested innocently.

I grinned. "H-O-R-S."

"B-R-A-T."

"Perhaps," I conceded. "But at least I'm winning."

She rolled her eyes. "Fine. But that means you have to buy me dinner."

"How do you figure?"

"Well, you've already destroyed my self-esteem. Do you want to deplete my bank account as well?"

I laughed. "You mean Jessica's bank account."

She shrugged, taking a seat in the middle of the court. "Hers. Mine. What's the difference? We share. She's like the sister I never had."

"What about Rachel?" I asked, slightly confused.

She gazed up at me with a smile. "Like I said, she's like the sister I never had."

I grinned. "Gotcha."

Alix looked at her watch for a moment, then leaned back on her arms, staring up at me. "Are you gonna shoot any time soon, or are we camping out here?"

I glanced up at the basketball hoop. I couldn't very well make the past couple of hours end in a few pointless games of HORSE. I sat down across from Alix. "Tell you what. If you make the next basket, I'll buy you dinner."

She glanced at me warily. "And if I don't make it?"

"Jessica's treat." I was pleased to see my smile reciprocated.

"Sounds fair to me," she said.

I grinned to myself and rose to my feet, looking around the court.

Where should I shoot from? Regardless of the spot, I doubted that she'd make it so it wasn't that big of an issue. But I couldn't let it seem like I was trying to let her win.

Finally, I decided on the foul line. It seemed fair enough. I shot the ball and watched it sail smoothly through the air, ending in a perfect swoosh through the hoop. With a satisfied smile, I glanced at Alix. She was in the process of retrieving the ball. "I think I'll order that lobster you mentioned earlier," I was saying, as she passed in front of me to take her place behind the line.

She shook her head and bounced the ball a few times. This time there was no look of concentration. She just let the ball fly. I watched it, suddenly feeling like everything was happening in slow motion. And then the unexpected happened.

She made the shot.

I blinked a few times, in pure disbelief. Then from somewhere far away I heard three little words:

"Lobster sounds good."

Chapter 4
Alix

New York was starting to grow on me after only a couple of days and it got me wondering why I'd never considered leaving Florida. Everywhere I looked something was happening. The most inconsequential things somehow felt important and I tried to take it all in, while at the same time trying to make sense of my time with Valerie.

Love was confusing. Women were confusing. How was one supposed to work with both of them together?

"You seem pensive," Valerie said, looking down at me.

We were walking in Times Square and I was staring down at the ground instead of up at the pretty lights and billboards. "What do you think about love?"

She seemed thrown by the question. "I suppose it's all right."

I smiled, my gaze finally rising to look around. Everything was so bright. Baldwin City seemed so far away at that moment. "No, I mean, do you think it can last forever? Or do you think it's a fleeting thing?"

Valerie was silent for a long moment as she contemplated my question. I'm sure she wasn't expecting to discuss the meaning of love while walking down the busy sidewalks of Times Square.

Finally, she looked down at me, a very serious expression on her face. My breath caught, as I waited for her deep and meaningful response; one that was certain to put to rest all my doubts and insecurities. I stared into her eyes as though I could find the most well-kept secrets of life hidden in their depths. Her lips parted and the words poured forth, escaping into the noisy air. "Laser tag."

I blinked. A few times. Then I voiced my thoughts. "Huh?"

"I think love is like laser tag."

"Laser tag. Right." Every time I thought I had this girl figured out she came up with something like laser tag to throw me all the way back to start. Talking to her sometimes felt like an endless game of *Sorry!*

"Would you like me to explain?"

The twinkle in her eye worried me. "I'm not sure . . ." Here I'd thought I was the weird one in this relationship.

"I'll do so anyway. See, to me, love had always been something to avoid. I didn't mind if someone fell for me . . . but falling for someone else was always something I couldn't handle. It always reminded me of a game of laser tag. Get them before they get me. Hurt them before they hurt me."

"Oh," I said, suddenly feeling sad. "Is that why you left? To hurt me before I hurt you?"

"No."

I grabbed her arm to stop her. I couldn't have this conversation while walking. "Then?"

Valerie looked uncomfortable. "You know why I left."

"No," I said seriously, trying to meet her gaze. "I don't."

She was looking anywhere but at me. If I hadn't known better, I would've sworn she looked embarrassed. "It hurt too much to stay," she admitted softly.

Silence. That's what I heard in spite of all the noise around me. Until that moment it had never occurred to me to wonder how Valerie must have felt about all of this. I'd played up my victim role to full capacity and it was time to let it go. This had never been about me, only I'd been too blind to see that. "I'm sorry," I whispered, stepping closer to her.

Valerie's eyes finally focused on mine. "You have nothing to be sorry for. It was all my fault."

I smiled sadly. "No. No, it wasn't." I took her hand. "Come on, let's go back to your apartment."

She seemed surprised by the gesture, but didn't take her hand from mine. In fact, she tightened her hold as we walked back to the subway station.

∅

"So," Valerie said, when we stepped inside the apartment a short while later.

"Why do you think I'm still in love with Jessica?" I asked.

Valerie sank down on the couch, caught off-guard. "Just a feeling."

I shook my head as I sat across from her. "No. There has to be a reason."

She sighed. "Whenever we would talk about anything, the subject would always go back to Jessica. It could never be just about us. You always brought her up."

"It couldn't be just about us, though," I said. "It was more about the two of you than it was about you and me."

Silence.

"I'd like you to come back to Florida with me," I said, bracing myself for rejection.

Valerie looked at me, her eyebrows narrowed. "Why?"

"Because I don't want to be apart from you," I answered, and suddenly wondered if I was asking too much of her again. Was it always to be about me? Did she ever get a choice? "But if you decide to stay here, then I'll transfer."

She shook her head. "I would never let you do that."

"It's not up to you to decide. I don't need your permission."

Valerie stood suddenly, and I was starting to worry that I was freaking her out. Maybe she wasn't ready for this. I'd never asked her what kind of relationship she was prepared for. I was willing to give up anything for her. But was she?

"Alix, what made you come here?" she asked. "Why would you want another chance with me?"

I wanted to say the words, but I was unable. "Because I want to be with you," I said instead, feeling like a coward.

Her blue eyes shone with sadness. "If I ask you something do you swear you'll answer truthfully?"

"I would never lie to you, Valerie," I said.

"When you are with me, do you pretend I am Jessica?" she asked softly.

I was completely floored by the question. It was definitely not one I was expecting. I frowned. "Is that what you really think?"

"Answer the question," she insisted and I thought she was going to cry.

I shook my head, trying to figure out what would give her such an idea. I was so hurt by the implication. "How can you ask me that?"

"Answer the question, Alix!"

I stared at her, then headed for the door. "I will not answer that," I told her as I turned the handle. "I'm going back to Florida tomorrow. Sorry I wasted your time." I closed the door behind me as I stepped out into the hallway, feeling completely defeated. I couldn't decide if I was more hurt or offended or angry. Maybe I was all of them.

Never for a second did I ever think Jessica and Valerie were interchangeable. They were as different as night and day. I couldn't have pretended one was the other if I tried. It was like someone pretending Rachel was me. Ha! Not even I had that good of an imagination.

But I supposed with Valerie's insecurities about my feelings for Jessica it was kind of understandable why she would think that.

I paused at the stairs. Maybe I should've gone back and talked it over with her. Assured her that I would never think something like that.

But ugh! How insulting that she would consider such a thing.

I continued down the stairs.

Somewhere between the first and second floor, I heard my name being called. I looked up to see Valerie racing down the stairs. She reached me a few moments later.

"I'm sorry," she breathed, gasping slightly. "I'm so sorry. I didn't mean to be such a jerk."

"I'm sorry, too," I said. "I shouldn't have walked out on you."

She stretched her hand out to me. "Come back, please?"

I hesitated only a moment before accepting her offer. I was beginning to understand that I had trouble denying her anything. One look into her eyes and all of my anger dissipated. That in itself was annoying. It's like she was a witch or something. I didn't completely dismiss that idea. There were a lot of things about Valerie Anne Michaels that I didn't particularly know.

Back in her apartment we stared at each other in silence. Then finally, I said, "Valerie, I'm not in love with Jessica. And even if I were I would never—"

Valerie stepped forward and placed her finger to my lips. "No. I shouldn't have even thought to ask you that question. I'm sorry. I just let my paranoia get the best of me." She went to sit on the couch. "I've never done this before, Alix. It scares me."

I sat beside her and faced her. "You've been in relationships before."

She smiled sadly. "I've never been in love before."

My heart skipped a beat. "Neither have I," I whispered.

Valerie turned to me, her eyes betraying her surprise. "But Jessica—"

I shook my head. "Jessica never felt like this." I took a deep breath. "Look, Valerie, that day in your apartment when you told me you loved me and I walked out . . . I'm sorry. I was overwhelmed. No one . . . had ever said that to me before. I kind of freaked. When it comes to fight or flight, I generally fly."

A smile passed her lips. "It's okay."

Okay? I shook my head again. "No. No, it's not okay. Because I'm in love with you. And I need you to know that. Even if I go back to Florida and you decide to stay here and I never see you again—"

Her kiss drowned my words, stealing my breath away. I couldn't even remember what I'd been talking about. I'd kissed her before but somehow this felt different. Its sweetness was tinged with an urgency that had never existed before.

Valerie pulled away first, looking like a child who'd just been caught doing something wrong. "I'm sorry. I didn't mean to do that. You were saying?"

Did she really expect me to remember? "Who cares? And why are you sorry?"

"I didn't mean to cross the line."

"You didn't," I assured her. Then I remembered what I'd been talking about. "I wasn't saying anything important. Just that I love you. But that can wait."

Valerie smiled. Then a troubled look passed across her features and she turned away.

"What's wrong?"

"There's something you need to know," she said. "I don't want to hide anything from you anymore."

Uh-oh, I thought. Whatever it was, I was sure I wasn't going to like it.

She took a deep breath. "Jade knew."

"Jade knew what?" I asked, suddenly confused.

"She knew the whole plan. She helped me. That's why she took you to Whispers that night. That's how I knew where you lived."

I nodded. "I kind of figured."

Valerie stared at me in surprise. "What?"

"Well, while I was in my fuming, angry stage I started thinking about everything, especially about the night we met. And everything just kind of kept going back to Jade. She wanted me to go to the club. She picked the club. She opened up a conversation with you. Then you told me that Jade had been at Whispers earlier and told you where I lived but she doesn't have a car so there's no way she could've gotten there. Especially not in the middle of the day."

I shrugged. "It started to make sense. What I couldn't figure out was why. But then I remembered Jade telling me this story about this girl Valerie that had pretty much saved her from getting raped one night. So all the pieces fit together."

"You're not mad?"

"Well, like I said, I was in my fuming, angry stage so I was enraged then. But I figured Jade never meant for things to get that out of hand. Don't get me wrong, we're going to have a big talk later, but I keep thinking that if none of this would've happened . . . we would've never met. And I'd rather go through this all over again than go the rest of my life without knowing you." I cringed. "Is that too corny? I'm sorry."

"You're amazing," Valerie commented, her gaze never leaving mine.

"Yeah, I think so." I smiled. "Any more confessions?"

Valerie paled slightly. "There're a lot of things about me you don't know . . ."

I took her hand. "Then you will tell me . . . later. I don't think I can handle any more tonight."

"I keep wondering what I did to deserve you."

"Maybe you were *really* good in another life," I joked.

Valerie laughed. "Thanks." She looked around for a moment, then cleared her throat. "Do you want to spend the night?"

I arched an eyebrow. "That was subtle."

"Not like that," she said, blushing slightly. "Just . . . sleep. It's getting late and I don't want you leaving at this hour. I don't really want you leaving, period."

I glanced at my watch to see what her definition of "getting late" was. Ten o'clock. I'd hate to know what she considered early. "Only on one condition."

"What's that?"

"You cook me something," I responded. "I'm starving."

ℒ

Several hours later, we were lying on her bed. Valerie lent me a pair of sweatpants and a tee shirt to sleep in. We had two bowls of popcorn between us, one with butter, one without. On the big screen TV, *Romy and Michelle's High School Reunion* was playing. We'd flipped a quarter to see who got to choose the movie. She'd lost.

"Romy or Michelle?" Valerie asked, grabbing a handful of popcorn and stuffing it in her mouth.

I stared at the couple on the screen. Which would I rather sleep with? Hmm. "Lisa Kudrow, definitely."

"You don't think Mira Sorvino is cute?"

"No she's cute too, but I'm loyal to *Friends*."

Valerie laughed. "Dork."

I munched away on some popcorn as I shrugged. "Romy or Heather?"

Valerie considered. "I have a weakness for bitter women. So I'll go with Jeanine Garofalo. Jennifer Aniston or Steven Tyler?"

"Steven Tyler," I replied without hesitation. "Catherine Zeta Jones or Jennifer Connelly?"

"Oooh! Tough one. Jennifer. I'm loyal to *Labyrinth*. How can you possibly choose Steven Tyler over Jennifer Aniston?"

"Easy. He's yum."

Valerie cringed. "I worry about you, I really do."

I laughed at her discomfort.

"Steven Tyler or me?"

I stared at her. "Steven Tyler, of course." I was rewarded with a handful of sticky popcorn hitting my face. "Thanks."

"I am officially not speaking to you," Valerie announced, looking very much like she meant it as she turned her full attention to the movie.

"You asked."

Valerie continued to eat her popcorn and focus on the movie.

"Fine, be that way." Two could play at this game.

The movie proceeded along. Fifteen minutes of silence went by before Valerie spoke. "Is it 'cause you'd rather be with a guy than a girl?"

I nearly choked on the mouthful of popcorn. I grabbed for the Dr. Pepper on the nightstand. "Huh?"

"Do you like guys more than girls?" she asked, quite seriously.

For someone who appeared so self-assured, Valerie was sure insecure about the oddest things. "No I don't like guys more than girls. In fact, I don't really like guys. Only Steven, and only because he's my idol. It's more about admiration than sexual attraction."

"But you'd rather sleep with him than me," she protested, almost pouting.

Laughing, I kissed her cheek. "I was just kidding, you dinkus. I would never choose anyone over you. And I wouldn't choose him over Jennifer Aniston either. I'd have to be insane."

"So you'd never pick someone over me?"

"Nope."

"Good to know." She appeared mighty proud of herself.

"Jennifer Connelly or me?"

Her mouth dropped. "That's not fair. You can't ask me to betray my loyalty."

I laughed. "All right, I'll put it this way. Say you were in a room with the two of us and you had to pick one and the other wouldn't know that you chose the other over them. Which would you pick? It's okay. I won't be offended."

"Okay, one moment." Valerie closed her eyes, appearing deep in concentration.

I continued to eat my popcorn as I waited.

Finally, she said, "You."

"You're just saying that to be nice."

"Nope. I'd pick you."

"Ahuh. And why?"

She grinned. "'Cause believe it or not, you're hotter."

I snorted. "Good one."

Valerie grabbed my hand and pulled me up. I nearly knocked the popcorn all over the bed. "Come on."

She led me to the full-length mirror in the closet and stood behind me as I contemplated my reflection. "Explain?"

Valerie simply motioned to the mirror. "What do you see?"

"You and me," I answered. "Do the questions get harder as we go along?"

"I'm serious." She turned me around to face her. "What do you see when you look at me?"

That was easy. "I see the most beautiful woman on the face of the earth." I meant that too. Jennifer Aniston had nothing on this girl.

"Why thank you," she said, turning me back around. "Now what do you see when you look at yourself?"

"I see me standing in front of the most beautiful woman on the face of the earth."

"You're gorgeous, Alix."

Shrugging, I said, "I'm okay."

"Gorgeous, yet frustrating."

"I like to present a challenge," I replied, smiling. I turned back to my reflection. I supposed I wasn't a complete ogre. In the right light, I even looked semi-human.

Smiling, I joined Valerie back on the bed. "So what are we doing tomorrow?"

"Packing."

I was confused. "Pardon?"

"We're going back to Florida."

Chapter 5
Valerie

So my plan to leave everything behind went full circle and landed me right back where I started and I wasn't entirely certain how that had occurred. There were many things over the past few weeks I couldn't quite explain. Like when did awkward silences give way to endless conversations? And how did "I had a nice time" suddenly start meaning "I love you"? I couldn't pinpoint the exact moment where dull aches turned into a searing pain at the thought of never being with her, yet looking back I can't recall what it was like when I didn't know her. Strange, that.

The clouds outside of the airplane window stretched out endlessly in a playground of possibilities. I wondered what it was about the sky that made everything seem possible. Perhaps the lack of boundaries, the presence of illusion that made the clouds appear more solid than they were. That's how I'd once imagined love to be, an illusion.

I gazed at the slumbering form beside me and felt my heart skip at the mere sight of her. It was unnerving yet exciting and I thought again of the tattoo on my skin and how I'd failed at living by its example. I'd thought myself strong for avoiding the weakening grasp love always seemed to have on those unlucky enough to fall for its deceiving allure. But now I saw myself as far more of a coward for running from the fear of heartbreak. Facing it was, by far, the greater challenge. I just hoped I was a strong enough candidate for the job.

Alix stirred in the seat, her green eyes slowly opening. "Was I snoring?" she asked with concern.

"Yes," I lied. "For a while I thought it was the engine. I thought for sure we were going to crash."

She slapped my arm. "Not funny."

I rubbed away the tingle her touch had left on my arm, pretending instead that she had hurt me with her sad attempt at inflicting pain. "Sleep well?"

"I always sleep like a baby on planes," she responded with a yawn. "I don't know why I'm so sleepy."

"Perhaps because you were up all night watching movies?" I suggested casually.

"Perhaps. But I think it had more to do with the fact that you kept kicking me."

"Me kick *you*?" I cried, shocked that she would have the audacity to suggest such a thing. "Do you want to see the bruises on my leg? You were probably a donkey in another life."

"Do donkeys kick?" she asked, the original argument momentarily forgotten.

Jade leaned forward in her seat beside Alix. "Rabbits kick hard."

I sent her a questioning glance that was voiced when Alix said, "What the hell?"

"A rabbit kicked me really hard once!" Jade argued, rubbing a spot on her chin.

Alix frowned. "I don't want to know why the rabbit was close enough to kick you in the chin."

"It's a complicated story," Jade stated. "Your simple minds would never comprehend."

"Thank God," Alix mumbled. She put on her headphones and started pressing buttons on her mp3 player.

Jade followed Alix's example and put on her headphones as well.

Bored, I turned once again to the view from my window. Such pretty patterns hovering over nothingness, breaking apart, breaking free of themselves and drifting nowhere. I contemplated the designs, attempting to find meaning in the meaningless forms floating with slow progression. I wondered briefly if clouds had any sense of self and if, like us, they basked in overrated self-glory. Did they realize they were going in circles? Did we?

I took Alix's hand in mine, amazed as always by the softness of her skin. Then I settled back in the seat and closed my eyes, succumbing to the safety and comfort her touch provided.

♋

We arrived at MIA shortly thereafter, and I was surprised to find Jessica waiting for us at the gate. Her presence made me feel terribly uneasy. I felt better when I saw that she looked equally surprised to see me walk out behind Alix.

The two of them hugged, and I stood by awkwardly, looking around as though strangers walking about were the most interesting thing in the world.

"I guess the mission was a success," Jessica said, glancing at me. I couldn't determine how she felt about the fact, but she seemed pleased that Alix was back.

It was then I remembered my hair, and felt suddenly self-conscious. It was an irritating feeling, one that left me feeling more angry than annoyed. Why should I feel embarrassed? It was my hair color. But the feeling remained even after we left the gate and stood by the carousel awaiting our bags.

"Catch my bag if it comes around," Alix said to me. "I've gotta run to the little nun's room."

Jade followed suit, leaving Jessica and I alone.

I tried not to clear my throat or make any other sound that would give away my discomfort. I tried instead to busy my head with plans of action. Like how I was going to get a car now that I'd sold the other one, for instance. I stared pleadingly at the line of bags cruising by, hoping one of them would turn into one of ours so I would have something else to do besides stand there in unbearable silence.

"So," Jessica said. "What made you come back?"

"I'm sure you know the answer to that," I replied.

She nodded. "Good reason."

"Yes, she is," I agreed, wondering if this was going anywhere or if she just wanted to kill time until Alix and Jade returned.

"They left on purpose," Jessica informed me, looking at me with her usual cool expression.

Reflexively, I glanced in the direction they had left. "How do you know?"

"Because Alix only says 'little nun's room' when she's up to something."

"Good to know," I replied, slightly jealous that Jessica should know something about Alix that I didn't. Reminding myself that they'd been best friends for years didn't make me feel any better. I had to get over this. "So what do you suppose she's up to?"

"This," Jessica answered simply. "Us talking."

"Oh," I said, not knowing what else to say.

Jessica turned to me, regarding me with a serious expression. "What would you be willing to give for Alix?"

"I'm sorry?" I asked. Did she want me to trade her for something? I was confused.

"Alix's happiness, how much is that worth to you?"

"Are you trying to buy me off again?" I asked, feeling my rage rising.

To my surprise, Jessica laughed. "Calm down," she said and her voice wasn't mocking so I did. A little. "I'm asking if Alix's happiness is enough to make you forsake your pride?"

I wasn't entirely sure where she was going with this, but I knew the answer to the question. "I would give anything to ensure Alix's happiness."

Jessica nodded, seemingly pleased. "So would I."

"I know," I told her, knowing it to be so.

She studied me for a moment, then asked, "Will you join me for lunch tomorrow?"

Her invitation shocked me, but I willed it not to show. "Will Alix be there?"

"No. Just the two of us."

I mulled the idea over. Then I thought of her question about me forsaking my pride and I instantly knew why she asked. "What time?"

"One. Is The Olive Garden okay with you?"

"Fine. If I can get there. I sold my car before I left." I have no idea why I told her that.

"I'll pick you up then." She seemed to debate something over in her head, then asked, "Do you have a place to stay?"

"I'll be at the same apartment," I said, thankful I didn't have to lie. I'd never needed anyone before and I wasn't about to start asking Jessica Heart for favors.

She nodded and said, "I'll pick you up at one then. Here they come. Act as if we've been standing here in silence the whole time."

I resumed my award winning brooding look just in time to see Alix and Jade round the corner. Jade carried a bag in one hand from a recent purchase. Alix carried a matching one.

"Bathroom having a sale?" I asked.

"Yes," Alix responded. "Toilet paper . . . hand soap . . . you name it. Quite the bargains too."

"Sorry I missed it." I smiled at her.

She smiled back, instantly making me forget that Jessica and Jade were both there, watching our interplay with undisguised interest.

"I'm sure you can still catch it," she replied.

I nodded to the bag. "So what'd you buy me? Toilet paper or hand soap?"

"Neither." She handed the bag over. "Enjoy."

Inside was a magazine with Catherine Zeta Jones on the cover. "Oooh . . . purdy," I said, petting the picture.

That's when I remembered that Jessica and Jade were still there.

℘

I never thought I would miss Florida but the moment I caught sight of the ocean, it felt good to be back. So far it had been an overly productive day. I'd returned from New York, gotten my apartment back, gotten my old job back, and last but not least . . . I'd made a lunch date with Jessica.

Who knew one could accomplish so many things in the course of a few hours? I still didn't have a car but that was something better left until tomorrow. For now I was content to sit on the sand and stare at the rapidly darkening waters of the Atlantic.

"Guess I'll have to add this to my list of places to find you."

I smiled at the voice and turned to find Alix walking toward me. "How did you know I would be here?" I asked, pleasantly surprised. We'd parted ways a few hours prior with no plans for the remainder of the night.

She took a seat beside me and stared straight ahead. "I didn't. I was on my way back to my car when I saw you sitting here. Lucky for me you're pretty easy to spot."

"Lucky for me too," I said, feeling happy all of a sudden. We sat there quietly for a few minutes, enjoying the cool breeze blowing in from the ocean and reveling in the beauty of sunsets. But I was curious, so I broke the silence. "So, what brings you by?"

"Few things," Alix said. "First of all, I wanted to know if you were okay . . . being back and all?"

I shrugged, then leaned back on my elbows. "Aside from not having a car, everything's good. I got my job back at Whispers."

"I was worried about how much you gave up before you left here," she said, a bit shyly. "I didn't want you to be homeless or something."

Her concern made me smile. "I wouldn't have returned then."

She nodded. "What are you going to do about getting a car?"

"Don't know yet," I admitted. "I suppose I can buy one. I'll be working more hours at Whispers now that I won't be going to school part-time."

This caught her attention and she looked at me with concern. "You dropped out?"

"I don't really have the time right now."

She frowned at this. "You should always make time to do something you love."

"I'll still be painting," I assured her. "Just can't deal with school right now. Maybe next semester."

Alix nodded and absently played with the sand. I could tell she was attempting to find the courage to say something. Finally, she asked, "Are you still considering Baldwin?"

Her question surprised me. I hadn't thought about it in a while. It had been a nice thought . . . but it had never been one I'd honestly expected to go through with. "I don't know." It was my turn to hesitate. "I suppose it would be up to you."

"Up to me?" she asked in confusion, the sand momentarily forgotten. "Why up to me?"

"Because I don't know if you would still want me to go there," I explained. The last thing I wanted was for Alix to think I was trying to suffocate her. I didn't want to seem clingy.

"I would love for you to go there!" she said, and her voice carried with it such resolve that I found myself smiling.

"Then I guess I'm still considering it," I said.

"Good," she replied, then resumed playing with the sand. After a few moments of silence she said, "The other reason I came by was to ask a strange favor of you."

My eyebrows rose. "Okay."

She appeared a bit embarrassed as she turned to address me directly, but her embarrassment was not enough to conceal her excitement. "I got a call from my agent about this audition that's coming up in a few weeks. It's for a film set in Miami. Anyway, the lead role is a girl who's a martial artist and they are looking for someone who already has some knowledge in the area. So I was wondering if . . . uh . . ." She trailed off momentarily. "If you could help train me," she finished quickly.

That was probably the last thing I'd expected to hear, but I welcomed the surprise. "Sounds like a great opportunity."

She stared at me expectantly.

I almost laugh at the look on her face. "Of course I'll help you. I'd be honored to. Just remember to thank me when you're accepting your first Academy Award."

She laughed and hugged me tightly. And I knew at that moment that she could've asked for my left arm and I would've gladly given it to her.

$\varnothing$

"So what's good here?" I asked, looking down at the The Olive Garden menu. True to her word, Jessica had picked me up at precisely one o'clock. I'd been surprised to learn that she drove a red Camaro. For some reason I'd expected a Ferrari or Lamborghini or even a limousine. I doubted I'd ever understand this woman.

"Everything's good," Jessica said.

"All righty then," I said, scanning the menu for something that looked appealing. Truth be told, my stomach was in so many knots I doubted very much I'd be able to eat anything I ordered. After much debating, I finally settled on a salad. I wasn't sure which one. I just pointed to something on the list when the waitress came to take the order.

When we were once again alone, I struggled to think of something to say. Finally, I settled on what was on my mind. "Why did you ask me to lunch?"

Jessica sat back, as if my question required deep contemplation. After a few seconds she said, "I'm not sure." The way she said it made it seem like a confession. And I supposed it was on some level.

"Jade spoke to me already about hurting Alix, if that's what you wanted to talk about," I said.

Jessica shook her head. "I know you won't hurt her."

"Oh?" I asked, surprised that she could sound so certain of something that even I wasn't altogether sure of.

"You came back," she said simply. "I didn't think you would."

"Alix is hard to resist," I told her with a shrug. I looked down, feigning interest in the pattern of the tiles. "I only left because—" I stopped abruptly, remembering who I was talking to. I had no intention of opening up to her.

"It's hard for you, isn't it?" Jessica inquired.

"What is?" I asked, avoiding her gaze.

"Seeing me as a real person," Jessica replied sadly.

Her tone forced me to look up. "No. What's hard is wanting to hate you and not being sure why."

"It wasn't my fault," she stated, and the way she halted slightly between words made me realize that it had taken her a long time to come to terms with that fact.

I suddenly felt ashamed to realize that I hadn't made that much progress. I blamed her for something that had been completely out of her control. What was I jealous of exactly?

"I know," I said, surprising myself. "Maybe I have trouble accepting that sometimes . . . but I do know it."

She nodded, suddenly at a loss. "I'm not entirely sure where to go from here. When Alix told me you'd left, I was selfishly glad that I wouldn't have to deal with this issue. I could just pretend it had never happened. Denial is easier."

I nodded, not wanting to interrupt in case she had more to say.

"But then I saw how sad Alix looked and how determined she was to find you and I was torn between wishing to never see you again and hoping you'd change your mind and come bursting through the door." She sighed. "I'm glad you came back."

"For Alix?" I guessed.

She nodded. "Mostly." Then she shrugged. "But I think for me, too."

I absorbed this information, unsure of what it meant exactly, but willing to give whatever it was a try. "Can I ask you something? And you don't have to answer if you don't want to."

"Go ahead."

"You said at the airport that you would give anything for Alix's happiness. You knew she was in love with you. Why didn't you . . . ?"

"Because I'm not good enough for her," she responded easily.

"So you do love her," I said, my heart sinking slightly.

"Very much so," she admitted. "Maybe not in the way that she wanted me to. Though who knows? But love her I do. Some things are just not meant to be."

I sat back, feeling defeated. If Jessica didn't find herself worthy of Alix, then why should I? Perhaps I should've stayed in New York after all. Allowed Alix to get on with her life, find someone who deserved her love.

"Whatever you're thinking, please stop," Jessica said. "You look seriously pained at the moment. Look, I wasn't trying to imply that you're not good enough for her either. That's not why I said that."

"So, do you think I'm good enough for her?" I asked, locking our gazes.

She smiled. "I don't think I'll ever think anyone is good enough for her. But she seems to think you're worth dropping everything for . . . and that's good enough for me."

Our food arrived then, interrupting the flow of conversation. I was pleased to note that my appetite had returned and the salad before me looked mighty tasty.

At some point during the course of our meal, I found myself asking, "Were you surprised that she forgave me?"

Jessica looked up from her food, an amused expression on her face. "Frustrated, yes. But not surprised. I knew she would."

"How did you know that?"

"Because that's what she does."

The way she said it sparked my curiosity and before I could think twice about it, I asked, "Has she ever had to forgive you for something?"

Jessica sighed, her gaze on her food. "Yes. But you'll have to ask her about that."

I left it at that, returning to my salad.

"Halloween is coming up next week," Jessica said casually and the change of topic was welcomed.

I realized then that she was testing me. "So what are you getting her?"

"What am I getting whom?" she said.

"Alix for her birthday," I clarified, though she knew exactly what I meant.

Jessica smiled. "Good. You know when her birthday is. That's always a good sign."

For a moment I thought she was patronizing me, but then I realized she was merely joking around. I relaxed a bit.

"I'm throwing her a surprise birthday party this weekend, if you're interested in assisting me."

"Count me in." If it involved Alix, I was gladly there.

"Cool," Jessica said.

The word seemed so strange coming from her lips that I found myself laughing. I almost stopped myself . . . but didn't. From here on end everything would be different. *I* would be different.

Chapter 6
Alix

My fingers played absently with the ring in my hands. The maze design stared up at me in a mocking fashion, reminding me of all the twists and turns my life had taken recently. I wondered if perhaps that was why Valerie liked the movie so much. Maybe she sometimes felt trapped in a labyrinth she couldn't escape from.

Or maybe she just had the hots for Jennifer Connelly. One or the other.

I lifted my head and stared at the ocean beyond the balcony of Jessica's bedroom. I'd been waiting for her for over an hour and no one seemed to know where she was.

"Alix?"

I turned around, quickly placing the ring in my pocket. I don't know why I didn't want Jessica to see it. "Hey, Jess," I greeted her, stepping into the room. "I came to see if you wanted to get lunch."

Jessica looked uncomfortable for whatever reason. "Ah, no thanks. I just ate."

"Oh, okay."

"Were you waiting long?" She walked to the closet and turned on the light. Then disappeared inside.

I leaned against the back of the couch. "About an hour or so," I called after her. "Where were you, anyway? No one would tell me."

"Lunch," she answered, from somewhere in the closet.

"I believe we established that," I reminded her. "With whom were you dining?"

There was a long pause, then, "Uh, Mathew."

I frowned at the answer, knowing it to be a lie. I'd seen Mathew earlier. Then he'd left for class. Now why would Jessica lie? "Oh, really?" I asked, playing along. "Where did you guys go?"

Jessica reappeared at the doorway and turned the light off. She'd changed into a pair of light blue jeans and a white shirt. "We went to The Olive Garden."

"Ah. That's nice that after all of these years together the two of you still take time to go out for lunch."

She smiled, but I could tell she seemed troubled. Jessica was a horrible liar. Even if I hadn't spoken to Mathew earlier, I would've known that she was lying. I sincerely hoped Jessica wasn't having an affair already. It had only been a few weeks since the wedding. "Yeah," she agreed, walking past me on her way to the balcony.

I followed close behind. "Especially since Mathew had to skip one of his classes to join you. That was mighty sweet of him."

Jessica avoided my gaze at all costs as she took a seat on one of the lounge chairs. "Yeah," she said, then must have realized she'd already said that and added, "It was."

I didn't say anything for a few seconds, hoping she'd come to her senses or at least come up with a better lie than that. But she didn't say anything. I rolled my eyes as I sat across from her. "Oh, come on, Jessica. I know you weren't out to lunch with Mathew because he was here when I arrived."

Jessica nodded, resigned. "Valerie."

I looked around. "Where?" Then I realized. "You had lunch with *Valerie?*"

"Yep."

"Huh," I said, sitting back. "That's interesting. She didn't tell me." Then I remembered how Jessica had lied about it and I figured that neither of them wanted to admit they didn't completely hate each other. I kept myself from smiling somehow. "Well, thanks for telling me. For a moment I was starting to think you were cheating on Mathew."

Jessica laughed. "It's nice to know you think so highly of me. I would never do that."

She said the last part more seriously than she probably intended.

"Well, I don't know, Jess," I said. "Maybe married life was finally getting to you. The pressures of living with the same person day in and day out, waking up next to them every morning . . ." Actually, that didn't sound particularly bad. I wouldn't mind waking up to Valerie every morning.

"Al, you trailed off there," Jessica informed me.

I attempted to backtrack through my thoughts. "What was I talking about? Perhaps I'm getting Alzheimer's at the age of twenty."

"Almost twenty-one," she reminded me.

Oh, right. It was a good thing there were people around who remembered such things as my birthday. I could always remember everyone else's but mine always seemed to slip my mind. Perhaps I was still in denial that I'd been born at all. "I'm going to have a burial service for my fake ID."

"I'll make the invitations."

"Thanks. So, what are you doing for dinner?" I asked.

"Eating seems likely," Jessica answered.

"Wanna double?" Actually, I wasn't entirely sure I could double, seeing as I hadn't spoken to Valerie since the day before. But I was pretty sure she was off and the girl had to eat.

Jessica thought it over, probably trying to decide whether or not she felt like spending two consecutive meals with Valerie. Finally, she shrugged. "I'll run it by Mathew."

I stood. "Very well then. I'll go run it by Valerie."

⌀

"Well, the first thing we gotta do," Valerie was saying, "is get you to start running." We were in her apartment, sitting on the couch, flipping through the channels on the TV. Since there was nothing on, we'd started talking about the training.

I stared at her, mouth agape. "Run? Me, run? Uh-uh. No way, Jose. I'll do those things where you jump around flailing your arms in the air—"

"Jumping Jacks?"

"Whatever. And I'll do the push-up thingies. I'll even lift a weight or two. But I will *not* run." I crossed my arms against my chest to further prove my point.

Valerie studied me for a moment. "Do you want this part or not?" she asked, quite seriously.

"Yes," I admitted, guessing what was coming.

"Then you've gotta run," she told me. "But if it makes you feel better, I'm running with you."

This could be interesting. "Really?"

"Yeah, I should start exercising again," she said simply. "I can't let myself get out of shape. Especially if I want to start teaching again."

I looked at her in surprise. "Teach?"

She nodded and smiled. "Yeah, ever since you asked me to train you I started thinking about maybe going back to teaching Karate or Tae Kwon Do. I did it for a while in New York when I lived there and it was great."

"Sounds excellent. You must be really good, then." We'd never really talked about her martial arts abilities. It somehow seemed interconnected with a past she appeared more than a little hesitant to talk about. But I was so incredibly curious to know everything about her.

Valerie simply shrugged and let the comment slide.

I decided to press on. "So, you could like, kick someone's ass, right?"

She grinned crookedly as she faced me. Her blue eyes shone with amusement. "Yes, I can."

I nodded. "Could you kill someone?"

Her amusement vanished instantly, and she turned her head away. Her gaze was focused on the TV but she seemed to be looking through it. "Yeah," she replied softly.

Uh-oh. I had stumbled upon a soft spot apparently. Common sense told me to drop the subject. That she would reveal things at her own pace. But at the rate we were going, I didn't see it happening any time soon. Curiosity killed the cat, I told myself. I hoped I had an extra eight lives to spare. "Have you ever killed someone?" It seemed surreal that I should be asking someone that question, least of all my girlfriend. But with Valerie, nothing really seemed out of the realm of possibility.

Valerie froze beside me. Slowly, she faced me. Her eyes were sad and distant. She wore an expression I don't remember seeing on her before and it tore my heart to shreds. I instantly regretted asking the question. Not because I feared the answer, but because her look of pain was unbearable.

I took her hand in mine, just so she'd know I wasn't going to bolt on her.

She seemed momentarily thrown by the gesture and she stared down at our hands for a long moment before responding. When her gaze finally met with mine, she looked more like herself, though there was a tinge of regret in her tone.

"Yes," she finally replied. "I have."

I simply nodded, not knowing how else to respond.

Valerie let go of my hand and sighed. "You can go if you want."

"Go?" I asked.

"Who wants a murderer for a girlfriend," she responded sadly.

Phrasing it that way sure put things in perspective. I wasn't entirely sure how to feel about the revelation. I couldn't say I was particularly surprised. Nothing shocked me anymore. "We are not defined by our past mistakes."

"Sometimes we should be," Valerie said sadly.

"Want to tell me what happened?"

"Not really," she answered. "But I will anyway. You deserve to know who you are with."

She paused as if to collect her thoughts, then continued. "Well, like I told you before, my mom left when I was thirteen and that sealed my fate. My dad went off the deep end of misery. I always came home expecting to find him dead. He decided to drag out suicide, though, I suppose, and just started drinking constantly. So he was pretty much useless as a father.

Aaron was ten at the time and he was already mixing with the wrong crowd. We didn't live in the best of neighborhoods, so you were either in with the wrong crowd, or dead somewhere. Sometimes there are no in-betweens. By then all the money my parents had gotten from Jessica's was gone.

"When I was fourteen I met Chris. She adopted me in a way. Aaron too. So I worked for her, selling drugs at the schools. My dad had me enrolled me in a martial arts school when I was four. I think that was the only fatherly duty he ever really performed. Anyway, I got into a fight with some kids who didn't want to pay, and Chris watched me beat them all to the ground. She was impressed and hooked me up with a friend of hers who gave me private lessons. I didn't realize it then, but she wanted to use my skills to her advantage.

"There was this man, he went by the name of Jake, but I doubt that was his real name. Anyway, this Jake guy owed Chris a lot of money. And he had it, too, which is what pissed Chris off the most. She hated being taken advantage of. So she sent me after him. I beat him until he told me where the money was. I got the money and brought it back to Chris. But she wasn't satisfied. She wanted to show him a lesson. So she sent me back to him, this time to kill him." She paused in her tale, her eyes watering. She shut them, pushing the tears away. When she opened them again, she sighed.

"I was only sixteen. I didn't know what I was doing. Jake learned his lesson the first time and had a bunch of his men standing around with guns, protecting him. They weren't very good or very smart. And eventually I got a clear shot of Jake. He never saw it coming." She fell silent for a moment, then said, "That was the abridged version."

I listened to the entire story, picturing it all in my mind like a movie. Sometimes I felt like Valerie's life seemed more fictional when she told the truth than when she lied about it. "So what happened then?" I was curious to know what caused her to get from there to here. Clearly she wasn't the same person she was then. I couldn't imagine this Valerie killing anyone.

"Well, Chris was so pleased with my work that she started sending me off on more and more adventures. By the time I was seventeen it all got to me. I found myself with a gun pointed at a girl, not much older than myself and I couldn't pull the trigger. I saw myself in her eyes. The fear and the repulsion. I dropped the gun at her feet, daring her to use it on me instead. She just turned at ran. And I went back to Chris and announced my resignation. Aaron refused to leave, though. He was fourteen and had already found his niche dealing with computers."

"Chris let you go that easily?" I asked, unable to keep my mouth shut.

Valerie smiled bitterly. "She didn't have a choice. I'd gone a bit mad at this point. I was on the verge of losing it. I threatened to go to the police. I threatened to kill her and anyone else who dared cross my path. She knew I would, too. In that frame of mind, I would've done many crazy things. Not that I hadn't already. I let her keep Aaron, one of my many mistakes. I will never forgive myself for leaving him there. But I was mad at him, too, for not wanting to leave with me. So I walked off. I ended up in New York City."

"Interesting," I found myself saying. Well, it was.

"You make it seem like I just told you a story from a book or something."

"Kind of seems that way," I admitted. "I believe you, of course," I assured her quickly. "It's just a reality so far from my own that it somehow seems like fiction."

Valerie nodded sadly. "I'm guessing once it dawns on you that all of that was real, you'll never want to see me again."

"No," I said sternly, frowning slightly. "I promise you that won't happen." I hoped she believed me. "So how long has it been since you spoke to your father?"

Valerie smiled, the first real smile I'd seen since we'd started this conversation. "I talk to him all the time. After I got my act together I went back to Boston for a month to see how he was doing. I was shocked to find he'd pulled himself together and was doing fine. We keep in touch. Email . . . or sometimes I call him, or he calls me."

This news made me happy, and I smiled back at her. "That's really good to know," I said, taking her hand once again. "Thank you for telling me everything."

"I promised you I would answer all of your questions," Valerie replied. "My fear is that one of these days you'll hear an answer you can't handle."

I laughed. "I can handle anything."

"I hope so," Valerie said seriously and seemed to relax. "My turn to ask you something."

"Shoot," I said, wondering what she could possibly be wondering about me.

Valerie played with her tongue ring for a moment. "I went to lunch with Jessica today."

"That's your question?" I asked.

Valerie laughed. "No. But it's relevant."

"All right . . ."

"She said you'd once forgiven her for something. She told me to ask you if I wanted to know that story." She smiled sheepishly. "I guess I'm curious to know what Jessica could've possibly done to you. Is it because she wouldn't go out with you?"

Her question surprised me. I hadn't expected that topic to ever come up. I was surprised that Jessica had even thought to mention it. It was so long ago. "Um, no. It happened long before Jessica and I were friends."

Valerie arched an eyebrow, interested.

"Well, it's not quite as compelling as your story, but I'll tell it." I started thinking over the details of the tale and suddenly felt embarrassed. "It's such a dorky story."

Valerie waited patiently for me to continue, regardless of my warning. Here went nothing.

"I first met Jessica in middle school and at that point she was a really big snob. In other words, she was a total bitch. But I was a total nerd, and the moment I laid eyes on her I was a gonner. Love at first sight and all that jazz. I was fourteen, she was sixteen. And I, in all my dorkyness, went up to her and asked her if I could be her friend." I rolled my eyes at myself. I was so glad I'd grown up into a much cooler person.

"Anyway, she laughed at me of course. Her posse of friends laughed along with her at the sheer stupidity of my question. But a few weeks later, Jessica was throwing a party. I heard about it through the grapevine, 'cause in spite of her rejection I was still majorly obsessed with her. You can imagine my surprise when Jessica walked up to me one day and invited me to her party. She apologized for laughing at me and said she wanted to be friends. I was elated. I was walking on air the rest of the week, counting the hours until the party.

"So, the fateful day arrived and the party was going wonderfully. I'd never been in a mansion before, and my jaw remained firmly planted on the floor for most of the night. All of her friends welcomed me into their circle with open arms and I couldn't imagine ever being happier . . ." I took a deep breath, then continued. "Then Jessica suggested we all go skinny dipping in the pool. Everyone thought it was a grand idea and I wasn't about to argue with my new friends. So Jessica led me to this room where I could take my clothes off and handed me a towel. Then she told me everyone was meeting in the living room.

"So I stripped and put the towel around my body and walked out into the living room, where I was surprised to find everyone else, fully dressed and standing around ready to sing Happy Birthday. When they saw me they started laughing hysterically. Jessica ran over and snapped the towel off of me so I was completely exposed. That's when her mom came wandering into the room, carrying the birthday cake. She dropped it on the floor when she saw me and cried out, asking what I thought I was doing.

"I was too petrified to speak. Jessica had dropped the towel at my feet and I quickly picked it up and tried to cover myself up. I was too scared to even cry. Her mom walked over and grabbed my hand and then told the butler to escort me to the outside gates of the mansion. I waited out there naked until my mom came and picked me up." I truly hated that story.

Valerie stared at me. "Wow," she said.

"It's okay, you can laugh," I said, shrugging.

"It's not funny," Valerie said, to my surprise. Everyone else found it hilarious. Jade had nearly fallen off the chair. "That must've been horrifying."

"Not quite as much as getting my diary posted all over school, but yes, I was quite mortified," I agreed. When she arched an eyebrow at the mention of my diary, I sighed. "This really evil girl found my diary and made copies and put them all over school. That's how Jessica found out I was in love with her. Yadda yadda."

"You could write a book of all your embarrassing stories," Valerie commented.

"Yes, so that I can immortalize the worst experiences of my life," I agreed. "I'll get right on that."

Valerie laughed and kissed my cheek. "Sorry."

"So how do you feel about having dinner with Jessica and Mathew?" I asked carefully. Better to ask when she was apologizing for something. It fared better for the chances of a positive response.

"Sure, when?" Valerie responded.

"Tonight," I answered. "I'll let you drive."

"The Bug?"

"Uh-huh."

"Excellent! I'm there."

I smiled, mighty pleased with myself. Some girls were just way too easy to please.

$\mathcal{B}$

We ended up at Friday's for dinner. I wanted to go to Wendy's but apparently Jessica and Mathew didn't think that would be an appropriate place for a double date. Instead of arguing, I simply expressed my disapproval by wearing all black. I tended to express my disapproval a lot.

"Cute shirt," Jessica mentioned, as Valerie and I sat down.

I smiled proudly at my recent purchase. It was a black shirt that read "I'm only wearing black until they make something darker." "Thank you, I like it."

"She was torn between that one and the one about the penguins," Valerie told them. "That's why we're late."

"Penguins?" Mathew inquired.

"'One by one the penguins take my sanity,'" I said solemnly. "I live by its wisdom."

"She's *your* friend," Valerie said to Jessica.

"*Your* girlfriend," she countered.

"Ladies, ladies," I said, holding up my hands. "There's plenty of me to go around." I regarded Mathew with mock seriousness. "You've only been married to her for a few weeks and already she's fighting over me. You must be doing something wrong. Are you making her wear that leash I gave you?"

Mathew laughed and blushed. "Well . . . uh . . . ."

"Whoa! I don't want to know," I said, catching his meaning. "You're both sick. Sick, sick, sick."

Thankfully, for all our sakes, the waitress appeared. I ordered a salad, because according to Valerie's new training schedule, I had to eat healthier. Apparently, Frosties and French fries weren't doing anything for me.

"Since when do you eat salads?" Jessica asked, when the waitress had gone.

"Since Valerie called me fat and demanded I go on a diet."

Mathew and Jessica glanced sharply at Valerie.

Valerie gave me an evil look. "I'm training her for this role she wants to audition for. She needs to eat *healthier*. Not less. And I did not call her fat." The last part she directed at me.

Mathew and Jessica looked at me for confirmation, and I nodded, letting Valerie off the hook.

Valerie sent me another warning look which I found more adorable than intimidating.

"So, Mathew," I said, staring at him. "How's med school treating you?"

"I love it," he replied, lighting up at the mention of it.

"You know that makes you a nerd," I informed him, in case he didn't already know. "When are you transferring to fashion design?"

"Are you trying to turn me gay?" he inquired.

"Dominique slipped me a twenty at the wedding so I'd suggest the idea," I replied. "And I think it's a lot cooler than med school. I mean, anyone can save a life. But to save a person from the evil claws of bad fashion sense . . ." I nodded gravely as I let the rest hang in the air.

"I'll consider it," Mathew replied with a wink.

"Oh, Alix," Jessica said suddenly. "Do you think we could celebrate your birthday a week late?"

"Hmm?"

"Mathew has a conference and I promised I'd go with him," Jessica said regretfully. "I didn't realize it would be the same weekend as your birthday. But it's too late to change the plans now."

I tried to hide my disappointment. "Yeah, sure. No problem." Who'd schedule a medical conference on the weekend of Halloween? Did these people have no sense of decency?

"We'll make it up to you," Mathew assured me.

Sure they would. I suddenly felt depressed, but tried to snap out of it. It was only my birthday. Jessica didn't have to always be present for me to turn a year older. It would happen regardless. But it suddenly felt like the start of a trend. What else would she be willing to miss? First my birthday . . . what next? My wedding? Maybe she wouldn't be able to make it to . . . whatever state deemed gay marriage legal that year.

Hmm . . . I was starting to notice my slight tendency to blow things out of proportion.

Chapter 7
Valerie

I arrived at Jessica's mansion shortly after one the next afternoon. I'd received an "urgent" message from her stating, and I quote, "Valerie, this is Jessica. You must be at my house tomorrow at one-thirty. It's urgent. Oh, and don't tell Alix. Bye."

And so I went, wondering what could possibly be so urgent.

"Mr. Collins is by the pool," Maurice informed me.

"And Jessica?" I inquired. Surely he didn't think I was here to see Mathew.

"She'll be down shortly," Maurice responded. "She'll join you outside."

"Thank you," I told him. I was a bit hesitant, knowing it was Mathew that awaited there. He seemed nice enough, but I'd never been left alone with him and wasn't sure I'd know what to say. Still, I couldn't very well stand in the foyer like an idiot waiting for Jessica to appear.

I found my . . . brother-in-law? The title sounded extremely awkward. In spite of the recent advances in my relationship with Jessica, we were still far from being friends. Even further still from being sisters. The entire concept felt as foreign to me as I'm sure it felt to her. Being sisters implied a bond that mere blood couldn't form. It saddened me in a way. Yet I had to accept it.

I found Mathew sitting on a lounge chair, dressed in jeans and a sleeveless tee shirt and surrounded by books. He was staring intently into a thick textbook whose cover was obscured from my view. But going by the other titles piled around him, I guessed the content of the book to be medicine-related.

Unsure of how to proceed, I stood still, studying him quietly. He was attractive in a boy-next-door sort of way. In a lot of ways he reminded me of Alix. Light hair. Green eyes. Soft skin . . . a beautiful smile that . . .

Er. Sorry. Back to Mathew.

"Having fun?" I found myself asking.

He looked up from the book and smiled. "As fun as Biochemistry can be," he replied. "Although, I think the entertainment factor is relative."

"So you *are* having fun?" I guessed, taking the liberty of sitting on the lounge chair beside his.

A lopsided grin was reply enough. He shut the book and placed it with the others. "Would you like something to drink?"

I had to admit that I was thirsty. But I did not like the idea of calling upon servants to perform duties I was perfectly capable of doing on my own.

Mathew stood. "What would you like?" he asked to my amazement. "I think we've got soda, juice, water. Milk probably. I'd fix you a drink but I don't know how."

I laughed at the sheer absurdity of the situation. Surely he wasn't serious. "I'll take a Pepsi," I said, out of morbid curiosity. Would he yell the order into the house? Perhaps he had an earpiece with direct communication to the staff.

"Be back in a jiffy," he said, then disappeared into the house.

Strange. Billions of dollars. A mansion by the sea. And the master of the household was studying medicine and fetching his own drinks. I'd wondered briefly how much of this marriage was based on love and how much was based on money. I distrusted people by default, having learned by experience not to set my expectations too high. So I'd written Mathew off as someone who'd married Jessica for the money. I'm sure it didn't hurt that she was beautiful. But I was starting to think that perhaps the boy deserved a chance.

Mathew returned shortly with a can of Pepsi. "Jessica's on the phone with her grandparents," he told me as he handed me the can. "In case you wondered why you're stuck with me."

I thanked him for the drink. "Is she close with her family?" I found myself asking. Since when did I care?

Mathew shrugged a shoulder. "Not particularly," he said, with a tinge of sadness in his voice. "They don't like the way she runs the business."

"What way is that?" I asked, suddenly curious.

He hesitated, unsure of whether or not to proceed. "She's kind and selfless," he stated simply. "They wish she were more like them."

I nodded, absorbing the information. It had never occurred to me that there would be a rift between Jessica and the rest of the family. I wanted to know more, but I knew that Mathew would not go into detail. I admired his respect for Jessica's privacy.

"May I speak frankly for a moment?" he asked.

"What were you doing before?"

He smiled, but quickly turned serious once again.

"Is this where you warn me about Alix and Jessica, and threaten to come after me if I ever hurt them again?" I asked, wishing to evade the blow. I couldn't deal with another lecture.

"No," he responded, shaking his head. "It's not my place to accuse or threaten. Neither is it in my nature. I trust that Jessica, Alix and yourself have settled matters on your own." He paused as if to reconsider his words. "Please don't get me wrong. I love them more than anything. Alix is like a sister to me. And Jessica . . . she's my entire life." For some reason, I didn't doubt his sincerity. "But they're also fiercely independent and I've learned with time to step out of their way and let them handle things."

"So what do you want to speak to me about?" I asked, now truly at a loss.

He leaned forward. "I want to thank you."

I stared at him in surprise. "What for?"

"For coming into both of their lives," he said. "I don't think you realize the effect your presence has had on both of them. For entirely different reasons, of course."

"I'm not sure I understand," I admitted. How much could I possibly affect another person? Positively, anyway. I was sure pain I'd caused plenty of. For a moment I worried that I'd suddenly be whisked away to star in my very own rendition of *It's A Wonderful Life*. Thankfully that didn't happen.

"I didn't think you would," Mathew said. "But I hope that you at least believe it."

I would have inquired further but Jessica chose that moment to make her appearance. "Sorry," she said, stepping out onto the deck. "Unexpected phone call. I trust Mathew entertained you?"

"He was telling me about the different parts of the cell," I said. "There was much I didn't know."

Jessica laughed, sitting next to Mathew on the chair. "Well, as long as you weren't totally bored."

"I'm here!" Jade announced, walking toward us.

Needless to say I was surprised by her unexpected arrival. I was also now remembering that I still had no idea why I was there.

"Good," Jessica said, rising to pull a chair over for Jade. We now sat in an ill-formed circle around Mathew's pillar of books. "Now we can start."

"Start what, exactly?" I asked. I had the uneasy feeling that at any moment Jessica would force us to join hands and start singing "Kumbaya."

"Alix's surprise birthday party," Jade said. "We try to alternate with the years so she doesn't expect anything."

Ah, now this I could get into. "What do you mean, alternate?"

"Well," Jessica began, "last year, Roxanne went to visit her family in Orlando. So we had Roxanne call from there and tell Alix that her car had broken down and that she needed us to come pick her up. But really we all met at Disney World and threw her a huge bash with Mickey and friends."

"I bet that was fun," I commented, wishing I'd been there. "So what's the plan this year?"

Jessica shrugged. "That's what we're here to figure out." She looked around. "Ideas?"

I tried to think of something special we could do for Alix. I envied Jessica the ability to get Alix anything. I could never compete with that, though I hadn't yet seen Jessica throw her money in anyone's face. "How about a cruise?"

"A cruise," Jessica repeated, considering it.

"She'd never expect that," said Jade, nodding.

"Definitely not," Mathew agreed. "Especially since she thinks Jessica and I are going away for the weekend."

I arched a brow. "You guys lied about that?"

"Of course," Jessica responded.

I laughed at their evilness.

Jessica was nodding thoughtfully. "Okay, I'll make the arrangements for the cruise."

"Can you make them on such short notice?" Jade asked.

Jessica grinned. "I know I can."

∅

I lay on my couch later that day, staring at the patterns on the ceiling and trying to decipher my emotions. I'd returned from Jessica's with mixed feelings and I couldn't quite define them all.

We'd spent at least a couple of hours discussing specifics. Jessica had called and made arrangements with the cruise line. She'd gotten a hold of Roxanne who'd been more than willing to partake in the plan. Everything would be perfect. I knew Alix would love it all.

I glanced around my meager apartment. Once upon a time, I could've bought Alix the world. Of course, she would've never loved me then. It's true what they say, you can't have everything.

And as much as I wanted to believe that Jessica did, I was starting to see that this wasn't altogether true. Still I did envy her the financial freedom to bring ideas to fruition. I couldn't compete with a cruise.

Sighing, I picked up the phone, pressing number one on my speed dial. It rang a few times before a voice answered.

"Yeah?"

I smiled instantly, her voice making me feel a billion times better. "Hey," I greeted. "I was wondering if you'd like to join me for dinner? I'm cooking."

"I can't. I have a date with my other girlfriend."

"Your vibrator can wait," I teased.

Alix started laughing. "What time do you want me there?"

"Seven," I said, thinking it would give me plenty of time to get everything prepared. "What would you like to eat?"

There was a pause as Alix considered. "I'll take that thing you made last time. That was yum."

"You got it."

"Do I have to stir the noodles this time?"

I laughed. "No, I'll take care of everything."

"Oh, good. Anything else?"

I arched an eyebrow though she couldn't see it. "Are you trying to get rid of me so soon?"

"I've got class in five minutes," she said regretfully. "When do you work again?"

"I'm off until next Tuesday," I replied. "I asked Dean to give me a week to settle back in."

"Good," Alix said. "Okay, leave me a message if you want me to bring anything."

"Just yourself," I assured her.

"See you tonight," she said.

"'Til then," I replied. I heard the click at the other end of the line, hung up, and rested my head against the arm of the couch. Loki stared up at me from the floor, and in one swift motion I had her settled on my stomach. "Oof! You're getting heavy. What have I been feeding you?"

The pug just stared at me, and I petted her, feeling guilty for all the traveling I'd put the poor puppy through. "Don't worry, from now on, we're staying right where we are," I promised her.

ॐ

I knew how much Alix loved the beach, so I decided to incorporate that knowledge into my dinner plans. I made the dinner and packed it away in a picnic basket, along with wine glasses, a couple cans of Dr. Pepper, and a candle. I left Alix a note on the door letting her know where to find me.

I'd spread out a blanket and set up the plates. I was in the process of lighting the candle when Alix appeared at my side. I'd been worried that perhaps she wouldn't get my note and think I'd stood her up. Or that she wouldn't like my idea. But the look on her face put my fears at ease.

"Wow," she breathed.

"I thought we could eat outside for a change," I explained, feeling a bit embarrassed. "Dr. Pepper?" I offered, holding up the can.

She smiled brightly as she joined me on the blanket. She took the can from me and poured the contents into the wine glass. "This is beautiful," she said, her voice conveying her sincerity.

I smiled back at her, happy that she seemed pleased. We were in a quiet area, far away from the buzzing of Ft. Lauderdale nightlife. The waves crashed near by and a gentle breeze blew in from the ocean. All in all, I thought it was the perfect atmosphere. "I'm glad you like it."

"I love it," she said.

"Hungry?"

"Bring it on," she answered. "I've been thinking of nothing else all day."

"Seeing me?" I guessed, serving the food.

She was staring hungrily at the plate. "Hm? Oh. Yeah, that too."

I laughed, proud that she liked my cooking so much. "Perhaps I should be a chef instead of a bartender."

"I'd hire you," Alix informed me, digging into the food with gusto.

"You couldn't afford me," I teased.

Green eyes sparkled with mischief as they glanced at me. "I'm sure there are other methods of payment."

I started choking on a piece of pasta.

"Are you okay?" Alix asked with concern.

"Fine," I managed to say through a fit of coughs.

"I learned the Heimlich in the ninth grade, I'm sure I can give it a whirl . . ."

I shook my head in reply. "Anyway, you were saying?" I asked, when I'd finally gotten my coughing under control.

"Not a thing," she responded innocently.

"No, no," I insisted. "I would very much like to hear about these alternate methods of payment."

Alix shook her head. "Sorry. It's clear that you're not mature enough to handle them."

I smiled, knowing she'd won. We ate the rest of the dinner in relative silence, commenting on random things here and there when we thought to mention something. I spent the time alternating between glancing down at my plate and trying not to stare at her. She looked so beautiful by candlelight.

When we were done, I cleared away the plates and put the basket aside. Alix sidled over and kissed my cheek.

"Thank you," she said. "That was really sweet."

I smiled, feeling completely content. I still had no idea what I'd done to deserve this. "You're very welcome. Anything for you." I wanted to kiss her but I was hesitant, afraid she'd pull away. So I settled for taking her hand.

"Close your eyes," Alix said softly.

I frowned slightly but did as I was told.

She removed her hand from my grasp and replaced it with something else.

"Open them," she instructed.

In my palm was a small box. "What's this?" I asked, surprised.

"Well, open it and find out," she replied.

Carefully I opened the box. I blinked a few times when I saw what was inside. "Where did you get this?" I asked, pulling the ring out. I was touched beyond words.

She shrugged. "I have my ways." She bit her lip for a moment. "Do you like it?"

"I love it!" I exclaimed. "No one's ever given me something like this before." I grinned at her.

"I've had it for a while," she said. "I was waiting to give it to you."

"Thank you," I said finally, putting it on. It was a perfect fit. "How'd you know my size?"

"Lucky guess," she replied.

I kissed her then, throwing caution to the wind. I wanted to show her how much I appreciated her gift, how much it meant to me. "I love you," I whispered when we pulled away.

"I love you too," she whispered back.

My heart skipped a beat at the words, which coated my broken spirit in a way that nothing else had. I wanted to say more, but didn't know what exactly. So I simply pulled her toward me, kissing her again. Hoping she understood what I was trying to convey, and knowing, somehow, that she felt the same.

Chapter 8
Alix

"C'mon, Alix," Valerie was insisting. "One more. You can do one more."

I glanced at her from my position on the floor. My cheek was pressed against the cool wooden floor of Jessica's private gym. "No more push-ups. That's enough. You are going to *kill* me."

"Just one more," Valerie pleaded.

She wasn't going to leave me alone. I was starting to realize this. Fine. One more. I could do one more. No problem. I got in position and prepared to lift myself up. Ugh! This was pure torture. Why would anyone subject themselves to this voluntarily? I managed to get half-way up before falling back down on my stomach. "Ouch."

Valerie nodded and sighed. "Two and a half push-ups."

"Is that bad?" I asked, sitting up.

"Are you sure you want to play this part?" she asked. "Isn't there a role that just requires you to sit there?"

I sent her a dirty look. "Hey, I admit I'm not in shape."

"There are no words for what you are." Valerie offered a hand to help me up.

I swatted her hand away and rose on my own. If she didn't start being a little more compassionate she was going to be sorry. I was tired and cranky and she was *this* close to feeling my wrath.

Mercifully, Jessica walked in. "You guys hungry?"

"Are you cooking?" I asked.

"Yes."

"Then no," I answered. I glanced at Valerie and gave her a look that I hoped would warn her away from the horror of Jessica's "cooking."

"Well, I'm officially offended," Jessica said. "If you guys want anything, you know where the kitchen is."

"Hey, that tuna thing you made that one time wasn't half bad," I said, hoping to make her feel better.

Jessica was confused for a moment, then she frowned. "That wasn't tuna."

♌

There are many things in life that I don't yet comprehend. Like why does Steven Tyler look so good in tight pants? And why does no one else see this? Or what is love, anyway? Is it like a chemistry thing? Or perhaps it's one of those diseases that everyone gets, like chickenpox. And why does it make me do stupid things like sit out on the beach all alone contemplating its muddled meaning?

I sat there watching the waves for a while, idly wondering the odds of the same drop of water touching the same exact spot on the sand more than once. How would one measure that? Could one put a little tracking device on a drop of water and then a sensor on the sand and . . .

"What are you doing out here?"

I didn't turn at the sound of Jessica's voice. "I'm jogging," I answered dryly. "Mental laps."

She sat beside me a moment later. "Where did Valerie go?"

"Home," I replied.

"Oh. Will you be seeing her again tonight?"

"What's with all the Valerie questions?" I asked, facing her.

Jessica shrugged, playing with the sand. "Just curious."

I nodded, relaxing in her company. "I think she wanted to take a shower and a nap. I doubt I'll see her again tonight." I paused. "So how are you feeling about the whole thing? Long lost sister dating your best friend . . ."

Jessica took a deep breath, staring at the water as if the answer lay out there somewhere. "Overwhelmed, I think." She glanced at me, then continued. "I'm not entirely sure how to feel."

"You guys need to sit down and talk," I said, knowing it was easier said than done. "I realize your stubbornness and pride may present a problem there, but I'm pretty sure you'll manage it somehow."

Jessica frowned. "Stubbornness and pride?"

"Ya," I replied. "I know you're dying to know about your real parents. About your brother. About her. And even if she doesn't admit it, I know she's curious as hell about you, too. But you both insist on pretending otherwise. And why? Cause you're stubborn and proud. Must be genetic."

She was silent for a long moment. Finally, she asked, "Do you know anything about them?"

I hesitated, unsure of how much I should say. "I met Aaron."

"You did?" she asked in surprise. "And?"

I tried to remember the brief encounter to the best of my ability. "Well, he's gorgeous. But I think unlike you and Valerie he actually knows it. Or at least, flaunts it. He hit on me. And then he left."

"Wow, you sure get around with the members of this family," Jessica teased, then must've realized what she'd said because she grew slightly sad. "It's so weird. I'm curious, you're right, but I'm afraid also. I painted everything up in my mind and to be faced with the reality of it . . . it's a lot to take in."

"I know," I said, wishing I could say something to make her feel better.

"And my parents?" she asked tentatively.

I bit my lip, unsure of what to say. "I think you should take that up with Valerie."

"I know," she admitted. "But I want to prepare myself." She stared pleadingly into my eyes. "Please."

Why did she do that? She knew I couldn't say no to her. "Well, from what I know, your mom left. Then came back. Then left again, and Valerie hasn't seen her since. But your dad is living in Boston. Valerie told me she speaks to him often."

Jessica nodded. "Thanks."

"It's weird," I said. "Every time she tells me something about herself or her family, I forget that it's your family too. That if everything hadn't happened the way it did, I would've never met you. I would've never met Valerie. It's so easy to forget that." I still wasn't sure which way Jessica would've had it better. She suffered either way, but at least had she been with her real family she would've known who she was.

It occurred to me that both Valerie and Jessica envied each other. I don't think either had any idea how much the other had suffered.

"So how are the two of you doing?" Jessica asked.

I allowed the change of subject, even if it wasn't so far from the original. "We're doing wonderfully," I said, grinning to myself. "She's really great, you know?"

"I'm glad," Jessica said, smiling at me. "You deserve that."

"So, how are you and Mathew doing?" I asked, thankful that the topic no longer tore my heart to shreds.

This brought a smile to her face and I was grateful. "We're doing great. We're thinking of moving."

The news shocked me. "Moving? Where?" I couldn't imagine Jessica not living at the mansion.

Jessica shrugged. "Not sure yet. But we don't want to live here for the rest of our lives. Two people don't need a house this big."

"So what are you going to do with it? Where are you going to go?" I had so many questions I couldn't spit them out fast enough. Were they going to move far away?

Jessica laughed. "Calm down, Al. We're not moving to the moon or anything. We're just thinking of buying a small house nearby. Someplace that's just ours. The mansion . . . it's just not us." She paused. "There's one by your mom's that's for sale. We could be neighbors."

I was honestly at a loss for words. Why would they want to give up this beautiful mansion? They were nuts. "Why don't you build one," I found myself suggesting. "By the sea, preferably."

Jessica nodded. "We talked about that too. Do you really think that would be a good idea?"

"Yes!" I said, excited all of a sudden. "You can get Valerie to help you design it. She's a great artist. You could make it really cool. Don't buy that stupid house by Mom's. I hate that house. It smells like cat pee."

Jessica started laughing. "I'll take your word for it."

"You should build one, Jess," I said seriously. "You can start everything brand new."

"We'll see," she said, nodding. "So what do you want for your birthday?"

"Honestly?" I asked.

"Of course."

"I want you and Mathew to be there." I really was upset that they were going to be gone for my birthday. "But since that's not going to happen, I want you to make me a promise."

Jessica stared at me. "What's the promise?"

"I want you to promise me that you will talk to Valerie," I said. "And that regardless of what happens with our relationship—hers and mine, I mean—you won't let it interfere with your relationship with her."

Jessica looked down at her hands. "That's what you want? Why?"

"Because I know that if you don't do it for yourself, you'll do it for me."

"I promise," she said.

Good.

"So is there anything else you want?" she asked. "Something I could perhaps purchase with my credit card?"

I laughed. "Yeah, how about one of those little islands in the Caribbean."

"If only you were serious," she said in mock sadness. "I've been dying to get you something expensive for years."

I patted her shoulder. "I would never give you the satisfaction of buying me a yacht."

She laughed. "There's gotta be something you want."

I racked my brain. "I'll take a pack of gum."

"What kind?"

"Surprise me," I said.

"Very well," she said. "A promise and gum it is."

I smiled. "Best birthday presents ever."

ℒ

The next few days passed by in a blur. School took up most of my time. I had a lot to catch up on since I'd missed about a week's worth of work while I'd been off gallivanting in New York. Only a couple of professors gave me a hard time about it. The others had been understanding. It still didn't mean that I didn't have to do the work.

Valerie started working on Tuesday and so our time together was cut even shorter. We talked on the phone a lot. She was still the only person I spent more than fifteen minutes conversing with. Every now and then I received an email from her. But it had been nearly a week since I'd last seen her. Luckily, we had plans for the weekend.

Unfortunately, it was still only Thursday and I was stuck in my dorm room attempting to memorize a scene for my acting class. It was a joint project with a playwriting class. They wrote the scenes. We acted in them. The one I'd been stuck with was bad. It was beyond bad. I was sure I'd have nightmares about it.

I was in the middle of practicing a line when there was a knock on the door. "Come in!" I called in a British accent. I don't know why.

Quite appropriately, Jade walked into the room. "How'd you know it was me?" she asked.

"I didn't. I was just being strange." I handed her the script. "Here. You're Rudolph."

"The red-nosed reindeer?"

"No," I said. "Rudolph the gorgeous yet misunderstood cowboy."

"I'm a cowboy?"

I stared at her patiently. "No. You're not a cowboy. He's a cowboy. You're a freak."

"Can I incorporate that into the character?"

"Whatever," I said. "Just read the lines."

We stood in the center of the room. I was playing Mary Sue, the gorgeous yet misunderstood barmaid who was secretly in love with Rudolph. He didn't love her back however for mysterious reasons. I suspected he was gay.

"'Howdy,'" said Jade/Rudolph, the only cowboy with a British accent. "'I've come for a drink.'" Jade frowned. "What kind of garbage is this?"

"Class project," I explained. "Some people really shouldn't be writing plays."

Jade rolled her eyes and continued. "'You are lookin' mighty fine there, Mary Sue.'"

"'Why thank you kindly,'" I said, glad I at least knew one line. "'What brings you into town today?'"

"'I was thirsty,'" responded Rudolph. Jade started laughing. Then composed herself. "'I come bearing sheep.'" She was trying desperately not to crack up.

"'They say a man's only as good as the size of his cattle.'"

That did it. Jade started laughing hysterically. "Please don't make me read this anymore," she pleaded, once she'd regained control of herself.

I took the script from her. "You're of no help. I have to have this memorized by tomorrow."

"You're acting in that?" she asked. "In front of people?"

"Unfortunately."

"Well, break a foot."

"Leg."

Jade rolled her eyes. "Is it really that bloody important which limb it is?"

I sighed. "Breaking a leg come from bowing at the end of the show. If you get to bow it's because you did a good job."

"Wouldn't it then be break your waist?"

"Girls curtsy," I answered.

"So what do you tell a guy?"

I opened my mouth but shut it again. "Never mind. It's all highly debatable anyway." I put the script aside and sat on my bed. "So what brings you by?"

"Just wanted to see how life was treating you," she responded, joining me. "How are things with Valerie? Any plans for your birthday?"

"Things are fine," I answered. "I haven't seen her in a while, though. But I get to see her tomorrow. She's taking me to Miami."

"Really? What for?"

"I'm not sure. Something about going trick-or-treating there."

"Cute."

Well, it was now or never. "Valerie told me. About you helping her with the whole thing."

Jade froze. Clearly she hadn't been expecting that. "Ah."

"You should've told me," I said, feeling sad. I'd figured it out in a way but the truth still hurt.

"I know," she said, looking down at the floor. "I never thought it would get so out of hand. I never thought you'd actually fall for her."

"So why did you encourage me to?"

"I don't know," she admitted, sounding sad. "I was so happy to see that you were interested in someone besides Jessica. I just wanted things to work out between you and Valerie. I knew she was lying but I guess I figured that even if you guys ended up breaking up then at least you'd be over Jessica. I really didn't think you'd fall so hard for her, Alix. When I agreed to help her, I figured the two of you would become friends at the most. And I never, not even for a moment, thought you'd actually sleep with her."

"I see."

"I owed her such a huge favor," Jade continued. "I didn't know how to say no. Especially since she seemed so desperate. I'm so very sorry, Alix. Truly."

I nodded. "It's okay. I understand."

Jade didn't say anything.

"But anyway, if you hadn't done that, then Valerie and I would've never met, so in a lot of ways I'm grateful."

She hugged me, a gesture so unlike her that I was stunned for a long moment. "I love you, Al. I would never do anything to hurt you on purpose. I hope you believe that."

"I do," I said, touched and shocked at the same time.

She let go of me, clearly embarrassed. She cleared her throat. "Anyway, the reason I came over was actually to give you your birthday present."

I frowned. "But it's not until tomorrow."

Jade ran a hand through the peach fuzz she called hair. "I know, but I kind of promised this guy I'd go to this Halloween party with him tomorrow night."

"Oh."

"But if you don't want me to go, I won't," she said quickly.

"No, it's okay," I said, feeling depressed. Why were they all abandoning me all of a sudden? If I didn't have Valerie I'd be spending my twenty-first birthday giving out candy to obnoxious kids.

"He's really cute, Al," Jade said. "I met him at the bookstore. He was in the Sci-Fi section. And I was going nuts trying to find this book I wanted to buy. And guess who was looking at it?"

"The really cute guy?" I guessed.

"Yes!"

"Well, as long as he's really cute," I said, not feeling any better at all. But I was an actress after all, so I could pretend otherwise. I wasn't about to ruin Jade's night. "So where's the present?"

"Oh, right," Jade said, and dug into her book bag. "Here you go."

She handed me a wrapped object which appeared to be a book. I tore the wrapper off and blinked at the cover. "*The Joys of Lesbian Sex.*"

Jade was grinning widely. "You're welcome. I had to buy it used because I think it's out of print. But I tracked it down."

"Used?"

"Well, don't fret, I wiped it off," she assured me. "Do you like it?"

I smiled. "Yes, thank you." I wasn't sure whether to laugh or blush.

Jade stood. "Well, I've got to run. I'll call you on Saturday and maybe we can get together and celebrate your birthday?"

"Sure," I said.

"Hope you have a good one," she said. She waved and disappeared into the hall.

I looked down at the new addition to my collection of classics. I was too embarrassed to open it, so I just put it aside for later.

I picked up the script and returned to memorizing the stupid lines. A few minutes later, the door opened, and Nicole walked in.

"Hey," she greeted.

"Howdy," I said. Perhaps the play was getting to me already. I needed a break. "Hey, do you want to come shopping with me?"

"What for?" Nicole asked, her surprise showing. We never did anything together.

"I need a costume for tomorrow."

"Got a party?"

"I'm going trick-or-treating," I replied proudly.

"How old are you?" Nicole asked, laughing. "Yeah, I'll go with you. I should probably pick one up myself. There're a few parties on campus I'll probably be crashing."

"Excellent," I said. "I'm not sure what I should be. A witch . . . a princess . . . a vampire . . . an elf."

"Straight," Nicole suggested.

I laughed. "Nah, I couldn't pull that off."

Chapter 9
Alix & Valerie

"Everything's set," I assured Jessica. "Alix doesn't suspect a thing. I told her we were going trick-or-treating in Miami."

Jessica laughed. "Good one."

I'd thought so too. Grinning proudly, I stepped in front of my closet to see what I could pull off as a costume at the last minute. I kept the phone to my ear as I rummaged through the articles of clothing.

"What time is she coming by?"

I glanced at my watch. "Soon probably," I answered. "I totally forgot to pick out a costume though."

"Smooth."

A knock at the door kept me from responding. "I think she's here," I told Jessica, stepping out of the room.

"Okay, you know where to be and what time, right?"

"Got it."

"See you there."

"Bye." I hung up the phone as I reached the door. In the hallway stood Alix, dressed as a pink fuzzy bunny, complete with an apron that read, "Pet me, I'm cute." I cleared my throat to keep from laughing. "Uh. Roger Rabbit lives two doors down."

Alix was not amused. "I have a little problem," she said as she stepped into the apartment.

Please God, I begged. Don't let me start laughing. She'll dump me on the spot. I closed the door and regarded her seriously. "Go on."

"Right," she began. "So I was in the girl's bathroom at my dorm, about to try on my very cool new costume." She held up an empty bag with a pictures of a weird gothic outfit clearly displayed. "Except that inside, I found this." She motioned to herself. "And I thought, 'Okay, I need to go return it.' Clearly." She looked down at the floor and hesitated a moment, blushing a deep red. "But um, I thought I'd try it on anyway. Just . . . because."

"Right . . ." I said, not sure where she was going with this. I smiled. She looked quite adorable in the bunny ears and pink furry body.

"Stop smiling," she said. "This isn't funny."

I covered my mouth with one hand and leaned back against the door.

She sighed. "Okay, so I got into the costume. But the um . . . the zipper got stuck. So I figured I'd get Nicole to help me. But when I got back to my room, the door was locked. And I didn't have the key."

"So you came directly here?" I asked. I could only imagine her walking down the street to the apartment dressed that way.

"Yes," she answered.

"How'd you get here without your keys?" I wondered.

"I had my car keys with me," she responded. She sighed again and dropped down on the couch. "I have two sets of keys. My car keys and my house keys. I generally lock them together into one but today I didn't feel like carrying around a lot of keys so I separated them. I wasn't expecting Nicole to lock me out of the room."

I grinned, walked over to her, and leaned down to kiss her nose. "Happy Birthday."

This at least brought a smile to her face. "Thank you. Now will you help me out of this thing?"

"Sure," I responded, offering her my hand. "I think I have a pair of pliers in my room." I took her fuzzy paw in my hand and led her to the room. "I kind of like the costume, Alix. It's very becoming."

"Shut up."

I grinned. "Okay, turn around," I instructed once we were inside the room. I reached up to grab the zipper. It reminded me of the first time we'd gone out and my grin turned into a smile. "I don't think you have much luck with zippers."

"I find myself in this position a lot with you, it seems," she agreed.

I laughed. "Maybe it's a sign." I tried the zipper but it wouldn't budge. "It's stuck."

"No, duh. Did you think I made that whole story up?"

"Hey, you never know."

She turned to face me, looking defeated. "So what do we do?"

"I think you should keep it on."

"Valerie," she whined. "I really have to pee. Come on."

I laughed, looking her up and down. "We can cut it."

"Yes! Get the scissors and rip the sucker!"

"Are you sure?" I asked, wondering if there was another way. Maybe if I pushed down really hard . . . But one look at her face let me know that if I didn't get her out of the costume and soon, there was going to be massive bloodshed. "I'll get the scissors."

ℒ

Valerie finally got me out of the dreaded costume from Hell. Its evil grasp had sucked me in. It was a satanic being, capable of destruction. It had to be stopped.

"Um, Alix," Valerie said carefully. "I'm pretty sure it's dead."

I kept on cutting through the pink material like there was no tomorrow. "Yeah, but this is fun." I held up a strip to her. "Try it."

"No thanks." Valerie turned her attention to the closet. "So what do you think we should go as? I've got a few old shirts we can tear up and spread blood on."

"Sure," I said. "Do you have blood?"

"Yeah. I picked up some make-up too."

"Cool. So what exactly are we going to be?"

"Bloody people with ripped shirts?"

"Awesome," I said, as she handed me a plain white tee shirt. "You sure you don't need these?"

"Yep."

Valerie left the room and I sat down on the bed. I started making holes in the shirt and then ripping them open with my fingers. A few moments later, Valerie came back and dropped a plastic bag on the bed next to me. Inside, I found a few tubes of fake blood and a pack of zombie make-up. I never knew zombies wore make-up. But who was I to judge?

It took us about half-an-hour to complete our desired looks. We looked equally hideous by the end of it all.

"Nice work," Valerie said as we stood together in front of her mirror. "We are getting lots of candy tonight."

I smiled. It had been a while since I'd celebrated my birthday the old fashioned way and I was looking forward to the free candy. For some reason, anything with Valerie seemed fun. "Hey, do you mind if we stop at my mom's house before we go? I'm sure she'd want to see me."

Valerie glanced at her watch. She'd been doing that a lot, and it was starting to annoy me. "Yeah, sure. No problem."

"Hey, is there somewhere else you need to be?" I asked. "We don't have to do this."

"Huh? Oh." She appeared to realize what she'd been doing. "I'm sorry. I just like to keep track of the time. I don't want to waste half of your day."

Not quite as bad a liar as Jessica, but she was still pretty bad. "Uh-huh," I said. Something was up. "Let's go then."

Valerie looked relieved. "Okay."

I let her drive. For some reason she enjoyed driving my crappy car and I wasn't going to complain.

When we arrived at my mom's house, I was surprised to see that her car wasn't in the driveway and the lights were off inside.

"Where the hell?" I asked, slamming the passenger door. I walked up to the door and rang the doorbell. The keys were in my dorm room, of course. I rang the bell a few times to no avail.

I turned to Valerie who was waiting by the car. I shrugged and went back. "I guess she's not home," I said, trying to hide my disappointment. "She probably went to the store to get something."

"Do you want to wait here?" Valerie asked.

"No," I replied, getting back inside the car. "Let's go."

We drove in silence for a while. I was staring out of the window, trying to look on the bright side of things. I was grateful that at least I got to spend my birthday with Valerie. It wouldn't have been a very happy one otherwise.

"Are you okay?" Valerie asked.

I smiled at her. "Yes. I'm happy you're here."

"I'm happy I'm here too," she replied.

I settled back in the seat, watching the scenery pass by. After a while, I knew we'd arrived in Miami. I wasn't sure where exactly we were going but Valerie seemed to know, so I just let her lead the way.

A short while later, she pulled the car off to the side of the road. I looked at her in confusion. "Are we here?" I asked, glancing around. There didn't seem to be much going on. In fact, it looked more like the entrance to a parking lot.

"Put this on," Valerie answered, handing me a black bandana.

"Is my hair bothering you?"

She laughed. "No, I mean, as a blindfold."

I arched an eyebrow. "I don't know how they go trick-or-treating where you come from, but we do things a little differently here."

"Are you going to be difficult?"

"Aren't I always?" I asked, glancing down at the piece of cloth in my hands. Was she serious about this?

"C'mon, it's a surprise," she insisted. "Put it on."

I was a little hesitant. After all, how well did I really know this woman? "Are you planning on kidnapping me and selling me to Columbian drug lords? Or the mafia?"

"Please. One day with you and they'd send you right back."

She had a point there. I put on the blindfold. Now I was completely at her mercy. Not that I hadn't been before.

The car was back in motion, even though I had no idea where we were headed now. A surprise she'd said. Well, it had better be a good one. I didn't appreciate this blindfolding business.

We drove for another five minutes before I felt the car roll to a stop.

"We're here," Valerie announced, killing the ignition.

Perhaps killing was a wrong choice of words. There would be no killing tonight. Of engines or anything else. "Can I take the blindfold off now?"

Valerie laughed. "You sure are impatient. No. Not yet."

"How about now?"

"Hold on a sec," Valerie said.

I heard her leave the car, shut the door. Now I was alone. A few seconds later, the passenger door opened and I felt Valerie at my side. She unbuckled my seatbelt and gently helped me out of the car.

Since I couldn't see a thing, I attempted to figure out my surroundings by using my other senses. But my sense of touch was busy enjoying the feel of Valerie's hand on my arm. And my sense of smell had just discovered it really liked Valerie's shampoo. What else did I have available? Hearing. I listened intently. I heard water lapping against something.

"Are you going to make me walk the plank and feed me to the sharks?" I asked.

"Yes," Valerie answered. "How'd you know?"

"Lucky guess," I replied.

Valerie finished locking up the car and took my hand. "We're almost there."

"I thought you said we were there already." Oh, no she was lying to me. She really was going to throw me to the sharks. I was too young to die. I hadn't even bought my first legal alcoholic beverage yet. She had to at least give me a chance to do that. Okay, I didn't really believe she was going to kill me. But it was the only logical explanation I could come up with in such a spur of the moment situation. What had happened to trick-or-treating?

She started leading me somewhere.

"There's a ramp," Valerie announced. "Careful."

And suddenly we were going up. The water was beneath us. I could hear it clearly now. Finally, we stepped off the ramp. We were inside someplace. Where the hell was she taking me?

"Surprise," Valerie whispered my ear and removed the bandana from my eyes in one swift motion.

I blinked a few times as my eyes adjusted to the sudden light.

We appeared to be in the entrance to a grand hotel, but that couldn't be right. I looked all around. Behind me was the ramp we'd walked up on, and below that was the water I'd heard.

There were people with suitcases wandering about the place. Some were wearing uniforms, others were dressed casually in shorts and tee shirts. If I hadn't known any better, I would've guessed we were on a . . . cruise ship?

"What do you think?" Valerie asked.

"I'm not sure I understand," I said, glancing at my girlfriend with what I hoped was a look that illustrated my sheer confusion.

"We're taking a cruise to the Bahamas," she said, grinning like a little kid.

"You're kidding," I said, now certain this was a dream. I was overjoyed for a moment. It meant that the bunny incident had never happened. I turned back to the surroundings. It all looked so real though. So detailed. Down to the intricate patterns on the black and teal carpet.

"Happy birthday," she said.

It occurred to me that perhaps this wasn't a dream. I couldn't believe it. I threw my arms around Valerie's neck and hugged her tightly. "I love you. This is wonderful."

"I love you too, and I'm glad you like it. Wanna go check out our room?"

Our room. I found I liked the sound of that. A lot.

I allowed her to take my hand since it appeared like she knew the way. It seemed like a dream. But I didn't think it was. I used my free hand to pinch my arm. "Ouch," I muttered and started rubbing the sore spot.

"Something wrong?" Valerie asked with concern.

"I was just checking something," I answered. "Where are we going?"

"Our suite's on deck 9," she replied. "I'm looking for the stairs."

"Ah."

A moment later we found them. Why couldn't I have landed myself a better phobia? Like feathers. Unless you were a farmer, you didn't really have to face feathers on a daily basis. And that's only if you housed chickens. But what were you doing raising chickens if you had a fear of feathers?

Eventually, we made it to deck 9. Valerie started down the hall in search of the room number. I was wondering how we were going to make it to the Bahamas with no luggage. I was also wondering how Valerie had managed to pay for all of this. Unless there was something else she hadn't told me, which was likely.

But hey I wasn't complaining. So far this had been a very welcomed surprise. I'd never been on a cruise before.

"Here it is," Valerie announced, standing in front of a door. "Ready?"

"Yup."

Valerie opened the door, and allowed me in first.

My first thought was that we'd gotten the wrong room, 'cause I noticed there were people already in there. But then . . .

"SURPRISE!" a grand chorus of voices yelled.

My jaw dropped as I realized that the people were all of my friends; Jessica, Mathew, Jade. Even my mom was there. Roxanne and Alisha were holding a big sign that read, "Happy Birthday, Alix."

"Wow," I breathed, totally overwhelmed. I'd definitely not been expecting this.

Jessica and Mathew stepped forward, grinning like little kids. "You like?" asked Mathew.

So far this had been the best birthday ever. I hugged them both, because I had no words to express how much this meant to me. "Thank you,"

They laughed and hugged me back.

"It was really Valerie's idea," Jessica said.

I turned to Valerie and kissed her, forgetting completely that my mom was in the group. Oh well, she'd get over it.

Valerie hugged me tightly. "Glad you like it. But you should really be thanking Jessica. She made all the arrangements."

I took turns hugging everyone, unable to stop smiling. When I got to my mom, I was suddenly embarrassed. "I went by your house but you weren't in."

"Now you know why," she said, and pulled me in for a hug. "Happy birthday, baby."

♌

Eventually, the crowd dispersed to their own rooms and Alix and I were left alone. I was beyond thrilled that we'd managed to pull this off. Alix looked so happy and it made me feel so good to know that I was in part responsible for the huge smile on her face. After all I'd put her through the past few weeks, she deserved to be happy.

Jessica had gone all out and gotten everyone suites. I didn't want to know how much everything had cost her. Just looking around the room gave me a fairly good idea that it hadn't been a cheap investment. But I also knew that when it came to Alix, Jessica had no reservations.

There were twin beds that folded together to form a queen. I sat at the edge of one and watched Alix. She was out on the balcony, looking out at the ocean. She'd changed out of her costume and wiped the make-up off her face. I'd talked to Nicole about preparing a suitcase with Alix's clothes. Somehow we'd pulled that off too without Alix noticing. So far, everything had gone perfectly.

Alix turned around, as if she could feel me watching her. She walked back into the room and sat down next to me. "I'm still in dream mode. This feels totally unreal."

I smiled. "It's real. Nothing has ever been more real." I wasn't sure I was still talking about the cruise.

She was about to say something, but the knock on the door interrupted.

"Come in!" I yelled.

A young man, dressed in a uniform pertaining to the cruise line's staff, stood in the doorway. He held a clipboard in his hand. "I trust everything is to your liking."

"Definitely," Alix answered.

He nodded and stepped inside. He opened a door I hadn't noticed was there. It looked like a small storage closet. "Life vests are in here. Please put them on and meet up on the side deck."

"Is the ship sinking already?" Alix asked.

"Just a safety precaution," he answered, not particularly amused. He nodded slightly and turned around to knock on someone else's door.

Alix and I followed directions to the letter. We ran into Jessica and Mathew outside. Soon after, Jade, Roxanne, Alisha and Alix's mom joined us.

"What is this all about?" Roxanne asked.

"They're just going to check that everyone on the ship knows where the life vests are and know where to meet," Jessica said. "It takes forever, because they have to call every single room, but it's for our own safety. They always do it."

"Fun," Jade commented dryly.

Someone from the crew called everyone's attention and then began to explain what was going on. She basically said everything that Jessica had told us, except with a lot more boring details. I listened anyway. One never knew when an emergency would arise. I'd seen Titanic. And though there wouldn't be any icebergs between Florida and the Bahamas, it didn't hurt to be prepared.

"Bring Alix by my room after dinner," Jessica whispered in my ear. "Presents."

I nodded my understanding. I'd given my present to Jessica earlier in the day, along with Alix's suitcase. It wasn't a very personal gift, but I knew she'd like it. I had something else I wanted to give her, but I wanted us to be alone for that. And I still wasn't all that sure I had the guts to do it. I let out a shaky breath. Fine time to be a coward.

All the rooms were called and after what seemed like an interminably long time, we were allowed back inside. There was to be a Halloween party after dinner on the Sun Deck and I thought that sounded like fun.

Back in the room, we put away the life vests and regarded each other.

"Hungry?" I asked.

"Of course," she answered. "What time's dinner again?"

"In half an hour," I answered, sitting down.

"I think I'll jump in the shower then," she answered.

I almost asked if she wanted company but I was scared to. We hadn't slept together since before the entire ordeal of her finding out about everything, and I was too afraid of crossing the line. I figured that once she was ready, she'd let me know. "I'll take one after you," I said instead.

"I'll make it quick," she said with a smile, then disappeared into the bathroom.

When I heard the water start, I dug into my pocket and took out the black velvet box I'd been hiding for days. I'd been saving to buy an art studio someday . . . but some things were more important. I didn't figure Alix to be the gold type of gal, so I'd opted for a platinum band. The jeweler had explained that platinum was more expensive than gold because it was an extremely rare precious metal. He also informed me that it was harder to mine and that it weighed more than gold. But he also assured me that in the end it was more durable. I'd taken his word for it. I didn't know the first thing about jewelry.

The diamond was 4 carats, surrounded by small opal stones. Opal was Alix's birthstone. The jeweler had informed me that it was a "beautiful and mysterious" stone. Beautiful and mysterious indeed. He'd called it the gem with a rainbow inside. This had caused me to laugh. How appropriate, I'd thought.

The water stopped, so I quickly tucked the ring away for later. I made a grab for the TV clicker. Information about the cruise was on. I pretended I was very interested in what the Captain had to say when Alix walked out.

"All yours," she told me. "I think I left you a little hot water."

I smiled. "Thanks, you're too kind." I grabbed a change of clothes from my still packed suitcase and walked into the bathroom. I hoped that a nice shower and some fresh clothes would prepare me for the night ahead.

But I knew I'd need a lot more help than that.

♌

Dinner was wonderful. Our waiter, Gaston—Daston?—was quite nice. Every time he came by the table, he wished me a happy birthday. He even brought a cake at dessert time so that all of my friends could embarrass me in front of the entire dining room by singing "Happy Birthday." Some of the staff joined in, just to top off my utter humiliation.

I was enjoying myself, though. When the day had begun, I'd never imagined that it would end like this. I was so touched that they'd all pulled together for the occasion. Even Jessica and Valerie appeared to have bonded, or something to that effect. They at least looked at each other and once in a while, went as far as exchanging a word or two. It was more than I'd hoped for, considering.

Some people from the crew were dressed up in random costumes as they walked around making sure everyone was enjoying themselves. I couldn't see anyone who didn't look like they were having a good time. Personally, I was ready to make camp and move into the ship. I could live like this.

After dinner, I felt Valerie take my hand. "Do you want to check out the party later?" she whispered in my ear.

I felt goosebumps pop out all over at the sensation of her breath on my skin. What had she just asked me? Oh . . . right. "Sure," I replied, though I'd been secretly hoping for some alone time with her. It had been so long . . . Well, a few weeks. But it felt like an eternity.

"Can we make a quick stop?" she asked.

"Of course."

I thought we were going back to our room, but we passed our door and I saw that she was leading me toward Jessica's room. I wondered what on earth was going on now.

She knocked lightly on the door.

From somewhere on the other side of the door, we heard, "Come in."

Everyone was standing around a table overflowing with presents. Did these people know no bounds? I smiled. "What's this?" I asked, needlessly.

"They're called gifts," Jade informed me.

"Never heard of them."

Jessica held out a chair. "Come and sit, birthday girl."

I complied with her request and stared at the pile of wrapped boxes in front of me. I had no idea where to begin. "Didn't you guys think the cruise was enough?" I asked. "I'm really not that materialistic." I picked up one present and shook it. "Unless Aerosmith is in here somewhere."

"You wish," Roxanne said.

I laughed. "Who is this from?" I referred to the mysterious offering in my hands.

"Alisha," Roxanne responded. "She picked it out herself."

I smiled at the little girl. "Well, thank you, Alisha." I ripped through the paper. Inside I found a Winnie the Pooh coloring book, complete with crayons.

Everyone started laughing.

"Can I borrow it?" asked the four-year-old.

"It's all yours," I said, handing it over. "Enjoy."

She gave me a hug and ran off to the corner to color.

"Well, then," I said, grabbing another gift.

"That's from me," Jade announced.

I glanced at her in surprise. "I thought you gave me yours already?"

She chuckled. "That was just to throw you off." She winked. "I'm guessing you'll still get some good use out of it."

I'm sure I blushed. I cleared my throat and turned to the present. Unwrapping it, I blushed even more. "Oh . . . my . . ." It was a vibrator.

"For when Valerie's not around," Jade explained.

Everyone cracked up. High fives were exchanged. I wanted to crawl under a rock and die of embarrassment.

My mom coughed from her spot on the couch, making everyone aware of her presence.

I closed my eyes. *Please God, kill me now.*

"Sorry, mum," Jade mumbled and hid behind Jessica. At least she had the decency to look embarrassed.

I opened my eyes and grabbed another present. This time I was fearful.

"It's from me," said Mathew. "It's rated PG."

I was grateful. Inside was a brand new chain wallet. "Nice!" I said, holding it up.

There was a chorus of oooh's and aaah's from the smartasses.

"Thank you very much, Mr. Collins," I said.

"You're very welcome," he replied.

I opened the next couple of presents. I got a new watch from my mom. And a gift certificate to Camelot Music from Roxanne.

Last but not least, was Valerie's present. I'd been wondering all day what she was going to get me. I saved the best for last.

I couldn't tell what it was just from looking at it. But whatever it was, it appeared to be framed. Maybe it was a painting of some sort. Probably something she'd drawn. I smiled in anticipation.

But it wasn't anything she'd made. Instead, a framed poster of Steven Tyler stared back at me. Autographed. I shrieked with delight and stood up to hug her. "Where did you get that?"

She laughed and hugged me back. "Umm, eBay?"

"You rock," I informed her.

"Pretty much."

℗

I stood on the Sun Deck a short while later, staring out at the invisible night beyond. The Halloween party was in full swing, and I'd left Alix with her friends. For some reason, I felt like I needed to contemplate my existence.

It wasn't long before another figure joined me against the railing. But it wasn't one I'd been expecting. I turned and offered my most polite smile. "Good evening, Mrs. Morris," I greeted.

Alix's mom smiled at me, green eyes sparkling in the moonlight. Her long blond hair was tucked behind her ears. She could've passed for a twenty-year-old if she wanted. "What are you doing by yourself?" she asked.

"Just thinking," I replied honestly, feeling extremely self-conscious. I'd never really talked to any parents before. I barely spoke to mine, save my father who'd just recently rediscovered his humanity.

She nodded as though understanding. "You make her happy," she said, not quite looking at me.

I was surprised by her admission. I didn't know what to say, so I remained silent, hoping she'd proceed.

"She hasn't been happy in a long time," Mrs. Morris continued, to my relief. "Her father's death . . . Jessica . . ."

I was surprised she knew about that.

It must've shown because she smiled. "I know my daughter, Valerie. More than she realizes." She looked at me for a moment. "Have your parents met her?"

"My father's in Boston," I answered.

"And your mother?"

I gazed down at the floor. "I'm not sure," I replied truthfully.

"I'm sorry."

"It's okay," I said, not wishing her to feel sorry for me. I'd done quite well for myself without my mother's help. Sometimes, I even managed to convince myself that I didn't miss her.

"I'm glad you two found each other," Mrs. Morris said. "It seems you need each other."

I looked at her, surprised by the comment. I'd never thought of it that way.

"Well, I'll leave you to your thinking," she said. "Good night, Valerie."

"Good night," I replied.

She patted my shoulder and walked off, leaving me to my thoughts.

♄

I was attempting to hold a conversation with Jessica, while keeping an eye on Valerie. I was very distracted by the fact that my mother was speaking to her. What on earth could my mom be telling her?

" . . . and you're not listening to a word I'm saying," Jessica stated.

"Sorry," I said. "I was sort of listening."

Jessica turned her head, in search of the root of my distraction. She found it immediately. "Ooh, what'd she do?"

"I can't imagine what Mom could be talking to her about," I said.

"Oh, probably the usual," Jessica said, casually. "Say no to drugs, don't drink and drive, use dental dams when having oral sex . . ."

I glared at Jessica sharply. "Like my mom even knows what dental dams are."

"What? You think she was born yesterday?"

"On the contrary," I said. "She was born way before sex was invented."

"Really? And pray tell, just how did you come into being?"

"The stork brought me," I replied, matter-of-factly. "And then he cloned my sister, because I was so perfect, there just had to be two of me. Only, I was so perfect there really could only be one of me. That's why Rachel turned out like she did."

Jessica laughed.

I watched my mom pat Valerie's shoulder and walk away, toward me. "She's coming over," I told Jessica.

"Which one?"

"Good evening, girls," my mother greeted.

"Hi, Mom," I said.

"Hi, Mom," Jessica echoed.

I smiled as did my mother. Jessica had been calling her "Mom" for years now. My mother found it endearing. "Can I have a moment alone with the birthday girl?"

"All yours," Jessica said. "I'll go mingle with the masses."

I watched Jessica walk away, then turned expectantly to my mother. What did she want to talk about? The vibrator? Please God, no. Anything but that.

"How does it feeling being twenty-one?"

I considered. "It feels a lot like being twenty. Only now I can toss the fake ID."

She didn't find this as funny as I did.

I gave her a crooked grin. "Kidding." I looked to where Valerie had been standing. She was no longer there. I frowned.

"You like her a lot?" my mom asked, knowing where my gaze was directed.

"A lot."

"I like her," she said. "She seems like a good kid."

I thought it best to keep Valerie's past from my mother. And everything else too. There were just some things parents didn't need to know. "She is," I agreed, knowing it wasn't a lie. Whatever Valerie's past mistakes, they didn't make her any less of a wonderful person.

"Are you having a good birthday?"

"The best," I answered at once.

"I'm glad that Jessica invited me. It was quite the surprise."

I smiled. "How was Rachel's day?"

"Jonathan took her out to dinner." She sighed. "Jessica invited her too but Jonathan didn't want any part of it, so she refused the offer."

"Oh," I said, not surprised. My sister and I weren't particularly best friends, which is odd for twins, I know. But I still loved her and would've liked to celebrate our birthdays together. Jonathan just sucked.

"Don't let that ruin your night, honey," my mom said, smiling. "You have a lot to be grateful for."

"I do," I granted, nodding my head. A lot, indeed.

Mom nodded, as if satisfied with the mother-daughter conversation. "Well, I'm off to bed. You kids have fun."

"We will."

She gave me a hug. "Happy birthday."

"It is," I assured her. The happiest ever.

♌

"Getting lectures already?"

I turned to find Jessica walking toward me, carrying a can of Coke in one hand. I'd retreated from the railing, preferring to sit down at one of the abandoned lounge chairs on the side. "She told me I made Alix happy," I said, still amazed.

Jessica nodded and took the liberty of sitting beside me. "You do," she admitted.

"Does that bother you?" I asked seriously.

Jessica smiled and sat back. "Perhaps," she said, looking out thoughtfully at the ocean. "Probably not for the reasons you think."

"Enlighten me, then."

She took a sip from her drink. "I regret being the cause of her pain for so long. It was frustrating to know that it was all in my hands. Her happiness and unhappiness. All up to me. What bothers me isn't that you make her happy, it's the knowledge that I could've tried and didn't."

"And why didn't you?" I asked. I felt a pang of envy at the thought of them together. It could've happened so easily, I realized. And Alix and I would've never been.

"I don't love her that way," Jessica said. "I love her more than anything and anyone. But not that way. She's like a sister to me." She glanced at me as she said the words.

How ironic. I would've laughed had it not been so sad. "Strange how things turn out."

She chuckled. "Indeed it is."

"You are not what I expected," I found myself admitting.

Jessica arched an eyebrow. "What did you expect?"

I hesitated, knowing I was on dangerous ground. I was willing to give Jessica a chance, but this was starting to get a little too personal and I wasn't sure I was prepared for that. But . . . what the hell? "When I was little, and Mom and Dad first explained to me about you, I thought it was the greatest thing. I would see you on TV and I'd brag to my friends that you were my sister. And none of them would believe me, of course, but I knew it was true." I felt embarrassed by my confession, but I'd already opened my big fat mouth, so I might as well keep on. "And one day, I was watching you on one of those interviews you used to do, and they asked you if you had any brothers and sisters and you said no. You said, 'I'm glad I don't, 'cause that way I get all the nice stuff.'"

Jessica cringed. "I really said that?" She shook her head.

I shrugged. "Well, from that moment on, I stopped telling anyone you were my sister. I didn't want to talk about it any more. If Mom and Dad brought up the subject, I changed it. I was ashamed of you . . . and I was hurt." I shrugged again, feeling stupid. "I was young."

"So was I," Jessica said sadly. "I'm really sorry."

"It was a long time ago," I replied. "I guess I just expected you to be that way still. That's why, in a way, I didn't feel so bad for wanting to take your money." I sighed. "But then Alix . . ." I let the rest hang in the air. "You know the rest."

Jessica nodded. "I thought you were different too. When everything happened."

"Well, I didn't make a very good first impression," I agreed, feeling ashamed. "I handled all of that terribly."

"Not that many ways to handle it," Jessica said. "I wasn't angry about the money. I was angry about you using Alix to get it. The last thing she needed was someone else hurting her."

I nodded, my heart aching for what I'd done. "I was desperate. My brother's life or Alix's feelings . . ."

"Seems like a pretty easy answer," Jessica replied.

"It was killing me," I said. "I was angry at Aaron. I was angry at the world. I finally find a girl that I can . . ." I hesitated. " . . . love . . . and I had to risk throwing it all away."

"Do you really love her?" Jessica asked, her tone revealing nothing about her feelings on the subject.

"More than anything," I answered at once.

Jessica considered this, taking another sip of her drink. Finally, she nodded. "I think the two of you complement each other well. And you make her happy. If nothing else, that's good enough for me."

I don't know why, but her words made me feel a whole lot better. Perhaps I was no longer that little girl who was in awe at seeing her older sister on television, but Jessica's approval meant more to me than I cared to admit.

"Strange how fate brought us together," Jessica remarked. "Through Alix . . . because of Alix."

"Maybe she's the center of the universe," I suggested, grinning slightly.

"Don't tell her that, she'll believe it," Jessica joked.

I laughed.

Jessica cleared her throat. "So, Valerie," she started, a bit shyly, "tell me about our family."

I blinked at her words, surprised but not at all upset. I smiled. "Um, what would you like to know?"

"Everything," she said.

♫

A couple of hours later, I was bored out of my mind. Jade, Roxanne and Mathew had done a swell job of entertaining me, but I really missed my girlfriend. I knew she and Jessica were talking, though, and that was one conversation I wasn't going to interrupt. I just hoped it was a civil one.

I turned to Jade. Roxanne had left to check on Alisha and Mathew had retired to bed. So the two of us were alone, watching drunk people in costumes stumble over themselves.

"I really am sorry about the vibrator," Jade insisted. "I totally forgot your mum was there."

"Yeah, yeah," I said, not wanting to talk about it. It had been embarrassing enough living through it, I didn't want to have to remember it.

"Oh, look," Jade said, looking over my shoulder. "Jessica's on her way over here. I'm gonna go flirt with some guys."

"The one dressed as Leonardo DiCaprio's definitely a keeper," I said.

"Oh, sod off," she said, shaking her head. She walked off.

I smiled to myself, then regarded Jessica. "Have a good time?"

"A promise kept," she said with a smile. "Here's your other birthday present." She handed me a small gift.

I stared down at the object in my hands. "What's this?"

"Well, open it and see."

I tore the wrapper off and started laughing. It was a pack of gum. "Watermelon," I said, nodding in approval. "Thank you."

"Happy birthday," she said with a wink.

I looked all around, my gaze settling back on her. "So how did it go?"

"Well. You can't change the stars in one night but there's definitely progress."

I nodded, knowing it was going to take time. "I'm glad you talked to her."

Jessica smiled. "So am I."

I smiled back. "Your husband went to bed."

"Your girlfriend's waiting for you in your room," she said.

"Are you coming up?"

Jessica nodded thoughtfully. "In a few minutes. I want to stare at the ocean for a little while."

I smiled. Some things never changed. I'd never asked her what she thought about when she stared out there. Perhaps she thought the answers to life were hidden in the great beyond. Maybe she just envied its freedom. Or perhaps she just found comfort in its consistency. But I would never ask, and she would never tell. Some things were better left unsaid.

"I love you," I said, in a way that made it feel final. Like the last period of the last sentence in a chapter of my life.

She smiled, if a bit sadly. "I love you, too."

I smiled my good bye and headed down to my room. I was dying to see Valerie. It felt like ages since I'd last looked at her. And it had only been a few hours. Jesus, I was in trouble.

"Valerie," I called, stepping into the room.

"Out here."

I saw her out on the balcony and joined her a few moments later. "Something interesting out there?" I asked, looking over the railing at the darkness below.

"Not anymore," she said, looking at me.

I smiled and hugged her, if only to feel the closeness of her body. I'd missed her. I'd missed feeling like we were connected. "I love you," I whispered.

Her arms tightened around my waist. "I love you, too."

When we pulled away, I noticed Valerie was holding something. "What's that?"

"Your real present," she responded. "But before I give it to you, I have to say a few things."

"Okay." I waited patiently for her to continue.

"Okay, I'm gonna do my best not to sound corny, 'cause I know you hate that," she began. "But I may fail miserably. Just a warning."

I laughed. "All right. I'll consider myself warned. Proceed."

Valerie took a deep breath. "Okay, here it goes," she said, closing her eyes. When she opened them, she looked right into mine. "I've never felt like I belonged anywhere before, but when I'm with you even the oddest places feel like home. I don't want to lose you again, Alix. I know you just recently forgave me and everything, but I am completely in love with you and that's not something that's going to change with time. So whether I tell you this now or five years from now, it doesn't matter. I want to be with you. Only you. Forever."

In spite of my usual hate for corniness, I was touched.

She handed me the present. "Please don't freak out. But. Happy birthday."

I took the box, my heart suddenly hammering in my chest. I opened it slowly and nearly passed out when I saw what was inside. I stared at her. "What does this mean?"

"Whatever you want it to mean," she said simply.

I took the ring out of its resting place and looked at it. It was beautiful. I wondered if she knew that opal was my birthstone? "I . . . um . . ." I had no idea what to say. "What does it mean to you?" I asked finally.

"That I'm yours forever."

I smiled, too happy to speak. Instead, I kissed her deeply, every doubt in my mind suddenly melting away into nothingness until there was just us and no one else.

Somewhere in the back of my mind, I felt the pages of a new chapter start to open.

ABOUT THE AUTHOR

Ingrid Diaz was born in the small island of Puerto Rico. Since then she's lived in exotic places such as Cooper City, Florida and New Brunswick, New Jersey. After landing a B.A. in English from Rutgers University, Ingrid packed her bags and moved across seas to Lyon, France, where she currently resides. She spends her days smiling and nodding at the French people (whom she still doesn't understand), and blogging for b5media. In her spare time, she enjoys playing World of Warcraft and terrorizing her next door neighbors by singing loudly and off-key. More often than not, she can also be found working away on her next novel.

Bedazzled Ink Publishing Company

http://www.bedazzledink.com

Nuance Books
Rebeccah and the Highwayman ○ Barbara Davies
Christie and the Hellcat ○ Barbara Davies
Remnants of Shadow and Light ○ Sias Bryant
A Nice Girl Like You ○ Tyree Campbell
Toe to Toe: Standing Tall and Proud
Alix & Valerie ○ Ingrid Diaz

Mindancer Press
Into the Yellow ○ Barbara Davies
Future Dreams ○ T.J. Mindancer
Present Paths ○ T.J. Mindancer
Emoria Campfire Tales ○ T.J. Mindancer

coming soon
Past Echoes ○ T.J. Mindancer
Adijan and the Genie ○ L-J Baker
Knight Predator ○ Jordan Falconer
Friends in High Places ○ Andi Marquette

Dragonfeather Books
Dragon Drool ○ C.A. Casey
Top of the Key ○ C.A. Casey

coming soon
To Live As Legend ○ Amy M. Smith, Lisa Victoria

Fletching Books
Running Through Roadblocks ○ Jerry Del Priore

Printed in the United States
121845LV00009B/29/P

9 781934 452042